WITHOUT HIM

Paperback ISBN: # 979-8-9890948-4-4
Hardcover ISBN: # 979-8-9890948-3-7
Ebook ISBN: # 979-8-9890948-5-1
Library of Congress Control Number: # 2025912416

Publishing Consultant: PRESStinely. PRESStinely.com

Printed in the United States of America.
Lindsay Law
LindsayLaw.net

"Sure on this Shining Night" from PERMIT ME VOYAGE, The Collected Poems of James Agee © 1934, Yale University Press

Scout's Vespers circa 1908, author unknown

Robinson Crusoe by Daniel Dafoe, published 1719

A Mighty Fortress is Our God by Martin Luther, 1529

Mad About the Boy, written by Noel Coward, published 1932

I'd Do Anything for Love [but I won't do that] by Jim Steinman 1993

Our House, by Graham Nash, pub. Nash Notes 1970

*"In the beginning was the Word, and the
Word was with God, and the Word was God.
All things were made by him; and without him was not
anything made that was made."*

St. John 1:1, 3

"Oh, isn't life a terrible thing, thank god?"

Under Milkwood by Dylan Thomas

WITHOUT HIM

—— A NOVEL ——

LINDSAY LAW

Dedicated to my dear friends and faithful readers.

CONTENTS

PART ONE

1989 – 2001

PROLOGUE

Nathan Winning puts on snowshoes, his parka, and scarf and walks into the heart of the howling blizzard. He hikes up a steep and narrow deer path, the strong winds and deep drifts slowing his progress until he finally reaches the overlook at Walker's Point. From here, he sees the broken trees, the downed power lines, and, in the distance, the town's traffic lights flashing orange.

With the lens of his Nikon camera he documents the storm's destruction, impressed by the dangerous beauty that has brought holiday celebrations to a standstill in his tiny Connecticut town. This is the second day of relentless snow and what had begun as a sentimental Currier and Ives landscape has now been transformed into something truly dangerous as the electricity fails, and the water pipes freeze, and his neighbors shiver in their homes.

He looks below and sees Lake Aspetuck, now fully frozen and covered by three feet of fresh powder. As he braces himself against the heavy gusts, he hears the abrasive whine of a chainsaw, and then it is gone, muzzled by the storm. He studies the wooly surface of the lake, looking north to south, wondering who could be out in such weather.

The chainsaw starts up again, on his right—south towards Nonnie Esmund's property. *Is it one of her grandsons?* He tightens the zoom and searches the white landscape with his viewfinder. Suddenly, in sharp focus, he sees a young boy alone on the ice, his red ponytail a near match for the bright orange saw in his bare hands.

Nathan studies the surrounding property, seeking clues to the mystery below. He spots multiple sledding tracks leading from Nonnie's house to the lake's edge, following a steep path that he and Jared and Rebecca had traveled many times in winters long ago.

One track branches away from the main route, leading towards the dock and ending at a large hole of agitated water where an active spring prevents the formation of ice. The redhead is now kneeling on the frozen edge of that black circle, his bare hand entering the roiled water, and then his entire arm.

Nathan's heart races. He tells himself to run for help, but he hesitates, wanting to capture the disaster taking place on the snowy lake.

He presses the shutter, again and again, horrified by his selfish instincts.

1.

'SURE ON THIS SHINING NIGHT'

Brighton screams, "Let go, Ezzie!" but his brother only tightens his grip on the ancient iron sled and it drags him into the freezing water, his new boots and green parka erased by the circle of inky blackness.

As the water bubbles, Brighton waits for Baéz to surface; he stares at the empty hole, his body shaking with fear. Nonnie would have prayed—Jared, too—but Brighton doesn't subscribe to their healing beliefs; he is uncomfortable with their devotions. Instead, he bangs his thick-booted foot on the ice, signaling his brother he is not alone. He then sees a flash of green under the ice, but then it is gone as a fresh blast of snow wipes out the image.

He knows they will blame him. This is his fault. He stares at the dark hole, and a powerful image suddenly fills his mind, a memory from their previous summer together when they experimented with various methods of breathing underwater.

He runs to the boathouse and grabs one of Jared's chainsaws, his exposed hands numb and fumbling. He fills the hefty saw with gas and oil and then spots the garden hose neatly coiled by his feet. *A way to breathe below the surface.* With pruning shears, he cuts off a ten-foot section, then runs back to the lake, forgetting his gloves as he tries to calculate how long Baéz has been under. One minute? Two?

He primes the saw, pulls the choke, and then cranks the starter cable. Again. Then a third time before the engine springs to life. He squeezes the throttle, the screaming motor adding a surreal dimension to the violence of the storm. Where should he cut?

He picks a spot twenty feet from the hole, figuring the current has moved his brother downstream, but as he lifts the saw, a tiny whirlwind springs up, sweeping clean an area of black ice farther to his left. He takes it as a sign and guns the engine, cutting a hole in the newly smoothed surface.

He feeds the hose into the water until only a foot remains above the ice. He kneels and blows into his end of the hose; the metal connector is cold and hurts his teeth, but he can hear the blast of bubbles as they travel through the water. Again, he blows, then a deep intake of breath, and more blowing, keeping the hollow tube open so Baéz can breathe.

The hose abruptly comes to life, being pulled from his hands and nearly disappearing into the freezing water. He grabs it and holds on hard. Brighton tugs on the hose and feels resistance—Baéz *is* there.

He fills his lungs again and slowly exhales into the hose, feeling his breath being pulled from his mouth. Moving the brass coupling to his ear, he can hear his brother breathing: loud, rhythmic gasps. Tears freeze to his face as he wills his body to stand, restart the chainsaw, and cut a new hole, large enough for Baéz to slip through.

The swiftly revolving chain covers Brighton in shards of ice. He stomps on the freshly cut circle until it shatters and dips below the surface. He kneels and puts his hand and then his arm into the water, his body shocked by the extreme cold. He searches for the green parka, hoping Baéz can follow the hose to safety.

A hand grabs his own, and he screams from the pain, his arm numb as he hauls his brother onto the ice. Baéz's face is blue, and his eyes are glazed. Brighton leans down, close to the body; he can feel the warmth of Baéz's breath.

"Don't leave me now!" he screams. "Stay with me!"

He stares into his brother's terrified eyes and then places his warm lips on the frosty mouth, attempting to transfer his own being into his brother.

Jared has been plowing the town's roads for hours. He sips the strong coffee from his thermos as the high-pitched trilling from his walkie-talkie grabs his attention. He pushes the green button.

"Jared Honor. Who's this?"

"Jared, it's Nate."

The voice is clipped, the connection poor.

"Speak slowly and push the 'talk' button firmly," he barks, annoyed that Nathan is using the town's emergency system.

"I saw your boys; they were on the ice, near the dam. One fell in. I was at Walker's Point, too far away to reach them."

Jared feels his heart skip and his body tense. Has he heard correctly?

"Who fell in?"

His childhood friend doesn't answer.

"Speak to me! Are they still in the water?" He makes a swift U-turn towards home, driving as fast as the icy roads will allow.

"Nonnie got to them," Nathan says. "I saw her pull the soaking boy onto a toboggan while the other kid dragged it up to your cabin. I called an ambulance."

Jared hears the fear in Nathan's voice as he tightens his grip on the wheel. His son is in danger. He shudders as he turns into the long drive that leads to his and

Nonnie's lakeside homes. He stomps on the brake as the deep snow explodes all around him. He throws open the door and runs to his cabin. He sees Brighton and Nonnie struggling with a toboggan. Jared goes to them and lifts his son, whose clothing is stiff as cardboard. Baéz lashes out at invisible demons and talks in gibberish as Jared carries him inside.

He removes the icy clothing and sees the goose flesh. Jared revives the fire on the stone hearth as Brighton covers his naked brother in blankets. Loud knocking announces the arrival of the ambulance crew. They struggle through the deep snow to get the stretcher in the house. As the attendants lift Baéz and strap him in, the boy continues babbling. Jared had once adored the nonsensical sound of his son trying out words for the first time, but now the babbling is terrifying. What's wrong with him? he wonders. He watches as Nonnie follows Baéz into the ambulance. She caresses the boy's face and then suddenly, almost magically, the jabbering stops.

As the ambulance siren blares, Jared runs to his idling half-ton pick-up. He sweeps the mess of tools and receipts and empty donut boxes to the floor and motions for Brighton to get in. They follow the flashing lights to the hospital.

"How long was he under?" Jared asks, his voice colored by dread.

The boy's hands are shaking. "I don't know, sir," he mumbles.

"Come on," Jared snaps. "If you had to guess, what do you think? Ten seconds? Twenty? Even longer?"

The boy looks at him and then away, clearly frightened by the harsh tone.

"Longer."

Jared smashes his fist on the steering wheel and curses as Rebecca's other son starts to cry. Jared doesn't know why his boy is so enamored of Brighton. Jared thought he was ridiculous, with his silly clothes and his girly hair. Ever since he came into their lives last summer, Jared has wished that the kid had remained in England.

They pull up to the hospital and see the ambulance crew roll the stretcher into the large brick building. Jared parks his truck and he and Brighton run through the snow and join Nonnie in the lobby. The room is dim, the hospital utilizing a back-up generator for emergency power. A doctor arrives.

"You were with him?" the doctor asks.

"Yes, sir," answers Brighton.

"How long was he in the water?"

"Several minutes, sir. At least three." The doctor raises his eyebrows as Brighton quickly adds: "He's stayed under longer! Last summer I timed him at four minutes!"

Jared looks at the doctor. "Will he be alright?"

"His pulse is weak, and his breath is shallow. We need to raise his temperature." He turns to a nurse who is waiting nearby. "Give him humidified oxygen and place warm compresses on his neck and chest." She nods and rushes down the hall. The doctor turns back to Jared. "His body has suffered a great trauma. I'll bring you information as soon as I'm able." He then follows the nurse down the dark hallway.

Jared stares at Brighton, unleashing his fury. "I told you both to stay off that lake! What were you thinking?"

Brighton shakes his head, angry at being blamed. "I *told* him to jump, but he wouldn't let go. He wanted to save your stupid sled!" Brighton, now close to tears, rushes after the doctor.

The accusation rings in Jared's ear. *He wanted to save your stupid sled!* Jared's father had been a blacksmith and had designed and crafted the elegant sledge with its ornate decoration. Jared often warned the boys to take care with its use. *It's a family heirloom,* he often explained.

"He's fine and perfect," says Nonnie. "Know that. Confirm it. Healing is happening right now. Do not be impressed by the hysteria that surrounds us."

Jared nods, hoping she is right. Nonnie is a metaphysical healer, utilizing prayer to cure the body. He has witnessed the recovery of many of her patients, but the concerned look on the doctor's face has filled him with fear.

✷ ✷ ✷

Brighton enters an all-white room where Baéz is being connected to a machine with many tubes and dials and flashing lights. Dr. Lee motions to him, and Brighton moves closer to the stretcher, taking his brother's hand.

"We are warming his blood. It leaves his body, goes briefly into this machine, for hemodialysis, and then back into his body."

Brighton nods and then leans down to speak into his brother's ear.

"Just like in *Teen Titans,* remember? When Beast Boy and Raven had to fight Trigon? Raven had her blood washed with aragonite, and her strength multiplied. You will be mighty, just as she was." He squeezes his brother's hand and thinks he sees a smile.

"Raven's my son's favorite, too. Why do you all like her so much?" asks an amused Dr. Lee.

"Because she's beautiful," answers Brighton as he spies a fancy contraption that looks like a rocket ship. "Is he going in there?" Brighton asks, pointing to the large hollow tube.

Dr. Lee nods. "Yes, it's a large 3D camera that shows what's going on in his body." He looks at Brighton. "This will take some time. You may wish to get comfortable."

Brighton whispers in Baéz's ear. "I'll be right back. Fear not—Raven is watching over you!"

✷ ✷ ✷

Jared devours snacks from the vending machines as snow continues to fall and daylight begins to fade. He turns to where Nonnie sits reading her Bible.

"I bet he dared Baéz to go on the ice. My boy would never be so foolish."

Nonnie stares at Jared, long and hard; she clearly is tired of the subtle digs and whispered complaints he utters whenever he speaks of the son that isn't his.

"That boy, who you treat with such disdain, saved your son's life today. Baéz didn't simply fall into the freezing water; he got trapped under thick ice, unable to find his way out. Brighton fed him a lifeline, a garden hose, through which your son breathed until Brighton could figure a way to free him."

Jared feels his face redden, as if slapped. In a shaky voice he asks, "How did he ever think of it?"

"A movie we watched last summer, the boys and me," answers Nonnie. "A man is trapped underwater, drowning, and a friend gives him a hollow reed."

"Nonnie's boyfriend is in it. That famous actor, not the President but—"

Jared looks up, startled, not realizing Brighton had returned. "Paul Newman?" guesses Jared.

"Yes, him!"

"He's not my boyfriend!" Nonnie scowls and then smiles, adding "But *Sometimes a Great Notion* is one of his best."

Brighton continues. "After seeing the film, Baéz and I tried breathing underwater using swamp grass and blue stem reeds. We had a mighty time!"

Jared sees the pleasure in Brighton's eyes. This boy, this *fancy boy*, as he derisively calls him, saved his son's life. He can't fathom it.

Brighton sits and finishes Nonnie's half-eaten sandwich.

"How did you know to come find us?" he asks. He turns to Jared, explaining, "No sooner had I pulled Baéz from the water than Nonnie was at my side with exactly what we needed—a toboggan."

She pauses before answering and then replies, "A voice, clear and strong, uttered a warning, so I looked out my window. One of you was missing, so I ran. The Lord is a very present help in trouble. Never forget that!" She then stands, smiling and retying her scarf. "Let's go visit our young man. It's time they are done with him!"

It isn't until later, when Baéz is safely resting in the hospital and Brighton and Nonnie have returned to her large Victorian home, that Jared tries to understand the mysterious events of this wild and stormy day. Much as he loves the Bible and all the people who live within it, he doesn't believe in miracles; yet how else to describe the doctor's baffling statement? *Your son cheated death today. His organs shut down, his body ceased to function, yet he's alive.*

Jared stands in the immaculate snow as a full moon illuminates the lake with an otherworldly glow. He stares at the black hole of freezing water that swallowed his son. He picks up the icy hose lying beside his orange chainsaw. He feels Rebecca's presence, and the tension and strain of this day is finally released.

Sure on this shining night of starmade shadows round
Kindness must watch for me this side the ground.

It's a favorite poem of hers. The words come easily to mind. *Kindness must watch for me this side the ground.*

He looks up at the sky. *As bright as daylight,* he thinks as he shivers and walks back to his cabin. He smiles and thanks Rebecca for keeping her boys safe.

✷ ✷ ✷

Nathan waits all afternoon for a call from Jared—a call to tell him the boys are okay—but it never comes. He isn't part of their world anymore. Not Jared's. Not Nonnie's. Not since Rebecca's death.

What he saw with those boys today has stirred him, and he is impatient to find what his lens captured. He is expected at a Christmas Eve party, but he wants to see his work first.

The loud spinning of tires draws his eyes to the large factory windows that frame his downtown loft. The sound of shovels scraping asphalt is drowned out by a dozen carolers who have braved the cold, bringing cheer to their neighbors.

Nathan goes to his dark room. The cameras, the lenses, the art of developing and printing his own negatives, is all new to him. A hip injury ended his promising tennis career, and now he is testing himself to see if he has the makings of an artist—a photographer. Returning to his childhood home has been the first step.

A red light illuminates the small space as he places the paper in the developing tray. It is the final image he wants to print, the last one on the roll. He wonders if he imagined it, or if the thickly falling snow might have obscured it. But as he gently moves the photo paper back and forth in its chemical bath, he can see that the image is as startling as he thought. A young boy surrounded by a world of white lies atop his brother and forces breath into his mouth as their lips tenderly meet. Nathan thinks the image resembles the religious paintings he has seen in churches and museums, with winged cherubs floating through cloud of white. However, in studying the angelic boys he also realizes the image is sexual, and he cringes, knowing that for the boy's safety, he must keep this glorious portrait hidden.

2.

MAYHEM AT THE WIDENER

More than a decade earlier, a different storm, a gentler one, also had a major impact on the lives of the brothers—or *half-brothers,* as both their fathers would insist. When heavy snow cancels classes and turns Cambridge into a ghost town, Elwynn Bethune's fellow students at Harvard Law convince their sober, redheaded friend from "across the pond" to let loose and join them as they purloin a stack of lunch trays from the cafeteria and use them as sleds to fly down the icy steps of the Widener Library.

Bowing to wisdom and seeing how treacherous the journey is for the first riders, Wynn rejects the suggestion of joining the daredevils until he sees a blonde coed look admiringly at their heroic exploits. She is cocooned in a thick white parka, her smile notable for the tiny gap between her front teeth. He decides he must win her heart.

He grabs a wooden platter from one of his fraternity brothers and with a running head start aims his coaster at the smiling blonde. He bumps his way down the steep incline, unable to slow or steer, the freezing snow finding its way beneath hat and scarf as he wildly waves his arms to warn the onlookers that he is out of control. His aim is true; her face gets closer and closer as a barrage of snowballs blinds him and the inevitable crash takes them both down. Wynn struggles to stand, wondering if she will greet him with a smile or a scowl. He brushes the snow from his woolen coat and sees her lying in a deep drift. She is neither smiling nor scowling as he goes to her and offers a hand.

"I am so sorry," he says. "I couldn't stop. Are you all right?"

She finally smiles at their predicament. "Yes, only my pride has been wounded. I'm usually quite deft on ice!"

He grins at her choice of words and then offers dinner as compensation for his carelessness. He learns her name is Rebecca Esmund. He loves three-syllable names and repeats hers quietly in his head as he listens to her soft voice in the French restaurant they have chosen.

"Ten more weeks, and we'll be clutching our diplomas, our futures waiting for us." Her face reflects excitement, but Wynn also hears fear. "For the first time I realize how sad I'll be to leave Boston," she adds.

He looks into her dark green eyes—something is happening; he feels lightheaded, giddy even.

"I'm not ready," she admits. "I'm not ready to leave here. There is still so much to learn! Cambridge still has much to teach us. No?"

He doesn't answer; he is pleased to remain silent and simply listen. He wants to study her and watch her. He wants her to see him as vigilant and thoughtful.

"I want more time; I love learning. I don't want it to stop." She laughs nervously, as if embarrassed, and then continues. "Last night I went to a concert. The snow had started, the air was crisp, the night held promise. As I entered the heated auditorium, there was an electric current in the air. Something was about to happen, and everyone felt it."

She closes her eyes; he wants to be part of the memory she is reliving.

"And what *did* happen?" he asks.

"A song cycle. James Agee poems. A graduate student set them to music. A small choir. No instruments. First performance. Ever. Brought tears to my eyes, and I'm not a crier. As the applause ended, we put on our coats and walked outside, the thick snow gently falling, our evening frozen in time. How do we guarantee such wonders will continue once we leave here?"

Elwynn, who had been desperate for graduation to arrive, now wants to stop the clock and allow their days at Harvard to continue forever. He memorizes her warm smile, a keepsake he will treasure from this dinner.

As it turns out, it will be the first of many. They work their way through the diverse cuisines of Cambridge—Korean, Mexican, German, Persian. They see each other nearly every night, shunning friends and ignoring studies. Only a few weeks remain on Wynn's student visa, but he wants to spend every one of them with her. And like Rebecca, he regrets what he has not learned. He wants to become expert in all things "American." He wants to impress her; he wants to be memorable. He begins to feel dependent on her, and that uneasy vulnerability is thrilling.

The impetuous nature of their affair pleases him. She imitates his tony accent and teases him about his habits, his politeness, and his gentility. Her main source of knowledge about his homeland is the popular TV series *Upstairs, Downstairs*. She asks if he treats his servants better than the infamous Bellamys treat theirs.

"I don't have servants!" he cries, displaying his empty wallet as they both laugh. Laughing comes easily, although neither are known for their playfulness.

He wrangles seats to the opening-day game at Fenway Park to demonstrate his adoration of all things "American." By the third inning, it becomes clear he has no idea how the game is played and doesn't understand any of the rules. He blushes at his ignorance and orders a hot dog.

She tries to explain. "The only game in history with the simple goal of returning home; hit the ball, run the bases, strive to reach home. An admirable concept, don't you think?"

He nods as she wipes yellow mustard from his cheek. He kisses her. Kissing Rebecca seems the only worthwhile thing to do.

As buds and blooms announce the arrival of a new season, Wynn is unable to grasp what is happening. Is this a great, last fling before the end of college, or are they falling in love? He becomes nervous, unsure of himself; words stumble from his mouth, and sentences are left dangling. Graduation is here, the chrysalis of college is being swept aside, and he doesn't know what to do. His only knowledge of love comes from the movies, so he decides to emulate the behavior he has seen in countless films. He books a table at the elegant Fairmont Hotel across the river. He tells Rebecca it is a celebration, a festive dinner away from campus to honor their accomplishments and bless their opportune encounter.

She checks her coat and scarf, and the maître d' leads her to a round table in the center of the restaurant. Wynn stands, a smile disguising his terror. A bottle of champagne is chilling in an ice bucket. The linens are sharply creased, and the crystal glasses act like prisms, refracting the soft light from the overhead chandeliers. After the menus arrive, the well-mannered Englishman gets down on one knee and asks Rebecca to marry him.

The second he sees her discomfort, he realizes how ill-advised this entire evening has been.

"Oh God, Wynnie, do you think? Are we sure?"

She smiles, and then she cries, understanding the hurt she is inflicting. He rises, awkward and agonized, looking about to see who has witnessed his humiliation.

She asks for patience. The melting ice in the champagne bucket shifts noisily. Both remain seated, stunned.

Wynn finally speaks, suggesting they talk in the morning.

Morning comes, but without the hoped-for clarity. Both are uncomfortable when he calls, nervous as teenagers.

"Time. Just give me some time." A long pause follows her entreaty. "The ring is beautiful," she adds.

The ring is beautiful, he thinks, but he wishes he could see it on her finger. As usual with Rebecca, he listens, listens carefully for any sign that he still has a chance.

"Give me the summer," she says. "My life is unfolding so swiftly, I feel like those divers who surface too quickly, and suffer, what, what do they call that?"

"The bends," he answers, wishing he could see her face.

He promises to wait and returns to London. She takes refuge on Lake Aspetuck. She spends the summer putting hundreds of miles on her sporty green convertible, searching for answers that never come.

"Becca, life is not meant to be this difficult!" her mother Nonnie says. "The decision to marry should be joyous, not troubling. Empty your head of all these conflicted thoughts and simply listen. You'll know if this is right."

"How did you know with Daddy? Were you sure?"

Nonnie smiles. "Yes, the minute I saw his eyes, I knew this was a man I could trust, and love."

Rebecca sinks into a pillowed rocker on the wide wooden porch, releasing a sigh of frustration.

"Oh, Momma, he felt so right in Cambridge. He was delightful and engaging and honest. And so smart! He made me laugh. But then he began, ever so slightly, to become afraid. I could see it. He lost confidence in himself; confidence in us."

"Invite him here. Let him stay with us. See if he's a good fit. There is no need to rush."

"I promised to go there. This fall."

"Something is holding you back. Remember, 'a perfect idea has not a single element of error.'"

Rebecca rolls her eyes in frustration. "Momma, you cannot throw Christian Science at him! He'll go running."

"Your beliefs are a part of you. Have you not shared them?"

"My beliefs come from many places, Momma. We've talked about this."

"To believe in everything is to believe in nothing. Don't be a religious dilettante."

"I don't even know what that means!" she angrily responds, annoyed by her mother's certitude.

"Well, is he a churchgoer?"

Rebecca stares at her hands. She wants to get back in her car.

"No, he's not."

The uncomfortable quiet is interrupted by a loud splash. Jared's tanned body skims the surface of the lake. Nonnie points in his direction. "Are you going to tell him?"

Rebecca pauses, wondering why her mother has asked such an odd question. "Jared? What do you mean?"

"You're going to break his heart."

"Oh, don't be silly. We're friends."

"Well, call it what you will. All I know is he comes up here each morning hoping for a glimpse of you. I tell him you've gone off on one of your drives, and he asks when you'll return. His eyes shine, then he runs back home to wait until he hears the sound of tires on gravel."

Rebecca ponders her mother's statement and whispers, as if to herself, "He's a kid!"

"That is not how he sees himself. He's in love with you." Nonnie stands to leave, but then adds, "You cannot marry a man I've never met! Invite him here, see him anew in familiar surroundings, safe surroundings."

The summer advances, and Rebecca continues to drive the country roads, lost in thought, wrestling with her future. She and Wynn write and occasionally speak on the phone. His voice is solid and his words reassuring. They plan a visit; she will fly to England for the August bank holidays, and he will come to America for Thanksgiving. These arrangements give Rebecca some room to breathe, and she begins to enjoy her summer.

Perhaps that's why in July, on a sticky, airless night in Flushing Meadow Park, beneath the totemic Unisphere that towers over Shea Stadium, she succumbs to the youthful zeal and passionate pleadings of Jared Honor, a boy who has always loved her. He isn't what she needs—he's seventeen—but his fervor and fire dissolves her anxiety and provides temporary comfort. They have grown up together, he lives on her property, she taught him to dance! His lovemaking is sweet and unskilled; she will treasure the feeling of him trembling close to her.

The next day she drives to Boston. She can't face Jared, and she can't talk with Wynn nor discuss it with her mother. A college friend has a roomy apartment on Boylston and helps Rebecca dodge the many calls from concerned friends. She hides away for weeks, surrounded by the landmarks of college that now feel so distant.

When the tenderness in her breasts confirms her worst fears, she flies to London and begs forgiveness. Wynn doesn't get down on bended knee, but he accepts her and the child that isn't his. They marry in a simple celebration in an ancient church in Dorset, and on a soft April morning, the tiny baby arrives. She names him Baéz after the folk singer she and the baby's father adore.

Wynn takes a job with an investment bank, and he and Rebecca rent a small apartment in Soho. The neighborhood is lively, and the rents are reasonable. Wynn is a nervous but caring father, but Rebecca feels the need to give him a child that is his, so before she becomes comfortable with motherhood, a second child is on its way. Nonnie flies over to assist her overwhelmed daughter, now the proud mother of two sons, separated in age by less than a year.

Nonnie stays at a small hotel nearby and arrives each day after Wynn has left for work. On this particular morning, however, she's greeted by the panicked face of her son-in-law.

"He's burning up. I called for the doctor, but he's at least an hour away. 'Becca is sick with worry."

Nonnie removes her coat and enters the room that holds two small cribs. Rebecca is seated in a rocker, still in her cotton nightdress, singing to Baéz. She smiles when she sees her mother. Nonnie takes the tiny bundle and sits in a side chair. Rebecca is tired, but smiling and unafraid.

Nonnie speaks quietly. "Your husband's fear is overwhelming this child. Can we send him to the store or something?"

Rebecca goes into the living room, asking Elwynn to buy more baby aspirin. He rushes out the door as Rebecca rejoins her mother.

"I promise to say this only once. I do not want to become one of those know-it-all grandmothers, but, Becca, you need to invite God into this home. These children deserve the protection and guidance of being acquainted with their maker, regardless of Elwynn's agnosticism."

"Momma, I know, but my hands are full. Please! One day at a time! My little Baéz is much better now. I've been sitting with him, singing hymns. My dear husband is indeed a fearful man, but I see him trying, day by day, to better understand life. He'll get there. He loves his boys."

When the doctor arrives, Wynn is pleased to be told that his son is fine, and his temperature is now normal.

"Your lovely young wife knows what she's doing, but perhaps I could prescribe a calming sedative for you?"

After a month in London, Nonnie packs her bags, confident her daughter has everything under control. Wynn stays home with the babies as Rebecca drives her mother to Heathrow.

"This is so sweet of you, but completely unnecessary!" Nonnie says. "I know you both treasure your weekends together."

"Momma, I need to tell you something."

Nonnie turns to her daughter, concerned by the tone of her voice.

"I am sorry I didn't tell you before. I wasn't sure how," Rebecca admits. "Wynn asked to keep it secret, for a few years at least, but it doesn't feel right."

"What?"

"Jared is the father of Baéz," Rebecca blurts. "He doesn't know. Please don't say anything until I figure out what to do."

Nonnie is surprised by her first thoughts upon hearing this confession. They weren't about her daughter and how sad this secret must be for her. Nor were they about her son-in-law and the surprising generosity he has demonstrated in taking this child and its mother into his life. Instead, Nonnie's heart aches for Jared, that sweet boy who has no idea that an alternate universe will one day be revealed to him, a universe he is completely unprepared for. How will he react when he learns he has a son being raised by another man, a man who also loves Rebecca?

Nonnie reveals none of these thoughts and instead does what is expected—she hugs her daughter and agrees to remain silent.

✶ ✶ ✶

The boy's cribs lie side by side in a small room. They watch each other every day, riveted, wisps of red hair on one and a thick mane of black on the other. Rebecca calls them her "her little bruisers." An expression from American football, she explains. They are a handful, and Wynn tries to lessen his wife's burdens by rushing home each day with take-out from one of the many restaurants in their neighborhood.

"A buddy at work gave me seats to Wimbledon for Saturday. Do you think Mrs. Devon can watch the boys?"

"What fun! Yes, I'll call her. My uncles were great tennis players, Nonnie's brothers." She laughs. "Maybe we could nurture our own doubles team!"

Wynn is good with the kids. Patient. In the evenings, he often sits alone with Brighton, cradling the child in wonder. He's noticed that the boys behave better apart, unable to egg each other on. With Wynn home on the weekends, Rebecca soothes her tired mind with the occasional drive in her sporty Triumph. With two children, the car is no longer practical, but she'd shipped it over anyway.

Rebecca is still adjusting to driving on the left. She speeds over the Ring Road, the top down, hair blowing, music blaring, smiling as she envisions her handsome husband pushing their toddlers in a wicker carriage through Soho Square. She races through the flashing traffic light, forgetting where she is, and turns into the wrong lane where the loud honking of horns is too late for her to correct course and save her tiny convertible from the oncoming crush of cars and trucks. At the moment of impact, her small voice utters a regretful "oh no" and then is heard no more.

Nonnie lost her father and brothers in the war, and her husband succumbed to an outbreak of pneumonia. Now, as she flies to London to escort Rebecca's body home, thoughts of her grandchildren fill her mind. They are all the family she has left but they will be raised an ocean away from her.

Elwynn neglected to file the adoption papers that Rebecca so painstakingly prepared. Legally, Nonnie can claim Baéz and bring him up on her own. Or she can inform Jared of his paternity, changing his life forever. Yet she fears she is being incredibly selfish. Shouldn't the boys be brought up together, as brothers? Is Elwynn a suitable parent? Will he allow her to be part of their lives? She has her doubts. Truth be told, she and Wynn are no better than strangers, and she fears for the children being raised in a godless home.

Nonnie finds an English barrister who specializes in family law. Her rights are clear, but the morality of her actions is not—not to her. She wants to do what is right for the child, yet like the indecision that plagued her daughter before accepting Wynn's proposal, Nonnie also hesitates, wondering who this man is.

A nurse sits with the boys in their tiny bedroom. Nonnie can hear her reading to them as they whimper and whine. Wynn pours tea for them both, his hands shaking, his eyes clouded with grief.

"I can't stop you, but I doubt 'Becca would have wanted her sons separated. Are you giving Baéz to that 'lawn boy'? Some kid?"

Nonnie cringes at Elwynn's tone. It is ugly and condescending. Who is he, and what did Rebecca see in him? She searches for the loving qualities that must have been present in their marriage, but all she sees is a bitter man overwhelmed by loss. All affection and tenderness has left him.

"I am taking Baéz to the States. It is my hope that at some future date the boys can be reunited. They should certainly know of each other's existence. I don't mean to add to your present sorrows, but I think this is best."

She speaks in an even tone, but he isn't listening; he's not even looking at her.

"Tell the nurse when you're coming, and she'll have Baéz ready," he says and then leaves the room. Nonnie has prayed and prayed, seeking guidance in handling this difficult situation. The words *mercy* and *grace* repeat over and over in her mind. But for whom? she wonders. For Elwynn? For herself? No, she finally reasons with sudden clarity, for Jared and the child.

Brighton grows swiftly, as if aware of the small measure of patience his father possesses. London offers no solace, so when a position in the firm opens up in Barcelona, they move. And when the Paris office expands, they move again.

Paris is sublime, and both learn French easily. A variety of male tutors and female nannies and the occasional ditsy girlfriend are charged with Brighton's upbringing. When Wynn stares at his son, the freckles on the boy's face is their only connection. He has his mother's eyes and chin, her excitable demeanor, and her laugh. A laugh that on some days he hears in nearby room and smiles, thinking she is near.

He is proud of the boy. Brighton is smart and observant. Wynn often wonders about the "other one." In the rare instances when he speaks of Baéz, that is how he refers to him—the "other one." Nonnie has sent pictures, but he doesn't share them with Brighton. He rebuffs her suggestions of Brighton coming to the States for a visit.

As Paris begins to feel comfortable and familiar, they move again—to Florence. Another language for Brighton to absorb, another city to wander and study. He is aware his father prefers the company of adults so he accommodates this knowledge as best he can, tossing aside childish behavior and habits. He is as likely to scream "*Merde!*" or wave goodbye with a friendly "*Ciao!*" as he is to kiss a friend on both cheeks. He is bright and effusive and conspicuous. He shops in secondhand stores, drinks coffee in streetside cafes, and enjoys European films.

"Oh, it was a mighty story. The audience applauded at the end. I've never seen that!"

Brighton has anointed "mighty" as his favorite new word. Wynn puts down his newspaper and looks at his son.

"What was it about?"

"World War Two, in France. A boarding school, where some of the boys are Jews hiding from the Nazis. Oh my, it was mighty, indeed!"

The boy is a sponge, absorbing everything around him. Wynn wishes his own appetite were as ravenous. "Isn't it time for a haircut?" he asks.

His son's red hair reaches past the collar. Today it is held in place with a checked headband, his jeans have holes in the knees, and his black boots have bright chrome hardware and thick soles. Florence is a city fixated on fashion, and his son is noticed everywhere he goes.

"Nope," Brighton says. "Going to wear it in a ponytail as soon as it grows a bit more. I'll be memorable!" And the boy laughs. "Memorable" is another favorite word.

Wynn's career has become the driving force of his life. Climbing the ladder within the reigning hierarchy of Banque Nationale de Paris is his sole focus. Personal relationships are brief and fleeting, hobbies are non-existent, and fatherhood is simply a responsibility that needs managing, like the stocks he so ably studies and recommends and trades.

When the center of world finance beckons, he accepts. New York becomes their fourth home, and they live together like members of a fancy club. Brighton calls his father by his given name, and Wynn refers to Brighton as "buddy." At the age of twelve, the boy reads *The New York Times* each morning while sitting opposite his father, both of them sipping coffee. At night Wynn and "Buddy" order meals from their neighborhood shops: Chinese, Mexican, sometimes prime rib from the steak house on the corner. If a sitter can't not be found, Wynn takes Brighton along on business dinners and even on dates. The girls all resemble Rebecca in some way—blonde and cheerful—but none are able to reawaken the man who has buried himself beside his one true love.

Brighton has his own credit cards and his own checking account. Wynn teaches him to look people in the eye. He shows him the mechanics of a proper handshake, the trick to tying a Windsor knot, and the elegance of cuff links.

"Nonnie called today," he announces, carefully checking his father for a reaction; any mention of Rebecca's family puts Elwynn in a sour mood.

"Yes? How is everything out there?" he asks, his tone neutral.

"Terrific. She asked if I could come out to Connecticut for the Christmas holidays. Can I?"

Brighton had spent the previous summer at Nonnie's lakeside home, and when he returned to New York, he was bursting with wild tales and crazy adventures. Elwynn was jealous, fearing his son was being stolen from him. Now he reminds himself that the boys are brothers, that they grew up in side-by-side cribs, fighting for attention, and now deserve the chance to know one another.

"You won't miss Christmas in the big city?"

"I don't have any friends here yet. Baéz is fun. I like him. A ton of snow is predicted. Could be memorable!"

Wynn completely understands. He is not the kind of father who takes his boy sledding or builds giant snowmen. He knows, somewhere deep inside, that he is a dull man who has fathered a luminous child.

3.

A BOHEMIAN SPRITZ

Baéz dreads bedtime. He knows the minute he closes his eyes, he will hear the deep, abrasive groans of the shifting ice overhead and cold water will numb his body, leaving him lifeless and floating like a specimen in a sea of formaldehyde.

"Perfect love casteth out fear," Nonnie advises. It's from the Bible. She and his dad are big fans. They each read aloud to him, morning and evening, his childhood defined by tales of lions' dens and fiery furnaces.

"Look around, see who you love, treasure them," Nonnie instructs.

Who do I love? he wonders.

He knows he loves his dad. Jared is thoughtful. Generous. Handsome. All the ladies say so. He is a jack-of-all-trades, doing the odd jobs no one else wants—emptying gutters, fixing roofs, cutting lawns, plowing driveways, felling trees.

He loves Nonnie, too. The consummate grandmother. Always a kind word, never too busy to listen. And Miss Talmadge. She is soft and has an exotic fragrance that follows her down the school hallways. She introduced him to Dickens and Hawthorne.

Brighton. Yes, he loves Brighton. A true best friend, like the ones in all the stories he reads. A year younger but a head taller. Brighton, spelled with an "O," meaning "one who is loved." He looked it up in the dictionary. Brighton is a wonder. When the dark limousine had pulled up to their drive last summer, this tall boy got out and received a huge hug from Nonnie. She walked him down to Jared's rustic cabin and introduced him as her grandson; Baéz's brother. Jared corrected her. "Half-brother," he stated, as if revealing some terrible family secret.

His brother is impressive, his smile inviting, his manner welcoming. He has a thick head of deep red hair, nearly burgundy. His eyes are large and colored a soft, watery green. Baéz memorizes the exotic features of a face that resembles no other.

Now, Baéz holds that face in mind as he tries not breathing while blocking out the reverberations of the unsettled ice, but he begins screaming anyway and is only released from this nightmare by his father, who is quietly rocking him in his arms.

Every morning.

The same dream.

"Shh, shh, quiet now. It's not real. You're not drowning. Not then and not now. Shh."

But it is real. To him. The fear is overwhelming, and neither his father's faith nor his grandmother's trust in an all-knowing God comfort him. They speak of Him like an old friend, a schoolmate they can always count on. He wishes he shared their conviction.

"Does B-B-Bright know? About my nightmares?"

"No. We've not said anything. He goes out early, shoveling sidewalks with my crew. He's a hard worker."

Baéz is pleased by this compliment. Before the storm, his dad would refer to Brighton as "that fancy boy," but now he is noticeably kinder. It is the only good result of his scary misadventure under the ice.

✳ ✳ ✳

A nurse at the hospital tipped off a friend at the *Hartford Courant.* The article, "Miracle on the Ice," is a perfect "feel-good" story for the holiday season, and soon other journalists follow, including the NBC affiliate in New Haven. Over and over the boys repeat their account, always ending with Baéz declaring, "He s-s-saved my life!" He speaks in a high, excited voice and has developed a stutter.

Freaked, Brighton begs Nonnie for help. "You have to make him stop! He whispers my name, over and over, saying 'He sa-sa-sa-saved me!' It's creepy!"

"Be patient with him. He's confused. He doesn't understand what happened."

"What doesn't he understand?" asks Brighton, throwing up his arms in frustration.

"The doctors confused him. They spoke of heart attacks and organ failures. These men should have kept their own counsel."

"Heart attacks?"

Now Brighton is confused.

"These terms have the power to create fear," Nonnie explains. "An intern at the hospital said he should be dead."

This stopped Brighton's harangue. "So, the papers are right? It is a miracle?"

She took her grandson's hand in her own, wanting him to understand.

"God is always in complete control, and his protection is ever available to everyone. You were simply an instrument helping Baéz demonstrate his enduring immunity from danger. There are no miracles in God's kingdom; simply the harmonious unfoldment of good."

They sit quietly, Brighton attempting to understand Nonnie's words.

"I hope our holiday activities haven't alarmed your father," she says. "Have you spoken with him?"

"No." Elwynn would accuse him of telling tales. "But I'm going back early; he's throwing a New Year's bash and asked for my help. I'll tell him then."

In truth, Brighton simply wants to go home. He wonders if his father is right. Wynn thinks all the Connecticut relatives are squirrely. He laugh when he says it, but Brighton knows he disapproves of them and frowns on Brighton's visits. They're not like other people. This he knows. Yet, some part of him trusts them; trusts their convictions and their opinions. They confuse him but also challenge him.

He stands and gives Nonnie a kiss on the cheek. "I'm going to go pack. Dad will send one of his guys to pick me up."

"I understand. Make sure to tell Baéz, okay?"

Brighton nods but he doesn't tell Baéz. When the dark limo pulls out of the drive, he sees his brother in an upper window of Jared's cabin, waving, his face a blank.

✳ ✳ ✳

Nicolas Tibor and Dušan Novotny are well-known in Elwynn's affluent neighborhood. They both drive for a local car service and, in their off hours, perform various tasks for nearby residents who can't handle a hammer or fix a toilet. They are polar opposites but are each other's sworn protectors. Proud Czechs with thick accents, their immigrant status does not dampen their dreams but instead increases their desire to become "players" in the great game of Monopoly known as New York.

Dušan is dangerously handsome, a pencil-thin gym rat with white-blond hair cut close to the scalp. A gothic tattoo is inked under the hair on his neck, and a metal bar creases his left ear lobe. He is a severe and formidable presence.

Niko is neither handsome nor formidable, but like a mutt lacking a pedigree, is adored by everyone he encounters. His accent fills the streets on the upper East side of Manhattan as he hawks pirated videos, counterfeit watches, and imitation Vuitton handbags. In December, he sells Christmas trees on the corner. He is friendly and wears a wide smile that contradicts his dark features. He has an ease that creates comfort, and his confused vocabulary is filled with odd expressions that put a smile on the faces of all passersby. As unalike as the two men are, they are inseparable, sharing an unheated loft in Little Italy.

Tonight, New Year's Eve, Dušan has been sent to Connecticut in a dented town car to retrieve Brighton. The young teen is frightened of him and had wished for Niko to pick him up. Neither speak as Dušan races into the city driving like a madman yet able to avoid the many holiday speed traps.

When they arrive, the limestone townhouse is teeming with activity; caterers and waiters and floral designers are transforming the spare, cheerless house into a festive space. After Brighton runs up the wide stairs and dumps his stuff in his bedroom, Nico calls up from the chef's kitchen that anchors the north end of the parlor floor.

"Perfect timing, Boy-O. Come on down and give me a hand! Your dad's invited a ton of people."

"Be right there!" Brighton answers.

He can already hear his father bellowing at everyone. This is why Brighton had gone to Connecticut—to dodge the false exuberance his father exhibits at holiday time. Elwynn is loud and boisterous, spouting drunken declarations of affection to all and everyone. He becomes sentimental, his accent thicker than usual, and then spends weeks mailing out notes of apology.

Brighton goes downstairs and changes the music. Madonna's "Like a Prayer" begins blasting through the house.

His father claps him on the shoulder. "Ah, the prodigal returns! Welcome home, buddy. Good to see you."

Nico interrupts, giving Brighton instructions. "I'm setting up by the fireplace. Grab the lemons, olives, onions, limes, and cherries. They're all together, on the same shelf in the back of the icebox."

Darnell, their housekeeper, greets the guests and takes their coats while Dušan circulates trays of appetizers, his tough demeanor softened by his beauty. The bar is the center of activity, and Nico is the star attraction—cracking ice, spinning glasses, and putting a smile on everyone's face. The hopeful promise of a new year envelopes the party, and Brighton is glad to be here.

"You seem like a lady who would enjoy a sparkly Negroni. Let me make one for you!"

The music gets louder, and laughter bounces off the clean white walls as Brighton sits on the stairs overlooking the living room, studying the handsome crowd of successful people, smiling at the beautiful women, impatient to become an adult. He nods to his father's colleagues as they crowd around Nico's bar, calling out their orders.

"Buddy, make me another. What do you call it?"

Nico laughs: this guest is already drunk, and midnight is still hours away.

"A Bohemian Spritz. Good for whatever ails you."

The man calls out to a buddy across the room. "Tug, get over here, you got to try one of these!" He lifts his glass while signaling to a tall, serious-looking man. "We're part of Wynn's crew. That's Tug, and I'm called Bill."

"I am Nico. Pleased to meet you. His crew? You sail boats?" He spins the shaker, bangs the lid free, and pours out a perfect concoction.

Brighton smiles. Nico knows they don't sail boats. He's simply winding them up, drawing them in with feigned naiveté. Brighton admires his ease and confidence. Both Dušan and Nico feel superior to this crowd; they think these spoiled bankers and brokers are soft and foolish, unprepared for the surprises sure to come their way.

"We work together, nearly everyone here," Bill says as he looks over the room. "A few I don't know. But myself, Tug here, Charley, and that blond crew-cut guy—we're all poker buddies. Every Thursday. It's a lot of fun, wouldn't you say, Tug?"

Tug answers: "Hard to say no to your boss."

"Mr. Bethune is your boss?" Nico asks.

"Yeah, and he's a real rainmaker."

"That is a good thing, a rainmaker?"

"That is a *great* thing; he pulls in lots of fees and showers us with the excess!"

"And are you allowed to beat your boss?" Nico shakes his head, doubtful. "Sounds tricky to me."

"Nah, he's fine. Good guy. His son too. Don't let the fancy Brit accent fool you. He's a killer. You play?"

Nico feigns confusion.

Bill laughs and then explains. "Cards. You play cards? Gamble?"

Wynn walks over and hands two empty glasses to Nico. "More of those grapefruit martinis, or whatever you call them, Nico. The ladies are parched!"

"Fire and Ice, that's what I call them. Two more coming up."

"Where'd you find this guy, Wynn? He's a master barkeep. We're trying to see if Nico has a feeling for cards. Maybe he could mix for us on Thursdays?"

Wynn looks over at Nico, and Nico shrugs.

"I gamble a little, but not cards," he insists. "I'm too clumsy for cards."

Nonsense, thinks Brighton. He often sees Nico in the parking garage playing cards with the other drivers. He rarely loses.

"What do you gamble on then?" asks Tug.

"Like you, with your stocks, I wager on probabilities, outcomes, winners and losers."

There is a silence, and then Tug's face breaks into a wide grin. "Sports. You bet on sports!"

Nico nods.

"What? Football? Basketball?"

He has their attention. The rest of the party whizzes around them, but the three men are glued to Nicola.

"Yes, and your baseball, and Bowl games."

"We can place bets with you on the football playoffs?"

Nico nods.

"Charlie, listen to this! Nico here is a bookie."

"Please, gentlemen. *Speculator*. Not bookie. 'Bookie' sounds cheap."

A tall, perfumed lady pushes her way through Nico's new fans and loudly announces, "That's the best fucking drink I ever had. Make me another, will ya, sweetie?"

"Another Christmas Bomb coming right up, missus."

"What's in it, doll?"

"It is aquavit and vermouth, with dash of bitters."

"I love how you say that." She turns to her host, smiling, and remarks, "Wynnie, you're not the only one at the party with a sexy accent."

"Guess not, Peaches. I guess not," responds Elwynn.

After Nico hands her a drink, she blows him a kiss. Then she walks by the wide stairs and sees Brighton perched there, eavesdropping.

"Can I bring you a Christmas Bomb, sweetheart?"

Brighton blushes and shakes his head. He is watching Dušan signal to Nico. They are up to something, and he is trying to figure out what it is.

"Careful of those two," warns Peaches as she gives Brighton a quick peck on the cheek. "They're up to no good!"

When a new wave of guests arrive, Brighton sees Dušan slip another item into Nico's coat pocket. The object is shiny. Maybe a bracelet, he thinks. To get a closer look, he begins to help Darnell collect empty glasses and crumpled napkins. The countdown to midnight is about to begin, and his father's voice is getting louder and louder.

"How about a Spritz, Boy-O?" Nico asks.

Brighton isn't tempted by alcohol, but he now understands what Nico is doing. He leans in close, whispering. "If your sleek buddy returns all the mislaid items, explaining how he discovered them behind the bar or left in the powder room, I'm sure no one will suspect."

Then he walks away, unsettled yet curious to know what the two schemers will do. Nico steps out from behind the bar, stares at the kid with an admiring smile, and then walks over to his partner, whispering discretely in his ear. Brighton watches from across the room as Dušan sends him a threatening look.

"Four—three—two—ONE! Happy New Year!"

The room erupts in cheers and kisses. Brighton watches as Dušan walks up to several women, explaining how he found their broach behind a cushion and their watch left behind on the bar.

Brighton never tells his father. He enjoys Nico. He can learn from him. Nico thrives in a tough world, and Brighton is learning that the universe is more complicated than he had thought. Young boys have heart attacks, and grandmothers wield magic. His Christmas holiday has been unnerving, but having such a cunning man in his debt might prove useful.

4.

HONOR BRIGHT

In the spring, Nonnie invites Brighton to celebrate Baéz's birthday.

"He misses you; we all do. Please say yes."

The boys have only spoken a few times since the incident on the ice, and the calls were awkward, peppered with long silences. Brighton is not at ease with the adoration his older brother now expresses.

Nonnie's sure, sweet voice continues, "Fear has settled within him. I am trying to teach him that fear possesses no power of its own, only the power he gives it, but I'm not sure I'm getting through. Please come up. You might be just the medicine he needs."

It's the damn sled, thinks Brighton. Baéz treats it reverently. "*A family heirloom,*" Jared always says, and Brighton is sure that's why Baéz refused to jump, choosing instead to be dragged to the bottom.

Maybe Brighton can find the sled, bring it to the surface, and let Baéz confront his fears. Could it help? Worth a try, he thinks as he accepts his grandmother's invitation. He goes out to Brooklyn, to a surf shop under the bridge on the East River, where he buys a rubberized wet suit to insulate him from the cold.

"Sprinkle a ton of talcum on your arms and legs; it makes it easier to slip the suit over your skin," advises the teen behind the counter.

"Do I wear underwear or what?" asks Brighton, embarrassed by his lack of knowledge.

"Nothing, man. Let it all hang out. When you first enter the water, take a piss in the suit, and it'll keep you plenty warm."

Brighton laughs. "Gross," he says as the kid folds the shiny suit into a box that features a buxom surfer riding a giant wave.

When he arrives on the weekend of his brother's birthday, Nonnie's yard is carpeted with daffodils and bluebells. He walks up the steps to the wide, painted porch where the summer furniture—wicker chairs and rockers and planters—is now in place. Before going inside, he takes a long look at the lake. The water is calm, but despite the clear sky, the surface appears leaden and unwelcoming. He rushes upstairs to the room he calls his own and puts his camera, his Discman, and a bag with his clothes on the bed. He takes the box bearing the lady surfer and runs down to the cabin.

Baéz's shiny yellow Schwinn is leaning against the porch post. Brighton calls out to him, rapping on the door of the equipment shed and then staring again at the lake. He sees the wavy disturbance in the middle, the air bubbles floating to the surface. *That must be where the sled lies.*

"Hey."

A small voice behind him. Quiet. He has cut his hair. He is taller. Fuller.

"Radical hair trim, guy. How are you?" asks Brighton

"Sp-sp-spring took forever. Very harsh around here. Gl-gl-glad to be outside, finally. What's in the b-box?"

"Wet suit. Thought I'd try it out and maybe find the sled. What d'ya think?"

Baéz takes a step back, his eyes wide, as if the very mention of the word "sled" has the power to weaken him.

"C-c-can't. Promised Nonnie I'd go into town and p-p-pick up some groceries for our dinner. That's why I got the b-b-bike out. Looks good, don't she?"

"Yeah, the color rocks. You do it?"

Baéz nods, obviously pleased, but Brighton hardly recognizes his brother; he is timid and shy, like they've never met. He realizes the stutter embarrasses Baéz.

"I'll bike into town with you," Brighton offers. "I can look for the sled tomorrow."

"Thanks, but no. D-d-dad will be pleased to get it back. The water is still freezing c-cold. You'll be alright?"

"Yes. The suit will protect me. At least that's what they say. I've got to try it out. Takes forever to put it on. It's like a second skin. Wait up, okay?"

Brighton enters the equipment shed. He looks at the rakes and shovels and then spots the chainsaw he had used that day. It's been cleaned and oiled.

Brighton removes his clothes and shakes the can of baby powder on his arms and legs. He wiggles his way into the thin rubber and then pulls the long string attached to the zipper up the back. The metal closure pulls the neoprene suit tight to his frame. He stands and smiles, feeling extremely cool. He walks onto the dock and sees his reflection on the lake's surface, his new outfit moving in sync with his own body.

"C-c-cat-woman's gonna love you!" comments Baéz.

Thanks to the upcoming film, the provocative poster of the man in shining black is plastered everywhere. Brighton is crushing on Cat woman, but Baéz is enamored of the tight suit of Kevlar worn by his winged hero.

"Slammin', ain't it?" says Brighton, smiling as he grabs a coil of nylon rope and dives off the dock. His feet and face are shocked by the cold, but his body stays warm inside the new suit. He does as the salesman suggested, releasing a stream of urine as he swims, and the sudden warmth that surrounds his midsection feels curiously pleasurable.

The water is dark, and visibility is limited; the sun hardly reaches the muddy bottom. He dives several times, stirring up the weeds and clay and sand. He looks up at the lake's surface, imagining the bright sky as a solid, impenetrable ceiling of ice. A shiver runs through him as he emerges to breathe in fresh air. He looks towards the dock, but Baéz is gone. Brighton hoped retrieving the sled would lessen his brother's fears, but now he wonders if he is simply triggering unpleasant memories.

He dives again, pushing these thoughts away. His foot strikes a large object. He turns his body upside down and searches the lake's bottom with his hands. There it is, he feels it—the iron sled. He ties the rope to one of the metal rails and then struggles to the surface with his heavy load. He reaches the opposite shore and pulls himself up the muddy bank, dragging his valuable treasure, rusted and covered in weeds.

Breathing hard, Brighton sits on a large boulder. Images from that day fill his mind—images of his brother in the ambulance, his body shaking, his smooth skin the color of blueberries. As he stares at the encrusted sled, he realizes this was a bad idea. He shouldn't have come. It's too soon. He promises himself he will finish what he started and then return home; he doesn't want to cause any more upset.

At sundown, when Baéz returns, the sled is on the dock, tied with a ribbon. It has been cleaned, the rust removed, and a note says, "Happy Birthday, Big Brother."

He runs to Nonnie's house to thank Brighton, but the bedroom is empty. A note on the desk explains that Brighton has returned to the city.

Baéz sits on his brother's bed, filled with disappointment. He tries to shake away the image of his brother in his sleek wetsuit. His brother is a superhero, his savior.

When they first met, Baéz had just returned from an overnight camping trip with several boys from My Redeemer Church, where they had learned "The Scout's Vespers."

Have I kept my honor bright?
Can I guiltless sleep tonight?
Have I done and have I dared,
In everything to Be Prepared?

Baéz thought the pledge *honor bright* was a perfect explication of their names—Baéz Honor and Brighton Bethune. He saw it as a signal that their friendship would be long and lasting.

Behind him, in the closet, hanging from a wooden hanger, the rubber suit is dripping water onto the wooden floor. He holds it, searching for any warmth still trapped within its folds.

What an idiot, he tells himself, embarrassed, while taking Brighton's note up to Nonnie's study. Her coon cat is sleeping soundly in the sun-filled room.

"I shared a cup of tea with that sinister driver as he waited to take Brighton back to the city. Did he tell you he was leaving early?"

"Nope, just this," he says, handing her the note.

"What's he mean? Sorry for what? Did you boys argue?"

Baéz shakes his head. "I embarrass him. My stutter." He shakes his head again. "I don't know. He didn't explain, he j-j-just left."

Baéz settles into the deep cushions of his favorite chair. Each day since New Year's, Baéz sits with his grandmother, and they read the Bible together. He wants to understand what happened that day. Why did a nurse say he died? He wants to study the art of healing. Nonnie's efforts, her clarity of thought and strong faith had restored him to life. He has decided to trust the spiritual component that she says is present in all our lives.

Nonnie is a metaphysical healer. Licensed by the Christian Science church, she utilizes prayer to heal physical ailments. She has lived in Sterling all her life and has rid many a neighbor of measles, sprained ankles, the flu, breast cancer, and blood diseases. She has also restored harmony to lives lost to addiction, domestic violence, and grief. She works with her patients to help them recognize their innate perfection.

"We can read and read, and talk and discuss, and fill your beautiful head with all the truths of the universe, but until you turn these beliefs into practice, until you go out and heal, you will not truly understand what it is we are learning. Belief is a powerful tool, and faith is a trusty companion, but only when these truths are understood will you see the real spiritual world that surrounds us."

Baéz nods. The men and women he reads about each day have no misgivings. They are confident in their view of the Lord.

"How do I apply this to m-my stutter?"

Nonnie shakes her head. "Don't call it 'my stutter.' It has nothing to do with you. Disown it; understand that God gives you your voice, that each and every time you speak, God is with your tongue. Moses felt insufficient and ill equipped to ask Pharaoh to release the Jews from their captivity. When he expressed his fears, the Lord answered, 'certainly I shall be with thee.' He is with us, guiding us, governing us. He made you perfect, and nothing can stop your ability to demonstrate that perfection. Right here, right now."

Baéz relishes her certainty. To be present with Nonnie is to understand that anything is possible. "What cannot the Lord do?" Nonnie's radical view of the world contradicts so much of what he sees and reads, but as he listens to her voice, he enjoys a confidence that warms him, making him feel safe. The image of his brother creates that same warmth.

Nonnie's words fill him; Brighton's image sustains him.

✳ ✳ ✳

When he learns that Jared's crew has raked and restored Nonnie's clay court, Brighton is anxious to play on it. His private school has let out for the summer, and Baéz's melancholy is preferable to being with his father and his silly new girlfriend. She has a high squeaky voice, and all her sentences end with a question mark. The house resounds with the thrum of her nasal sibilance, and Brighton is anxious to be elsewhere.

The court sits on a level acre of land overlooking the lake. Enclosed on three sides by chain wire fencing, the fourth wall is solid, made from wooden boards and painted deep green with a horizontal white line painted at net height—a practice wall. A player can hit balls over the "net" and have them bounce back without needing a partner.

Brighton finds the equipment he needs in the shed below Jared's cabin, and he spends the mornings hitting the yellow balls against the wooden wall. *Thwack. Thwack. Thwack.*

"You know you are d-d-driving Nonnie crazy, right? Bang, bang, b-bang. Sounds like a gun range over here."

Baéz is standing outside the fence, his fingers entwined in the narrow-gauge wire.

Brighton continues to hit the ball. *Thwack. Thwack.* Baéz is undeterred.

"You have a strong s-s-troke. Where'd you learn?"

"School. Paris. You play?"

"A little. Dad's friend, Nathanael Winning, gave me a few lessons at The Aspetuck Club. They have a clay court too, right near the ninth hole."

Brighton nods.

"I could get another racquet, hit some back to you. Save Nonnie's sanity."

"You are a selfless person," jokes Brighton, smiling, providing Baéz the permission he needs to race across the huge green lawn and find a racquet.

From her study atop the house, the sudden quiet is a relief. Nonnie looks out the window and sees her grandsons attempting to hit the ball over the net. She grins and reaches for her phone, calling Nathan.

"Hello, young man. I'm glad I found you."

"Glad to be found! Preparing for another splendid summer on the lake?"

"Indeed, I am. And word has it you have snagged an important client. I hear you're creating a splashy brochure for the Sterling Spa and Resort!"

"Your network of informers is impressive. I haven't told anyone yet!" He laughs.

"Small towns, you know," she explains.

"Yes, indeed. Keeps me on my toes. And why have I been so fortunate as to be on your call list today?"

"My grandsons. I need some help. I hope you can provide it."

"How so?"

"They are trying to find their way back to each other but are still spooked by the incident on the ice. Today, I saw them attempting to play tennis, and it reminded me of my brothers and their enjoyment of the game. Maybe this is something Baéz and Brighton can share. Could I engage your services for some lessons?"

"Of course! I'll come by tomorrow and talk with them, see what we can arrange."

"Thank you!"

The black-and-white photo of the tall boy breathing life into his frozen brother is still pinned to the corkboard in his dark room. He thinks it's his best work, but he keeps it hidden. He's never told them he was there that day.

✷ ✷ ✷

Nathan is a born teacher. He loves to share what he knows. During breaks, he rewards them with stories about the lake, tales of his own childhood, and occasionally, a tidbit about their mother. Both boys listen quietly, anxious to hear about the woman Nathan describes as "a tenderhearted beauty." Both boys fantasize about her and her life with the polar opposites who had fathered them.

Within several weeks, Nonnie is rewarded with the gentle sounds of one of the most elegant games in the world. They play in the early mornings before joining Jared's lawn crew and then resume in the late afternoons when work is finished.

They emulate the distinctive traits of their favorite players and imitate their foreign accents. At the close of each day, Nathan has them run a gentle five-mile trail. They jog barefoot and shirtless on the old logging path that borders the golf course and leads down to the lake. The silence of the forest is restful, and soon they discover more and more things they want to talk about.

"Does your father bring home girls? On dates, I mean. Women, you know?"

"He used to. They were a p-p-pain. They couldn't cook. They had terrible taste in m-music. They messed with my hair. None have been invited lately. Usually they c-c-came from our church."

Baéz comes to a sudden stop, holding out his arm to restrain his brother. His eyes wide, he holds a finger to his lips, signaling silence.

Two balls of fur cry out as they run across the boys' path and scuttle up a tree. Brighton stares as they climb to the uppermost branches.

"Wow! What kind are those? Black, brown?" asks Brighton.

Baéz doesn't answer. He looks straight ahead, frozen by the large eyes of the mother bear. He whispers, "Don't move. Freeze."

When Brighton looks over, the huge animal stands tall on her hind legs. She makes a loud sound, calling to her cubs. Brighton feels exposed, dressed only in shorts, no shoes, no weapon.

"Do not move. Stand tall. Put your arms high in the air. Puff out your chest. Make your body look as large as possible."

He does as instructed, staring at his brother and not the bear. The bear growls, greatly displeased by their presence.

"Do you think we could make it to the water?" Brighton asks.

"She'll tear us to pieces before we get ten feet down the path. Stay calm. No sudden moves. Keep your arms up."

They are not alone. This is what Baéz tells himself. They are safe within God's care and no harm can come to them nor to the protective mother.

Brighton watches as his brother adopts a mean scowl and scrunches his eyes. The mother stands taller as her cubs cry out, and she edges forward, but Baéz does not retreat. He makes a low guttural sound and then slowly advances.

"What the fuck are you doing?" Brighton whispers.

Baéz then claps his palms together and begins barking like a dog. The bear looks at him, confused, but dismisses him as a threat. She lowers herself to the ground and walks on all fours to the wide base of the maple.

The brothers slowly walk down the packed dirt trail. They don't dare breathe until they are in sight of the lake. They dive in and swim all the way home, neither speaking a word. When they reach the dam, they pull themselves up on Jared's dock, exhausted, their chests heaving. They plop down on lawn chairs, their wet shorts dripping, both still silent.

"You want to tell me what just happened?" asks Brighton.

Baéz turns to him, an enigmatic smile playing on his face. "Don't know. I must have read that somewhere. Pretty cool though, wasn't it? She was big!"

"And mean!"

The sun is setting, and the cool air announces the approach of summer's end. Baéz closes his eyes and smells the newly mown hay they baled earlier that day. He can feel his brother's stare, still wanting a more thorough explanation. He decides to change the subject.

"I have an idea you're not going to like, but I think you've got to try," Baéz says.

"Yeah?"

"You know how you hold a pencil with your right hand, but a throw a ball with your left?"

Brighton nods—he's ambidextrous.

"I think you should play lefty. Your best shot is your two-handed backhand, and I think it's because your left hand has more strength. If you played one-handed, with your left, it would be so much more beautiful."

"Like Andres Gomez?"

"Exactly."

Gomez is a favorite because he is from Ecuador, like Enriqué and Rio, who are part of Jared's lawn crew. He won the French Open by beating nineteen-year-old Andre Agassi. They love the young Agassi but are impressed with how fluid and graceful Gomez plays with his stinging left hand.

"It'll be like starting over again."

"No. It won't. There'll be some adjustments; some time will be needed, but not much. And you will be much better. Stronger. You could be unbeatable!"

Brighton stares at his brother and then looks away, realizing Baéz no longer stutters.

Nico beeps the horn and waits in the drive. When the front door opens, Nonnie and the kid are laughing. The boy carries a racquet and a paperback book.

"Nothing for the trunk? No bags?" he asks.

"They're both growing like weeds," answers Nonnie. "He's outgrown all his clothes. No use packing them for the city."

Nico opens the rear door, and Brighton gets in. Nonnie waves as they depart.

"So, my Boy-O, I come especially for you. End of summer, end of our pleasant little trips together."

"What do you mean?" Brighton asks.

"I no longer driver. It is not becoming for me." His broken English always gets a laugh, even though he is sure the kid sees through it.

"Well, I will miss you. How can we make it *becoming* for you again?"

Now they both laugh.

"No, you see, I now own the company. So, it is not right for me to drive any longer."

"You own it? Fantastic!"

"Yes, some clients hit a bad patch. Many debts."

"You won it? In a bet?"

The boy's surprise pleases him; he is more than a driver; he is a businessman.

"I have luck, as you know. She be on my side. She helps poor immigrant boy!"

"Oh, eat my shorts! 'Poor immigrant boy,' indeed!" Brighton shakes a bony finger at Nico. "I have your number, you know. I see you take Wynn and his buddies for a ride. Don't steal it all. I need some for college."

Nico isn't sure if the boy is joking, but he raises his eyebrows to signal he understands.

"Do you make your living on bets?" asks Brighton.

"In this world, my boy, anything is possible. People like to take chances. I am merely middleman, guiding them in their chance-making. This line of work is not for everyone, requires strong constitution. My Dušan gets too afraid. Needs be fearless!"

The kid leans forward in his seat. "How does it work?"

Nico beams: he is proud to explain his business.

"I give them odds on the team they hope will win. Let us imagine they pick the Giants to beat the Steelers. I say the Giants must win by at least seven points. They plunk down fifty bucks, and when the Giants only win with a three-point field goal, I pick up the money. They spread their bets over many games, hoping to even out their losses with some wins. On a good weekend, they come out even."

"And on a bad one?"

Nico smiles and looks into the rearview mirror. "That is how I now own limo company. And a few parking lots, too!

"Truly?"

"Yes. I am a natural. I learned from my father. He was a born gambler. He gambled with our lives. He gambled on the West and defected to come to America and play for the New York Rangers. He is my example. Can you imagine? At first, I only bet on my father's hockey games. I hung out in the locker room; I would notice when a player was limping, or someone stayed in the ice bath too long. I hung out with the trainers, too. They always let slip some important piece of information. Loose lips. I encouraged such conversations. I invest many beers for such tips."

He laughs as he steers the car onto the six-lane highway to New York.

"You must study. Statistics, players' morale, who is getting divorce, who is behind on his mortgage. I am good with numbers, but no matter how much you know, how much you study, on any given day anyone can win. Never bet more than you can afford to lose, because sometimes, no matter how smart, you will lose. Unless . . ."

Here he shrugs and rolls his head, dreaming his favorite scenario.

"Unless what?"

"Unless you control player. Have them shave points, miss a tackle, hit into an easy double play."

"That's cheating, Nico. That's not skill."

Nico laughs. The innocent boy will learn the difficult ways of the world. Not everyone is shuttled in comfort from lake to home; not everyone is encouraged to wear silly clothes or grow their hair like a girl. The kid will learn, and he will grow, and Nico will make sure he is safe. He owes him. The kid has kept Nico's secrets.

✳ ✳ ✳

The lock jiggles. The alarm system switches from green to red and then back to green. Wynn hears something clang on the front hall table. The ugly Chinese vase vibrates from the heavy steps of the intruder. The smell of grass clippings and sweat and some musky new cologne penetrates the air.

Wynn had forgotten Brighton was coming home today. School begins soon. *What day?* He should know these things, but work has been brutal. The market is skittish, clients are unhappy, and his bosses are unreasonable.

He rubs his eyes and prepares for the perpetual motion machine that is his son. Brighton never stops moving, never stops talking, never stops smiling. *Where does he get such liveliness?* Elwynn wonders.

"Did you know Nico owns the limo company now? Isn't that cool?"

"It's not a limo company; merely a car service."

"Still, it's a big step. I mean, cripes, he used to sell Christmas trees on the corner."

Why does he do this? Why disparage Nico's accomplishments? Who does that benefit? Nico is the smart one. Wynn and his pals are the fools. They owe Nico a handsome sum, and the debt grows larger every week.

"That was a big storm you had, no? I saw dramatic footage on the news. Aspetuck Lake, right?"

Brighton pops into the living room while throwing a handful of peanuts in his mouth. "You saw that? So fine! Came out of nowhere; caught the whole town off guard. Power went out, boats on the lake were damaged, the roads flooded—it was very cool! Ezzie and I helped his dad sandbag the river to prevent flooding."

Ezzie. Wynn hasn't heard this nickname before.

"What can't that man do, huh?" His sarcasm is clear, embarrassing him. Why is he trying to diminish his son's excitement?

Brighton ignores the comment and continues with his story. "He's on the town's emergency crew. We went out in the firetruck, armed with chainsaws, keeping the roads open."

"Uh-huh" was all Wynn could muster.

"Oh! And we got a dog! Ezzie did. A chocolate lab. We named him Choco. Baéz rescued him when we were working on the river. The dog got caught in the raging waters, and Ezzie didn't hesitate. He dove right in, caught the dog by his collar, and swam him ashore. Whatever fear the water once held for him is gone. It was a mighty rescue!"

His son rushes in and out of the kitchen, talking and pouring milk and throwing Pop Tarts in the toaster. The house feels alive again. All the noise and disorder and mess are welcome after a summer of silence.

"A dog. Not for here?" he asks.

Brighton slows but answers brightly. "No, don't worry. Choco is staying out there, but Baéz might come in for Halloween, and bring the dog with him. Wouldn't that be great?"

Everything is described with superlatives. Life is either "great" or "brilliant" or "rockin'." Brighton is his mother's boy. Joyful and filled with an effervescence that enriches all who come near. Wynn notices certain habits that replicate those of Rebecca, the way his son pushes a lock of hair behind his right ear. And now his son is enthralled by the same cast of characters that had peopled her life. He should never have encouraged these Connecticut visits. Rebecca's people are stealing his son.

"Be careful out there. Be smart. Your stories make me nervous. Chainsaws and river rescues. Jared caused a big mess for your mother, you know."

He watches for a reaction, but there is none.

Nonnie has called to discuss arrangements for sending Brighton to a special tennis academy. She explained both boys love the game and want to continue their lessons. "They have become inseparable," she said.

Wynn flashes on an image of the boys in their cribs, crying softly. Losing Rebecca had been horrific, but losing Baéz too, separating the boys, had been cruel. He will never forgive Nonnie for taking the boy.

5.

SUMMERS ON THE ASPETUCK

Nonnie treasures the late summer afternoons when the sun glances golden on her wide wooden porch and cooling breezes blow gently across the lake. The sound of rubber balls hitting soft strings lulls her into a state of repose. Her brothers, the twins Edward and Thomas, used to play matches that began during their parents' cocktail hour and continued until darkness forced them inside. They were large and bulky, manly, with blond crew-cut hair. They smelled of sweat and Old Spice, their faces all teeth and nose, their arguments rough and callous.

Brighton and Baéz are softer, leaner, prettier. She worries about them and prays for them every day. But on these bright afternoons, she craves the music they create with their rackets and their constant chatter across the net. They narrate their games, imitating the announcers they hear on the bootleg VHS tapes Nathan Winning finds for them. Borg and Connors, McEnroe and Becker, and the present-day players who have become their idols—Sampras, Agassi, Chang and Courier.

These summers with her grandsons all run together, their ages increasing without her noticing, their height forcing her to look up to see their faces, with whiskers that attempt to shadow their chins.

After their games, when darkness arrives, they listen to her stories. She weaves the past into a rich tapestry of tales they never tire of hearing. Stories about their uncles, their grandparents, their mother. Nonnie brings new life to these ancestors, replacing the medals and news clippings stored in the attic with something more tangible, more real.

She tells them about their great-grandfather, Austin Rivington, born in 1899.

"He was imbued with the excitement promised by the new century. He learned to fly and became the youngest pilot in the 27th Aero Squadron, a forerunner of our Air Force. When the first war ended, he flew the mail up and down the east coast. On one of his flights, a massive snowstorm forced him to seek shelter. He saw a great field of white and landed his beautiful De Havilland plane on this frozen lake. A game of ice hockey had been in progress, and the rough boys threw down their sticks and raced to the plane. The boys carried the mail ashore as the young woman who lived here, in this very house, walked out and chided the pilot for being so reckless. And she married him. That was my mother!"

"She was named Lillian, right?" asks Baéz, although he knows the answer.

"Yes. Lillian Cartwright."

"And then?" eggs Brighton, knowing how the story unfolds but loving her telling of it.

"My dad taught my brothers to fly. He built an elaborate hangar right on the water's edge, pounding huge posts deep into the lake. The handsome barn-like building floated magically atop the liquid surface. My brothers flew that seaplane on and off this lake as if they were simply going into town for a quart of milk. They would wave to us and tip the wings. When the Second World War broke out, Dad sailed for England and became an instructor with the Royal Air Force, teaching young Englishmen how to fly. And his sons, my brothers, soon joined him at an air base in Hounslow."

"The war hadn't yet come to our shores, but these Americans teamed up with the Brits to fight the Nazis. They were confident, strong, and with their flat American accents they told glorious tales of life on the tobacco farms of Connecticut, winning the hearts of their British colleagues. They told stories about Mother and me, and, as Dad explained in his letters, we became characters in a novel, visited again and again."

At this point, Baéz and Brighton would lean back, place their hands behind their heads, and relax in comfort as their favorite part unfolded. Nathan could also recite it by heart, as could Jared, because years earlier, sitting with Rebecca, they too had listened to these remembrances of love and war.

"In July of that awful summer, with England fighting with its last breath, a daring mission was designed to send nearly seventy planes over the German cities that manufactured their superior armaments. Dad, who was there as an instructor and not as a pilot, felt he must join this mission. He led the attack deeper into German territory than had previously been attempted. Managing the fuel would be as difficult as getting in and out of enemy territory alive. They would be flying on fumes, if they were lucky."

Nonnie sees Brighton smile over at Baéz, knowing this part of the story always makes his brother cry.

"The damage inflicted that night set the German war effort back many months. But the Royal Air Force was also devastated. The Germans shot down eleven planes. Among the pilots lost were Edward, Tommy, and Austin. In the nights that followed, the men shared remembrances my brothers had told them, and worried about Mother and me. They could not accept the idea that some unknown American soldier would arrive at our door to inform us of our losses. This soldier would not have known the boys, or their base, or their comrades."

A full moon has emerged, shining its cold blue light on the heavily scuffed floor as Nonnie pauses and then continues with her tale.

"So, in an unprecedented action, their commander went to the War Office and asked permission to send one of their own across the sea to deliver the news. The chaplain of their unit, Geoffrey Esmund, sailed to America on a supply ship, his bag filled with a letter from every flyer in the unit. He docked in New York harbor, where a naval officer drove him to a tiny town in Connecticut. He knew all about the lake, the landing in snow, the clay tennis court set above the water, the impossible blondness of the sister and infectious laugh of the mother. He stepped out of that car and walked onto the wide surrounding porch that looked exactly like all the airmen had imagined. So many of the tales about home had been set on that porch. And he could see the airplane hangar on the water as he stiffened his back and knocked on that door."

Here the brothers would let out a sigh. They loved the ending, as had Rebecca and Nathan and Jared in tellings long past. The merciful gesture of England's Flying Squadron #6 had resulted in the glorious union of Geoffrey Esmund and Dolores Ann Rivington, their Nonnie. The two were married three weeks after VE Day.

It is from Austin and Geoffrey, Nonnie thinks, that her grandsons have inherited their spirit. Integrity, fearlessness and ease came from her father; joy, benevolence and morality from her husband. More importantly, she tries to teach them that God is their father and mother, their creator.

Boys are such strange beings, she thinks as she begins to prepare their dinner. They speak a language she doesn't understand. Baéz is still in thrall to his younger brother. He is in a fever each summer that only breaks when the boys part each fall. None of the meanness that defines so many male friendships is present—no teasing, no bullying, no fighting. From sun-up to sundown, they never stop talking. Meals are loud and funny, filled with code words she doesn't understand and people she doesn't know. But she misses it when summer ends. Her hope, for the boys' sake, is for these summers to continue and for Wynn to stop his efforts to keep Brighton away from her family.

"Where do you think she is now?"

The brothers are walking up Madison Avenue, playing a game where they pretend their mother is alive, her car crash an elaborate government cover-up. They invent scenarios in which she thrives.

"Kuwait, ministering to soldiers behind enemy lines," Baéz answers.

Brighton smiles. "Yes, good. She writes letters home for the injured soldiers. They are all in love with her."

"Like on *China Beach.*"

"Yes, exactly! But is she Colleen or Cherry?"

"Not Cherry; she's too dumb. Rebecca's smart. Dana Delany plays her."

They call her "Rebecca," not "Mom" or "Mother." They study their fathers' pictures of her, and they ask Nathan again and again to tell his stories about her.

Nonnie has treated the boys to Ground Passes for the US Open Tennis Tournament. This sporting event is the final Grand Slam of the season, lasting two weeks on either side of Labor Day. Brighton and Baéz are familiar with all the players, they have their favorites, and they can't wait to attend.

Baéz is not at ease in New York City. He is unnerved by the summer smells, the heat of the subway, and the dissonant screeching of the iron wheels on steel tracks. Brighton knows this and always meets his brother at Grand Central, so he won't be alone.

"The old man is taking us to the Harvard Club. I don't know why. He usually takes clients there, to impress them. I suggested a great Mexican place around the corner, but no, he said, 'The poor boy only comes to the city once a year. Let's give him a treat!'"

Baéz shrugs. His excitement for tomorrow's tournament has been dampened by his fear of tonight's dinner. He isn't comfortable with Brighton's dad. *The man is mean*, he thinks.

Brighton opens the front door, and the boys run up the wide wood stairs. The hallway is lined with oversized black-and-white photographs of Wynn and Brighton, neither smiling, their formal poses resembling a magazine ad for life insurance.

"The Club requires jackets, so you can borrow one of mine. And a tie. Wynn's going to meet us there."

✶ ✶ ✶

Wynn stands as the boys enter the fancy dining hall. Seeing Baéz startles him. He has met the boy only once before, but it had been Halloween, and the boys were in costume, their faces covered by masks. Seeing him now, standing beside his brother, they are two sides of the same coin. The resemblance to Rebecca is uncanny—and unsettling.

They shake hands and then sit. Brighton takes his napkin and puts it in his lap as Baéz mimics his move. They each order a ginger ale as the wine steward tops up Wynn's glass of Barolo.

"So, is our fair city treating you kindly, Baéz?"

The boy mutters, "Yes, thank you."

Brighton rolls his eyes. Speaking with teens is not Wynn's forte.

"What do you boys think about the strike? The Yankees cheated out of a World Series they were certain to win!"

There is silence, but then Baéz answers.

"My dad says the greed of the owners is ruining a great sport. They want to keep all the money for themselves."

Wynn sips his wine. Brighton is silent, reading his menu.

"The owners took the risks," responds Wynn. "They invested the funds, so when the gamble pays off, they deserve the rewards. The players risk nothing. They get paid to play games! Come on!"

A man at a neighboring table turns, so Wynn lowers his voice. Both boys look at their menus.

Wynn is upset by his son's silence. They read *The Times* together every morning. Certainly, Brighton has an opinion on the biggest sports story of the day! He must teach his boy to assert himself, to defend his point of view.

"Do you enjoy your studies, Baéz? Do you know what you want to pursue in college?"

Baéz looks up, a deer in the headlights. He stares at Brighton, hoping for a sign, but his brother looks away.

"I think religious studies could suit me, or maybe English; I like to read."

Wynn scowls, his disapproval plain. He nods to the attentive waiter and then orders. "I'll have the double-ribbed lamp chops, with heirloom beets and potatoes Florentine." He turns to Baéz and asks, "What's your pleasure?"

"The Cambridge burger, rare, with fries, please."

Wynn frowns. "No, no, come now, you can't come here and simply have a burger. Bring him the liver and kidney pie, a specialty in my country. Try it. That's the point! Try new things, not the same old burger!"

Baéz looks to Brighton for guidance.

"For God's sake, Wynn, let him eat what he likes!"

"So American. So unimaginative."

He sips again as Baéz returns to the menu.

"Okay, I'll try the Yorkshire pork belly."

"Any sides with that?" asks the waiter.

"Whatever Mr. Bethune recommends!"

Wynn isn't sure if the boy is mocking him, but he completes the order and watches as his son makes the dull choice of roast chicken.

"So, tell me, in the exciting world of tennis, who will you see tomorrow? Who are today's stars? I don't follow the sport. Fill me in!"

Only then does the table come to life. The boys talk over each other, laughing and mentioning names Wynn doesn't recognize. They argue and disagree. Their enthusiasm should have been contagious, but Elwynn finds it distressing. They sound like sweethearts, teasing and taunting, their laughter exuberant.

"Our family never put much store in sporting activities; the outdoors, all that!" says Elwynn

"My great uncles, *our* great uncles"—Baéz turns to Brighton to include him—"were terrific athletes, especially tennis and lacrosse."

"Rebecca's uncles," Brighton clarifies.

Elwynn raises his eyebrows. He sees an image of their cribs, side by side, each baby reaching through the little wooden slats to find the other.

A collection of waiters present the main courses, an elaborate display that ends with the removal of the sterling domes from the white porcelain plates. After nodding to the waiter for another glass, Wynn watches the older boy use his salad fork to eat his entrée. He wonders how his son puts up with such a dull fellow.

"How's your father? What does he busy himself with at this time of year?"

His own son responds. "Oh, it's so cool!" He pokes Baéz on the arm. "Tell him. His dad's up in Nova Scotia rebuilding an enormous church steeple!"

Baéz's face wears a proud smile. "Yes. It's the tallest steeple in Eastern Canada, and they hired my dad to take it down, restore it, and then put it back up! We saw a video of the huge crane placing it back on top. So cool."

Wynn is displeased with the reverent tone. Jared is a handyman, for Christ's sake! No way for a grown man to make a living. This American habit of honoring manual labor is a mystery to him.

"Yes, well, he wasn't always such a clever fellow, was he?"

He feels a strong kick to his leg. His son shoots him a dirty look as Baéz stares at his brown entrée.

"Jared makes a mean burger on the grill, rare with the perfect amount of char. Right, Ezzie?"

Baéz nods as Wynn stares. Passersby in Soho Park used to stop and admire his beautiful babies, lying side by side in the wicker carriage on sunny Sunday afternoons. They, too, ignored him.

"Your dad created a mess for your mother and me," he says. "She wasn't so sure what to do about you."

Brighton looks at him with pleading eyes; he has heard these terrible stories before. "Dad, maybe some coffee would be good, huh?"

"No, they have such a fine cellar here. A shame not to take advantage." He looks over at Baéz. "Does your dad drink? I seem to remember—"

"Nope. But he did as a teenager, he told me. He tells us both to stay clear of alcohol."

"Yes, he was undisciplined. A big drinker. Luckily, I was able to convince Rebecca—"

Brighton knocks over his dad's wineglass. As the scarlet stain spreads across the white tablecloth, the waiter arrives and covers the spill with a large linen napkin. He asks if Wynn would like another. Brighton stands and signals for his brother to follow.

"We're going on home, Wynn. We've got an early morning. I gave the man our account number."

Rebecca also became dismissive when he drank too much. Impatient. Like Brighton.

Wynn stands and shakes hands with both boys.

"Thank you, Mr. Bethune, for a lovely dinner." Baéz bows and then both boys run out of the Club, untying their ties and laughing.

Wynn sits as the waiter brings him a fresh glass.

"Anything else, Mr. Bethune? We have a fine chocolate mousse tonight."

"Thank you, no."

The waiter nods and leaves.

What kind of man tells lies to children? Wynn asks himself.

He sips the heavy Borolo, neither shocked nor surprised by his behavior. He tells himself that his lies have done no harm.

Elwynn is wrong; his words have stayed with Baéz, but he refuses to be upset. He is sure they are lies, but he figures he should ask Nathan.

They have started playing twice weekly, at an indoor court, so Baéz can keep up with Brighton, who is now studying at an elite tennis academy in Manhattan.

"When did you last see her?" asks Baéz, wiping the sweat from his face as they head to the locker room.

Without answering, Nathan retrieves shampoo and soap from his bag and then removes his clothes and enters the shower, testing the water and soaping his rangy body.

Baéz is shy about nakedness; he doesn't know where his eyes should rest. He removes his clothes and turns on the shower next to Nathan's.

"Should I not have asked?"

"No, you have every right to ask. I was thinking back to that day."

"When?"

"Can you keep a secret? Knowing that if you told, it could hurt someone?"

"I promise. Can I tell Brighton?"

"He already knows. He understands the pain if Jared were to learn of it."

"My dad? Is it something awful?"

Nathan quickly speaks. "No, no, not bad. Simply sorrowful." Baéz hears him sigh. "I was in Casablanca, a small tournament. I was the only American in the draw and had made it to the semi-finals. This was my first year on tour, still a teenager; my career was on the upswing. One day, I get a message at my hotel: Rebecca Esmund has called. A phone number in the UK. To this day, I don't know how she found me. I called back, and there she was, same as ever, telling stories, laughing. She explains that she is getting married. A small church in Dorset. A few friends. Nonnie is the only one flying over from the States. Could I come and walk her down the aisle?"

"And did you?"

Nathan nods. "A glorious church, ancient, like everything in Europe. I met Elwynn Bethune and his family. A short service, followed by a sweet dinner at a local restaurant. The entire weekend felt improvised, planned at the last minute. But your mother was radiant."

"Dad doesn't know you were there?"

"No. Nonnie and I felt we were betraying him, but of course, we loved your mother and did as she asked. At the time neither of us knew she was carrying you."

Baéz doesn't know what to think. He leaves the shower and quietly dresses. He loves hearing stories about his mother, but this tale creates discomfort. He feels bad for his dad. He doesn't like owning this secret.

6.

'SPEED ON IN YOUR SPEEDOS!'

Their voices carry in the night, over the boathouse and all the way to Jared's cabin. The lights are out, but their conversations continue. It is their last summer before college, and they have many things to talk about.

Jared lies in his bed, listening, comforted by the gentle buzz of suppressed laughter and urgent whispers. At thirty-six, he is the father of an eighteen-year-old boy who is in love with tennis and captivated by his half-brother.

Jared knows the signs. He recognizes the lethal combination of joyful expectation and painful heartache. He will not judge his son. He will not warn him away or be the extinguisher of this flame. The oddly striking boy with the ponytail and the Hawaiian shirts had saved his son's life, and Jared will never speak against him.

The brothers have spent the summer honing their tennis skills while working for his landscaping business. They blend well with Jared's diverse crew of immigrant laborers. Brighton, with a vocabulary acquired from living in many countries, converses with them in their own language while Baéz heals them. This fact is far more unsettling to Jared than his son's affections. He doesn't understand it. He isn't even sure he believes it. He has enormous respect for Nonnie and for the religion she practices, but it is so hard to know, so hard to accept.

The evidence of things not seen. He has often puzzled over this phrase from the Bible. He has faith, a faith he discovered while still in high school. After his parents had died in a freak accident during the July Fourth celebrations on the lake, Nonnie had become his guardian. A nearby mega-church took him under their wing. A youthful congregation, a Sunday school with kids his own age, and lots of friendly activities—Bible classes, dances, concerts of contemporary Christian music—but that faith was sorely tested when Rebecca married Elwynn.

Over the years, he was the handsome parishioner for whom the ladies baked an endless supply of cakes and casseroles. He is comforted by his faith but knows he lacks genuine understanding. His son possesses that understanding; Baéz's belief has grown beyond faith and into a knowledge that has true substance. This is Nonnie's doing, he knows, and he will never begrudge her influence on his son. If not for her, he never could have fulfilled his duties as a father.

He had been nineteen years old, running his own business, when early one morning the phone rang in his lakeside cabin, his hangover so severe he called out in pain as he lifted the receiver. It was Nonnie. Could he please come up to the house? She had something important to discuss. His clothes were scattered about the room, empty beer bottles sat on the nightstand, and a used condom lay on the floor. He showered as the coffee brewed. Each morning he swore off these drunken evenings, but then night would fall, and Blackie's Tavern would beckon.

As he dressed and combed his long hair, he wondered what could be so important for Nonnie to call so early. The sun was rising as he knocked on her door.

"For goodness sake, come in. Why waste time with knocking?" she said.

The kitchen felt odd to Jared. Normally, it was spotless, but this morning unwashed dishes remained in the sink, crumbs were scattered on the countertops, and several cabinet doors remained open.

She looks tired, he thought.

"I once made a promise to my daughter, a promise that greatly displeased me. But there is sad news this morning, and I am no longer bound by that pledge." She looked him directly in the eye. "You, and your parents before you, have always been a part of the history here at Hill House. I would never wish to do anything to harm you, yet I fear I have done so."

Jared felt lost, not understanding what she was trying to say.

"I found out a few months ago but was sworn to secrecy. For this, I ask your forgiveness."

"Say it plain, Nonnie. You know my simple mind." He smiled in the beguiling way that always won hearts.

She swallowed. "You have a son. You are the father of a one-year-old boy named Baéz Bethune Honor."

He did not immediately grasp the meaning of Nonnie's words.

"Is Rebecca here?" he managed to ask. He looked out over the lake, as if a vision of his first and only love might magically appear.

"I am sorry to tell you that Rebecca was involved in a car crash early this morning, outside of London. She was alone and did not survive."

The silence in the kitchen magnified the plain sounds of morning—a radiator releasing steam, a dripping faucet, the insistent cawing of the crows in the yard. Jared realized he should hold her, comfort her, but he was frozen in place.

She reached for his hand. "Would you like to see him?"

He nodded. His son was named Baéz, after Joan Baéz, his and Rebecca's favorite singer. *"There but for fortune, go you and I."*

Nonnie opened a kitchen drawer and withdrew a black-and-white photograph, which she handed to Jared. As he saw his son for the first time, an astonished smile filled his face.

And now that son is getting ready for college, Jared tells himself as the voices of the brothers gently fade. Jared wonders what Rebecca would think of them.

He thinks they are both miracles and he loves them very much.

✶ ✶ ✶

Brighton and Baéz's usual routine of chopping fruits and vegetables for their smoothies has been interrupted by the arrival of the morning mail. An envelope with a return address of Wake Forest University has been delivered, but both boys are too frightened to open it. Brighton received early acceptance several months earlier, but they've been waiting to see if Baéz would also be accepted. They have dreamed of attending college together and spent months studying the catalogues of dozens of universities until they settled on the school in Winston-Salem, North Carolina.

Baéz uses his army knife to open the paper sleeve. Brighton stares at his brother's face. He can read its every mood and expression. He knows when to steer clear and when to hold him close. The small tear forming in Baéz's left eye tells Brighton everything he needs to know. It is a tear of joy, not sadness, and they both raise their arms in triumph.

After sharing the exciting news with Nonnie and Jared, they get on their bikes for the ride to the Aspetuck Club. As they pedal up a steep hill, Brighton, in the lead as always, hears Baéz makes a confession: "I don't dream of breasts; of touching them, licking them. Doing anything to them."

"What?" asks Brighton, amused by his brother's statement.

"You said last night that you dreamed of breasts, were obsessed with breasts. I thought about it, after you told me, and I realized I'm different—I don't dream of breasts."

Brighton laughs as he increases his speed on the steep, curvy slope. He knows his brother doesn't dream of breasts, or of girls, for that matter.

"You didn't have my advantages!" he answers. "Partially clothed au pairs running about the house, young nannies giggling as they snuck in their boyfriends, not to mention my father's collection of brainless companions. None of them could help me with my homework, but they did teach me how to win the heart of any girl—*just listen to them,* they advised."

He can tell Baéz isn't paying attention.

"I'm taking the train into the city tonight," he says, changing the subject. "Our housekeeper is turning fifty, and there's a big party planned. My dad won't remember. Totally hopeless!"

"But you'll be back tomorrow?"

"Yes!"

They skid their bikes to a stop in the parking lot. The Club has one clay court, which overlooks the lake with a view across the Litchfield Hills. A small set of bleachers sits on one side, and Nathan and several other men are seated on the weather-worn planks. Nathan is trying to get the boys accepted to a program for exceptional players at Yale University. This morning is their audition.

"Okay, listen up. I need twenty minutes of great tennis. Don't hold back, use everything you've got, play to win! Understand?"

"Yes, Coach," they mutter, each wearing a smirk on their face.

They never call him coach. Nathan chuckles as the boys play their hearts out, just like they do each and every day. When they finish, Nathan gives them a thumbs-up and they began the five-mile trek back to Nonnie's for their second breakfast.

"I've got to stop at the Elgars," announces Baéz. "The guys are mowing the fields today, and I'm the only one who knows the boundary lines."

Brighton is pissed. "Come on! I told you I was going into the city today. We've got to make time for our practice before I leave! Skip this shit. They'll figure it out."

"Don't be such a dick! This will take two minutes! Come on."

Brighton follows him as he turns his bike into a gated drive. Jared's trucks are parked to the side, but as the boys get near, several of the crew are pointing towards a fallen worker.

"It's Enrique!" Jesús calls out. "He drove his mower over an underground nest. The bees have swarmed him! I've called for an ambulance! He can't breathe!"

The bees are still circling the idling mower. Enrique is rolling on the ground, trying to kill the stinging bees, but there are too many; they are everywhere. Enriqué's smooth skin is covered in welts. Tears flow from his swollen eyes. He is gasping for air.

Baéz rushes to his anguished friend, ignoring the bees and their stings. Brighton watches and listens as Baéz lies on the grass beside Enriqué.

"Look at me, 'Riqué. Look right at me. Look into my eyes. Forget the bees. You are God's perfect child; he is your refuge and strength, and you are exempt from danger. He has bestowed all his blessings on you; he has given you dominion over his entire creation. He did not make you vulnerable to the sting of a bee."

The young man's breathing is raspy, and his eyes reflect his growing panic. He tries inhaling bigger and bigger breaths, without success. Baéz grasps his arms, holding him.

Brighton leans in to hear the words his brother whispers.

"Fear, leave us alone!" commands Baéz. "There is no cause for fear. God gave you life and breath and all things. You lack nothing. You have no lack of breath, no shortness of breath, no difficulty finding breath. It is right here, all you need. Do you hear me, 'Riqué? You are the Son of God, powerful, strong, filled with the breath of life. Look right at me, buddy, and know what I say is true. Declare it to be true. Now, BREATHE IN, BREATHE OUT, slow gentle drafts, no impediment, no swelling, no fear. Only perfection."

He holds Enriqué's hand, oblivious to everyone around them.

"You are fine. You are perfect. Never forget this!"

Enriqué sits up, clearly embarrassed to be holding Baéz's hand. He stands and Brighton sees all the bees fall from his body, from his hair, and out his ears. Enriqué walks back to his mower in a trance. His skin is smooth and unmarked.

The crew is unnerved by what they have witnessed, and they stare warily at Baéz.

Brighton is also mystified by this episode, but it's not the first. He is confounded and annoyed and a little bit afraid.

The two ride home in silence.

✶ ✶ ✶

As Brighton had feared, Elwynn has forgotten Darnell's birthday. As he jogs from the lively party in Queens to his father's lifeless home in Manhattan, he tries to control his anger while dodging the heavy traffic.

He opens the front door and is greeted by loud voices. He hesitates, and then remembers—it is Thursday, poker night. His dad and his buddies from BNP still play every week.

The house is freezing, the air-conditioning on high. He drips salty sweat on the highly polished oak floors.

"Boy-O, what a sight for these eyes. Hello!"

Brighton is surprised to see Nico—he no longer tends bar for the bankers. The others stand, greeting Brighton with quiet hellos.

"What are you doing here?" asks his dad.

"It's Darnell's birthday. I told you I was coming in."

His father nods, not listening, as his anxious colleagues stare at the floor, chomping on chips and pretzels. Only Nicola wears a smile, looking sharp in a midnight-blue suit and tie.

"Is it still so hot? You are a soaked chicken!"

"I ran here from Queens, over the bridge. I'm in training. Coach will kill me if I miss a day."

"Coach is Mr. Tennis?"

"Yes, Mr. Tennis." Brighton still laughs at Nico's expressions; he knows the mangled English is a put-on, but he finds it endearing. "And speaking of Mr. Tennis—Wimbledon begins in three days, so let me help you with your bets! Brother Baéz and I have gone over the draw, and if you stick with us, you can't lose!"

He thinks he sees the men wince as he utters the word "bet."

"Gotta shower first," he says. "Be right back."

After he disappears, Nico breaks the uncomfortable silence. He swears he will never be like them—dependent on their jobs, on the market, on luck.

"Well, isn't that the breath of fresh air we needed, eh, gents? Now before he returns, let's review our situation, yes?"

"What's the idea?"

Tug is the hopeful one. Charlie and William simply stare at Nico with daggers for eyes; his success makes them crazy.

"Well, boys, I have been enlarging my interests. I have some unneeded cash to park and could use some guidance from pros like you. You specialize in pharmaceuticals. I see these drug companies can advertise on TV now, not only aspirin and Rolaids, but prescription medicine. Bypass the doctor; go direct to consumer. Very clever. Very lucrative, I think. I ask some help in stocks, which companies I should watch, who might be coming out with valuable new drug, or which test is failure. You know such things, am I correct?"

He knows they understand. Insider tips. Privileged information not available to the public. Very risky and very lucrative. And very illegal.

"I will erase your debts in exchange for information."

"We cannot do that," answers Wynn.

"No? Then maybe a session at Gamblers Anonymous would be advisable!" shouts Nico. He has won a lot of money off these men and their colleagues, but their stupidity infuriates him. "Do you think we are playing here? This is *my* money we are discussing! Not your fancy bank's, not some gambling parlor's, but mine. Nearly a hundred thousand dollars! I want its return. We are too long in this friendship for me to threaten. It is beneath me, and it is beneath you."

His angry voice reverberates up the stairs where Brighton is listening. Sensing something was wrong, he had left the shower running as he tiptoed down the hallway to eavesdrop.

Their first Christmas in New York, the year Baéz fell through the ice, he and his father bought their holiday tree around the corner from a bearded kid with a thick accent. Now this kid is in control of these smart money managers, telling them what he needs them to do. Their losses are out of control. Their weakness has placed them in danger.

Brighton returns to the shower, turning the dial to cold, and stands in the frigid water, wishing he could forget what he heard.

✳ ✳ ✳

Nathan Winning had hoped to avoid the bane of all photographer's careers—weddings, baptisms, and bar mitzvas. But he had to start somewhere, and initially these assignments were amusing, and he began to feel comfortable again in his hometown. But then his career received a seismic jolt, pitting neighbor against neighbor over their support or opposition to his frankly erotic photo spread of the boy's wrestling team at Sterling High. He was accused of sensualizing the sport, placing the team in compromising poses with their singlets displaying their manhood in all its glory.

The uproar subsided, he lost a few friends, but he was deluged with new and lucrative assignments. His skill with a camera, with shadow, lighting, framing, was suddenly rewarded. From a sexy and silly ad campaign for Victoria's Secret to a vastly misunderstood but widely admired collection of revealing photos of the actor River Phoenix, he was in demand and finally able to make a living doing what he loved.

When the head of marketing for the Australian swimsuit behemoth, Speedo, contacted Nathan for help in shaping their upcoming anniversary campaign, he readily accepted, newly confident in his skills. American men shun Speedos; they are only worn in athletic competitions and are rarely seen on beaches or playgrounds or public swimming pools. Speedo wants to change that.

Nathan suggests an elegant, oversized catalogue in black and white, printed on fine paper without any words, only pictures. Joyous images of summer and skin and Speedos.

He will photograph a group of young men at play—kayaking, canoeing, snorkeling—making these young men and their activities irresistible.

The pure simplicity of Nathan's proposal makes the marketing executives nervous, but they give their approval.

He decides that Brighton and Baéz will be the only models. They are no longer the pretty boys he had captured on the ice but uniquely charismatic and masculine brothers with a powerful mutual affection. Nathan simply has to capture the ease of their seductive natures.

He stages them chasing each other with water guns, floating in inner tubes, and swimming with their dog, Choco. They play soccer with beach balls and float frisbees; they paddle in canoes and kayaks; they fish from boats and from shore. They cycle and skateboard with their long wet hair, their skin shiny with perspiration.

Nathan takes them to the inlet famous for its red clay and has them wrestle in the mud. He gives them a football, and they struggle to run and tackle and catch. As their favorite tunes blare from a cheap boombox, Nathan snaps away, imbued with the contagious energy of his models.

Baéz screams out, "Stop, stop, give me a sec! My eyes. The mud!"

He runs to the clear water and splashes his face, removing the luxurious gunk. In truth, he needs time to tame his embarrassing erection. He has been afraid this would happen, prancing around all day in a skimpy swimsuit. *Or is it the beautiful freckles on his brother's back?*

He sits down in the cold water, his skin clean, and his hair free of the lubricious muck. He tucks his parts back into place and walks over to rejoin Brighton, staring into the camera he is learning to loathe. His heart slows its frenzied beating as he listens to Meatloaf screaming their summer anthem.

Will you cater to every fantasy I got?
Will you hose me down with holy water, if I get too hot?
Snap, snap, snap goes the camera.

✳ ✳ ✳

On a sweltering August evening, as the familiar drone of tree frogs mixes with the unnerving screech of flying bats, Baéz is awakened by the sound of careful footsteps on the wooden dock.

He rises from bed. The stars are bright, and he can make out the shape of his brother pushing away from the pier in their aluminum fishing boat. He hears the small trolling motor kick in.

This is the third night Brighton has crossed the lake.

Baéz spies his old wooden canoe bobbing in the water. He decides to trail his brother. He puts on a shirt and then he follows the low thrum of the fishing boat's engine as he listens to Brighton humming Meatloaf's summer hit. He rows quietly and passes the forested finger of land that juts into the lake and separates Nonnie's property from all the other waterfront homes. He hears a party in the distance.

He tells himself to turn around. This feels wrong.

He sees Brighton tie the aluminum boat to a dock lit by tiki torches. He hears a girl's high-pitched giggle.

"You made it!"

Baéz recognizes her: Bethany Alcott, home from college. They had cut her lawn earlier that day.

After kissing Brighton, she leads him to a screened gazebo lit by candles. She removes his T-shirt and kisses his chest and shoulders. Brighton smiles but does not move, his hands hanging by his side as he passively accepts her caresses. She reaches into the waistband of his faded workout shorts; the ones he wears every day.

When she eases the shorts down his brother's hips and over his erect penis, Baéz knows he should look away, but he is fascinated; he feels a perverse pleasure in sharing the sexual joy his brother is experiencing. He hears Brighton's low moans as they travel over the water—*yes, yes, yes,* he hears him say, until Baéz suddenly climaxes in his shorts, mortified.

He puts the oar in the water and turns the canoe around, his heart still beating as he paddles back to Nonnie's side of the lake. He tries to forget about this night's events as he climbs into bed, but the sticky wetness between his legs reminds him of his shameful behavior.

✳ ✳ ✳

Brighton doesn't engage the motor. He fits the oars in the locks and quietly rows, wondering what to do about Baéz. He had felt his brother's presence and then saw him in the green canoe, rowing away. The consequence of being constantly together has recently caused a friction that pains Brighton. Their rapport is so thorough, so exclusive, that it has begun to feel claustrophobic. For the first time in their long friendship, he dreams of an escape, a need to start over, elsewhere, and this instinct saddens him. The desire for freedom saddens him. He doesn't want to relinquish the thrall that pleases them both but knows he must if they are to survive and grow.

As he secures Jared's trawler to the dock, he gets more and more agitated. He walks into the boathouse, the shadows as familiar as his brother's labored breathing.

"Did you enjoy that?" he shouts as he turns on the bright overhead light. "Huh? I know you're awake. Get up!" he screams, grabbing his crotch and making an obscene gesture. "You want some? Huh? Wanna shoot your load?"

He sees his brother cowering, the result of his mean and menacing words. He has never spoken to his brother like this, and although he is angered by this invasion of privacy, he is also embarrassed by his behavior.

"I am so sorry," says Baéz. "I didn't mean for this to happen. I simply wondered where you've been going every night."

"Why is that your business?" Brighton asks, trying to temper his rage.

"It's not, I know! I said I was sorry."

Silence hangs in the air. Brighton moves to the large hassock in the middle of the room. He sits down and waits for his heart to slow. He speaks clearly, knowing his words will wound.

"We are too much together. Nonnie calls out to me when she means you; Jared confuses our names; there has to be a place where you and I begin and end."

Baéz nods. "College will be different. We'll have new friends, different friends."

Brighton stares at his brother, heartbroken by the news he is about to share. "I'm not going with you, Ezzie."

"How do you mean?" Baéz's face is contorted by fear, and Brighton knows he must tread carefully; he is entering territory they have always avoided.

"We can't always be together. We must begin our own lives!"

"I don't understand. What are you saying?"

He takes a deep breath.

"Pepperdine held a space for me. A full scholarship and a starting position my first year. I've withdrawn my acceptance from Wake Forest."

Brighton has always appreciated his brother's simple, transparent nature. Baéz is not clever and doesn't disguise his feelings. His face now reveals the deep hurt that Brighton has caused. They had planned to attend college together; they had been planning it for years.

"California?" is all Baéz says, his voice tiny, making the Golden State sound as far away as Jupiter.

"Ezzie, I love you; you know that. I will always love you and I know you love me. That has to be enough."

Another long silence. Baéz hears what Brighton leaves unsaid. He knows that within the love he feels for Brighton there is something else. He tells himself it is simply admiration, yet that doesn't explain his beating heart. All he truly understands is that life is more fun when Brighton is around.

Brighton stands and says, "I've got to shower."

Baéz stops him, asking the one question he has never dared.

"When you pulled me out of the water and lay me on the ice, I felt your lips on mine. You kissed me. Why?"

A motorboat flies by; a midnight run. The waves splash over the dock as the joyful screams of teenagers hover in the humid air.

Brighton remembers the fears of a twelve-year-old boy. "I'm not sure about anything that happened. That day is wrapped in mystery, the memories at odds with each other. Some called it a miracle. Nonnie said it was the harmonious unfolding of God's day."

Brighton stands and goes to sit on his brother's bed, taking his hand, wanting him to understand.

"I thought it was my fault you were under the ice. I thought I would be blamed. I talked you into one more run, even though you were freezing. And then you and your dad's sled disappeared into a black hole, like a special effect in a movie. Poof! I thought you were going to die!

"It's the first time I ever prayed, if asking favors from God is considered praying. When my hand found yours and I pulled you out and lay you down, I said, 'Thank you, Lord.' At that moment, my shivering stopped. I was no longer cold. I looked down at you. You were beautiful; you looked like those angels painted on the ceilings of churches. You know? Your lips were a deep purplish-blue, and your face was whiter than the snow that surrounded us, and I simply wanted to make sure you were real, that you were alive. I leaned down and I felt the warmth of your breath, and so I kissed you, in gratitude. I've tried to forget that day, tried to deny the existence of those events, but Nathan's clandestine photos verify my fears, reminding me how close we both came to death."

Brighton stands and walks to the bathroom, turning on the ancient shower.

Baéz lies back down on his bed. Nathan had only recently shared his photos of that terrible day, and he and Brighton had been upset by the disturbing memories that came to light. Baéz had been traumatized by that day, and Brighton had emerged as the hero. Baéz has never realized that the day was equally painful for his brother.

The clanking water pipes usher him into a jittery sleep where he is struck by a vision so clear and so detailed that he is sure it is real. In it, he sees his brother, triumphant, being cheered by a large crowd as Baéz watches silently from the sidelines—all alone.

✳ ✳ ✳

Speedo initially ships twenty-five thousand catalogues to their best customers—clothing stores, sports outlets, surf clubs, aquatic centers. The classy handout flies off the shelves, and the publisher cannot keep up with requests for additional copies. After four printings, nearly a quarter million copies are in circulation. The images of the two young men cavorting in their Speedos grace teenage walls around the country—both boys' and girls'. Within the gay community, the brothers are deified.

Some chord has been struck. The images please people, reminding them of the joys of summer, the simplicity of youthful contentment.

Nathan thinks the elegant supplement has a further life and he gets permission from Speedo to approach publishers regarding a hardcover edition that utilizes additional photos from the shoot.

A German publisher, known for expensive high-end art books, is willing to invest considerable sums, utilizing thick papers and rich inks, and commissions the pop poet Rod McKuen to write an introduction extolling the virtues of youth. Titled *Summers on the Aspetuck,* Nathan adds a few of the racier photos Speedo had nixed and even includes a few casual nudes.

For the cover, he gets the boys' permission to use the image he has labeled "the kiss." Enough years have passed that the image no longer embarrasses them. Even though they are dressed in parkas and covered in snow, they are recognizable as younger versions of the boys inside. There is a congruity between the boys on the ice and the boys on the water; a connection that is communicable and pleases the eye and the mind. Nathan convinces them that the juxtaposition is not sensual, but virtuous; a manifestation of brotherly love, not desire.

There are no names, no pagination, no explanatory titles, but led by the over-ripe McKuen introduction, the book is seen as a love story.

No one, not even the experienced publishing house, could have predicted the book's success. And everyone wants to know the names of those beautiful boys.

7.

THE SEPARATION

An old cow barn on the far side of the property serves as Jared's equipment shed. Large halogen lamps hang from the thick wooden beams, illuminating the massive space. The smell of animal dung and rotted hay fills the air, and hundreds of bats hang from the rafters, creating piles of guano that add to the agrarian stench.

The crew begins and ends their days here. A large refrigerator holds their lunch sacks, and a row of coffee makers urges them awake each morning. Jared is seated on a low stool, sharpening the cutting blades of his mowers. The slow, careful activity seems to relax him as Ricky Martin's addictive tunes echo from a tape player.

"Did you ever want to go to college?" Baéz asks as he sits on a milk crate opposite his father.

"I don't think so. Your mother was big on the idea, so I sent away for catalogues to impress her, but it was simply an excuse to talk with her. I had started my business by then and was doing fine. It was enough for me. 'The love of money is the root of all evil.' That's what the good book says. I'm grateful I never had that desire, that longing. I hope you know that you will always have what you need. That's all we can ask."

"Yes, sir, I do know."

Jared puts down the rough file and switches to a fine sanding cloth.

"Have you heard from Wake Forest?" he asks. "Did they assign Brighton as your roommate?"

He hasn't told his dad. Each time he tries, he feels tears nearby. *Don't make a big deal of it*, he tells himself.

"No. Brighton accepted an invitation from Pepperdine. They promised him a starting position, which is rare for a freshman."

Baéz tries to speak the words without color or emotion.

"I'm sorry, son. I know you were looking forward to being together at Wake Forest."

"He flew out this past weekend. Had to happen sometime," states Baéz with a practiced air, having repeated these words over and over to himself.

Jared moves to the next mower, removing the dings and dents from its blades.

"You know I won't need any funds from you, for college," says Baéz. "What the scholarship doesn't cover, I can pay."

"You saved that much from our work? I'm impressed."

Baéz wonders how to explain and then simply blurts out the truth.

"The money is coming from a book. A book Nathan created from last summer's Speedo catalogue."

He hates reminding his father; hates even saying the word "Speedo."

"I thought that nonsense was over!"

"Nope, he's made a handsome book out of it. An art book. You know the kind that sits on people's coffee tables, gathering dust. There are new photos and an introductory essay. You might think it's a bit racy." Baéz smiles, trying to gloss over the fact that he and Brighton are naked in several of the shots.

He watches his father absorb this new information.

"And people will buy this, in bookstores?" Jared asks.

"That's the hope, sir. They paid Brighton and me a handsome advance."

"And the folks at Wake Forest will be okay with this? The Divinity School isn't rethinking their decision to accept you?"

Baéz chuckles. "Who knows? Maybe a naked minister will put more folks in the pews!"

The minute the words leave his mouth, he knows his attempt at humor is misguided.

Jared shakes his head and puts down his tools. "I thought you had more sense than this!" He stands, his disappointment clear. "Did you pray about this? I am curious how you arrived at this decision. Was it the money, or Brighton, or some desire to flaunt your good fortune?"

The Speedo catalogue had embarrassed his father, Baéz knew, but Jared would never say why. Only that he disapproved of the two of them posing in "their underwear," as he called the swimsuits.

Baéz looks at his father, exasperated. "I cannot pray about everything in my life. There would be no time left for living!"

Jared will not hear it and begins quoting scripture, a habit Baéz hates. "'Pray without ceasing,' Paul says. Your role in this world is to daily praise and celebrate your creator. He did not say 'carve out some private time for tennis.' Life and prayer are not separate activities."

His father's anger, so rarely on display, rattles Baéz. He is lost without his father's approval; Nonnie provides the foundation, but his dad is his keystone, the element that allows him to stand.

"Maybe you're not cut out for this—the discipline of being a preacher," his father says. "It's not a painless calling. People come to you with their sorrows, rarely their joy."

Baéz thinks his father is overreacting, but the criticism pains him. "It is the subject which interests me, sir. The goal of my studies is to gain a better understanding of religion, of God, of my connection to him. It is a course of study, not necessarily a vocation."

Jared turns off the coffee warmers, then the lights, as the setting sun colors the barn orange.

"Sir, please don't walk away. I go in a week. I would like to think you are supporting me in my endeavors." Baéz swallows hard, feeling a collapse of the ramparts he has built to protect himself. "My brother has abandoned me. I would hate to think my father has done the same."

He cannot hold it back any longer. His eyes release a flood of tears. The agony of a broken heart.

Jared stares at his son and understands his grief. It's what he felt when Rebecca left.

"I am so sorry. I would never do that. I love you and I'll always be here for you."

He places a hand on his son's shoulder as the boy wipes his face clear of tears. Jared never cried as a boy, not even when his parents died. He knows his son is a softy, just like his mother, and he loves this about him.

8.

'MAD ABOUT THE BOY'

As Baéz adjusts to life on his own, three thousand miles away his brother is thriving. Brighton arrived on campus early to give himself time to settle in. Having grown up in four glamorous cities, he is practiced in navigating new surroundings, new friends, and new pleasures. Having escaped his father and Baéz, he is pleased to discover that this hip little town on the edge of the ocean feels like home. He enjoys his studies, and his new teammates are talented and welcoming. He rooms with another freshman player, Jimmy Royale, a born and bred Angelino who takes great pleasure and pride in introducing Brighton to all things Californian.

"Bethune, take your freshman buddies down to Bill's Barbers and get a proper haircut. Tell Eduardo to put it on my tab. Today. Is that clear? I won't have my team looking like a bunch of pirates for our first match."

Brighton opens his mouth to speak, but the tough, tanned coach barks, "No argument, you hear me?"

"Sir, I'm not arguing. Give me one minute, and then I promise we'll come back looking like boy scouts."

"One minute, Bethune." Coach looks at his fat Timex as if measuring Brighton's promise.

"Sir, I'm a proud member of an organization called Wigs for Kids. They collect donated hair for children undergoing chemotherapy. Jimmy and Walt have joined me. We're scheduled to have our lengthy locks trimmed at a big fundraiser in November."

He pauses. Coach isn't screaming, but Brighton knows this is a bit much to take from the new kid. He decides to try a bit of humor.

"They are especially eager for my red hair, sir. It is rare!"

"I'm sure it is, Bethune. I'm sure it is." Coach keeps a straight face, but Brighton thinks he detects a smile beneath the gritty demeanor. "Make sure the University gets credit at your fundraiser, son. Now, everyone to the showers. That was a good practice. I'll post the line-up at seven tonight."

The nine male players are standing above the beautiful hard courts overlooking the Pacific Ocean. Pepperdine is situated on eight hundred rolling acres in the exclusive enclave known the world over as Malibu. The seven thousand students in this Christian college are reminded daily of their good fortune as they view the deep blue waters on their way to class.

"USC is good, right?" Brighton asks.

Steam rises as the lean, tanned teammates laugh and taunt one another in the showers.

"Yeah, bud, they are scary good. We'll have our hands full. Are you working tonight?"

Brighton is a waiter two nights a week at a popular oceanfront restaurant.

"Yup."

"Is this one of Scottie's nights? Is she playing?"

"Hope so."

Several players nod, smiling. Scottie is the restaurant's attractive owner and can occasionally be coaxed to sit behind the piano.

"Beware, my man. She's famous for taking young athletes under her wing—if you get my meaning."

"Nah, it's not like that. She's nice, I enjoy her."

"Good! She's a looker. Be careful is all I'm saying."

"Message received, Jimmy. Message received."

He dismisses Jimmy's warning as simple jealousy and then waves farewell to his new teammates as he hops in his used VW and drives to the restaurant. He enters the dining room as the sun sits atop the water's edge, hesitates for a long moment, and then slowly sinks below the horizon. The cocktail crowd quiets momentarily and then returns to their light, genial conversations. Tipping is generous, and Brighton often finds a random business card tucked beneath the bill.

Scottie Morris finds Brighton's appearance unusually notable. In a land where handsome men and beautiful women are the norm, Brighton's copper locks and welcoming smile outshine all the others.

The walls of her restaurant are floor-to-ceiling glass. At high tide, the waves crash into the rocks upon which the restaurant sits, sending a salty spray into the air. In the center of the dining room, perfectly lit and set against the endless ocean, is a grand piano, black with an impossible shine and featuring a giant bouquet of white roses. She is seated on the polished bench, her voice strong and clear.

Mad about the boy.

I know it's stupid but I'm mad about the boy.

Her eclectic repertoire ranges from Joni Mitchell to Phoebe Snow to Noel Coward. She acknowledges the light applause as the song ends and Brighton delivers her preferred drink of Jack and soda.

"You know the boy's mad about her too, right?" Brighton doesn't smile; he doesn't need to. He simply makes his statement.

"So, you were actually listening, Mr. Bright and Early?"

"Always. Although I prefer Bright and Breezy. Excuse me, a customer calls."

She watches as he walks over to a young woman sitting alone at a table set for two. The woman smiles and looks Brighton up and down, but he simply jots down her order and walks away.

He returns to Scottie's side after giving the lady's order to the bartender. He whispers in her ear. "The boyfriend is late. Second time this week. She's pissed."

Scottie smiles. "Well, you didn't seem very sympathetic. She was waiting for a comforting word. A disappointed woman is a poor tipper."

"Are you suggesting I flirt with the customers to boost my gratuities?"

The candlelight illuminates the deep cleft in his chin. She punches him on the arm, not caring that she is being too familiar with him in public. She sips her drink and takes in the view. She owns the building after an effortless divorce from a movie executive and now lives in the apartment above the restaurant. She leads an easy, uncomplicated life—one that has become more fun thanks to the attentions of Brighton Bethune.

"Tell me about your accent; I can't place it. Or you. Who are you?" She laughs because she already knows; she quizzes him every night.

"I'm the tennis player. From Pepperdine. Remember?" he jokes.

"Ah, yes, I recall now! And the accent?"

"An amalgam of every place I've lived. Barcelona. Paris. Milan. But that's all I can say. My au pairs always advised me to hold something back. Never give it all away on a first date!"

"You were brought up by au pairs?" She leans in close. "They gave you dating advice?"

"Those girls from Finland and Sweden taught me everything. How to make an omelet, how to balance stripes with plaids, and how to treat a woman!"

Scottie laughs, flattered by his care, but she wonders what it would be like to be part of a couple where your handsome mate is noticed first.

✶ ✶ ✶

The last customer waves goodnight as the valets count their tips and the busboys place clean glasses on the shelves.

Brighton follows Scottie's instructions, leaving with his colleagues, then making a U-turn at Los Flores Beach and returning to the now-empty parking lot. A polished steel staircase leads up the side of the restaurant to a shiny metal door.

"All clear," he announces as he steps into the modern space which resembles the deck of an elegant yacht—polished teak and tinted glass. She has changed into Capri pants and a T-shirt, looking more like a perfect doll than a grown woman.

She must order children's sizes, he thinks.

"Something to drink?" she suggests. "I've got everything."

"Indeed you do, but I never drink. Lemonade, iced tea, water is fine."

He walks into her galley kitchen, places his large hands on her shoulders, then leans down and kisses her neck. He breathes in her lovely fresh scent, a perfume that is new to him. He thinks he should shower after working all night, but she is impatient, pulling him close.

She is beautiful, covered head to toe in freckles, her skin a mirror image of his own. She has tiny breasts, with the most perfect nipples. He kisses her all over, devouring her sweet, freckled spaces. They don't speak, moving slowly as they explore each other's bodies. The sculpted red hair of her wet vagina is also scented, and he lingers there as he memorizes her smells and savors her skin.

"You are lovely." He smiles, pushing his hair out of his eyes, tracing her face with his fingers, his voice low and colored by warmth. He can feel her heart swiftly beating.

"Thank you," she answers, kissing his fingers.

Later, they sit on the balcony off her bedroom, counting the endless planes circling overhead.

"After 7:00 p.m., aircraft can only approach LAX from the ocean, lessening the noise for these waterside towns," she says.

Brighton looks up. "Yes, here comes the three-fifteen from Copenhagen."

"Do you think they saw us?" giggles Scottie.

"I hope so."

What a pleasant surprise, Brighton thinks. *A real woman. Not a girl.*

"What are you thinking?" she asks.

He holds her hand. Perhaps he shouldn't return to the dorm tonight. He doesn't know what she expects.

"I feel good. The water is all shiny. Let's go for a swim."

Her employees begin to suspect but know better than to gossip. When she starts to attend his matches, all pretense about their "friendship" ends. They feel no need to define their relationship; they simply enjoy being together.

9.

CHOOSE CAREFULLY

The huge, purple-carpeted gaming hall reeks of cigarette smoke.

"Another card for you, sir?"

Wynn looks at his hand; it totals eighteen. He shakes his head. "No thanks."

The two college buddies on his left each ask for an additional card. So does the Texan, his stomach hanging over a large turquoise belt buckle. The heavily rouged dowager on his right also holds.

When the dealer turns over his cards, they total twelve. He deals himself a seven and holds at nineteen. The college boys are the only winners with a pair of jacks and a pair of tens.

An attractive, scantily clad waitress arrives.

"Another, Mr. Bethune?"

"That would be lovely, thank you."

The Texan, he learns, is a cattleman who served with the military—he wears a bolo tie and keeps his cards close. The dowager tells tales of her years as a Rockette and the handsome suitor she married. She enjoys chatting with the college boys who are raking it in. Wynn assumes they are card counters.

They all amuse him with their light banter and bad jokes. Atlantic City does not resemble the European casinos he once enjoyed; he is reminded of the bingo castles of his native England, not the baccarat tables of Monaco. Still, he is a frequent visitor to "the Taj." Everyone loves him—they love his tony accent, and they love his tall tales.

On some visits, he is a journalist. Other times, an inventor, or a publisher. Often, he is a member of the British secret police. This last occupation is forced out of him after many drinks and many hints, his interlocutors finally exclaiming, "I knew it!"

A stock analyst is never one of his disguises.

The poker nights with his buddies ended after a year of feeding insider tips to Nico. With Brighton at school, the crisp duplex on 68th Street has become uncomfortably quiet. No footsteps tromp up the stairs, no music blares from the speakers, no phones ring in the middle of the night. Wynn lives well and earns good money, but he doesn't want a swell sports car or a cabin by the beach or a closet of bespoke suits. Inhabiting another life, residing within a fictional creation, even for a short while, is the guilty pleasure he enjoys, but his losses at the casino are mounting.

The waitress delivers his drink as the college boys rake in more chips. They are Brighton's age.

"You guys ever bet on college sports?" Wynn asks.

"You can only do that in Vegas. Not legal here."

"Officially, that's true. But there are many 'unofficial' bookmakers. Or does your proficiency with numbers only apply to cards?"

They smirk knowingly as they win another hand.

They remind him of the young men at work, the well-dressed, winnowed crowd that arrives each year from the elite business schools. Daredevils, risk-takers, sharks. Know-it-alls, too, but he likes them. He likes their spirit, their enthusiasm, and their hunger for riches. They challenge him to stay current, to be on top of his game. He is terrified of becoming the old fogey whose colleagues merely abide his presence.

Wynn has kept up to date on the technologies affecting his business. Five years earlier, only five percent of Americans were invested in stocks. Now that stock trading has gone to the internet, that number has risen to twenty, and the young whizzes who surround him are creating new ways to reel in more and more customers every day. Wynn is not a trader, but an information broker exclusively focused on pharmaceutical companies—their strengths, their weaknesses, and the new drugs being brought to market. He excels at his craft. Gambling with cards is more fun than betting on stocks and his companions at the Taj are far more colorful than his colleagues at Bank Paribas, but neither can provide the rush he felt from his exploits with Nico. He misses the peril that danced on the periphery of Nico's existence.

As he settles his account with the cashier, he takes out his Nokia and flips it open. Does Nico still live in the unheated loft with Dušan? The voice in his ear answers his question.

"*Dobrý-den!*"

"And a good day to you too, my friend!"

"I was just talking about you. You must come and see all the new trouble I have created!"

"Perfect! That is why I called. Life has become boring! I need a little trouble."

✳ ✳ ✳

The thin, flexible tubing covers the forest like a hastily thrown pot of spaghetti; narrow strands of blue plastic lead from tree to tree, terminating at an enormous aluminum tank. Baéz stares at his creation, wincing at the diminished beauty of this grove of maples.

"You sure she won't see this?" he asks his father.

"Nope. Nonnie never comes here. The goats prevent her walking this way."

They both smile, recalling the run-in between Nonnie and a mother goat on this distant acreage. "I'm fine," Nonnie had insisted when she came limping back from her afternoon walk. "They're all God's creatures," she explained, "though I do wish you had chosen to raise lambs instead of those rude goats!"

Jared's herd roam this hilly parcel, keeping the brush low while adding their distinctive sound to the rich choir of local livestock.

The two men are boring holes in scores of trees and then inserting a disposable tap that connects to the hollow tubing, creating a huge grid of hoses through which the sap flows.

Jared built the handsome sugaring house. Three large kettles sit inside, perched on wood fires that burn for several days. A barrel of maple syrup sells for fifteen times the price of oil. Baéz figures his operation will be profitable within the year.

"What's your brother doing with his share of the royalties?"

"Tuition, room and board. Pepperdine's an expensive school, but that book has generated a considerable sum." Baéz grins; he loves needling his father about how much money he, Nathan, and Brighton earned from their Speedo endeavors.

"Is he doing okay?"

Baéz shrugs. "Best I can tell. We haven't spoken in a while. He's never home when I call; I get Scottie. His calls are forwarded to her house."

"You like her?"

Baéz knows his father's irritating curiosity is simply a reflection of his concern, but he is tired of questions about Brighton. They spent seven summers together before going off to college; now their summers are spent apart. The maple syrup operation keeps him busy and provides the distraction he seeks.

"She's older, she has a lovely voice, and a delicate laugh. Other than that, I can't say, but Brighton seems quite taken with her."

Both men retreat into silence; the subject of Brighton is awkward for both of them. Nonnie too. Yesterday, she had found him napping in Brighton's old room. "I forgot what I came up here for," he explained, "and then I lay down. That was an hour ago."

"It still smells like him," observes Nonnie. "That cologne!"

Baéz nodded; that was why he came up there. To breathe in the perfume of vetiver, an exotic grass from India useful for inducing sleep.

"How goes the workhorse?" she asked.

"Fine. I'm fine, Nonnie. I am. It's a lot of work and I get tired, but it's a pleasing fatigue. I enjoy it."

Baéz finds their concerns exhausting. He realizes how fragile they think he is.

He turns to his father, who is inserting a tap into the last maple. "The agricultural inspector is coming today. He has our certificate."

Jared nods, a pleased look on his face. "Congrats. You've done fine work. "

Baéz smiles, pleased with the compliment from his dad.

✴ ✴ ✴

The image of the gun lingers in Wynn's mind. Metallic blue with a matte finish resembling the veneer of fine racing cars. He doesn't understand why Dušan carries a gun, but it does create an unforgettable picture, like a handsome gangster in a hip European film.

The compact room where they are sitting was once the projection booth of a movie palace. A wall of one-way glass provides a view of the transformed space below, including a sixty-foot-long bar sheathed in copper, twelve regulation pool tables, a batting cage, and surrounding it all, twenty large television monitors. Nico has spent a fortune on Panasonic's innovative flat screens, forty-eight inches wide and twelve thousand dollars each. This daring investment had paid off handsomely—the bar is packed at all hours.

The TV's play baseball games from Chicago, tennis matches from Dubai, street races in Monaco, and live soccer from Germany. At two o'clock on a Sunday afternoon the cavernous space is crowded as bartenders spin their concoctions and handsome waiters dressed in clingy wrestling gear brave the gauntlet of handsome, handsy patrons. Nico has named his gay sports bar "Singlets."

"I recognize the footballer, David Beckham," Wynn says. "Should I assume those other portraits are athletes, too?"

The walls below are papered with life-sized photographs of Oscar de la Hoya, Thierry Henry, Troy Aikman, Michael Jordan, Alex Rodriguez, and Andre Agassi.

"Yes, all famous athletes. Except for the large one over the bar. Two brothers and a dog playing football in a field of mud." Nico laughs. "They are the patron saints of our customers."

Wynn never criticized Brighton for agreeing to appear in the revealing book; the profits are putting his son through college. The only element that rankles is the inscription. *Dedicated with love to Rebecca Esmund.* Her maiden name.

He looks around the private dining room. Dušan is on his left, his skinny suit unbuttoned, revealing the holster that holds his gun. His electric blue eyes shine through the scruffy beard that covers his baby face. He is tanned, and a small cross is tattooed on the back of his head.

Opposite him is Allison Green, a tall woman of indeterminate age. Her bright-red lipstick gleams neon against her dark chocolate skin. She was once a champion forward on UConn's basketball team.

Wynn lifts his Bloody Mary and takes a sip. He nods to the others but stares at Dušan. "Does a gay sports bar attract a level of violence that requires a gun?"

Nico laughs, but Dušan scowls—Nico's humorless partner has never liked Wynn.

"No, this is a safe, solid moneymaker," Nico says. "No violence. It is our gambling interests that make Dušan nervous. He wants me safe. And pairing the blue of the gun with the blue of his cashmere suit makes for a striking picture, no?"

And again, he laughs, patting Dušan's back.

The tall woman smiles. "Forgive my boys, Mr. Bethune. They are still celebrating. After many weeks of waiting, and many official forms and many interviews—"

Nico interrupts. "Not to mention many thousands of dollars in kickbacks and bogus fees and charitable gifts and weeks in an overpriced hotel—"

"—in Antigua, mind you. Don't feel badly for us. We succeeded. Nico is now licensed to run gambling sites on the internet. A new world."

"It is your Wild West, Wynn, and we are in at the beginning. My partners are in Prague, but I am focusing on American sports, all of them."

"And Nico has opened a management division," adds Allison. "We are representing athletes from many disciplines. So, yes, we are celebrating these recent triumphs."

Wynn smiles. He'd known this lunch would be interesting. A gay sports bar, a gorgeous black woman, a handsome thug, and crazy Nico. *Better than a night at the Taj,* he thinks.

"How is my Boy-O? Still with his tennis?"

"Yes. Out in California. Couldn't get any farther from the old man!"

"No different than we were at his age, eh?"

Dušan dives into his breakfast sausage. He is a noisy eater. Allison smiles as she demurely picks at her salad, waiting for her boss to begin.

"We read your proposal," explains Niko. We have some questions of course, but you are right, these odd little businesses could be a good fit for us. Health and Sports. How did this come about?"

Elwynn answers. "My boss at BNP has an old high school friend—an unsavory friend some might say—and he has promised this friend to find new owners for several questionable businesses. Protein powders for gym rats, diet powders for the obese, energy drinks, male potency pills, pills to reduce hair loss, pills to enlarge your penis. The products are sold in the back of muscle magazines and on TV in the middle of the night. They are unproven but also unregulated. And they sell for many times the cost of their manufacture."

This last point gains everyone's attention as Wynn continues. "I thought with some clever marketing, better distribution, and a big upgrade in their packaging, you could have a gold mine here."

"Yes, and for you . . . what? A lifetime supply of penis pills?" Nico asks.

Even Dušan laughs.

"Thanks, no. And I'm not losing my hair either. Maybe a finder's fee and a modest ownership stake? Silent, of course."

"Of course. We wouldn't want your boss to know what unsavory company you keep!"

Nico chuckles, clearly enjoying himself. Wynn stands and looks at the teeming crowd below. It is hard for him to admit, but he has grudging respect for what Nico has created.

"A goldmine, eh, my friend?" asks Niko as he shakes Wynn's hand, cementing their deal as a waitress arrives and delivers a fresh round of drinks.

Niko names his new company HARDBODY, after an expression Allison used when she saw Brighton in the Speedo catalogue. He likes the term; he thinks it's crisp and sexy. The products *are* a good fit with his gambling empire and his sports management company. He is impatient to reintroduce these pills and potions, anxious to recoup his investment, but Allison is a steadying influence, advising him to move slowly. He needs endorsements; he needs sports pros and doctors and dieticians to recommend their merchandise.

Surely, he thinks, *there are coaches and physicians in need of a little pocket money!*

✳ ✳ ✳

In the lobby of the Divinity School, between the drinking fountain and a map detailing the emergency exits, is a large corkboard covered with a colorful collage of photographs, index cards, and brochures, all advertising a myriad of diverse opportunities: apartments for rent, summer internships, tutoring, and even the sale of a wedding dress, "never worn."

It is here, in the last warm weeks of May, as his junior year comes to a close, that Baéz discovers a leaflet advertising a contest to choose a new minister for a church in Texas. A six-week audition process will be filmed and then televised on The Faith Channel, the winner taking home a $100,000 prize. Ten people will be chosen to participate, and a panel of religious scholars and ministers will pick the winner. The contest will be filmed in New York this summer.

Baéz removes the flyer, intending to share it with Alonzo, his roommate. They often watch the Faith Channel for class assignments, seeing ministers preach the power of success while an 800-number urges viewers to reach into their wallet and buy salvation.

"Why do they do this?" classmates ask. "These preachers are stealing from the poor!"

Their professor answers, "Exploiting God is nothing new. Religion and money have always been paired; promising the impossible for a hefty fee."

For Baéz, the choice of what to believe has always come down to Nonnie's warning: "The thoughts you hold in your heart will determine your existence. And the fears you give power to will limit your potential. Choose what to believe and choose carefully."

She would send the boys out to play, yelling after them, "Go with God, choose carefully, celebrate perfection!" They heard it every day, after breakfast, on the phone and running for the school bus. When Baéz was reading his college course descriptions, Brighton had whispered, "Choose carefully," in his ear, and they both cracked up. But the concept remained, ever-present in their thought.

Alonzo suggests they both apply. He is a film major, minoring in religious studies and fascinated by the power of belief.

"A summer in New York could be great," he explains. "I'll approach it as an acting exercise. Can I convince these judges of my sincerity, my originality, can I move them? Come on, it will be fun. We can do this. Faith Channel, here we come!"

Baéz answers the lengthy questionnaire and writes his essay. He reads it one last time before sealing the envelope:

My father is a steeplejack, but no one is building churches today. Luckily, he has other skills. He's good with cars, he's a fine roofer, and he even knows how to train dogs. Yet each year he must hire an accountant to file his taxes, having neither the time nor the inclination to study accounting.

We turn to trained experts in fields we do not understand. If our car is making a funny noise, we take it to an auto mechanic. If our bodies ache, we visit the doctor. And as the world we live in becomes more complex, there are more and more things that we do not understand. Discoveries are made each day, and old truths are proven faulty. Pluto is no longer a planet; bloodsucking leeches do not cure illness. In another hundred years, will today's discoveries also be found erroneous? Are the truths we are living with transitory and temporal? Are we enjoying a life comforted by false evidence? What is true? What is eternal? And who do we hire to resolve these questions?

In 500 BC, the King of Babylonia, King Belshazzar, was partying with his princes and drinking wine from gold and silver vessels stolen from a temple in Jerusalem when suddenly he saw the fingers of a human hand writing on the walls of his palace! He was scared. The sight of the floating fingers tortured his dreams. He had to know the meaning of the message, so he called for all the alchemists and soothsayers, the prophets and diviners, the oracles and seers to come and translate. These men possessed the greatest knowledge of their time, yet none could decipher the markings.

Then Daniel appeared before the King. Young Daniel possessed the breath of the Gods, and the message was revealed to him. The writings were an admonition to Belshazzar to change his ways. Had he learned nothing from his predecessor's downfall? Had he not seen the writing on the wall?

We give power to those who can explain things we do not understand. Accountants. Economists. Doctors. Priests. Soothsayers. Whoever can interpret the writing on the wall will be greatly valued and recompensed. They will hold the strings.

We are living through an explosion of information unprecedented in human history. The World Wide Web can help us create a perfect soufflé, craft a stylish racing car, or show us, step by step, how to build a nuclear bomb. But can "ones" and "zeros" lead to Truth? Can they explain this life and the reason I am here? What is Spirit? Is there a God?

Whoever can lead us through this existential minefield and help us understand our purpose will be a successful minister or rabbi, priest or imam. This is my role. This is why I study. This is why I am here.

He licks the stamp and drops the envelope in the mail. He is unnerved by embarking on this adventure without consulting his brother, but he is learning to exist on his own and to find everything he needs within himself.

That same summer Brighton moves into Scottie's Malibu home, where he embarks on an intensive training regimen to increase his strength and stamina. College tennis competitions are the best of three sets, but the four major tournaments—Wimbledon, the French Open, the Australian Open, and the US Open—are the best of five, often requiring three or four hours to complete. Brighton has never played a five-set match.

The summer of 1999 becomes one long grueling workout. He runs in the mornings and evenings. He lifts weights, jumps rope, and jogs on an obstacle course. He lowers his body-fat index from nine percent to six percent, until Scottie says he feels like a piece of finely polished furniture. She tolerates his obsessive calorie tracking but also warns him to be moderate. Already his cheekbones have become sharp as knives. His large green eyes stare out from a face that is nearly inflexible.

"I think I should go for it," he announces. "Not wait. If nothing else, I'll get a taste, so I'll be better prepared next time."

They are seated on Scottie's balcony, drinking smoothies and grilling shrimp. The sun is slowly reaching the horizon where a cluster of surfers float on the expanse of blue.

"Would you like me to come? The restaurant won't miss me."

"But you'll miss all this." He opens his arms, framing her house and the ocean beyond. He turns the shrimp and then looks at her. "Baby boy has to fly off at some point."

She returns his gaze. This day has been arriving since they first met. She once suggested that he manage her restaurant or perhaps oversee Pepperdine's summer tennis clinic, but Brighton is choosing to leave.

"Kimbro has a great place in Manhattan," she says, mentioning her ex-husband. "Told me to use it. He's never there. Why waste money on a hotel?"

"Maybe. That could be perfect. Thanks," he says.

He wants to avoid Wynn. When they last spoke, his father described Nico's new business ventures. "Managing stocks has always been easy for me, but Nico's projects add some excitement to my life. You'll see. You'll be impressed!" Brighton wants nothing to do with either of them.

He sips his mango smoothie. "I have to survive three qualifying matches in a six-day period so I may be back in no time!"

Was he crazy? His top-ten college ranking provides him entrée into the qualification rounds of the U.S. Open, but he's told no one, not even his teammate Jimmy Royale, who has been his practice partner all summer. He feels bad keeping his decision secret, especially from Baéz, but he wants to avoid the pressure of their expectations.

"If you are going to do this, then let's make it right," Scottie says. "Make it momentous. And that starts with a distinctive look. An image. The way you carry yourself. The way you are photographed. Let me call Reynaldo. He can create a line of athletic wear to light up the world of tennis!"

He is grateful for her enthusiasm. He puts the shrimp on plates, serves them each a salad, and then sits. They eat slowly, quieted by the spectacle of the flaming sun sinking into the dark blue water. This glorious evening and the affection he feels for the woman across from him makes him smile.

"Thank you, for everything," he says. He eats the tasty lime-seasoned shrimp while wondering if their breezy relationship can withstand the rigors of him turning pro. He has learned that tennis is a jealous mistress.

10.

BEAU BRIGHTON

Corona Park is built on a mountain of ash collected from coal furnaces in the early decades of the twentieth century. The nine-hundred-acre greensward is now home to Shea Stadium and the National Tennis Center. And within this impressive complex, Brighton Bethune sits on a bench staring at court Seventeen where he will play his first match.

His court is at the end of a long line of similar blue courts, some with small grandstands, others with only a few rows of wooden bleachers. These distant courts allow die-hard tennis fans the opportunity to watch great players in a truly intimate setting.

The three large stadiums on the northern edge host the high-profile matches that provide the bulk of the television coverage, but with more than a hundred matches played each day, many famous faces are forced to play on these outer courts, players such as Tommy Haas, Patrick Rafter, Lleyton Hewitt, Marat Safin. Some of the era's greatest players, players Brighton worships.

"You okay? You look a bit lost."

Brighton looks up to see a young man with a thick head of dark hair and a winning smile. Brighton stands. "Nervous. This is my court."

The pleasant young man sticks out his hand. "My name's Taylor. Taylor Dent."

"Brighton. My match is in an hour."

"Trying to qualify?" Taylor asks.

"Yes."

"First time?"

"Is it obvious?"

Taylor's face breaks into a wide grin. "Yes! But we'll get you past this. Do you need to warm up?"

"I do. I thought I could find someone here, but I guess it doesn't work that way."

Taylor reaches down and grabs Brighton's bag. "Come on, follow me. Have you reserved a practice court?"

Brighton feels so stupid. "Uh, no."

"Okay, don't worry. We'll get you ready."

The young man leads the way to the other side of the center. At the practice courts, he exchanges a few words with an official, signs a form, and signals Brighton to follow.

"Who's your opponent?"

"Nicolás Massú."

Taylor stops and turns to face Brighton. "The Chilean?"

"Yes. You know him?"

"I lost the Junior Doubles Championship to him and his partner. Come on, you can get revenge for me."

"Is he good?"

"Good? He's great. He beat me, right?" Taylor chuckles.

They begin hitting the ball back and forth, easily at first, warming the muscles.

"Are you in the tournament?" Brighton asks.

"Yes. Got a wild card, so I can skip the qualies. I'm here today to support a few friends who are doing what you're doing."

"Does anyone come to watch these early matches?"

"Are you kidding? This place will be packed. And the crowd will support you. They always cheer for the American. Be ready. It's a trip. I mean it. Feed on it. You'll need it. Massú is a fine player."

"How do you know all this stuff?"

"My folks play. I've been around these courts all my life. Don't worry. After today, you'll know exactly what you're doing. We've just got to get you past this first match."

"What's his serve like?"

"Strong. Great first serve, not necessarily fast, but great placement. The second serve is weak. He has no confidence in it. If you get a second serve, step way into the court, you'll unnerve him."

"Okay. What else?"

"He's a baseline player, but he's most comfortable on clay. Move him around a lot; he'll get frustrated at being unable to slide. Understand?"

"Got it."

"And favor his forehand—it's his weaker stroke. He has good power from both sides, but his accuracy is wobbly on the forehand. Let's get right into it. Ready?"

"Ready."

They are well matched, both fast, both strong. Taylor has a powerful serve, faster than any Brighton has faced. They play for thirty minutes, both sweating as the temperature rises, until the official signals their time is up. The teenager helps Brighton pack up his racquets and they walk towards the locker rooms. The Center is getting crowded as people rush to find good seats. Brighton is beginning to feel excited.

"Now what? Do I wait here or go to the court?"

"Stay here. They'll come and get you and walk you over. Seventeen, right? I'll drop by."

"Thanks."

"Okay, good luck. Nice to meet you."

"Thank you. You've been a godsend."

"It's up to you now. Go do it. Three wins, and you're in."

The next day, Jimmy Royale walks into the large reading room of the Payson Library, which carries the daily newspapers of more than twenty-five American cities. He sits down with Tuesday's edition of *The New York Times* and immediately turns to the "Stats and Scoreboard" page. His high school buddy, Ranger Holmes, a UCLA player, is competing in the qualification rounds for the US Open. As he reads down the list of yesterday's matches, his eye is caught by a tiny entry: *B.Bethune def. N. Massú 1-6, 6-3, 6-3.*

He doesn't even look for his friend's score. He runs out of the library and calls his teammates.

Two days later, Fletcher Hill and Jimmy Royale walk into the Payson Library, their hearts filled with fear and excitement. They open Thursday's edition of *The New York Times.* Slowly, Jimmy turns to the Stats and Scoreboard page again. He can hardly look. Finally, he sees *B.Bethune def. M. Hall 6-3, 3-6, 6-3.* The teammates looked at each other in amazement.

On Saturday, the entire Pepperdine Tennis Team, players and coaches, walk into the Payson Library. Silent prayers and secret talismans are called forth as Coach approaches the newspaper display. He slowly turns the pages and looks for the correct listing. On the bottom left he reads *B.Bethune def. JR Lisnard 6-1, 6-0*

He smiles. "He demolished him!"

A huge cheer erupts, shocking the normally placid building.

Jimmy Royale has tears on his smiling face as he announces: "We got to get there!"

★ ★ ★

A few miles east of Court Seventeen sits a neighborhood of two-family houses stacked on tiny plots of land. The noise of the Grand Central Parkway mixes with the takeoffs and landings at nearby LaGuardia Airport, creating a constant thrum that irritates and annoys. Each home has two entrance doors, one for the first floor and the other for the family above. Some yards are cared for, while others are still sporting last year's Christmas decorations.

This is Baéz's third day of going door to door discussing the Bible. Sporting a tiny surveillance camera in his ball cap and a microphone sewn in the placket of his shirt, Baéz feels like an intruder, invading the privacy of the trusting residents. But after many conversations, he forgets the electrical devices and greets each resident warmly and simply.

Wearing sharply creased shorts and a crisp long-sleeved shirt with the cuffs rolled to the elbows, he stands out among the other pedestrians in their torn T-shirts and lace-less sneakers. His longish hair is curling from the intense humidity. The white Faith Channel van is parked down the street, recording the images and sounds from his electronics.

It is a neighborhood of immigrants—policeman, subway drivers, toll collectors, nurses. His unthreatening appearance helps gain entry to many houses, and to his surprise, they are willing to accept his gift of the New English Bible and to discuss it. A stranger talking about God is not unwelcome here.

The ten contestants on *The Divine Road* are dropped off in a different neighborhood every morning, accompanied by a producer driving a remote video van. Morgan, Baéz's producer, initially despaired when she was assigned him. His quiet manner is in sharp contrast to the wildly animated demeanor of the others, but as she follows him each day, she finds his conversations compelling. He is getting good footage. People open their doors to him and speak freely.

This morning, Baéz is tired. He stayed awake until the early hours preparing for this day's "crusade." That's what he calls it. A crusade. His father never turns away the Mormons and Jehovah's Witnesses who occasionally knock on their door. Instead, he listens, nods, and then wishes them a good day. Jared always says that people are shy about God. He has respect for those willing to go out and risk the humiliation of a slammed door while they attempt to share the "good news."

The first house of the day looks abandoned—the grass is dry and uncut, and a thick layer of grime covers the windows. The pressure of his knock opens the flimsy door.

"Hello? Anyone home?"

A blast of warm air greets him, adding more curls to his damp hair. "Hello?" he calls again, a bit louder.

A female voice answers. "In here. Please."

He walks through the empty foyer and into the living room. On the floor, a thin woman is breathing in loud, short gasps. Her forehead shines with perspiration. He reaches into his pocket for his phone.

"I'll call an ambulance."

"No, please, don't. Let me lie here."

"But you need help, ma'am."

"We all need help, young man. Leave me be. Please. I've been in that hospital more times than I can count. I doubt they want me back!"

He looks around the spare living space and gets a pillow from the worn sofa and a glass of water from the spotless kitchen. He sits beside the prone woman, gently lifting her head and placing a pillow beneath. He offers her the water. She takes a few sips, most dribbling down her chin. He wipes her face with the sleeve of his crisp white shirt.

"Damn, boy, who starches those shirts for you?"

He smiles and looks into her tired eyes. "I do, ma'am. I should look nice if I wish to be invited into a stranger's home."

"We're not strangers. I know you."

"Ma'am?"

"You're the angel come to take me home. A damn handsome angel, too! Come on, now. It's time"

Baéz closes his eyes. *Listen*, he tells himself. *Be quiet and listen.* He looks down at the women. She is shy of sixty, with close-cropped hair that shows care in its cutting, eyes covered in a layer of fog, and a beautiful wide nose that leads to full, chapped lips. He lies on the floor beside her, propping his head on an elbow. He sees her as perfect. An idea of the Divine Mind. He dismisses her loud breathing as a lie and denies the existence of rheum in her eyes.

"Does God love you?" he asks.

"I believe he does, yes."

"And God made everything, didn't he? He made you and me."

"Yes, he did."

"Well, I don't think he made you to be sick. I don't think he made sickness at all."

She looks at him as if he is blind, or maybe crazy. "Well, someone done made it. Look at me. Been sick for months now."

"So you say. But God doesn't see you as sick. He sees you as he made you—healthy and loving, not a touch of illness. And if that's what God's eyes are telling him, then I think you should adjust your own view. Away from the body, and towards the perfection of God. Do you know the story in the Bible where Jesus comes across the funeral procession of a young man accompanied by his widowed mother?"

A smile forms on her lips. "They are carrying her son to his burial."

"Yes, and Jesus walks over to them."

"Yes. I love that story. She is adored in that village."

"Yes, and Jesus tells that boy to sit up, doesn't he?"

"Yes, he does."

"You have that same authority. And you are also going to sit up."

"Young man, I am not Jesus, and I have had a stroke. I ain't sitting up any time soon. I can't move my arms or my legs."

"Well, today we are going to rid you of these complaints. Do you hear me?" Baéz finds himself shouting over the sound of a plane flying overhead.

"I most certainly do hear you."

"You are not vulnerable. God loves you and made you perfect. You are here to glorify and stand witness to that truth. Stand and bear witness. Banish sickness from your thoughts. Hold only expectations of good. Hold only thoughts of wellness, of perfection, of love. Can you do that? Do not look inside and try to find a cause for these material symptoms. God is the only cause. Do not listen to false evidence. Know only good. Only God. And let that truth set you free."

His voice possesses a calming certainty. The woman knows he's not lying, but he is speaking so loudly. The upstairs neighbors will be furious. They have a young baby. She rises up from the floor to ask him to lower his voice and then walks over to her favorite chair and sits. She stares at him unblinking through clear eyes.

"My name is Clarice."

"Well, Clarice, it is nice to meet you. I am called Baéz."

Sitting in the video van, Morgan doesn't understand what she has witnessed, but she knows it will make compelling television.

✳ ✳ ✳

The producers of *The Divine Road* have rented a large, multi-roomed loft in lower Manhattan to house the contestants and crew. They eat, sleep, and shower here and are constantly being filmed. Imitating the structure of MTV's successful series *The Real World*, the tensions and day-to-day interactions of the ten participants serve as background for the daily assignments they each must complete.

"What's the writing on your shirt?" T'Shawn, a fellow contestant, points to Baéz's sleeve which reads HonorBright.Com.

"It's a website I created in college. An online congregation."

"You kiddin' me? Real people?"

"Yes. Four hundred registered initially, but only about fifty remain."

"Let me see."

Baéz turns his laptop so T can look at the page. Baéz designed the site to be a healing resource. In addition to Bible stories, he included testimonies describing the various healings he has experienced. The site is interactive and invites people to share healings or request prayers for a problem they are experiencing. Some entries are clearly pranks, but he also receives heartbreaking appeals for assistance.

"And you respond to them all?"

"I try to."

The phone vibrates in his pocket. The caller ID says *Tennis Rules!* He smiles and answers, apologizing to T'Shawn. One of the many cameras is focused on him, invading the privacy he seeks.

"Hey, brother, what a pleasant surprise!" He says the words with warmth, intending no irony. This is how they are now. Baéz has adjusted his behavior to fit the relationship that is comfortable for Brighton.

"Hey, big guy, what's the deal? Where am I calling you?"

Baéz wonders how to explain. "I'm part of a TV show. A documentary, I guess you'd call it. Ten of us, vying for a cash prize, being tested for our suitability to become the pastor of a church in Texas. We're in New York, a sweet loft near Crosby Street. Did you get my T-shirts? I mailed them to your Pepperdine address."

"Yup, I did. Thanks. Listen, what are you doing tomorrow? Can you come out to the Tennis Center?"

"What? Are you in New York?"

"Yeah, staying at a friend's pad, Scottie's ex. Lying low."

Baéz tries to accept this information as simple fact, but he feels his body tensing. "What, you got seats? Ashe Stadium, finally?"

"Nope, sorry, fella. Not Ashe. Court Seventeen."

"Our first court. Mats Wilander won, but it took five sets!"

"Yup, and that's where I'll be playing."

Baéz isn't sure he understands. He takes a deep breath, calming his heart. "You're in the Open?"

"Yes, I won my three qualifying matches, and tomorrow is my debut. Can you be there?"

It's just as they had dreamed, playing in the Open, yet he is upset Brighton hadn't shared his plans. He wants to express his excitement but must hide the hurt he feels at no longer being a trusted confidant.

"My God, Bright, this is huge! I mean, congratulations! This is so exciting. You're not joking? You are actually *in* the U.S. Open?"

"Yes, my first opponent is some Spanish dude."

"They're all Spanish now. Who's in your draw?"

"Too scary to consider, so I didn't look. Going one day at a time. Can you come?"

Baéz shakes his head, knowing his brother fully expects him to drop everything and rush out to the tennis center. "I'm filming tomorrow. The schedule is set. It involves lots of people, not just me." He pauses. He can't believe it. "I'm so sorry."

"If I win tomorrow, my next match will be Thursday. Can you make that?" Brighton asks, his voice betraying an urgent need.

"Win tomorrow, and I will make every game you play. That's a promise!" responds Baéz.

He hears a loud car horn over the phone.

"Gotta go," says his brother. "A van's picking me up."

Baéz folds his phone closed. His fellow contestants are arguing in the kitchen, calling to him. He doesn't want to join them. Not now. His mind flashes on the disturbing dream he had in school, standing on the sidelines, grim-faced, while his brother wins it all. He tells himself to celebrate his brother's accomplishments. The camera follows him as he plasters a smile on his face and joins his rambunctious competitors.

✷ ✷ ✷

Jared and Nonnie drive in from Connecticut and meet Baéz at the food courts in the middle of the Tennis Center. Nonnie is telling anyone within earshot that her grandson is in the next match. They are keeping an eye out for Brighton's college teammates, who will be wearing green Pepperdine T-shirts.

They have caught the TV highlights of Brighton's win against the Spaniard and are now eagerly awaiting his second-round matchup with the Russian player, Marat Safin. The contest is scheduled for The Grandstand, a beautiful court that seats six thousand people. It will be the largest crowd Brighton has ever played for.

"You're nervous for him," Jared says.

"Terrified. I want to play the game *for* him. Win it *for* him. We sat right here, six years ago, excited kids who dreamed of playing here. Now he's done it. He's actually here. I still can't believe it." His eyes are wet, and he is embarrassed. He laughs and looks in his father's eyes. "Sorry."

"Don't apologize for your feelings."

They sit quietly, neither saying anything further as Nonnie rests at a nearby table sipping a coke. Jared points to the giant aluminum Unisphere at the far end of Flushing Meadow Park.

"They built that in 1963. A sign of the future. The bold logo for the New York World's Fair. This tennis center hadn't yet been built yet." He looks over at Shea Stadium. "You were conceived here, you know."

Baéz's eyes widen; he knows no such thing.

"We had come into the city to see the Mets play. The Mets and Cubs. I had tried all summer to get Rebecca's attention, but she spent the summer driving her convertible all over the county. I could tell something was bothering her, and I hoped it wasn't a boy. I wanted to fix the trouble, whatever it was. Mr. Campbell had given me his seats, right behind home plate. I pleaded with her to join me, anything to escape the boredom of that stifling summer."

Jared wears a smile his son rarely sees. Baéz leans in to catch every word, every inflection.

"I don't know why she said 'yes,' but she did. I prepared sandwiches and cold chicken. Deviled eggs. I filled an old thermos with sangria. I had a cloth-topped Jeep in those days, and we drove in, singing with the radio, screaming out the lyrics of some Carly Simon tune. The city was sinking into bankruptcy, graffiti covered every surface, and the police were hunting a killer called 'Sam.' Neither of us had experience with New York City. We weren't comfortable here.

"We parked in a giant lot by Shea, weeds sprouting everywhere, broken glass covering the asphalt. The smell of piss filled the air. But when we entered the ballpark, we were pleasantly surprised by the beautiful field of green. Perfectly manicured. Such a wonderful contrast! Paths of red clay led to pristine white bases. As we took our seats, she smiled and looked at me. 'What could be better,' she said, 'than a game whose sole purpose is to find your way home!'"

Baéz is flabbergasted—his father never tells wistful tales about Rebecca.

"The Mets had a firm grip on last place, and the fans were frustrated, especially since they had just traded Seaver. No one was buying tickets; the stadium closed off the upper decks. But I was determined. They were my team. They were my heroes." Jared clenches his fist and shakes his arm in jubilant remembrance. "We shared our food with everyone around us, we cheered our team, we jeered the Cubs, and we had a grand time. This is life, I thought. This is life as an adult."

His expression darkens as the memories come flooding in. "At the top of the sixth inning, the stadium goes dark. Flashes of heat lightning illuminate the clouds as emergency lights switched on and a voice on the public address system says the game is over. New York is in the midst of a blackout, he explains, and the subways are not operating."

Jared shakes his head. "We don't know the roads, we can't see the signs, and we get lost leaving the stadium. Traffic is a nightmare, nothing is moving, and everyone is honking. We are driving beneath the elevated tracks, and the passengers above us are screaming for help. Kids are running everywhere, excited, yelling threats, and then a brick or a pipe breaks through a window. And then another. Rebecca is frightened; only a thin covering of canvas protects us, and the heat is so great we have to drive with the windows down. More storefronts are shattered as a fire breaks out. Sirens begin to scream, and all color leaves Rebecca's face. I see how scared she is, so I lean on the horn and begin to drive on the sidewalk, screaming bloody murder."

Baéz's heart is pounding, as if he himself is in danger. He watches his father, barely recognizing him.

"We get back to Roosevelt Avenue, and I can see the outline of Shea Stadium against the sky. I aim for it, and we are back where we started, in Corona Park. There is no hysteria—folks aren't rioting but are roller-skating, and the only fires are the ones in the barbecue grills. We calm down. We breathe easily, and I park near a picnic table. I lay out our meal. We say nothing. I kiss her. She kisses me back. Out of gratitude I think, for getting us away from the danger."

He looks over at his speechless son and smiles.

"I don't recognize any of it. Only the Unisphere looks the same. Not sure where we parked, or which table was ours, but from all the chaos of that scary night, we found comfort for a while and created you."

Baéz doesn't know what to say. "And she simply left?"

Jared nods. "She returned to Wynn, begging forgiveness. They were married at the end of that summer. Only after Rebecca's death did I discover that you existed. You were nearly two years old."

"Jesus, Dad, why have you never told me this?"

"I don't know. I truly don't. But today, seeing your emotions so close to the surface, seeing you so proud and content with everything Brighton has accomplished, I wanted you to realize that I understand the sorrow that comes from loving."

As Baéz whispers a thank-you to his dad, he sees a bunch of guys in matching green shirts wandering in his direction. Brighton's teammates. They call Baéz "Ezzie," and are thrilled to meet Nonnie.

"Shall we get our seats?" Jared asks.

"Yes, sir. Let's go!"

✶ ✶ ✶

It is Mary Carillo, one of the USA Network's sportscasters, who first gives Brighton the moniker "Beau Brighton." With his witty clothes, his red ponytail, and his joyful smile, she teasingly says he reminds her of the eighteenth-century fashion plate Beau Brummel. And they nickname his opponent Marat Safin "The Russian Slugger." A year younger than Brighton, Safin is ranked twenty-ninth in the world.

Desperate to increase their ratings, the network asks the Open officials to move the match to the last afternoon slot, knowing it will stretch into primetime.

As the stadium announcer introduces Brighton, cries of "Beau! Beau! Beau!" greet his arrival. He wears black sneakers with bright yellow soles and yellow laces. He wears tall socks, striped yellow and black. Peeking out from below his yellow satin trunks are black compression shorts. The largest break with tradition, however, is on his head. Instead of a sweatband or a baseball hat, Reynaldo has designed a yellow-and-blue madras cap with a narrow black bill. Baéz thinks he looks like one of those newsboys in an old black-and-white movie.

"You don't think he looks silly?" Nonnie asks.

"No, ma'am. He looks great," answers Jimmy Royale. "And everyone will remember him. He's a genius at self-promotion."

"I thought you had to wear all white," says Nonnie

"Only at Wimbledon. Here in New York, anything goes."

Down the row, one of the younger teammates asks, "How does he get away with it? If I wore that outfit, I'd be laughed off the court. He wears it, and they give him the prime evening slot!"

The guys all nod in agreement.

"He looks like a bumblebee," says Nonnie, smiling.

As the players begin their warm-up, Baéz makes sure everyone has what they need. It has been a horrible day for the Americans. Five have already tanked, including the winner of the French Open, Michael Chang. Bethune is expected to add to the carnage.

As Baéz orders hot dogs and cokes, a television over the food stand shows his brother while Mary Carillo prepares her audience for an exciting match.

"**S**inglets" is packed, but only one flat screen is tuned to the tennis tournament. The large crowd is there to watch the Red Sox/Yankees game. The three-night series featuring the archrivals has been sold out for months.

Dušan is filling in tonight and working the quiet back bar where a few college jocks in polo shirts and khakis are glued to the Bethune match. The crowds amuse him. They don't root for teams; they root for players, the cute ones, speculating on their sexuality and commenting on their hair, their eyes, and their "package." Of the seven sports bars Nico owns, this is the only gay establishment but also the most profitable.

The college guys are laughing and arguing as they point to the large sepia photograph above the bar. Two boys in Speedos, covered in mud and throwing a football, as a large dog tries to steal it. One of the guys calls Dušan over.

"We think one of the men in that photo is the same one playing on the TV. Do you know?"

Dušan doesn't know the story behind the portrait, but he certainly sees the resemblance.

A scream comes from the circle of college guys. "Look, look, it's the other one, I swear it is!"

The image on the TV switches to a shot of Baéz sitting in Brighton's box.

"It must be him. What are the chances, huh?" says the excited customer as his buddies lean in.

Dušan calls his boss at home.

Nico answers angrily. "What? You can't leave me alone for one night?"

"And a good evening to you too, boss. Listen, something curious has come up here. You know the guys in the photo above the bar, the ones who aren't famous?"

"Yeah, what about them."

"Does one of them play tennis?"

"They both play tennis. Why?"

"Because there's a guy on the TV playing tennis who looks a lot like our guy on the wall."

"You making this up?"

"No. We have some excited customers here who are sure they are right. And bets are running high. Turn on your TV, the USA Network. I'll hold."

The guys at the bar are looking to him for an answer. The voice on the other end of the phone becomes loud and excited.

"Jesus Christ, that's Brighton. How do we not know this? Has Wynn not mentioned this?"

"Never, boss. We don't spend a lot of time chatting."

"Well, that's his son. Haven't seen him in years, but that is definitely him. I'm coming down there. Pour me a Glen Livet!"

✶ ✶ ✶

Brighton breaks Safin's serve twice, and the set is over in twenty-five minutes. The clothes Reynaldo designed don't breathe properly, and his cap is not absorbing the sweat from his brow. Worse, the compression pants are causing a rash on his thighs.

Stop it, he tells himself. *You've won the first set. You can do this!*

The matches on the outer courts had been fun. Small stands with rambunctious crowds. But this large stadium is something entirely new. Thrilling, but also disconcerting. The fans scream out his name like they know him. They applaud his every move. The groan in unison when his ball overshoots a line.

He drinks his Gatorade slowly, replenishing his sweating body.

He looks up at his box. Jimmy Royale is explaining something to Nonnie as Baéz looks on and laughs. They are all here, in his box, cheering him.

Stop this. Focus. His backhand is killing you. Stay away from it. Move your serve around more. He is getting better and better at guessing where you are going. He doesn't look a bit tired, and he is so angry. Play that. Force him to make mistakes.

✶ ✶ ✶

Nonnie is a wreck. Years earlier, when she watched her brothers play, the game seemed gentlemanly and civilized. The pleasant sound of the ball hitting nylon strings, the fluid motion of the racquet through the air, even the arcane scoring procedure, with the term "love" meaning zero. But she also recalls that the game was named for the French verb *tenez,* meaning *watch out,* a term that was shouted before the server hit the ball.

She tries viewing the game as a simple manifestation of the beauty of man—his grace, his strength, and his intelligence—rather than as a competition. But the crowd continually reminds her of where she is and that there has to be a winner and a loser. And she realizes how much she wants Brighton to win.

"How are you holding up?" asks Baéz. He has switched places with Jimmy.

"My heart is in my throat. Will he win?"

"Maybe. No one knows."

"Oh, come on, if anyone knows, you know. Can he win?"

"Of course he can, but he has to be smart now and win the mental game as well as the physical."

Yes, of course, she thinks. The universe is nothing more than a mental construct. That is how she heals. Correcting the thought, not the body.

✹ ✹ ✹

Brighton also wins the second set, but then Safin roars back and wins the third and fourth. They are now tied. Brighton is soaking wet, and his clothes are sticking uncomfortably to his body. He asks the umpire for a bathroom break. He has to pee, and he has to change. He reaches in the bag that holds his racquets to see if he has any more dry clothes but can only find the T-shirts Baéz mailed him. He feels a stab of quilt as he remembers stuffing them into his bag and not giving them another thought.

In the restroom, he stuffs the vest, the tall socks, and the soaking singlet into a trash can. He squeezes as much moisture out of the satin shorts as possible and holds them under the hand dryer. As he puts on Baéz's shirt, he notices discreet lettering circling the armhole. A dot-com address. He hopes that doesn't violate tournament rules. The writing is tiny. HonorBright.Com. Maybe no one will see it.

He steps into the semi-dry shorts without underwear. On certain summer days Baéz used to announce, "Today we play commando!" They would laugh, enjoying their near-nakedness and the freedom it allowed. But at Pepperdine, Coach had forbidden the practice. "Don't want your female fans to faint, Bethune" was all he would say, smiling.

Too late to worry about that now. He has to play his smartest set of tennis ever. He has to corral all his resources. And he has to believe.

✹ ✹ ✹

"Jesus, I'd go down on him in front of my mother!" says the guy in a pink polo shirt.

The randy fans are laughing and swooning over their new heartthrob. The first—and as it would turn out, the last—slow-motion shot of Brighton playing without the support of underwear stuns the boys into awestruck silence.

"Zoom in!" they beg as the satin shorts sway back and forth.

"You actually know him?" they ask Nico as he sips his scotch. He is no longer the owner chatting up some customers, but a friend of the gods.

"Can we buy copies of this game? Do they sell them like Super Bowl videos?"

"Fellas, tell you what. I got friends out there and if you are serious, I can book a block of seats for you."

"Well, first we gotta be sure he's going to win, dude."

Nico smiles. "Fear not; he's a finisher."

One of the young admirers throws his head back and howls. "Oh God, yes! Finish me, finish me, please!"

✳ ✳ ✳

Loud cheering comes from the sports bar behind Wynn's blackjack table. Customers are filing in, standing five-deep at the bar as they stare at the overhead screens. His fellow players asks the dealer to explain the commotion.

"A young American kid is wowing them at the Open."

One of the players asks if they can bet on him.

"Sorry, ma'am, only in Vegas. At least officially!"

With this, he smiles at Elwynn as if they share a secret.

Wynn's string of IOUs have been bought up, and the second mortgage on his duplex has been repaid. This was Nico's method of expressing thanks for the purchase of the HARDBODY line of products. Wynn is grateful for Nico's discretion. He is glad to play at the Taj again.

Tonight, he has taken on the persona of Huntly Cross, an early investor in *The Phantom of the Opera* and a trusted adviser to the office of the Exchequer. Americans are suckers for British aristocracy, but maybe he should actually be spinning a tale of being the father of the tennis player currently playing on the Grandstand.

A huge cheer goes up, and the bar begins to empty. The excited crowd bursts into the casino's main hall.

Wynn looks for a friendly face and asks: "Did the young American win?"

"Yup, in spades, buddy, in spades! A great game!"

Wynn smiles, wondering how his son might be of use to him. He will call Nico in the morning and see what he suggests.

✳ ✳ ✳

The wait staff are cleaning up as Dušan closes the register.

"Boss, tell me something."

"Certainly, Duše."

"With all the famous athletes on our walls, why is it the two unknown brothers who generate the most excitement? They're like good-luck charms for our customers."

Nico laughs. "Easy. Youth and beauty. People want to be near them. We should invite Boy-O to come visit. Maybe he could DJ one night, sign autographs, no?"

"Yes, boss. Maybe. And maybe you can convince him not to always play so incredibly well. There must be some days he feels less than one hundred percent."

"That's what I've been thinking. See what dad is up to. Perhaps he needs some fresh cash!"

11.

THE PERSIAN BOY

Baéz sits in the top row of seats in the circular Grandstand, staring down on the court where his brother beat Marat Safin the night before. The stadium is quiet. Today's opening match is hours away, but Baéz wants to study the arena and remind himself what last night's upset had felt like. He wants to write about it. The final challenge on *The Divine Road* is to deliver a homily to several hundred churchgoers. In searching for a theme Baéz recalls the wildly enthusiastic fans cheering for his brother and how strongly they resembled a mob. "Beau, Beau, Beau" they chanted as they placed their hopes on the shoulders of a stranger—celebrating him, exalting him, wishing to unite with him.

To Baéz, the behavior felt extreme, and he wonders what it would take for that confederacy to shift, to become hostile. He thinks about the adulteress in the Bible and the mob that wished to stone her. They were also cheering. Taunting. Condemning. Jesus himself had an enthusiastic crowd reverse their affections and attempt to throw him off a cliff. Will Brighton's new fans abandon him if he stops winning?

In the final set, Brighton had changed into one of Baéz's tee shirts with the name of his website circling the armholes. Baéz had wondered if the logo was legible to the crowd or to the viewers at home. His answer arrived when he logged in this morning—internet traffic to his site had increased ten-fold. Their identities as the boys in *Summers on the Aspetuk* is now public knowledge, as are Baéz's stories of falling under the ice. Comments from visitors ranged from heartfelt congratulations to rampant homophobia.

The secrecy provided by the internet emboldens the toxic bigotry of its users, and Baéz is saddened to learn how easily the joy of athletic achievement can be transformed into something ugly. If he hopes to uplift his churchgoers, he must find a different subject for his sermon.

"You were afraid, and he saw it in your eyes. Your fear betrayed you," yells a coach at a young player on the court below. Baéz looks down and sees a once-promising Czech who is on a losing streak.

Baéz thinks about the coach's words. He realizes Brighton didn't *win* last night's match; Marat Safin *lost* it. Safin exhibited fear, and Brighton saw it, providing the spark he needed to win.

Baéz smiles. He has found his subject.

✷ ✷ ✷

Brighton is on the practice courts, hitting serve after serve, moving the ball closer and closer to the white lines. A few photographers are following him, and the multitude of shutter-clicks are annoying, yet Brighton finds the attention pleasing.

"Hey, Mr. Lucky, looking good, but could be so much better!"

The crowds often yell at the players as if they were animals in the zoo.

"Smile when you're playing; it will unnerve them. Your beauty will unnerve them. I know. It unnerves me!"

Brighton gives in and laughs—a witty heckler! The jokester is a darkly tanned fellow with wild, unruly hair. Pretty as a model, with a lopsided smile and colorful clothes. Brighton recognizes him. He's one of the ball boys and is the talk of the men's locker room. An Australian player had asked him to dinner, assuming such beauty could only be possessed by a woman.

"You are in need of practice partner, and I am here to save the day!" the kid announces.

"You're the smug Persian boy?"

The young man laughs and walks onto Brighton's court.

"Yes, that is me. Taylor must have told you. I work with him and his doubles partner. *He's* a dreamboat, don't you think?"

Brighton shakes the boy's hand. "Usually I am the dreamboat!" he says, making the young man laugh.

"Well said, and so you are. Hello! I am Kaveh Havari. At your service!"

Brighton is drawn to people with a sense of humor, so he likes the kid right away. "Are you ready?"

Kaveh smiles, raises his eyebrows, and answers, "For anything, sir."

They play, relaxed at first, then harder and faster, working up a sweat and forcing each other to run, chasing down balls and trying to impress. The kid is good—unschooled but with natural talent. After an hour, they towel off and walk to the busy food stands, dodging the eager spectators who rush from court to court.

Kaveh looks askance at Brighton's order of a cheeseburger with waffle fries. "The player's cafeteria has a much healthier menu, you know."

"Yes, but I like being out here, with the crowds, feeling the energy."

The pretty kid nods. "Kiefer's next?"

"Yes. Know anything?"

"He's good. Top twenty."

"Fifteen. Strong serve. Fast."

"Did you see any tapes?"

"No. How?"

"Oh, come on, you can always get tapes of your opponents. I'll take care of that. You worry about winning, okay?"

"Who are you?" Brighton laughs as he says this, surprised by the kid's cocky nature.

"I'm from the left bank of the Tigris, land of Persians, Ottomans, Mongols, and Turks. I was born beside the hanging gardens of Babylon. And I am the best player on the Iraqi National Tennis Team!"

"Is tennis popular back home?"

Kaveh laughs. "No. If one of us get sick, it is difficult to find a new player!"

The boy's eyes resemble glass marbles, lit from behind and touched with blue.

"*Goodly is your beauty, honeysweet!*" says the boy. "Do you know this poem?"

Brighton shakes his head, mystified by the question.

"Oldest poem ever written. Part of Gilgamesh's adventures in seeking eternal life. I love tennis and I love poetry, but my father explained I had to choose one. I didn't know how to make a living spouting beautiful words written eight thousand years ago, so I got myself a round ball and threw it and kicked it and caught it until it felt natural. And then I bought a racquet, and the rest is history!"

"Poetry's loss is tennis's gain, eh?" jokes Brighton

"Yes, but I still study every day."

Brighton sees that Kaveh is serious. "Then you will teach me about poetry, okay?"

The boy raises his eyebrows, not sure if Brighton is teasing. "Okay. I shall read from the earliest days of Uruk, my homeland, the cradle of civilization. In Arabic. Yes?"

"Yes. And if I am lucky, as you say, and win today, either Tommy Haas or Hicham Arazi will be next. Can you find tape on them?"

"Yes, but Haas will beat Arazi."

"You know this?"

The boy nods, grinning. "Yes. I know this!"

"**F**ear. Fear of flying. Fear of failure. Fear of being chosen last on the team. Fear of death. Fear of disease. Fear of the dark. Fear of losing. Losing your job, losing your money, losing your wife, or maybe your health. A popular president once stated that we had nothing to fear but fear itself."

Baéz's words carry over the large auditorium of Trinity Baptist Church in the Bronx. The attentive crowd leans in and listens.

"What is fear, and why do we allow it to rule our lives? Fear is the dread caused by anticipating danger. An expectation of danger. We live under God's protective care, so why do we expect danger? Life is not dangerous; it is glorious, and we should celebrate this fact every day!"

He pauses and studies his audience. Bright sunlight streams through stained glass windows, tinting the transept and the domed ceiling.

"A buddy of mine grew up on the ocean, his hair bleached white by the salt and sun. He and his friends surfed the waves, and they cherished the hours riding those swells, surrounded by nature's beauty. During a nasty storm, he and some of his pals took on the challenge of the turbulent waters. They thought they understood the ocean's many moods, but on this day, they were punished and pummeled, dragged to the sandy bottom and held there until they were finally released. When they rushed to the surface, they were choking and terrified."

Baéz sees the quizzical looks on the faces of his audience as they wonder what he intends with this tale. He continues, his voice dropping in volume and forcing the crowd to edge closer.

"He never mentions the riptide that dragged him under. He never talks about how he thought he was going to die. He was afraid, so he stopped surfing.

"I ran into him one day at the Y. He was swimming laps. Hours in the pool every day. He wore electric orange Speedo jammers, so you couldn't miss him. We got to talking. He explained he was in training. 'For what?' I asked. He smiled and answered, 'To rejoin the ocean.' He was attempting to wean himself from this debilitating fear by entering the pool every day. I said to him that his fear wasn't real. I told him he had dominion. This dominion was God given and could not be taken away. His unease, his fright, was not a part of his perfect being. It was a lie, and he could undo the effects of that lie by proclaiming and celebrating the existence of his creator."

Baéz takes a deliberate pause, smiling before beginning again. "Well, as you can imagine, this new friend of mine looked at me oddly and asked what I'd been smoking."

Some gentle chuckles can be heard from the congregants.

"I didn't see him for a while. He wasn't at the Y. One evening, I found a seat at the fish shack at the end of the pier and ordered oysters and a beer. Tourists were everywhere. One young couple asked me to take a picture of them looking out to sea. I stood, they leaned against the railing, and I framed the picture, making sure to get the waves and water in the background. And then, through the lens, I saw a man in bright orange Speedos rise up on his board and float into shore. It was my friend. He had been released. The fear had left."

Baéz steps away from the solid oak lectern and looks directly at the men and women who fill the pews. He feels the cameras focused on him but pays them no mind. His solid baritone echoes off the plaster walls.

"The Bible clearly states, '*Fear not—for it is your Father's good pleasure to give you the kingdom.*' The Bible is filled with advice for those who live in fear. David in his Psalms tells us, '*The lord is thy light and thy salvation—who shall I fear?*'

Baéz stops and listens. There is only silence. They are with him.

"Mark equated fear with a lack of faith. '*Why are you so fearful?*' he asks. Our fidelity to God can deliver us from fear. Hebrews advises, '*Deliver them who, through fear of death, were all their lives subject to bondage.*' Living in fear is living in bondage. Who would choose to live in bondage? None of us. Pray, honor God, and be released from these fears."

He pauses and then slams his fist onto the wooden lectern. The forceful sound shocks the crowd as he increases his volume and intensity.

"We must listen when we pray! Instead of telling God what we want, we must be silent and hear what we need. Listen! Humble yourselves. Stop all these petitions of 'I want, I want.' Stop these attempts to negotiate with your Father! 'Oh Lord, I will stop drinking if you will save my little girl. Oh, please God, get me this job, and I will never again stray from home! Please God, save me.'"

His voice becomes louder, and he wonders if he is going too far—is he alienating the parishioners? But he continues with a firm voice, a finely tuned instrument climbing musical scales.

"God has done all he is going to do. He has given you everything you need. He has made you perfect. He has made you wise. He has made you loving. *There is no fear in love, but perfect love casteth out all fear. For God hath NOT given you the spirit of fear, but of power and of love and of a sound mind.'* A sound mind. Perfect love. Think on that."

He takes a deep breath and then raises his arms out to his sides as if embracing a giant globe. "People!! Fear God and follow his commandments. FOR THIS IS THE WHOLE DUTY OF MAN. Your duty. To love, to recognize the greatness of God, to be in awe of God, to honor him and his wonders, to reflect his greatness because he made you perfect. He did. And as Genesis states, he not only made you perfect, but he gave you dominion over everything on this earth. Everything! In your prayers, affirm your dominion. In your prayers, see your brothers and sisters as perfect too. And most important, in your prayers, LISTEN!"

He wipes the sweat from his face. He has to convince them. This is the task of every minister, every preacher, and every rabbi. He understands this now; if he can convince them, if he can get them to believe him, their lives will be so much richer. Through God. The promises of God.

He smiles. "I WILL HELP THEE. These are not merely words; they are a promise. A promise from our Father/Mother. Thoughts to keep close with you all day. Not fear. Not envy. Not anger. These drown out the Lord's voice and allow fear to enter your realm. Set yourselves free!" he cries, his voice filling the auditorium. "Honor the Lord and praise his creation, for as John says, *'Without him, was not anything made that was made.'* Renounce fear. Demonstrate your dominion. And as Isaiah promises, *'The trees of the field shall clap their hands.'* Yes, CLAP YOUR HANDS! Praise him, praise him in the highest, praise him, praise him. Clap your hands! PRAISE HIM! Renounce fear! PRAISE HIM! Renounce bondage! PRAISE HIM! PRAISE HIM! PRAISE HIM! God bless you all!"

Baéz leaves the stage, his face dripping, and his shirt having soaked through to his jacket. He loosens his tie and unfastens the top shirt buttons. He is gulping for air, fighting for breath, but feeling great. He pumps his fist, feeling like a winner.

Down, pride, he tells himself.

As Kaveh had predicted, Brighton *is* lucky and wins his next match. Haas also wins, and now Kaveh and Brighton are studying tapes to prepare.

"Beautiful backhand. Lethal," says Brighton. He loves examining a player's habits and mannerisms, trying to uncover their secrets, their strategy, their flaws.

"Not as pretty as yours. Your shots will smoke him!" The kid laughs and Brighton smiles as the apartment buzzer rings. The doorman. Brighton rises from the floor and answers. "Yes? Yes, fine, send him up!"

The excitement from tonight's win begins to diminish. Brighton replaces the phone, staring at the view from this immaculate glass box. Cruise ships and barges are moving up and down the Hudson River.

"It's my father." Brighton has feared this possibility ever since he spotted Nico sitting courtside two nights earlier.

Kaveh stands. "I should go. Tomorrow at eleven?"

"Yes, but don't go. He'll leave sooner if you're here. Keep watching the tape. I'll take him to the kitchen."

His father is grinning when he opens the door. "Hey, Buddy, good to see you. What is this place?"

He waves his father in, offering neither a handshake nor an embrace. He points to a set of barstools in the high-tech kitchen. He watches as his father examines the impressive view. "Why are you living here? I would have welcomed your company."

Brighton pours them each a club soda. He has no time for this.

"I wanted to minimize distractions. This place is perfect—chilly as an old girlfriend."

"Okay. I get it. I wish you had called, that's all."

"I'm sorry, you're right. I didn't tell anyone, not even Ezzie."

His father stares at him. Brighton cannot read the expression, but for the first time he realizes they are strangers. He was a teenager when he flew off to college and has never returned. A few phone calls, a Christmas present, and some e-mails. That is the extent of their relationship.

Wynn looks at the match playing on the living room TV.

"That's my practice partner, Kaveh," Brighton explains. "We're studying tapes of my opponents."

"Okay, got it. I won't be long. I know you saw Nico, after your game."

"Yes, he was full of good cheer; high-fiving me and explaining his new endeavors. Sports management, protein shakes, weight loss."

"And Allison? Did you meet her? She's the liaison with his athletes."

Brighton now understands the reason for his dad's visit.

"Yes, we met. I remember her. Baéz and I drove to Storrs several times to see her play at UConn. She was the number one basketball player in the country until she was named in that point-shaving scandal. But it makes perfect sense for her and Niko to team up. A pair of grifters, fleecing the crowd!"

"Charges dismissed! Never proved!" snaps his father as Kaveh swiftly turns his head, missing nothing.

"Good to know. Still, she might find it hard to get licensed as a manager."

Brighton watches as Wynn composes himself, forcing a smile. "I'm not worried about that girl. She's smart and savvy; you'd be lucky to have her on your team."

"Wynn, in case you've forgotten, my major at Pepperdine is sports management. This is what I know. This is not your field. And it's not Nico's field either."

"He's been a good friend, to you and to me. And he wants you as a client. He's willing to spend heavily to add you to his roster."

"And do some of those funds find their way to you?"

As he watches his father pretend not to hear the question, he wonders if Wynn knows that Nico used to steal from them.

"I have a lawyer, a solid fellow; he'll negotiate my deals," explains Brighton.

"Yes, a good lawyer is valuable. He can protect you. Fine. But you need someone looking out for your interests full time. Let the lawyer take care of the big picture, but let Allison and Nico do the grunt work. Please. If it doesn't go well, your lawyer can build in protections that allow you an out. Think about this. I *need* this!"

Brighton is startled by his father's desperate tone. Wynn had always taught him to never let your opponent see you bleed. He wonders what Kaveh thinks of their loud voices.

"Are you betting for me, or against me?" Brighton asks.

His father's face hardens. "That's a terrible thing to say! I'm your biggest fan, always have been."

It *was* a terrible thing to say, but Brighton is dead tired and needs to end this. He has to maneuver his father out the door. "I now must focus on playing and leave business aside. But if it pleases you, I will listen to their pitch and I will take it seriously."

His father does not smile, but his relief is plain. Brighton calls out to the living room. "Kaveh, let's pick up tomorrow. My dad's going, why don't you leave with him."

Kaveh grabs his backpack and shakes Wynn's hand. "Nice to meet you, sir."

"Yes, well, take care of this boy. He's a treasure!"

"Yes, sir."

Brighton opens the apartment door and pushes the "down" button. Kaveh calls out to him. "Eleven a.m.? Exercise room?"

Brighton nods.

✶ ✶ ✶

On the elevator, Kaveh sizes up Elwynn Bethune. Kaveh has a practiced eye for recognizing fellow scoundrels, and Brighton's dad reeks of deceit. Kaveh had not chosen Brighton randomly but had studied him, his game and his bearing, understanding that Brighton would one day be worth a great deal of money. Kaveh wanted to be nearby when that happened. He wanted to insinuate himself into Brighton's team and gain Brighton's trust. He was pleased to see the hunger in the father's eyes.

"So, Bright will meet with your guy, but he made no promises, simply a meeting. How much is it worth to you if I get him to sign with your guy?"

Elwynn looks up, caught off guard.

Kaveh explains. "He trusts me, and it's clear he does *not* trust you." He watches the father's face and decides to push harder. "He will listen to me. He honors my advice. So, how much?"

When Elwynn grins, Kaveh knows his instincts have been correct.

"Twenty-five hundred," says Elwynn Bethune.

"Don't waste my time. Your son's looks and skill will generate millions of dollars. You may as well share in it. Give me an offer that shows you're serious and not just a bumbler."

Wynn's eyes widen as Kaveh meets his icy stare.

"Okay, ten thousand now, and ten thousand in three months," responds Elwynn angrily.

Kaveh reaches out and shake Wynn's hand. They have a deal. The elevator doors open, and they part.

✳ ✳ ✳

The next day, Brighton meets with Nico's partner. Much to his surprise, Allison Green is impressive. She is knowledgeable. He likes her.

"I want you to play all the European contests this fall, get some wins, get your ranking up, get invited into tournaments instead of having to qualify. By Christmas, maybe you're in the top hundred; if you perform well, top sixty. We should hold off committing to endorsement deals—they'll pay much more in a few months."

She also reveals that she wants him to be the face and voice of Nico's line of men's health and grooming aides.

"I'm nervous about becoming too connected with Nico's universe," he admits. "I assume you are aware of the rumors that follow him. The gambling, the whispers about monies paid to an English football club. I need you to keep me away from all that."

"Dušan runs the betting sites. Nothing to do with us. We'll be fine."

Brighton's lawyer and schoolmate, Tolliver Brigham, advises against the deal but also understands the pressure of family obligations. He pushes for a hefty signing bonus and warns Brighton to keep a close eye on these bounders.

✳ ✳ ✳

As the players are announced, their names generate massive cheers. Brighton tries not to be overwhelmed. Andre Agassi is a New York institution and has already won five Grand Slam tournaments.

Brighton surveys the enormous crowd, row upon row of happy spectators, and then he sees her, walking down the steep aisle that leads to his player's box. Beautiful as ever, stylishly attired in a lavender-print dress, Scottie wears a large-brimmed hat that guarantees all eyes will be fixed on her. Brighton feels his nerves slip away. He waves as

Baéz turns to meet his girl. She extends her hand. He knows Baéz will blush and find her smile infectious.

She sits as the umpire calls for the match to begin.

Brighton wins the coin toss and elects to serve first. He is standing in the largest tennis stadium in the world, competing in the quarterfinal match for the US Open. He knows his body is too tired to win but he is thrilled to be here. All 23,737 seats are filled, and a huge overflow crowd is watching on the giant video screen outside the stadium. The atmosphere is electric.

Kaveh is seated on a small patch of lawn, eating the meal he packs each day—cold kebabs and saffron rice. He stares at the video screen; Brighton's liquid serve is a joy to behold and the first one flies past Agassi—an ace.

"Kaveh? Kaveh Havari?"

A tall, striking man with an enigmatic expression stands above him. He has an exotic accent and wears a tightly tailored blue suit that matches the arctic blue of his eyes.

"Hello, Mr. Ugly, how are you? Have a seat!"

His greeting takes the man by surprise. Kaveh smiles, thrilled by the danger he senses in those eyes.

"Sit, sit. How can I help you?"

"My name is Dušan," the man says. "I am part of Brighton's management team."

"Yes, of course you are!"

"Can I have a quick word?"

"You can have anything you want!"

Dušan again hesitates, a confused look on his face. He sits, careful in his linen suit. "You will be traveling with him, yes?"

"I will," answers Kaveh proudly.

"I would like you to consider a special arrangement for additional monies, sums his manager and I would deposit directly in your parents' accounts in Mosul. Mr. Bethune's father informed us of the valuable assistance you have already provided. We thought you might be keen for additional opportunities to serve. For information, private information, nothing more. The arrangement is between us, not to bother the ears of Mr. Bethune."

How does this man know Kaveh's parents live in Mosul?

"Please, join me for a drink," suggests Dušan.

"Now? The match is on!"

Dušan's eyes narrow. "I was told you were a clever boy, eager to make a buck. Was I mistaken?"

Kaveh follows Dušan to a distant bar that serves beer and lobster rolls. He is shamed by his own weakness; shamed to be so easily seduced by the evil that glistens behind this handsome man's eyes.

✷ ✷ ✷

As Brighton suspected, his luck finally runs out, but he is all smiles as he shakes Andre Agassi's hand.

In the following weeks, Brighton creates headlines wherever he goes. He and Scottie are photographed at the splashy new Cité Restaurant, and *New York Magazine* catches them touring the recently reopened Museum of Modern Art.

"What's our budget?" she asks.

Brighton flashes his new platinum card as they sit in the back of the town car he's booked for the day. "There's no limit."

"Fine. Let's start at Bergdorf for Men." She leans forward and speaks to the driver. "Fifth and 58th please. And can you find some decent tunes on that radio?"

She loves spending money and is clearly pleased to be here. She calls ahead and arranges for a personal shopper to greet them.

Brighton tries on suits, pants, sweaters, scarves, and ties. He dons dinner jackets, dress shirts, shorts, vests, and trendy caps. He buys Armani, Zegna, Lanvin, Yamamoto, and Chanel. Tailors measure him, pinch him, and stick him with pins as they serve Scottie champagne and croissants in one of the private rooms set aside for special clients.

Forty-seven thousand dollars later, they head downtown for a late lunch.

"Your brother is adorable. Your whole gang is devoted to you. I hope you know how lucky you are."

"I do. Thanks. You were sweet with them. Baéz loves so easily. He trusts everyone. I worry about him."

"Don't—he's fine. He understands the world and still loves it. That's rare. If I were you, I would look out for Nico and his gang. A bunch of handsome thugs. Especially the kid, the Persian boy. That beauty is masking a true opportunist!"

Brighton laughs and pays the bill and then they climb back into the limo.

"You need to be smart," she says. "You will become an American brand, like Tiffany's."

"Or Hershey's Kisses?" He snuggles up to her, surrounded by their purchases. She laughs and pushes him away.

"Do you know what I am saying? Don't leave your hotel in Vienna dressed in sweats and flip-flops. Don't spend a night on the town in cargo shorts and sneakers. Be a new vision for American athleticism and carry your brand with swagger. It will immediately separate you from every other athlete in the country. People will notice. Got it?'

"Got it, ma'am. Can we go home now and take off all these clothes?"

She laughs and kisses his smiling face.

✶ ✶ ✶

A massive rainstorm has stalled over the East Coast, delaying his flight to Stockholm. Brighton and his guests wait in the elegant first-class lounge of the TWA terminal.

He is sitting with Allison, reviewing last-minute details of the fall tour across seven European capitals. By making the semi-finals, he is now eligible to enter several of the tour's most prestigious tournaments. Alison is guiding and advising the next steps in his career, and he is comfortable trusting her.

He sees Scottie chatting with his lawyer, Tolliver Brigham, as Nathan hovers nearby, recording images with his ever-present camera. Even Dušan has made the trek to the airport, representing the absent Nico, who knows to stay away.

"It doesn't rain in Southern California," explains Tolliver as he looks at the thunderclouds that hover over the runways. "We have no experience with rain," he tells Jared as they both laugh.

"The boy will be fine. Rain can't dampen his spirits!"

Tolliver, nicknamed 'Ollie' by all who know him, nods in agreement. "Yes, you're right; he will always be fine!"

"Baéz didn't make it?" Scottie asks. "I was looking forward to seeing him again."

"He's not good with goodbyes," explains Jared. "A family trait. We tend to get all weepy!"

Brighton overhears this and nods. He turns back to Allison. "You've done a great job. Thank you."

The PA system crackles to life, announcing the start of boarding. As his friends stand, Brighton looks for Kaveh. He shakes Jared's hand and gives Nathan a quick hug. Scottie is last, and he holds her close. He had been seventeen when they met, and the adventure of discovering love has been a thrill for him. Love will never again be so tender or so true.

"Don't forget, the boy's still mad about you!" He kisses her, and she smiles. They had said everything the night before, but she knows their relationship has entered a new phase; the luster of youth is short-lived, and tennis will now fill his every thought, not her.

He watches as she passes Dušan, who is deep in conversation with Kaveh. "Handsome thugs," she had called them, a very prescient observation, yet Brighton could not be dissuaded from his trust in them.

✳ ✳ ✳

"**N**o one needs to know," explains Dušan near the boarding gate as he hands Kaveh an international cell phone with a built-in antenna.

The kid looks at him, his face a mask, but Dušan knows this boy will pay off handsomely. He will be their fox in the henhouse.

"Let me know if someone is sick, if someone is under the weather, if someone is going through a mental distraction that might adversely affect his game—a divorce, a lawsuit, financial trouble."

"And this will improve your betting?"

Dušan doesn't answer. "In the locker room, look around, listen, notice things. Don't fail me. Don't fail your parents. Tell no one!"

These last words are whispered into Kaveh's ear as Dušan slips a thick envelope of cash into the kid's pocket.

12.

"SELF-PORTRAIT WITH STRIPED SHIRT"

Images of Brighton are everywhere. His face stares out from tall buildings, from the sides of buses, and from scores of magazines. His copper hair, his deep-green eyes, and his tightly muscled stomach are on full display in the new Calvin Klein underwear campaign. As Baéz travels from Grand Central to the TV studio, he sees his brother's nearly naked body at every turn.

A young woman greets him in the lobby where posters for *Maury* and *Sally* cover the walls. Sally is number three, after Jerry Springer and Oprah. She's the one with the large red glasses. Nonnie doesn't care for her, and Jared tried to talk him out of appearing. The producers of *The Divine Road*, however, begged him to accept Sally's invitation. The series premiered the previous week with the story of Clarice's stroke. She was then invited on the TODAY show where she attributed her recovery to God and to "that lovely man, Baéz." The attention the show is generating far outweighs its modest audience.

Baéz hopes he doesn't embarrass himself. As he sips his coffee, he hears loud applause welcome Sally's first guest—a long-distance trucker with a nice smile and a friendly face. He has two families, each living on opposite ends of his trucking route. The mothers of his several children are seated nearby and flipping through piles of magazines, wiping scent strips on their wrists and giggling. Now they stand and join "their man" on stage.

He knows Sally Jessy won't be as generous as Katie Couric. She will try to discredit him and make him look like the other nutjobs who make up her stable of guests. He closes his eyes and shuts out these worries. She is simply a woman making a living. He will not judge her. She is a beloved daughter of our Father/Mother God. That is what he sees as he sits opposite her.

The audience screams, clapping and sighing. On the screen behind him is a huge blowup of Brighton's underwear ad.

Sally smiles. "This is your brother, am I correct?"

"Half-brother, actually. We have the same mother, different fathers."

"Being a man of the cloth, what do you think of the blatant sensuality of this ad? Is this a good example for a popular athlete to be setting for our children?"

"I'm a divinity student, not a 'man of the cloth.'"

"Okay, fine," she snaps. "But do you approve of what your brother is doing here?"

"Half-brother. And yes, of course. Listen to your audience. They applauded. Should he be criticized simply because he is beautiful?"

The audience cheers, answering Baéz's question.

"You don't find it odd, calling your brother beautiful?"

"Half-brother," he says for the third time as the audience laughs. She ignores them and continues grilling Baéz.

"You're a bright guy, college educated. Wake Forest, am I right?"

"Yes."

"Studying for a degree in comparative religions?"

"Correct."

"Whatever possessed you to appear on The Faith Channel and compete to become the next Elmer Gantry?"

Baéz sighs, irritated by the question even as he remembers to smile. "Elmer Gantry, Father Coughlin, Tammy Faye Bakker. Some evangelists, real and imagined, have provided a great deal of fodder for those wishing to tar all preachers as crackpots. But every profession has its villains, even a few talk-show hosts have been reviled of late, no?"

The audience "oohs," wondering how Sally will respond.

"Oh, come on! Dueling sermons, faith healing, the show's a snake pit. It demeans true religion. Why did you agree to be part of it?"

He takes a deep breath and calms himself before answering. "My grandmother, a wonderful woman who has spent her life studying the Bible, says a lie is nothing more than the absence of truth, the same way that darkness is nothing more than the absence of light. They have no reality of their own; they are defined merely as the absence of something else. I assure you that these programs are truthful, the contestants unblemished."

"You are telling us that you actually healed that woman of a stroke?"

Her voice reveals not only disbelief but contempt. He stares at the red frames, reminding himself that the forces who wish to silence truth have no power.

"God does the healing. I am simply a messenger, helping Clarice see what is real. Life is what is real; the stroke was not. Like the darkness and the light, the stroke was simply the seeming absence of health. I declared the presence and reality of her health. Don't make it more complicated than it is. Don't mock something simply because it falls outside your experience."

"Tell us about Clarice," Sally says, changing tack. Baéz senses her displeasure; she is losing the sympathy of her audience. Her hand goes to her chest, to the tiny microphone attached to the placket of her blouse. Baéz understands she is feeling pain, and the discord of their interview stems from that. He says a brief prayer asking for them both to be lifted out of the suspicions and doubts surrounding this interview. Then he smiles at her, and she looks surprised, relieved, as if her affliction had melted into nothingness.

✶✶✶

The thrill of touring never lessens for Kaveh. The four-star treatment, the cars and drivers, and the restaurants that always have a ready table, are luxuries he treasures. He feeds Dušan more and more information, week after week, and never views his gossip as a betrayal of the friends he is making on tour.

As they arrive in each new city, whether it's in Europe, South America, or Asia, Kaveh accompanies Brighton through crowds of cheering girls. This is their second swing through Europe, and Brighton is teaching Kaveh Italian. In exchange, Kaveh gives lessons in Arabic. Like exotic animals loosed from the zoo, people stare at them wherever they go.

"He looks like you, no?" asks Kaveh with a pleasant smirk.

They are in Vienna's Leopold Museum, studying a series of self-portraits by Egon Schiele

"He looks crazed and troubled. Is that how I appear?"

"No. He is handsome; peaceful; at rest. He is not crazy, as you say. Your eyes have fatigue, yes?"

"My legs have fatigue. My eyes are fine, and you are blind."

"Ah, you Americans. You move too hard. Stop, and look at it. You will see; he is handsome."

Brighton is dressed in shades of green, the perfect complement to his rusty-red hair. He has followed Scottie's instructions to the letter. Kaveh, however, wears only one outfit. A white Henley matched with white jogging pants. Bare arms and bare legs are frowned upon in Iraq.

"We should go practice," Kaveh suggests. "With a win tonight, you will move into the Top Ten!"

"Don't jinx it! You go on ahead. I'm going to wander a bit."

He returns to the gallery where the Schiele self-portraits are hung. He stares at one that caught his eye; a thin-faced man with curly, untamed hair, midnight blue, nearly black. The spitting image of Baéz. They once dreamed of visiting Europe together.

He misses him; his misses their rambling conversations and the explosion of words that poured from their mouths, delighting them both.

✶✶✶

Baéz sits on a wooden fence, staring at the young man named Crosby, who is leading a chestnut Appaloosa out of the barn. Alonzo Dewey, affectionately called "Lonnie" by Baéz, is standing inside the riding ring and focusing the lens of his small video camera on the horse's flaxen mane, which perfectly matches Crosby's hair.

"Beautiful, isn't she?" asks Crosby. "She was our first save, three years ago. Now we have twenty. Elderly carriage horses rescued from the glue pots. We've got a full-time vet, and the high school set up a program for special-needs kids to come and work with the horses. 'Animal-assisted therapy,' they call it. Our desire to help old horses has become a blessing for these youngsters. I feel a real pleasure in it. Something almost holy, you know?"

A perfect ending. Baéz will turn the footage into a fifteen-minute inspirational tale for the "Good News" section on his HonorBright website.

He had won the hundred-thousand-dollar prize on *The Divine Road* but declined the offer to minister a church in Texas. Instead, he used his winnings to upgrade his website and began accepting limited advertising in the form of sponsorships. With Lonnie's technical know-how, he bought a color camera and a digital editing system. Lonnie also chose not to return to Wake Forest for his final year, anxious to dive into the real world, the working world. Like scores of other young men, he wants to direct films. Shooting and editing these "feel-good" pieces allows him to experiment with his storytelling skills.

Crosby walks into the golden light from the setting sun as the men pack up their gear. The boy clicks his tongue, and the horse follows, nuzzling the back of his head.

Lonnie looks over at Baéz. "You don't suppose we're a bit ridiculous, thinking this stuff actually helps people?"

Baéz shakes his head. "I don't know, but I hope not." Lonnie's question is one he constantly asks himself. How can you measure your impact on another human being? He lifts the heavy equipment bag. "Let's get back. I need your help installing Nonnie's new contraption."

The drive home takes less than an hour, but the lengthy instructions for hooking up the TiVo take all evening.

"Okay, try it now. Click the green button. Yes?"

"I see it. I see it. I'm not blind, you know."

Nonnie has spent five hundred dollars on this elaborate invention so she will never again have to watch commercials. The remote control has more than twenty buttons, and Baéz is patiently explaining them to her.

"Okay, now I've programmed your favorite shows, and of course Tom Brokaw."

Tom Brokaw is Nonnie's chosen guy for the news. She watches him every night, but now the half-hour is littered with commercials for medications to cure every ailment known to man. Some feature Brighton. Every night she sees his face, smiling at a gorgeous girl before they kiss, and then he emerges from a tiled shower, steam surrounding his tanned torso as he shakes out his wet hair, looks into the lens and says, "Assure your performance—get HARDBODY!"

She is furious with him.

"Now we can watch the news whenever we like, Nonnie, and when a commercial comes on, simply hit the 'skip' button. Easy-peasy!"

Baéz enjoys living at home. He sees Nonnie every day and finds great satisfaction nurturing his online parishioners. He assumes his life will be lived alone; no one he meets interests him, not romantically. Instead, he pours his considerable energies into major construction projects. First, he, Jared, and the lawn crew winterized the boathouse, installing a kitchen and bath, and created a sleeping area in the cantilevered balcony that overlooks the lake. Now, he is drawing up plans to transform his great grandfather's airplane hangar into a sanctuary where he can preach. He has already named it. "The Lakeside Meeting House."

Later that night, he climbs the stairs to show Nonnie the new sketches. She is seated in her favorite chair, reading *Sports Illustrated.* Brighton is on the cover. In the past year, he has graced the covers of *GQ, Men's Health, Vanity Fair,* and *PARADE*, while a polarizing article in *Rolling Stone* focused attention on Baéz and his Bible-based health-and-wellness website.

Brighton's influence on American men is evidenced everywhere. When he wore clam-digger shorts at his second US Open, The Gap made a killing. When he revealed in the *GQ* article that the Abercrombie scent *Orchard* was his favorite cologne, they sold out. Newsboy caps nearly outsell baseball hats.

The phone rings and Nonnie puts down the magazine. Baéz is seated nearby.

"What a lovely surprise! Hello!"

Baéz looks up. The pleasure he hears in his grandmother's voice can only be caused by one caller—his brother.

"No, never fear. Remember, you have dominion. Your harmony cannot be invaded by any lack of ease, by tainted food, or by a loss of sleep. So, go out there and demonstrate your dominion."

She listens, nods several times, and then says, "Yes!" as she continues to console and comfort. "You will be fine. You don't have to win but do him the honor of showing up. Yes. Yes. I love you too!"

✱ ✱ ✱

Brighton has been sick and fears he will have to default on today's semi-final match with Juan Carlos Ferraro, but Nonnie's voice has calmed him.

Kaveh hears the last part of their conversation as he enters Brighton's hotel room. He sees his cell phone in Brighton's hands.

Kaveh walks over to Brighton's bedside to retrieve his phone. "Do you need this any longer?"

"Oh, sorry. You said it made international calls."

"No, it's fine. I forgot I told you about it."

"It keeps dinging. All morning. Not like a phone call, something else. And there were messages on the screen. Lots of them. I'll show you."

Brighton clicks the "on" switch. Kaveh tries to explain.

"They're texts. Cheaper than a phone call. They're new. You don't have them in America."

Brighton is reading the screen above the tiny keyboard. He pushes a button, and the screen changes, again and again. He looks up at Kaveh, surprised and confused.

"Who are you discussing my illness with? And why?"

"I am so sorry. It's my dad. That's why I have the phone. To speak with him. Sometimes he asks my advice about who will win. There is a tiny gambling operation out of Mosul. He plays." Kaveh begins crying. "They are so poor now; things get worse for them every day."

"Can't you help them? You're well paid."

"Yes, of course. But he's running a bicycle shop now. He used to work at the Embassy! He is crushed!"

Brighton scrolls through more messages.

"You give him updates on the players, who is sick and who is not?"

"Yes, occasionally. I don't know. This is the second, maybe the third time."

The young man is weeping, blowing his nose, mortified to have been caught betraying his friend and employer.

"Kaveh, sit here. Stop. Listen to me."

Kaveh does as instructed and looks directly at Brighton.

"This is illegal. You may think you are simply helping your dad, and no one will know, but what if your dad shares the information with friends of his, and then those friends spread it further and go online and tell more? If a certain match generates an uncommon amount of activity on these betting sites, the officials investigate. You work for me; I could be banned from the sport! Don't you see how serious this is?"

"I did not know. I will call my father and say to lose what I said. And never again. I promise."

"Okay. And you should get rid of this phone. The Tiber might be a good spot for it."

Kaveh raises his eyebrows in alarm.

"I am serious. Throw it away!"

✳ ✳ ✳

Strong spirits don't agree with him, but he sips the proffered drink out of politeness. The man who gifted it is not what he is looking for.

The large watch on the wrist of his suitor reads three in the morning. He nods to the fellow, places his beverage on the bar, and makes his way to the exit. One of the ball boys from today's match rushes in from the busy dance floor.

"That was a remarkable comeback today, didn't you think?"

"Yes," answers Kaveh. "A close one. Mr. Bethune woke with a churning stomach and then midway through the second set, he was back to normal. An unexpected win!"

Kaveh *had* been amazed. Brighton had never been the subject of Kaveh's bulletins, and now he feels like a traitor. He has to figure out how to extricate himself from the web the ever-handsome Dušan has woven around him.

"Want to dance?" asks the sweet ball boy.

"Thanks, I was about to leave. It's late. See you tomorrow?"

The kid nods.

As Kaveh walks down the slick street away from the disco, he hears footsteps behind him. Probably the guy in the white suit. The one who bought him the drink. He knows he smiles too easily, and it gives the wrong impression. He should deal with it now; he doesn't want a scene in the hotel lobby. Word could reach Brighton.

He turns and flashes a friendly smile, but it isn't the man in the white suit. Instead, he faces a muscled thug with a knit cap and a tattered scarf covering his face.

"We do not like misinformation. You will learn, pretty boy."

The first punch from the gloved hand breaks his front teeth. The second, his jaw. Then he sees the knife.

✳ ✳ ✳

Brighton sits with Kaveh as the doctors catalogue the injuries—three shattered ribs, a broken jaw, internal bleeding, and forty stitches to close the wounds carved in his face.

Nothing was stolen. Not Kaveh's money, or his watch, or his Iraqi passport. The sole purpose of the attack seems to have been destroying his beautiful face. Had he jilted a pursuer at the disco? This is the police's theory.

Brighton is trounced in the Final and withdraws from the following week's tournament in Gstaad. He stays in Rome with Kaveh until his young practice partner is able to fly home. They watch the Swiss matches on TV, talking about tennis, only tennis.

"Did you insult someone at the club?" Brighton asks.

"I don't know. Maybe."

"Was it because of my swift recovery from an expected loss?"

Kaveh looks up, but his face is blank. Brighton tries again.

"That new website, Betfair? I checked in with them. Anonymously. My match against Juan Carlos generated huge sums of money. Many losers that day."

Kaveh simply nods his head. "I will be safe in Baghdad. No one can find me there. And when I am gone, you too will be safe. I am sure. I never made it to The Tiber. Forgive me." He reaches into his pants pocket and withdraws the cell phone. "It is Dušan's. Perhaps you can return it for me?" His pointed look confirms Brighton's worst fears.

"Oh Jesus, Kaveh, I am so sorry."

He holds the shaken boy, careful of the heavily bandaged face. He is ashamed that his own team has lured this young man into their dirty tricks.

Scottie, of course, had been right.

✳ ✳ ✳

Brighton rejoins the Tour, playing the North American hard-court tournaments that lead to the US Open. His third try. "Three is a lucky number," Kaveh would have said.

Now he sits in a rented conference room at the Hampton Court Hotel, across from the LaGuardia terminal where he will catch his flight to Montreal. He sips a cup of lukewarm coffee as Allison and Nico enter the room

"My bright, talented boy." Nico grabs him in a tight bear hug while Allison pours herself a coke. "Tell us, what is so important we had to take a fifty-dollar cab ride to see you?"

Brighton takes an envelope from his leather satchel and places the contents on the table. Allison recoils from the police photos of Kaveh's mutilated face.

"Your buddy hired someone to take a razor to Kaveh's face. My practice partner was feeding information from the locker rooms to Dušan. Some of it turned out to be untrue."

"I have no knowledge of this. Do you, Allison?"

She looks up in surprise, then shakes her head.

"Do you have proof of this?" asks Nico in a strident voice.

"I know what Kaveh's little international cell phone was for. There are tons of messages between him and Dušan discussing the health and welfare of various players. Including me. I can prove this but cannot bear to put my friend through the humiliation. And your arrogant boy would probably find a way to reach out to Baghdad and have him killed."

Nico's face hardens. "I did not give him that phone. You will have to look closer to home to find the devil in this tale."

Brighton can hear Nonnie advising him to allow the universe to repay this debt. *Back away and remove yourself from this infected atmosphere.* He doesn't listen but instead reaches into his satchel and brings out another manila folder.

"Several agents were anxious to sign me, but my dad told me to trust you. You and your handsome thug. Well, you and I are done!"

"He is not a 'thug,' and I have no knowledge of his activities. Perhaps you should ask your paterfamilias about their business."

"Brighton," Allison says, "these accusations are terrible and scary, and I have no idea where the truth lies, but even a hint of this could destroy you. If someone in your employ was passing on information, you will be guilty by association. And if this trail leads anywhere near your father, your career is over. We should not be trying to pin blame here, although the attack on Kaveh is unforgivable. What we need to do is figure out how to minimize the spread of this information. Am I right, Nico?"

"Yes, there is much to protect, and everyone has a stake. Don't be so quick to cut old ties. As my Allison says, a well-placed whisper could destroy you, my Boy-O!" Nico's face twists into a lopsided grin. "Be careful!"

✳ ✳ ✳

Since the attack on his practice partner, Brighton Bethune's game has suffered. His young friend was brutally attacked as he left a gay club in Rome, and now Bethune's ranking has dropped from number seven to number eighteen, which will have serious repercussions in his draw for the Open. Tennis experts have been advising Bethune to simply return to basics, sharpen his serve, and improve the accuracy of his forehand. "Easier said than done" add many sports psychologists, who say such a traumatic event could have a lasting impact on Bethune's game.

Baéz reads the article in the weekend edition of *The New York Times*. Sports journalists are mystified by Brighton's lengthy run of poor play. He isn't following their script. They had predicted that this year's Open was his to lose.

A new team has been hired to prepare Brighton for the year's final Slam, but for moral support, he turns to the only expert he trusts—his original teacher, Nathanael Winning.

"What do you think is going on?" Baéz asks Nathan.

"I wish I knew. Often a talented player rises too fast, gets ahead of himself, and neither his mind nor his body are able to adjust, like a deep-sea diver getting the bends. But that's not Brighton."

"No, something has spooked him, like me with my underwater nightmares. Is it his friend Kaveh? Is he still in danger?"

"Don't know. That whole story sounds like something out of a bad horror film, "says Nathan. "Let all these pros push and pull him in whatever direction they think best, but you guys should play with no one watching and no one instructing. Remind him what he loves about the game."

Nonnie's house is transformed into an elegant spa with professional chefs creating healthy meals and sports therapists devising new strategies to strengthen Brighton's body. Each afternoon, Baéz plays a gentle game with Brighton, often in shorts with bare feet, hitting and laughing and finding their way back to an earlier simplicity—no pressure, no goals, nothing but easy hitting.

"Where do you suppose another decade will take us?" Baéz asks one day after a lively workout.

"Haven't a clue. Right back here, I suppose, would feel good. Always has." Brighton looks over at Baéz and smiles. "Any sightings of Rebecca lately?"

Baéz thinks before answering. "I imagine she's nursing folks in Yemen."

"Yes. Yemen. Of course."

They are lying in the orchard, their hands cradling their heads as the sun shines through the branches heavy with fruit. They each feel a strange satisfaction by imagining their mother alive.

"You know, there was this sweet boy at Browning," Brighton offers. "Popular with the girls, nice to everyone. I taught him to dance his senior year."

"You taught him to dance?" responds Baéz, raising his eyebrows in mock alarm.

"Yes, remember, it was a boys' school. There were no girls available."

Baéz laughs, wondering where this conversation is going.

"He embodied a humble perfection; he had an ease with knowing what was right. And when I get all full of myself . . ."

"Which is often. . ."

He laughs. "Yes, which is often. I picture him. I keep his image close. And I correct course."

"Did I ever meet him?"

"No. This was years ago. He was two grades ahead of me. So, the other day, I Googled him. And he's dead. He's been dead for three years. Some freak accident at Dartmouth. I never felt the loss. He's been clearly present with me."

"Then he's not dead. The body, sure. But the essence of him, his consciousness, moves forward, continuing to manifest life."

"That's weird."

"I guess. But I think it's true. We spend so much time fearing death. Defining it as some leave-taking, an ending, when in reality it is nothing more than turning a corner."

Brighton considers this abstract statement, and then asks, "Do you think turning that corner is simple?"

"Can be. Yes. But what are you asking? Is this about Kaveh? Did he nearly die?"

"No. That poor fellow succumbed to the nefarious plotting of Elwynn and Dušan. They wanted to let me know who's in control."

Baéz looks at him, surprised. "I am so sorry. Your father's an odd duck, but do you think him capable of violence?"

"I don't know what to think. I doubt it was his idea, and maybe Dušan acted on his own, but at their core they are gamblers, and gamblers don't know how to stop."

Baéz shivers as he realizes how little he knows of Brighton's current life or of the people who surround him.

✳ ✳ ✳

The crowds at Flushing Meadows Park grow larger every day and are rewarded with many thrilling matchups. In the quarterfinals, Sampras knocks out number two Andre Agassi in four tie-breaking sets while Andy Roddick dispatches the top-ranked player, Gustavo Keurten. In the semi-finals, Brighton needs five sets to beat Roddick while Sampras easily dispatches Brighton's nemesis, Marat Safin. The loud and loyal fans will get an all-American Final.

The smart money is on Bethune. Sampras has not won the Open in five years, and his most recent appearance was an ugly loss in a lackluster match.

Jimmy Royale is holding court in Brighton's box. He takes drink orders, delivers food, and makes sure that everyone has what they need. Jared is pacing while Nathan hides behind his camera. Nonnie's nerves are frayed. Scottie sits with Baéz, both quiet, blocking out the noise, blocking out the import of the moment. They are an odd comfort to each other, both loving a man who has left them behind.

A tall, handsome, well-dressed fellow is shaking hands with several of the Pepperdine players. Baéz turns to Jimmy, whispering, "Who's that?"

"That's Ollie! Haven't you met? He coached the doubles team our freshman year. From the law school, a few years ahead of us. I think Bright's a client." Jimmy calls out to his college friend. "Ollie, get over here, let me introduce Brighton's family."

Ollie wears a sharply creased French-cuffed shirt with a colorful silk tie. His mop of light, unruly hair is his only accommodation to his youth. He squeezes between the seats and introduces himself to Nonnie and Baéz.

"Hello. I'm Tolliver Brigham, friend and lawyer to Bright. I've always wanted to meet you."

He shakes Nonnie's hand and then gives a smile and a nod to Baéz. Baéz holds his gaze longer than is comfortable. Even Nonnie takes note of the sudden atmospheric change.

"How does he seem?" Nathan asks as Tolliver take a seat next to Jimmy.

"Odd, to tell the truth. On edge. His father was there, glad-handing and wishing everyone good luck. If I didn't know better, I'd say he wanted to rattle his son."

"Now, now," says Nonnie. "It's a big day for him too."

Baéz looks around, trying to absorb this moment. He is trembling. He feels eyes on him. When he turns, he is rewarded with a smile from the impressive lawyer.

The announcer's voice comes over the speaker. The players are introduced, and the crowd erupts, the cheers deafening.

Sampras is a big guy with dark, thinning hair that dominates his plain face and simple smile. He has won thirteen grand slam victories, including four US Opens, and he possesses one of the greatest serves in tennis. Two weeks earlier, he turned thirty, which some thought marked the downward slide of his career. He is consistently losing to younger players.

Scottie takes Baéz's hand and kisses it. She senses how nervous he is. "He would enjoy seeing us so unhinged!"

Baéz laughs and nods.

The players' warm-up is over, and both men return to their seats, sipping water from bottles and toweling their arms and faces. Sampras wins the toss and elects to serve first. The umpire signals to begin. As the crowd quiets, thunder can be heard in the distance.

Sampras sends the first ball over the net. An ace. And then another. And a third! Brighton returns the fourth into the net. Four serves, three aces. Fifty-seven seconds into the match, and Sampras has laid down the challenge. He still has plenty of fire.

Brighton tosses the ball for his serve, but the wind is strong, and he has to catch it. He tosses the ball again, not as high as usual, and hits it squarely into the net. Another weak ball-toss, but this one lands in the service court and Sampras smashes it back for a winner. Baéz hardly recognizes his brother's game. It is erratic and unsettled. Is it nerves?

Baéz feels several raindrops and looks up. The sky is churning with dark, threatening clouds.

The Pepperdine teammates call out a cheer, trying to inspire their friend, but Brighton doesn't respond. After only twenty-five minutes, Sampras is serving for the set with a score of five games to one. He smashes a ball over the net at 130 miles an hour and, as Brighton lunges for it, his legs give out. The crowd gasps, then lets out a communal groan.

Brighton hits the ground hard, his elbow and knee bloodied. As a final indignity, his stomach regurgitates his breakfast and lunch just as the funereal sky lets loose with heavy rain. The crowd runs for cover.

Jimmy Royale herds Brighton's guests to a protected section of the stadium. No one knows what to say or where to look.

Standing by his seat, Elwynn watches his son limp back to the locker room. Nico gives Wynn a quick stare. They know the rules: a bet cannot be withdrawn after the fourth point of the first game.

Standing in the heavy rain, Wynn sees one of the uniformed guards collect Brighton's water bottles and protein drinks and place them in a cloth satchel with NYC POLICE stenciled on the side. He stares at the sky, hoping it will soon clear. He needs his son to lose, and it has to be today.

✳ ✳ ✳

Brighton lies on a long, padded workout bench as the doctor cleans and bandages his wounds. He is breathing heavily, his mind fogged. When the doctor explains the body is rejecting a poison or a toxin, Baéz immediately asks the Tournament Director to come to the locker room. Brighton's food and liquids are gathered from the court, and no one is allowed to enter the premises. The Director and Baéz both agree to keep their suspicions private. They could be wrong.

Baéz pulls up a chair and holds his brother's hand, which is warm and vibrating from an increased flow of blood. He asks one of the many security men to find Nonnie.

Brighton's lips are moving as if engaged in a lengthy conversation. Baéz leans into his brother's ear and speaks softly, not wanting to be overheard.

"Nothing inharmonious can enter into being. Food cannot harm you, neither a lack of it nor an excess of it. God is right here, and the first thing we must do is forgive your father."

Brighton's eyes open wide. A tear escapes his bright green eyes.

"Don't think about it; it never happened. Whatever hatred or greed directed this action, it has no power over you. There is only Love. Right now, right here. Nothing can take away your strength, your skill, or your grace. Evil cannot harm you; evil has no power. Forgive him. Pardon him."

Brighton nods, acknowledging his brother's entreaty. He then smiles as he sees Nonnie enter the room. "Hello, my angel," he says. "I am so sorry about this."

Baéz finds a chair for Nonnie.

"Nonsense. There is no 'this,'" she says. "You will rise up; perfect as the day you were born, tanned as Tecumseh and equally strong. No one can hold you back, my son. Don't think that for a second. And remember, God is a present help in trouble. Now get up and give your grandmother a kiss!"

She smiles as Brighton sits up. A variety of fruits and sandwiches sit on a tray nearby, and he absentmindedly reaches for them and begins to eat. On the overhead monitor, they can see that the rainstorm had ended and a bevy of workers are drying the court with blowers. Mary Carillo and Dick Enberg assure viewers that a Final will indeed be held today.

When Sampras serves out the first set, the crowd is relieved to see Brighton able to move and play. They no longer need him to win but simply wish him the strength to finish.

As the sun breaks through the clouds, Brighton looks up at the sky and hears Baéz's voice, as clear as the golden light now washing the court. *There is only Love.* He looks over at his box, full of anxious faces all dear to him. The sole exception is Baéz. He isn't anxious; he is beaming. It was Baéz who made him the tennis player he is today. It was Baéz who made the outlandish suggestion that Brighton should play left-handed. And it was Baéz who patiently practiced with Brighton during the painstaking process of reversing his muscle memory.

There is only Love. He had misunderstood his brother's love, rejecting his affections as they both struggled to understand their bond. Brighton ran three thousand miles away from the brother who would do anything for him; from Scottie, too, truth be told, centering all his devotions on the game of tennis. Now he must demonstrate his love for the game and prove it is worthy of his sacrifices.

He sees them barefooted on Nonnie's clay court, their feet and ankles covered in red dust as joy fills their hearts. Joy. Love. He smiles and looks into the crowd, grateful for their presence. He throws the ball in the air and then strikes his sweet spot, smashing it over the net for an ace. The crowd cheers, and Brighton keeps smiling. He plays for Baéz, and for his uncles, and for Nonnie, and for that sweet boy he once taught to dance as the aces continue to mount.

By the third set, the cheering has given way to a stunned silence as the crowd watches Brighton demolish one of the sport's top-ranked players. In less than two hours, Brighton completes one of the most thrilling comebacks in tennis history.

He collapses at the baseline as the crowd roars its approval.

After he meets Sampras at the net, shaking hands, he bows to the four corners of the stadium, thanking the crowd for their faith in him. And then he raises a defiant fist, searching the stands until he sees his father.

What follows the match is a blur. The speeches on the court, the presentation of the trophy, the celebratory dinner, the touching tributes from his friends and family. Monday morning's newspapers and news programs are filled with Brighton's face, his wide smile displaying his contagious joy. He makes a surprise appearance on *The David Letterman Show* and the audience refuses to let him to leave.

His new ad for Calvin Klein is released to coincide with the Championship, and his pensive face is everywhere. In the sexy ad, Brighton's entire body is covered in red clay, his green eyes and white briefs standing in stark relief. His moment has arrived. The planets are in perfect alignment.

What could possibly stop him?

And then comes Tuesday morning. Never has a champion had so little time to bask in the thrill of victory. As the twin towers disintegrate, Brighton's world, like the worlds of so many others, collapses.

PART TWO

2002 – 2011

13.

THE RANGERS

"**S**ay it again, sir."

"*Eid Milad Majeed.*"

The skinny kid with the ever-present smile repeats the words.

"*Ma-JEED,*" corrects Brighton.

The kid tries again, his Southern accent fighting him.

"*Ma-Jeed!*"

"Better."

"And that means Merry Christmas?"

Brighton smiles. "Not precisely. A literal translation would be 'Glorious Holiday of Birth,' but the idea comes through; they will understand your intention.

"Thank you, sir."

Back in October, the United States Congress authorized a new war, this one in Iraq, as the fight in Afghanistan was thought to be won. Small teams from the Special Activities Division of the CIA and from the Army's Task Force 20 are covertly mapping Northern Iraq, identifying targets for the forthcoming invasion, locating water and electric plants, and verifying the coordinates of airfields and military bases. And, like today, meeting with influential chieftains and seeking their support.

"*Hal toughrak al-aradi al mounkhafida kilal moussem al-matar?*" Brighton asks.

"*Tartafih al anhar, lakenaha naderan ma toufid ann hudurihah.*"

Brighton Bethune is speaking with their Iraqi guide while trying to control his anxious palomino. His main rifleman interrupts. "Hearing the harsh sounds of their language pour so easily from your pasty face as you sit atop a magnificent Arabian horse may well be my most memorable keepsake from this fucked-up assignment!"

Brighton laughs. Raven Jameson is not yet twenty and shaves but once a week. He wears glasses with thick lenses, yet he has perfect scores on the shooting range and is now their designated marksman. He and Brighton attended Ranger school together—jumping from planes and helicopters, learning the art of up-close combat and the trick of killing with a simple twist of the neck. Both men survived the grueling training and are now prepared for the fight of their young lives.

There are ten in his crew, including re-con, special ops, sniper, and spotter. The other men wait in their armored Humvees several miles below the craggy ridge that Private Raven Jameson, Corporal Brighton Bethune and Sumar Ackah are slowly climbing on horseback. The tribesmen picked this elusive location knowing the unobstructed views provided safety.

Neither Brighton nor Raven are officially here. The Pentagon and the State Department deny the existence of military personal in the region. The men in these elite units travel under cover of darkness, with small wood fires for warmth and MREs for nutrition.

Their horses follow a broken path upwards as the cold wind whips their faces.

"Ranger school taught you well," remarks Private Jameson as Brighton maneuvers his horse across the uneven terrain. Raven Jameson trained racehorses in his native state of Kentucky. There isn't anything he doesn't know about the animal, and he admires a skillful rider.

Brighton tightens up on his reins and looks at the empty landscape. "Stone fruits are becoming rare," he tells Raven. "This land has been decimated by droughts."

"Excuse me, sir?" the kid asks, confused.

"For Christmas. For you. I looked for cherries. I asked everywhere. *Alkarz* is the name in Arabic. I spoke with shop owners, farmers, everyone."

Raven smiles. His mother made cherry pies every Christmas. Cherry pies with a herringbone crust. One lonely night when he had been missing home, he had shared this fact with Brighton.

Their guide brings his horse to a stop. All three men dismount. They can see the small village below, which sits beside a huge generating plant. A group of boys are playing kickball. The wide river winds south, carving the arid land in two. From the eastern side of their promontory, they see several riders approaching, covered in large blankets with rifles slung over their shoulders.

"Do you think we'll be killing these people in a few months?"

"Above my pay grade, Private Jameson," Brighton says.

"We were not attacked by Iraqis. How do they threaten us? Tell me that!"

None of his fellow soldiers has an acceptable answer.

✶ ✶ ✶

Three months after the Glorious Holiday of Birth, "shock and awe" arrives. Fire and rain fall from the skies. As the troops march towards Baghdad and fleets of bombers deliver their devastating payloads, Brighton's small cadre of specialists carry out guerilla missions, searching for Saddam's leaders and convincing them to surrender or be killed. His task force is always on the move. His unit is nimble, a deft killing machine. He keeps them safe and sane. They trust him. Many of them enlisted because of him.

Prior to shipping out, Brighton posed for the Army's new recruitment campaign. Standing rigidly at attention with his right hand holding a firm salute, he wore a tight T-shirt tucked into tailored cargo pants as his serious green eyes stared directly into the lens. His close-cropped hair and his stern demeanor stirred many young men and women to enlist. "An Army of One" was boldly printed at the bottom.

It was the last impression many Americans would have of Brighton Bethune for a very long time. News of him shipping out to Iraq was embargoed. He is a high-profile target, and the Army needs to protect their valuable poster boy.

His unit never remains in one place for more than a few days. Tonight's campsite is a dense thicket of riverbank scrub. Salex and poplars are shedding their foliage as another season slips by. Some of his men have reached the end of their first deployment.

Raven is on watch, and Brighton lies nearby, under their 7500-pound Humvee. His men remain in the cab, some lying down, some seated, but he prefers to be outside in the cold night air; it keeps him sharp.

Brighton's skills as an interrogator who is fluent in Arabic are being utilized to grill the former leaders of Saddam's government. Kaveh Havari had taught him the basics—the alphabet, pronunciation, simple conversation—but the Army made him completely conversant. He also speaks a bit of Persian and Turkish.

"That was a close call today. You alright?" asks Brighton.

"Yes, sir. I keep seeing him, though. In my mind. Do you truly believe he was a major in Saddam's army?"

They had found one of their targets at an outdoor market. The man spotted them and began to run, but Raven squeezed the trigger on his high-speed rifle and the man's head exploded.

"What do you mean?"

"He looked like a farmer to me, sir. Hardly a threat."

"It is not our job to determine who is and who isn't a threat. We go where they send us, soldier. We kill at their command."

"But, sir, can you imagine the reverse? You're waiting in line at a farm stand, surrounded by all that is familiar—your neighbors and friends—and suddenly, from the woods, a forest you have known since boyhood, comes a bullet that ends your life."

"He was a bad guy, Raven. He did bad things. Tomorrow we will be back at Camp Packhorse. We'll eat some real food and finally get some rest."

Brighton tries to gauge the level of Raven's distress. The night is dark, and he can only sense the boy's presence. The troubled young man stands.

"See you in the morning, sir."

"If you want to talk, soldier, I'm here."

"Sir, unless you can give me a steaming cup of coffee and a blowjob, you're of no use to me."

Brighton chuckles and then closes his eyes, but sleep does not come. He sees the major's head exploding.

✳ ✳ ✳

The weather is turning. The cold rests in their bones. Gus Tanner is driving this morning, and Brighton senses tension in his crew.

"What's on your mind, Tanner?"

"It's that jokester, Ahmed Chalabi. He got my goat today."

"What he do?"

"Well, isn't he meant to be the next president?"

"That's what they say, but I wouldn't put money on it."

"In *Stars and Stripes*, he says this war is gonna take at least two more years! Two years! What nonsense!"

"I told you to ignore that paper."

"Yes, sir. Where we headed?"

"You and the guys are going to Tikrit. More interrogations. Raven and I are taking a side trip to the Ninevah Plains. Some unpleasant business. We're driving under cover of a Red Cross jeep, no protection; the trip is 'off-record.'"

"Delivering condolence payments, sir?"

The most hated chore in the Army. Reimbursing the families of citizens killed in error. Brighton often wonders how such a sophisticated army makes so many lethal mistakes.

✳ ✳ ✳

That evening, after rejoining their crew, Brighton tries to catch up on his sleep as Raven crushes his cigarette in the dirt.

"They wanted to kill us, didn't they, sir? That's why they screamed at you, right?"

The townspeople did not take kindly to the blood money Brighton delivered. An angry citizen thrust a dead child in his face.

"Let's forget today, soldier. Tell me about Kentucky. Tell me about your horse farm!"

Brighton sounds tired, but the blood is still rushing through his veins, preventing sleep. The image of the dead child is hard to erase.

"Well, sir, spring's coming on fast, and the horses are skittish, requiring extra care."

Brighton looks forward to these stories. He feels like he's in the middle of an epic novel, and each evening another chapter is read aloud by an engaging actor. He fears the end, though, which he thinks is swiftly approaching. Brighton's afraid to learn the true reason for his sniper's enlistment.

"A prince arrived from Saudi Arabia. A fortune from oil, and now he's investing in racehorses. Two of his finest were boarding with us, preparing for the Derby. I wasn't allowed to ride them, but I took them out of their stalls each day and exercised them. One night, as I was combing the big one, this prince came into the stall, pushed me against the wall, stuck his hand down the front of my pants, and kissed me on the mouth. I punched him in the jaw and kicked him as he fell. Several times. Many broken ribs.

It didn't matter what I said; his story was the one they had to believe. He was investing in the farm. They needed his money. I had to go. And you know the rest. Here I am."

"Yes, here you are."

★ ★ ★

"*Fakat, ukhbereny ma ra-ayit*" instructs Brighton.

The man sits in his soiled uniform, frightened and unwilling to talk.

"*Aaielatak satakun be-aman. Ouw-edaka bizalika.*" Brighton tries to reassure the man. The soldier looks at Brighton's face. He clearly wants to believe. He wants the interrogation to end.

"*Lan ya-alam ahaad. Satakun ameenan. Roubama bahd al maal lee tabdaa hayat jadidah.*"

Brighton dangles an offer of funds for a new life as he hands the man a cup of boiled coffee. The man places the cup against his cheek, warming himself, and then takes a sip, nodding his thanks. He reveals the whereabouts of a maid who is married to one of Saddam's drivers.

Most interrogations involve an inquisitor and a translator. Two faces, two different tones of voice, two different methods seeking information. But Brighton is a package deal. There is no confusion. Just one voice. One face.

"*Kuntum damon takmahou, khademan?*" He asks when they bring her in.

She is pretty, with striking eyes, showing no fear. "*Mo 'abden!*" she corrects him. She is his maid, not his servant.

Brighton had chosen the wrong word. She is staring into his green eyes. He remembers Kaveh advising him to use his beauty as a tool, and he smiles in remembrance. The woman begins answering his questions and tells him about a family compound nearby.

They are getting close. Day after day, Brighton speaks to family members and former employees, seeking small bits of intelligence that will lead to a precise location.

"*Kam yubeid almanzil ean almadina?*"

This teenager is nervous. He is afraid for his sister.

"*La astateeh an akuul. Sa yu-zunahah.*" Brighton promises to protect her. He speaks slowly, never rushing, always assuring, sometimes touching him on the shoulder, on the arm, on the hands. The boy finally provides exacting directions to this new compound.

Now they are going in. Six hundred men, twenty-five Abrams tanks, air power. Tomorrow night.

"I want you with us. I want you to be there. To speak with him. We need him alive."

Raven and the other men from his unit are part of the outer perimeter, charged with preventing escape, while Brighton travels with a cadre of small-arms specialists, guns at the ready, slowly walking to their destination and meeting no resistance.

The first house is empty. A radio crackles in the silence of the dark night as the Lieutenant grimaces and turns it off. Brighton follows, his heart swiftly beating, his body on full alert. Using simple hand signals, the men spread out, moving toward their second target: a one-story mud house. Brighton puts his hand on the wall. The chimney is cold. No one home. The disappointment on the men's faces is plain.

In the distance, Brighton sees an apple orchard, its rotted fruit still hanging from bare limbs. A car parked in the middle of a palm grove stands out due to its distinctive colors of orange and white. In nearby Tikrit, these are the colors of a local taxi service. Brighton wonders why a taxi is parked here. There are no roads.

Brighton walks to the car and feels the hood. Still warm. He signals the lieutenant, who sends several men to assist him. A wooden hut stands by the orchard. A worker's shack. Brighton opens the door. Clothes are hanging from a loose line of yarn. Threadbare rugs cover the white plaster walls. There is a single bed and a chest piled with books. Another room serves as a kitchen. Unwashed plates and plastic bottles are everywhere.

Outside, safely surrounded by more and more men, Brighton searches the ground with his flashlight and finds a large chunk of Styrofoam, serving no obvious purpose. Brighton kicks it, revealing a square hole outlined in neatly cemented bricks. A tunnel. He shines his light as men line up behind him. It is a tight fit, and he must put down his rifle. The lieutenant hands him a pistol. Brighton kneels, preparing to enter the hole, when suddenly a man's head appears.

Brighton yells, "*An-ba-the*! GET DOWN!"

The dirty, heavily bearded man looks at Brighton and then says in English: "I am Saddam Hussein, President of Iraq. I am ready to negotiate."

Brighton repeats the words his commander had given him. "President Bush sends his regards."

Someone snaps a picture and Brighton turns swiftly away. The lieutenant knows to get Brighton clear of the area. Several men rush him to the outer cordons where he is reunited with his crew.

The photo is a problem. Brighton hopes he turned fast enough.

He must not be identified.

"**W**hat is it, soldier?"

Another night sleeping under their battered vehicles. The ground is hard, and the air is cold.

"Well, sir, we've been trying to remember the nickname for three aces," Raven says. "Two aces is pocket rockets, sometimes Alan Alda, but now, with Hussein, we've got three aces. What's that called? Do you know?"

His father would know. Elwynn rarely comes to mind, but he does thinks about Nonnie's father and her brothers, and the war that killed them. They were the inspiration for his signing up. All those stories on long summer nights. Now he will become a part of those stories. He prays to be allowed to share his tale in person. If not, perhaps Raven will explain it all.

"It's a good hand, soldier. Be proud of it. No matter what it's called. We've done what they asked." He takes a quick puff of the hand-rolled cigarette Raven has made. "You know, growing up my brother and I were greatly enamored of a comic book character named Raven. We loved her. We asked her blessing."

"Her?" asks Raven, chagrinned.

"Yes, she was a goddess from another planet. When my brother was in the hospital, I prayed to her. I asked her to watch over hm."

"And did she?" Raven asks.

"Yes," answers Brighton as he studies the unlined face of his sharpshooter.

His men aren't afraid of dying in battle. What they fear is performing poorly while under attack or causing harm to a fellow soldier through carelessness. That is their nightmare.

Brighton closes his eyes. He tries to think about home, but all he can see is blood. Blood pouring from ears, from eyes, through bad teeth, from chests and arms and necks.

His crew is good. They are careful. They are patient. There aren't many cards left in Rumsfeld's deadly deck.

FOB. Forward operating base. Brighton can't remember the name of this one. Nothing fancy, but twenty kilometers down the road, the 101st is camped in a former palace, complete with gold faucets, hot showers, and real food.

He walks outside to a line of latrines. He brushes his teeth over the open ground with tooth powder and bottled water. Attached to the privies are several plywood cubicles, the Army's version of a portable shower. He enters the grimy space and undresses. He attaches a gray vinyl bag to an overhead hook. He twists the nozzle and releases a thin trickle of cold water. He has to work fast. The water only lasts nine minutes.

He looks down at his body. He has new muscles in his stomach but has lost some of the thickness in his arms. His perfectly smooth skin, "fine as furniture" as Scottie liked to say, is now pocked with scars and cuts and burns. Bodies take a terrible beating in a war, and Brighton takes pride in every mark and divot and discoloration.

He towels himself dry and reaches for clean underwear. Clean is a luxury. An extravagance. He feels almost human.

He finishes dressing and finds his way to the mess hall. He spots Private Jameson talking with his mouth full as the diminutive woman seated beside him laughs. She has dark hair, cut short, and possesses a pretty smile.

"Gotta help me out, sir. She doesn't believe me."

The female soldier suddenly becomes shy as Brighton reaches out his hand to shake.

"He's a terrible fibber, ma'am, so be warned. I'm Corporal Brighton Bethune. Pleased to meet you."

"Yes, I know who you are. My brothers didn't think you deserved to be on the Wheaties box, but my mother and I stood up for you!"

"Boys are serious about their heroes, ma'am. They think only football, baseball, and basketball players should be on that box. I understand their dilemma. Wheaties has taught you my name; may I ask yours?"

Raven quickly stands. "Sorry, sir. Allow me to introduce Private First-Class Ruth Powers. She and her crew have been assigned to overhaul the engine on our Humvee!"

Brighton raises an eyebrow. "You work with field maintenance?"

She laughs. "I *am* field maintenance, sir. I run the crew, and we got a bulletin to take your machine out of rotation while we patch her up."

"Well, good for you, Ruth Powers."

"Yes, sir. Thank you, sir. There are several women on our crew. Guys aren't the only ones who like to play with engines, sir."

Brighton finally sits, preparing to eat some rubbery pancakes and glutinous oatmeal. "Now what lies has my buddy been telling you?"

"Well, sir, when you and your men came in last night, you all looked a wreck. Many days of living in tents, or worse; we've seen it all. And usually, men who have been out from base for that long acquire a certain odor. But not you two. We named you 'Mr. Sweet.'"

"And did my buddy here spill our secret?"

"Yes, he said 'talcum powder.'"

"No, Private Powers, not any talcum powder, but talcum made by Lanvin!"

Raven laughs aloud. "That's what I told her!"

"Keeps us fresh for days!" explains Brighton, enjoying her look of surprise.

She smiles and sips her coffee. Then her face turns serious. "Sir, on behalf of our entire base, may I congratulate you on the capture of Saddam Hussein."

Brighton's face tightens. "The identity of the forces that captured Hussein is secret, soldier. Do you understand?'

"But the guys—"

"Do you understand? Or do I need to discuss this with your commanding officer?"

Her eyes widen at his harsh tone, but she quickly nods.

"Thank you."

The information officer at the base has tipped Brighton to the news that was circulating. The military will neither confirm nor deny that Brighton had been part of the Task Force that captured the Iraqi president. The US media is cooperating and does not report the rumors, but the Al-Jazeera Network has run footage of Hussein crawling out of his hole, and the back of a redheaded soldier is clearly visible.

"If this news goes public, sir," he said, "the Army may pull you out of here.

$$14.$$

GOD HAS THEIR BACK

The night is clear and cold; a nearly full moon creates strong shadows on the white landscape. Baéz greets his friends and neighbors at the modern glass entry to his new Meetinghouse. A steady plume of white flows from the two chimneys, and the kerosene lamps dance with their unsteady flames. Every seat is taken, and scarves and hats and gloves are strewn across the dark chestnut floor. A young man at the piano is joyously playing Christmas carols and a twenty-foot evergreen, decorated for the season, dwarfs everyone. A wall of tall schoolroom windows looks out on the frozen lake.

Baéz walks to the lectern, studies his notes, and turns towards his neighbors.

"Merry Christmas and welcome to the Lakeside Meeting House."

The crowd answers back. "Merry Christmas."

"'For God so loved the world that he gave his one and only Son that whoever believes in him shall not perish but have eternal life.' Tonight, let us join in celebrating the birth of that son named Jesus. Picture that tiny village, overflowing with people who have come to pay taxes to their distant rulers in Rome. Tradesmen and sellers of spice; adventurers and innkeepers; shepherds, tentmakers and bakers of bread. And in a small barn where donkeys and horses and sheep are kept, a mother whose time has come lies in the straw and delivers a child.

"News of this event is not covered on CNN, nor is the birth announced in a thousand emails. A single bright star signals the arrival of an exceptional child, a child whose birth has been prophesied for generations. And that star points the way for wise men and kings to come and greet this child, giving thanks to God. And that child will grow and flourish and teach us how to live, how to love, how to heal. His lesson is simple—love God supremely and love one another as you love your own self. So, on this Christmas Eve, let us be silent for a moment and think on his lessons. Let us be grateful for his birth and praise the Lord who created him and created each and every one of us."

Baéz bows his head and expresses gratitude for this gathering, this building, and this night.

"This is our first Christmas here at the Meetinghouse. I want to thank you all for your support, for your thoughts, and your deeds. We can each be a light in our community, and our time together in this lovely building prepares us to be better disciples, better listeners, better mothers and fathers and neighbors, and better practitioners of the lessons that Jesus shared with us.

"As many of you know, the benefactor of this church, the man who financed the transformation of my great-grandfather's airplane hangar into this warm space we now inhabit, is my brother Brighton. If you don't mind, I'd like to read an interview with him from northern Iraq. I think his message is timely as we prepare to celebrate Christmas and participate in the many rituals that surround this holiday."

When Baéz mentions his brother, the murmurings begin. Everyone loves Brighton.

"This was printed two days ago on the front page of *The New York Times,* and we couldn't have asked for a better Christmas greeting if had he called each of us personally."

The fact is Brighton doesn't call. Ever. Baéz knows the operating bases are all equipped with internet service, but Brighton is rarely at base. He said being a good soldier requires leaving family behind. He can't be worrying about life in America while trying to keep himself and his men safe. Baéz accepts this, but he misses his brother.

"God Has Their Back"

by John Bee

I can hear the cold in his voice. The winter's first snow has covered the ground, and he and his men slept under their trucks last night, unable to light a fire for fear of giving away their location. They are a unit on the hunt. Their mission is to capture the senior members of Saddam's government and army—alive, if possible.

"I can't give you our location, but we are in the north, and winter has come on swiftly. The landscape is bleak and rocky, and the people are poor. Small buildings of cement or mud serve as their homes; nut trees provide their food. I feel as if I've awakened in biblical times. I am a Pharisee chasing the Chaldeans. When the snow began falling yesterday, I thought of the season, Christmas coming, and the rich history of this area. Noah built his ark in Iraq; Jacob met his Rachel; Peter preached here after the death of Jesus. These inspiring people all walked the ground we are walking. They are with me."

Bethune's missions in Iraq have been off-limits to the press, the Army fearing for his safety. But two weeks ago, he was recognized in news footage of Hussein's capture in Tikrit. Mr. Bethune, it turns out, is a proud member of the Rangers, an elite Army division. It is rumored that the Rangers arrived in Iraq well before the "shock and awe" campaign began in March, but the Corporal would not comment. I asked his plans for Christmas and his thoughts on the season in a foreign land.

"My men and I will be leaving the road and going to one of our forward bases for a traditional meal. We're going to watch the Blue-Gray Bowl in the middle of the night. Also, a tennis match. I am playing a Marine recruit who was the top player from UCLA last year. An old palace of Hussein's has an indoor court."

I asked him what difficulties the soldiers face being away from home at Christmas.

"You know, it's a tight group. We look out for each other. Although we are not in Bethlehem, we are in the Holy Land, and that registers with my men. The people here pray five times each day. We hear the calls from mosques in the many towns we travel through. Abraham, the father of three major religions, is from Iraq. This resonates in a way that holiday decorations at the mall do not. Prayer is part of a soldier's day. Americans at home may want God out of their schools and out of their government, but here we welcome him. Here he is close. He's got our back."

When asked if he had any holiday greetings for folks back home, he answered, "Yes, please go to your local post office and buy a phone card for a soldier. It's simple and easy, and it helps. Eid Milad Majeed. Allah Maak.*"*

Merry Christmas in Arabic. And then "May God go with you."

The tennis world's loss is certainly the Army's gain.

The crowd smiles as Baéz asks them to rise and join in singing "Silent Night." As they sing, his vision turns blurry, the room spinning, and he feels an electric jolt. He grabs the podium and looks over at Nonnie. All color has left her face.

A children's choir sings next, followed by the story of the birth of Jesus as told in the Book of Matthew. Jared reads it in English, followed by Rio who reads it in Spanish. One final carol ends the service, and then the many families rise and gather around the food tables. Baéz overcomes his uneasiness and thanks everyone. He finds Nonnie, deep in prayer, in a far corner away from the heat of the stoves.

"Something's wrong, isn't it?" he asks

"We must pray to know that nothing is wrong, nothing is out of place in His kingdom. Nothing."

His skin becomes gooseflesh, as it had that evening under the ice. He kneels beside Nonnie and holds her hand. She recites a portion of the 91st Psalm.

He that dwelleth in the secret place of the most high
shall abide under the shadow of the Almighty.
I will say of the Lord, He is my refuge and my fortress: my God; in him will I trust.

They damp the stoves, extinguish the candles, and return to their homes. Baéz looks at the moon, knowing that the firmament above covers both him and his brother in the safety of God's love. He remembers Paul's many escapes from danger—the viper rendered harmless, the shipwreck that landed him safely ashore, and the prison cell unlocked by an earthquake.

In a room at the top of her house, Nonnie opens her Bible and reads.

When the powerful Centurion approached Jesus, asking him to heal a dying servant, Jesus agreed. He asked the man to lead the way, but the Centurion said a visit was not necessary—Jesus had only to say it was so and the servant would be well. Jesus had not seen so great a faith in all of Israel. Returning home, the Centurion was greeted by his staff who informed him the fever left in the selfsame hour as his visit with Jesus.

Nonnie knows that proximity is not necessary for healing. Man can never find himself in a predicament where divine Mind's control is absent. She prays to know that God's truth is ever active and will correct any seeming lack of harmony. Brighton reflects all the intelligence he will ever need to solve any problem he might find himself trapped within.

✷ ✷ ✷

Laith Halevi finishes dressing in near darkness, a single candle beside him as he kneels on his prayer rug. He has been called in early. The entire team has. Not a good sign.

He pulls into the parking lot astride his Honda Scrambler. The bright red helmet with the orange flames and tinted windscreen conceals his Middle Eastern features, providing him the anonymity he welcomes. His dark skin and thick, unruly hair are hidden, as are the blue eyes that make him such a catch at the gay bars he frequents.

As he parks the bike on its stand and removes the helmet, his face is caught in the stream of headlights pulling into Fort George G. Meade, the sprawling five-thousand-acre complex shared by the Army and the National Security Agency. Employees pour into their respective sections. They are a league of nations—men and women—who share a gift for languages and computer coding. Their families are from Turkey, Iraq, Iran, Syria, Israel. They speak Arabic, Hindu, Pushtan, Persian, Turkish, Hebrew, and Kurdish.

They are all citizens of the United States, in their twenties, single, and most living in a bland apartment complex in downtown Baltimore where the NSA provides patrols and surveillance. There is increased harassment of Muslim Americans, so these young workers keep a sharp eye.

The sun has another hour before it rises, and the cold fluorescents are humming overhead. The rich smell of home-brewed coffee fills the air as they pour the first of many cups from their thermoses. Their supervisor, Dunya Eshe, calls for quiet.

"Listen up. I know the holidays are here, but they pulled Hussein out of some hole the other night and we have to be on top of our game. Somebody, somewhere, is going to be inspired to retaliate. We need to increase our searches, be creative in our word choices, and be diligent. And share. Talk to each other. Find patterns. Something. Anything. You are your country's eyes and ears. I encourage you to be paranoid. Get to it."

Laith is an intelligence analyst. He reads the transcriptions of phone calls, emails, text messages, and any other communications their satellites sweep up. These are fed into mainframe computers that are programmed to search certain words, phrases, and proper names. "Bomb," "green zone," "Kabul," "Kalashnikov," "armor," "suicide," "Taliban," in ten languages and three alphabets. It is his job to read the transmissions that include these keywords. These stolen transmissions are collectively called "chatter."

His desk is a gathering point as his coworkers compare notes, share stories, or simply discuss the previous evening's episode of *The West Wing*. His cubicle features the *People*

Magazine cover for the "Sexiest Brothers Alive." He tells anyone who will listen that Nathan Winning's photograph of the boys skateboarding shirtless beneath the Unisphere broke Farrah Fawcett's sales record.

As a senior analyst, Laith has some discretion in choosing their search words, and he often comes up with odd combinations simply to alleviate the sameness of his days. Last week, he added the phrases "boy band" and "blond" and discovered the Middle East is infatuated with Justin Timberlake. Today he will try a new variation. "Tennis shorts" and "Brighton Bethune." His main man. His inspiration. His right hand's best friend.

✷ ✷ ✷

Three trucks will make the trip with fifteen soldiers. Since the route is much traveled, there is little fear of roadside bombs. Raven is joining them because a stable of undernourished Arabian horses has been discovered at the palace and the crew needs guidance in handling them. Ruth is coming because she asked. Brighton enjoys her company.

The three climb into the middle Humvee, with a driver and two marksmen. Brighton doesn't know the soldiers, but Ruthie does. There are nearly five hundred men and women living in the tents and stables of Packhorse, and she knows them all.

Raven has shaved and even trimmed his hair. He raided Brighton's pack and smells of Lanvin. The more familiar scent of diesel fuel fills the air as the Humvees pull out. They are driving fast, creating huge clouds of dust that forces them to leave hundreds of yards between their vehicles. Brighton thinks they should slow, reducing the dust, and stay neatly on top of each other, but he isn't in charge. These are not his men.

"A lovely drive on Christmas day. To grandmother's house we go."

Brighton is slouched in his seat, speaking softly.

"The horses got apples on Christmas," Raven responds. "I went from stall to stall, carrying a bushel basket."

"Sledding with your brother?" asks Ruthie.

"Yup, Brother Baéz. He found God on Christmas Day and now preaches to the masses."

"Pretty cute for a preacher."

"Dangerously cute for a preacher! What'd you do, Google him?"

"Just for a minute. You. I Googled you. Thousands of pages. But he was in there too. Has his own website. Some crazy shit."

Brighton doesn't want to think about Baéz. He resents God for stealing his brother. He had basked in the warmth of Baéz's adoration. Now God was the recipient of Baéz's praise.

"We losing you, sir?" Raven says. "Wake up. It's a beautiful day in the neighborhood."

Ruth adds, "Could you be mine? Would you be mine?"

Raven laughs. "Mr. Rogers goes to war. What a powerful concept."

Brighton smiles. "He was a subversive guy. I'm sure, had he known his little charges would one day end up in a war, I'm sure he would have had a song for us to sing so we wouldn't be afraid."

A loud explosion interrupts their thoughts, and they grab their rifles.

✷✷✷

Laith now dreams in English. His mind is so adept at absorbing multiple stimuli that this simple alteration in his daily life has gone unnoticed. There is a lesson in this, he realizes. Proud of his sharp mind, he now understands that something unremarkable could slip his attention. He has to work harder. He can't simply study the impossible, the improbable; he must give equal thought to the obvious, the simple. Otherwise, something important could slip by.

His entry of "tennis shorts" into the mainframe search engine has returned a wide variety of responses. He had intended the search simply as a diversion, an amusing trigger to make his colleagues laugh.

He is no longer laughing.

A tennis team in Iraq has been brutally murdered, pulled from their van and executed at point-blank range, their bodies left to rot in the street. The players' only offense was wearing shorts in a district that banned them.

Camp Ironhorse has scheduled an exhibition match pitting Bethune against a recent college grad. A supply officer spent days trying to locate tennis balls in a war zone. Bethune has been identified as part of the team that captured Hussein.

The chatter increases and multiplies, but Laith cannot discern a cause. The Iraqi murders and the Christmas Day exhibition match keep appearing again and again.

Why such interest in a supply officer tracking down tennis equipment? The obviousness of the message stuns him.

Rushing to his station, he sends the memo that will haunt him and his bosses for months to come.

"Plans in place to kill US tennis star on Christmas Day."

✷✷✷

The Humvees are too far apart when the insurgents attack. A remote-controlled bomb disables the front vehicle, injuring everyone on board, while a barrage of mortars immobilizes the third, sending shrapnel in all directions.

The middle Humvee withstands the barrage, but thick black smoke hides the attackers.

"Ruthie, can you operate the turret?" screams Brighton. She answers "yes" and moves to the middle of their vehicle, opening the hatch and stepping up to the large gun.

"Raven, got any grenades?"

"Never without, my friend."

Brighton places the end of his rifle in the gun hole and begins firing. Raven's grenades light the landscape. Ruthie triggers her gun, swiveling the turret nearly two hundred degrees and sending an endless fusillade of bullets into the dark. One combatant breaks through and covers their vehicle in kerosene as more enemy soldiers move in and set their vehicle on fire.

"This tin can's gonna blow! We gotta get out of here!" screams Brighton as the flames surround him.

They try to escape but the bearded soldiers overwhelm them, kicking them to the ground. A battered truck approaches, and the three are thrown in the back amid shouts of victory. As the truck drives through the smoke and carnage, Brighton looks back and sees a highway littered with American soldiers.

"Where are you taking us?" he asks in English, not revealing his language skills.

No answer.

The soldiers laugh, and the tall one remarks that Brighton has nice teeth. Brighton hears a reference to Samarra.

Ruth's body is coiled in fear. Brighton tries to offer some hope but measures his words carefully. "They will find us. We are in the steppes; a few helicopters should be able to find an errant truck."

"As long as they do it soon, before we enter a city," cautions Raven.

They sit looking at one another, wondering what comes next. No one speaks until Raven asks the question that is preying on their minds.

"Why didn't they kill us?"

Brighton knows the answer. "They're going to make an example of us. Retaliation for Hussein. They have obviously targeted me. It's going to be some ransom demand that the US can't possibly meet. I am so sorry. Something told me this was a frivolous trip, yet I agreed."

When night falls, all hope for a swift rescue disappears. Raven hums *Mr. Roger's* theme song. They try not to think. The options are too grim to consider.

The trucks slow and pull up to a series of small buildings constructed of packed mud and cinderblock. A crevice carved in a rock wall camouflages a satellite dish. Several cedar trees hide digital transmitters and a generator rumbles nearby.

They are taken to a windowless room with vertical wood beams. Dim lights hang from a tin ceiling. An oddly elaborate carved table sits in the center.

Brighton sees four men, heavily armed. Their clothes are clean, their beards trimmed. They are not monsters; they allow Ruthie, Raven, and Brighton to use the outhouse and have a drink of water.

"I heard a horse whinny," Raven says. "I'm feeling a bit of a Jesse James moment here, an elaborate escape on horseback. Very cool. Very sexy. Saddam controlled the bloodlines of some great thoroughbreds."

"Got a plan, Jesse?" Ruth asks. Raven looks over at her as Brighton studies her face, wanting her to be strong, hoping she doesn't cry. What soldiers hated most about having women in the Army were their tears.

"It'll reveal itself. Don't worry. Stay strong and be ready."

Brighton closes his eyes, finally daring to think of what lies ahead. He knows this is some kind of communication center. They are going to force him to recite some anti-American statement, or they are going to torture him. Whatever it is, they are going to do it on camera for the entire Arab world to see.

He tries to prepare himself. He reminds himself he is strong. He can withstand pain. He remembers what Baéz told him about his time under the ice. "Did you think you were going to die?" Brighton had asked. "No," his brother answered. "I never thought that. I was afraid I would try to breathe, so I focused on breathing being unnecessary. I saw the ice above me as something I had to get through. I knew I needed to enter a different plane of experience. That's how Nonnie would describe it. I had to see myself above that ice, existent elsewhere. I wasn't in danger; I wasn't under that ice; I was safe somewhere my eyes couldn't see but my mind could. I truly believed you would know what to do to get me to that place."

Existent elsewhere.

He focuses on those words as he hears the jangling of keys, and then a wide door swings open. Three men enter, carrying electronic equipment and trailing a series of wires. They place a laptop on the table, then set up a simple tripod that holds a video camera. A fourth man, talking on a cordless phone, follows them in. He says it is noon in America on their biggest religious holiday and then asks if they are getting an image. Two men go to Brighton and pull him roughly to his feet. Ruth lets out a scream.

They untie Brighton and motion for him to remove his clothes. He unties his boots. A hidden knife lies in the heel, but he can't overpower this many men, even with a knife.

He removes his shirt and then his tee, carefully folding each item and placing it on the table

The man with the phone leaves, and the other two station themselves behind the camera, rifles at the ready. Another man enters and places a box-cutting knife, a hammer, and a pistol on the table. From a bag, he removes a long cotton bandage and a syringe.

Brighton looks the man directly in the eye. He will not focus on the items on the table nor allow them into consciousness. He must enter a world where this is not happening. He denies the evidence of hatred, revenge, and danger. His initial fear that they are going to disfigure him, cut him, damage his body, dissolves into thin air. The pride he takes from his handsomeness leaves him. His desire for life leaves him.

"I have a statement for you to read." The man takes out a single page and places it on the desk.

"I will not read it," announces Brighton, flinching as he sees the fist coming towards his face.

The images recorded in that mud hut are sent via satellite to a server in Samarra. From there, the signal reaches a web address that Al Jazeera has been advised to monitor. Al Jazeera then bounces the signal to its own website, streaming the images live in English and Arabic. The NSA is ordered to stop the signal, to shut down the servers, but they are unable to do so.

The Army, AT&T, and the governments of Egypt, Saudi Arabia, and Qatar are trying to track the IP address to learn of Brighton's whereabouts. American hackers, appalled at what they are seeing, try to stop the video but are unsuccessful. The suffering continues to be broadcast everywhere—except in Brighton's mind, where it simply isn't happening.

✳ ✳ ✳

A volunteer on Sterling's ambulance crew is a ham radio operator and often spends his Christmas chatting with fellow operators and wishing them a happy holiday. A buddy who lives in Ankara offers condolences for the captured tennis player who is being streamed live on the Al Jazeera Media Network.

The ambulance driver calls Jared, not sure he is doing the right thing, and tells him what he heard. He gives Jared the IP address for the Middle Eastern TV network.

Jared is stunned. *If it is true*, he thinks, *wouldn't it be all over the news?* He turns on his TV and flips across several stations. He finds a hockey game, the weather report, and Jimmy Stewart in black and white. He types the Al Jazeera address into his search engine, and magically Brighton's face appears on his screen. Brighton is sitting behind a table, shirtless, blood dripping down his face, a man screaming at him in English and Arabic. The man hits him, hard, again and again, as tears from Brighton's eyes mix with his blood. His face is covered in cuts, each bleeding profusely.

Jared is frozen in place. He is watching a horror film and is unable to turn it off. He looks out his window. He doesn't know where Baéz or Nonnie are, but he prays they are not seeing this.

The tall man hands Brighton a piece of paper. "You will read this, or you will die. Do you understand?"

"I won't read it," comes the response.

Hearing Brighton's distinctly accented voice, the voice he knows so well, breaks Jared's heart.

The neat, bearded man unties Brighton, placing his prisoner's hands on top of the wooden table. Brighton struggles, but another man comes to assist. They both force an opened hand onto the table as the tall man takes the claw hammer, raises it overhead, and then smashes the delicate flesh and bone. Brighton screams. The sound is loud and reverberates off the cinderblock walls. The steel hammer comes down again, harder. Blood and bone splash onto the camera lens as Brighton's torturer strikes once more.

Jared throws up on his desk, choking on bile and mucus and tears. He runs to the bathroom for a towel and begins to clean his face as the ghastly sounds continue. He hears his back door open, and Baéz calls out to him. He rushes from the bath to turn off the computer.

"Dad? Dad?"

His son has turned to the images on the computer. The tall, bearded man throws a bucket of water on Brighton, the blood and bone clearing from his face and shoulders as he slowly regains consciousness.

Baéz stares at the violent scene, uncomprehending. Then he looks at his father, seeking an explanation.

The man in the video yells. "STAND UP!"

Brighton slowly rises.

"READ IT!" the man instructs.

Brighton shakes his head and whispers, "No." His muscles tense. He stares into the eyes of his tormentor and then, drawing on a last burst of strength, he screams to the heavens. "*ALLAH YAGHFIR LAK! ALLAH YAHMIK!*"

Hearing those words, the attacker loses control, shouting furiously and striking out with a final punch that knocks Brighton to the ground. His bloodied body falls out of frame, and the picture goes dark.

Baéz screams, and Jared rushes to him, preventing him from collapsing to the floor. "Oh, my boy, my boy, my boy!"

✶ ✶ ✶

The Saudi Arabia desk of *BBC News* breaks the story. Brighton's last words to his torturer are translated as "Allah forgives you." These words become the headline on newspapers around the world. Brighton's bravery makes Americans proud. On that Christmas Eve, he becomes everyone's son, everyone's brother, and everyone's husband.

The story darkens, however, when a massive earthquake strikes Northern Iraq, complicating rescue efforts. The Army declares a news blackout and issues a terse "no comment" when asked the whereabouts of Corporal Bethune. What the Army cannot say, and certainly will not admit, is that they are unable to locate Corporal Brighton Bethune.

✶ ✶ ✶

The sun is rising when the young Iraqi turns onto the Arbataash Tamuz Bridge, which leads to the International Zone. The entry point is guarded by troops from the Florida National Guard. He keeps his hands visible, his arms at his side, his jacket unbuttoned. Then he walks up to a guard and says in perfect English, "This is your lucky day, soldier. I have information on the whereabouts of Brighton Bethune!"

In a matter of minutes, a jeep careens towards the entry point, and the Iraqi is driven to the As-Salam Palace and led to a large room lit by giant crystal chandeliers. A tall man in uniform points to a chair that sits behind a desk decorated in gold leaf.

"What is your name?"

"Kaveh Yavari."

"And you claim to know where Corporal Bethune is being held?"

He hadn't known Brighton was a corporal. He doesn't understand military titles, but it sounds important. "Yes, sir."

"And how do you come to know this information"?

"I saw the video. On my computer. I've been to those buildings."

"Under what circumstances?"

"Delivering supplies; to Tikrit, Samarra and Tuz."

"What kind of supplies?"

"Guns, telephones, food. Whatever they asked. They killed my teammates for wearing shorts in a district that had banned them. I was spared. I was wearing long pants."

The soldier doesn't understand. "You're sure you've been there before?"

"Yes, sir. I recognize the table. It is rare and valuable"

"The table?"

"Yes, sir. There is large Saad and Haa carved in the top. Hand-crafted. Stolen from here, from this palace."

"What?"

"Look above you."

The soldier stares at the ceiling. Thousands of tiles with the 'S' and 'H' in Arabic are in the ceiling.

"Hussein's initials, sir."

"And could you find this room again?"

"I wouldn't have come here if I couldn't lead you to it."

Kaveh once called Brighton "Mr. Lucky."

He hopes the nickname still holds true.

When the mud hut collapses, everything goes dark as the earth trembles and quakes. A fallen roof beam strikes Brighton, pinning him to the cold ground and increasing the agony of the wounds inflicted by his captors. He calls out to Raven and Ruthie and is grateful when each confirms their survival.

Their captors are silent. Even the horses are silent.

As the rubble settles around him, he fears the aftershocks will cause further collapse. He can't move. He can't think. His mouth is filled with dirt and debris, and breathing is only possible through his nose. He is filled with fear as claustrophobia heightens his suffocating anxiety. He realizes he is undergoing a delayed reaction from his tormentor's beatings; the pain has become unbearable.

Is this how life ends, he wonders, *buried alive in a foreign land?* For the sake of his men and to assure his own survival, he has held himself together for the past two years by never allowing the wickedness of the world to encroach upon his thinking. Now, in pain and nearing death, his entire being is unravelling.

A light breeze cools his face, and he understands he is lying in the open; there are no walls, there is no roof. He hears Ruthie mumbling prayers as Raven gently repeats the words of an old country tune. A light flickers in the distance. A star, maybe—or a spy satellite, trying to locate him. Should he wave? He's pretty sure he's hallucinating.

He closes his eyes and the flickering stops. He wants to cry. He wants to go home. He wants to be elsewhere.

Existent elsewhere.

Disconnected images float in and out of his mind. He sees Scottie in her lavender dress. They are walking down the beach near her restaurant and notice a handsome house, all glass and steel, standing tall as the tide threatens. Scottie wonders who lives there, and Brighton leaves a note under their door. He jots down the address—Pacific Coast Highway. So exotic.

He coughs, spitting up dust. His feels his heartbeat slowing. Scottie stands on the balcony of the glass house, waving goodbye. He bows to her, and she walks inside the house, which he now realizes is his. He remembers buying it before shipping out.

A hand caresses his face. Warm and smooth, and smelling of Vetiver. How kind God is, he thinks, allowing him a final breath scented with his favorite cologne. It feels so good to be touched. He curls into the embrace and gets an erection. *Angel Lust.* That's what they call it. Men getting erections as they are about to die. *What a grotesque betrayal of the body,* says a voice in his head.

He feels the world slipping away. He hears voices, loud voices. And a strident thrumming. The light is blinking again, far in the distance. His heartbeats are farther and farther apart. He tries to speak. He wants to ask what's going on. Raven has stopped singing, and Ruthie is crying.

He hears another voice. A new voice. A voice he knows.

"Over here, under this beam. Yes, help me move it. Oh my God, they're alive. Hold on, we've got you. Just hang on a bit longer, okay? Let us get you home!"

As he slips from consciousness, he hears Kaveh weeping.

15.

'A FOREIGNER OF BREMON'

Walking the hallways of Germany's Landstuhl Medical Center requires enormous concentration. Pain hangs in the air, tangible, with a sickly metallic odor. The atmosphere is troubling, and the bright fluorescents hurt the eyes.

At the nursing station, a young intern points the way to Brighton's room. Baéz slows his walk, telling himself not to be alarmed by his brother's physical condition.

Brighton is asleep, his face covered in bandages. His blanket is askew, his torso exposed. A tray holds congealed eggs and untouched toast. Baéz moves it, the smell mixing with disinfectant and the sugary-sweet air freshener. He can't image a space less conducive to healing.

Brighton's ribs are darkly bruised, and his once-smooth chest is covered in burns. His crushed right hand is encased in a plastic mold and wrapped in a thin layer of black rubber. Baéz pictures his brother in his wetsuit, all sleek and shiny.

He moves a chair towards Brighton's bed and sits. The room is a soundtrack of hisses and beeps and whirrs. The window looks out on other buildings filled with other broken soldiers. The pain and fear behind all those windows bears down on him, so he closes his eyes. Medical science has achieved wonders when it comes to fixing broken bodies, but to Baéz, the world is a mental creation. Instead of believing what he sees, he sees what he believes. And he believes his brother is perfectly well. That is what he needs to see. Right now.

He reaches for Brighton's left hand and holds it. Brighton's eyelids are twitching, and his face registers agitation. A low moan escapes his lips, and his head begins thrashing on the synthetic pillow.

"I'm right here, buddy. Everything's fine. Let your thoughts take you someplace pleasant. Out of this room. Out of this situation. Away from this haze of impairment."

A doctor enters and introduces himself. He wakes Brighton, who stares blankly at his surroundings.

"What medications do you have him on?" Baéz asks. "He hardly seems conscious!"

"A sedative, anti-seizure treatments, anti-depressants, and pain medication," answers the doctor succinctly. "Lots of pain medication, nerve blockers we call them, to relieve anxiety and distress. The air evacuation was not restful, and he has experienced episodes of extreme anger and confusion. A manifestation of severe trauma, both mental and physical. His body is protecting itself."

Baéz nods, taking in a world with which he has no familiarity. He reminds himself that man is the reflection of one omniscient Mind, the only true cause, the effect from any other cause being false, nullified by the Truth.

"Can I assume you saw the video, saw what they did to him?" the doctor asks.

Baéz nods.

"This will take a while. But it's good you are here. He needs time. Healing takes time."

Without thinking, Baéz answers, "Healing takes love, not time. It can even be instantaneous."

Baéz sees the doctor frown at his words.

A young soldier enters the room, addressing Baéz as the doctor leaves.

"Good evening. I am Lieutenant Frobish. Information officer. I work with the press. And, as I am sure you're aware, the press has an unhealthy appetite for news where your brother is concerned."

"To be accurate, Corporal Bethune is my half-brother."

"Which means what?"

"We share the same biological mother."

"Okay. Half-brother it is. So, this is the situation. Each morning, two doctors and I have been giving the press an update. Each day is the same. There is no news. With your arrival, they are grasping at straws. They are asking if you are applying faith healing, if you are taking him off his medications, if you are interfering with our work."

"And you would like me to do . . . what?"

"I would like you to join us tomorrow and answer their questions, assuring them that your brother is receiving excellent care, and his treatment remains unchanged by your arrival."

"Fine. I can do that."

"Excellent. I will pick you up 0900 hours."

They shake hands and Frobish departs.

Baéz goes to the cafeteria and gets a sandwich, washing it down with milk. He wants one of Nonnie's grilled cheese creations; he needs Nonnie's nourishment. The stale, chemical odors cycling through the hospital's air ducts make him feel weak and vulnerable.

He empties his trash and slowly walks back to the patients' wing. He fixes his gaze on the worn linoleum floor, avoiding the view of open rooms with their mangled fighters.

He has to get Brighton out of here.

He has to get Brighton home.

✷ ✷ ✷

The press conference begins promptly at ten hundred hours. Lt. Frobish and the doctors repeat what they have been saying for several days—Brighton is receiving excellent care, but while his right hand might regain some movement, it will never again be fully functional. He is heavily sedated to aid the healing, and they are pleased with his progress.

All eyes turn to Baéz, who holds the only potential for actual news. He looks at the scores of reporters, representing outlets from around the world. He closes his eyes for a brief moment and hears "I am with you." He smiles as the tension leaves his body.

"On behalf of my brother, and on behalf of our family and friends, I want to thank the thousands of people worldwide who sent their prayers and good wishes to Brighton. Thought has power, thought has weight, and it can alter a landscape. The violence and hatred so graphically displayed in the gruesome video that was viewed by millions has left a mark on us and on my brother. I would like to ask the many websites and news organizations who continue to make this video available on the internet to take it down. It is pornography."

He senses the mood of the journalists; they are leaning in, listening carefully.

"Whatever fear that video created within you, whatever anger rose to the surface as you witnessed the terrorists' attempts to destroy my brother's body, you must denounce. Do not be impressed by evil. Please, take down this video. It can be the first step in my brother's healing. Against this faceless foe, my brother is presently speechless. Help give back his voice. Remove these images not only from the internet, but from your minds."

Baéz continues, the room completely still.

"I would also like to send my gratitude to the sports journalists who never pointed out that my brother has triumphed in tennis as a left-hander, not a right-hander as the terrorists believed. That man with the hammer did not steal my brother's ability to play tennis. Brighton will play again, he will triumph again, and he will transcend the forces arrayed against him. Thank you."

Baéz steps away from the lectern, and the reporters begin shouting their questions. As they seek to stir the cauldron, trying to get Baéz to explicitly condemn the war, Lt. Frobish rises and attempts to introduce some order to the room. Baéz simply displays his quiet smile, knowing he must not misstep.

"Were you aware the National Security Agency warned the Army of an attempt on your brother's life twelve hours before the attack?"

The room buzzes, impressed by the boldness of the French journalist.

"When we are the sowers of our own destruction, a voice in the wilderness warning us off our path is rarely given credence. I was gratified by the bravery of that young analyst for making his warning public, although I understand he has now been placed on leave. Truth will survive. It cannot be silenced. You are each messengers for truth, and I urge you to never let up. On Christmas Eve, Brighton's grandmother and I each received a strong message that Brighton's safety had been compromised. But we did not ignore it. We acted. We got down on bended knee and affirmed that God was present right where the trouble seemed to be. And twenty-four hours later, an earthquake did what our Army could not—it freed him."

Once again, the swarm of journalists begins screaming and wildly waving their hands in the air as one yells out a question.

"Are you suggesting that your prayers resulted in an earthquake?"

Baéz shakes his head, smiling. "No, sir. I simply like the symmetry of it. Earthquakes frequently opened the gates of prison doors in the Bible."

✳ ✳ ✳

"Eh, Preacher Man, come in, come in. Take a seat. Bring me your cup of cheer."

The man in the bed is shirtless. A black patch covers his right eye, and a metal hoist holds his raised leg, which is covered in a plaster cast.

"Doing the rounds today?" the man asks. "Bucking up the spirits of our best and brightest?"

Baéz ignores the sarcastic tone. He moves a chair to the man's bedside and sits. The face before him is young, the skin smooth but tough, like a polished hide. His one good eye is as gray as gun smoke and firmly focused on Baéz.

"They send you down here to reason with me?" the man asks.

"A nurse mentioned your predicament and wondered if I might offer some advice. As a member of my brother's team, I was desirous of making your acquaintance."

"Desirous?"

Baéz laughs. "It's the preacher in me. I love words. But you already knew that. What gave me away?"

"I come from a family of snake handlers. The Church of Holiness. Bible thumpers and Jesus-savers from way back. I recognize your type."

The man's voice is low, like a country singer's, but not warm, not welcoming.

"'And the Lord shall give you power over serpents and scorpions,'" quotes Baéz. "I know the practice, but I fear snakes, always have."

"That's a good thing. My Uncle Jotham had no fear, yet he died on a Sunday morning, writhing helplessly in front of his congregation. The poison from the fangs didn't take but ten minutes. Some mighty large doubts were sown in those churchgoers that day."

"I bet. My name's Baéz, I'm brother to—"

"Brighton, I know, I know. And I suppose you know I'm Raven Jameson, rifleman extraordinaire." He let loose a low cackle, enjoying his private joke.

"I know your name, but little else. When Brighton joined the Army, he fell off the map. His years as a Ranger are known only to those of you who served with him "

The words come out clipped and short, the resentment undisguised.

The man in the bed smiles, but his facial muscles do not relax. "Your brother led a unit charged with tracking down and assassinating the officers of Saddam's army. He was also my spotter. Do you know what that means?"

"I'm afraid I don't."

"The spotter gauges the distance to the target, the wind speed, the angle of the bullet's descent, that sort of thing. Based on his calculations, I adjust the riflescope. He also keeps the target in view through his binoculars, so we know if our calculations are correct. My scope and his binocs brought us images we cannot erase. Heads exploding, blood spraying, men we never met falling to their knees as death overtakes them. We had to ignore those commandments you preachers lay such store by, and I think that bothered Brighton."

Baéz stares at the soldier, barely old enough to have enlisted. The soldier stares back.

"How is he? Suffering in munificent silence?" The white skin is drawn into rigid smile. "I too enjoy words."

Raven is tightly wound, but Baéz won't judge him.

"Patched up, stitched up, and pumped full of drugs, I'd say. I'm trying to get them to ease off the meds and see who emerges."

"Yeah, careful with that. The docs are big on pain management, but the euphoria that follows can be lethal."

He pauses and swallows a thin white pill.

"He mention Ruthie or me?"

Baéz shakes his head. "Nope. He's not speaking."

"Odd. He was talking a blue streak when they found us. Not all sensible, but tons of words. The Iraqi kid is bawling like a baby, trying to dig us out with his bare hands. Ruthie is shaking and screaming and hugging every soldier she could reach. Their joy upon finding your brother alive was something to behold. Their impossible mission was a success. Ruthie and I were afterthoughts."

"They were grateful you were safe. Pictures of you were all over the news."

"The news," spits Raven. "What a joke! I saw your press conference. They asked all the wrong questions." Raven becomes agitated. "And you, sir, are a false prophet! You make your brother weak. Do you know that? You intrude on his thoughts, in battle and at rest. He worries what you think and how you regard him. You are a burden. Your care and affection diminish his strength."

This man loves Brighton, thinks Baéz. He isn't suffering from the bloody carnage he caused or the violence he perpetrated. He is suffering from his inability to protect Brighton from Zarqawi's soldiers; shamed by his helplessness.

"My brother's strength or his weakness, his beauty, his wounds, they are all his own. I have nothing to do with it. I am here as a witness and to shine a light. If you wish to celebrate darkness, I cannot stop you."

Raven struggles with a pitcher of water, pouring out a glass. He takes several swallows and then wipes his chin. His demeanor softens and he speaks in a gentler tone.

"We slept together, under the trucks, sharing the day's last cigarette. We would talk and talk; there was no end to our words. We spoke about our troublesome dads, our older brothers, our first girlfriends. We fell asleep to the soothing sound of the other's voice. For that brief period each day, I felt safe. And then morning would come, and we'd take a piss, pack our things, and kill some strangers. All for five hundred nineteen dollars a week. We were far from tennis courts and horse barns, from everything and everyone we trusted and treasured, but I guess that was the point."

Raven stops and looks into Baéz's eyes. "He saved my life. Several times. Thought nothing of it."

Baéz nods, understanding. "Yes. Me too. It's something he does. He's good at it. There is no possible 'thank you.' Believe me, I've tried. Stop worrying about it. He's not."

Raven pauses while gathering the words for his response. "He didn't describe it as saving your life. He said he witnessed your discovery of God. For him, it was a holy moment, one he was pleased to be present for."

Baéz is baffled. He and Brighton have different memories of that day.

Raven adds, "He believes you possess the understanding he lacks."

Baéz is quiet and then says, "We are each searching, in our own way."

Raven adjusts his pillow and then stares at the ceiling. "We were sleeping on the soil where your biblical heroes once walked. He found this enormously moving."

"Was it for you, Raven?" Baéz likes saying the man's name.

"I don't know. Those Bible folks are mighty far away. I recall Uncle Jotham telling me that King David had red hair, just like Brighton. The boy who felled Goliath had red hair. Imagine!"

They remain quiet, neither speaking, until Baéz asks, "Would you like me to pray with you?" He's still not comfortable praying with strangers, yet he feels a kinship with Raven.

"No, but thanks. I will be in his prayers, and now, yours too, I imagine. That will suffice."

"Why were you traveling with my brother on that day? To watch his tennis match?"

"No, sir. I teased him about his choice of sport. 'Not a man's game,' I complained. Ruthie came for the tennis and to get a hot shower. She walked away without a scratch and is still over there, tuning engines—a knack of hers. My knack is horses. Thoroughbreds. Saddam owned some fine breeding stock. We were planning to visit a herd of horses they wanted me to examine."

"Were you in that room with my brother, when they beat him?"

He doesn't know why he asked. Everyone has those images ingrained in their memory. He wonders how others remember it, what remains, and what has been discarded.

"Yes. Ruthie too. He told us to be unafraid. He asked us to banish fear from our hearts. I couldn't do it." Tears roll down Raven's face. He does not attempt to hide them or wipe them away. "It would do me a world of good to see him before they send me home. If you could try."

"I will. I'll try, but the doctors are slow in reducing his meds. He's still not speaking."

"Be careful with him. Those pills create a world of trouble," warns Raven. "Make sure you've got all of him when you take him home. I've heard tell of soldiers who have returned home but think they're still on the battlefield."

"I'll take care. That's a promise."

✶ ✶ ✶

I *was born in the year 1632, in the city of York, of a good family, tho' not of that country, my father being a foreigner of Bremen, who settled first at Hull. He got a good estate by merchandise and leaving off his trade lived afterward at York, from whence he married my mother, whose relations were named Robinson, a very good family, in that country and from* *whom I was called Robinson Kreutznaer, but by the usual corruption of words in England, we are now called, nay, we call ourselves and write our name Crusoe, and so my companions always called me.*

"Ah, our beloved 'foreigner of Bremen!'"

These are Brighton's first words. They had read *Robinson Crusoe* many times as kids. Baéz found a copy in the hospital library.

"Garbo talks!" Baéz announces.

"Yes. I must stop you, though. It is a majestic sound you make—like your father—reading his Bible."

Baéz has been speaking for hours, day upon day, as the doctors slowly reduced his brother's dependence on painkillers. Baéz described the construction of the Meetinghouse, the expansion of his father's business, the many new patients that Nonnie is treating, his collaboration with Lonnie creating "feel-good" video pieces, even a few brief, but unsatisfying, affairs. When he ran out of news, when invention finally failed him, he read aloud from books as they had done when they were children.

"You heard it all?" Baéz asks.

"I think so, although I have many questions about your romance with Tolliver."

"I don't know why I told you. Please don't mention it; he will be embarrassed and also disappointed in me. I don't think I could bear his disapproval."

"What about my disapproval? You can't find your own friends? Have to sleep with mine?"

Baéz knows to ignore Brighton's prickly mood. His brother is in pain, all kinds of different pain, mental and physical. Baéz is here to help dissolve the pain, not engage with it.

"So, the silence was what? A conscious act of willfulness? Anger?"

"No. I would love to claim credit, but it was not conscious. I was beyond help or healing. I did hear you, but I couldn't have named you. I lived inside that voice, your voice, drowning in blood. I see it everywhere. Always. Like you being underwater. And then, the blood ebbed, the tide went out, the sky cleared, and there was only you."

The silence that follows is awkward, so Baéz shares more news.

"I met Raven Jameson. He would like to see you. I can wheel you down there. If you would like."

"A regular 'Charles in Charge,' aren't you?"

There is no rancor in his words, but Baéz knows he is trespassing. This is Brighton's world, Brighton's military, Brighton's crew.

"I know you're upset with me," Baéz says. "You want to do this on your own. I understand. I know the cost, for people like us. We believe in our own competence. We resent help because we fear the burden of gratitude. It has taken years for me to not feel diminished by my debt to you."

Baéz lets those thoughts settle over the room and then adds: "I spoke with Elwynn. I discouraged him from joining me on this trip."

Brighton opens his eyes wide but says nothing.

"Don't worry. He can't get here. He doesn't have two nickels to rub together. He thought it was a free flight."

Brighton snickers. "Perfect. A free flight to Europe. Maybe he can take bets on my recovery. How many weeks until my piss runs clear! How soon until I play tennis again?"

Baéz doesn't mention that Elwynn sold the duplex because Bank Paribas forced him into "early retirement" and that Nico sold HARDBODY to Afidcorp, a pharmaceutical giant, to cover his losses. Now they both work for the new owners.

"The boy who found you. Kaveh?"

Brighton sits up at the mention of his friend's name. "Is he alright?"

Baéz answers quickly, wanting to dispel the fear he sees in his brother's eyes. "He's fine. The Pentagon prevailed upon the State Department to allow him into our country. For his safety. We put him in your house in Malibu. I hope that's okay."

"You might want to lock up my watch collection!" Brighton grins but doesn't explain.

"We can find him a motel if that's more suitable," suggests Baéz.

"No, I'm sure he's learned his lesson. Does he have money?"

"Tolliver is providing funds until we come up with a more permanent solution and Scottie checks in on him."

There is a long pause which neither dares break. Scottie. Brighton hasn't asked, and Baéz hasn't offered. He doesn't want to intrude. He knows so little about their relationship. On the day after the Towers fell, with all flights grounded and no way for her to return home, Brighton asked Baéz to shepherd Scottie to the safety of Connecticut. On that same day, Brighton enlisted in the Army, telling no one. A brief letter soon followed, explaining his need to serve. His words were plain but did not assuage their heartbreak. Nonnie blamed herself for sharing all those heroic tales of her father and brothers. "I should never have glorified war for the boys!"

Baéz was the only one who understood. He had received a separate letter in which Brighton said he would need to put family aside while preparing to go to war. "I need to do this well, to dedicate myself to my country and to my fellow combatants, and to do this, I must leave you all behind. Don't write. I'll be fine. And I know I'll be in your prayers. That will be enough." Also enclosed was a sizeable cashier's check to cover whatever was needed while he was away.

"Kaveh's a lucky devil! It's a beautiful house. And with Scottie just up the road, I'm sure he'll be fine."

Brighton lays back down and closes his eyes. "Read some more. You have developed a fine preacher's voice. Truly."

Baéz understands Brighton doesn't wish to talk about home or the people who live there, so he does as asked—he reads. Many hours, every day. Defoe is followed by Dodge and then Dickens, and sometime during the final passages of *Bleak House*, Lt. Frobish announces an Army transport will be taking them to Andrews Air Force Base later that evening.

"What is left for our reading pleasure, brother?"

Baéz picks up his satchel from the floor. He removes a book in a bright, colorful dust jacket. "A short American melodrama! Perfect for the flight home!"

Brighton takes the book and studies the cover with its bombastic early twentieth-century illustration. Blood-red letters scream the title: *Abel's Curse*. A muscular man with a blond beard, dressed as a minister, shakes his fist at the heavens as bolts of lightning strike the earth around him.

"What is this?"

"A bestseller from 1908! A man of the cloth torn between his love of God and his love of the flesh."

"A page-turner?"

"Hope so. Lonnie, my college roommate, has written a screenplay based on it. He wants my help filming it."

"Well, let's go, brother. Pack a bag and let's see if your roomie's story is any good!"

Baéz is wary of his brother's jaunty mood—he fears it is disguising a world of hurt that still lies hidden. He packs their few possessions and prepares himself for Brighton's reentry into present-day America.

16.

FREAKS BENEATH A CARNIVAL TENT

The Boeing C-17 is a flying hospital. Baéz helps Piet Ullner wheel the stretcher up the ramp and through the rear of the enormous cargo plane. Brighton and several other ambulatory patients are boarded first, while a dozen litters holding seriously wounded soldiers are loaded last, allowing them a swift exit when they arrive at Andrews.

The aluminum floor is heated, and the high ceiling is crisscrossed with the wires, tubes and machinery that operate the sophisticated equipment required to service up to thirty-six stretchers holding America's rarest treasure—her wounded combatants.

There are twenty-four airline seats, twelve per side. Piet and his team of nurses take these spots, monitoring the patients whose stretchers are affixed to special latch pins in the floor. The plane's cavernous cargo hold resembles an ingenious erector set, all silvery and shiny, with bolts and cleats and outlets attached to every nook and cranny.

The patients and nurses tense as the winged infirmary speeds down the runway, but once airborne, Piet unclicks his belt and roams the space, checking on his patients. Brighton leaves his stretcher, walking from litter to litter, introducing himself and seeing if the soldiers need anything. His heart aches as the predicament of his fellow combatants is placed so starkly in view.

"Buddy, over here," calls out a haggard soldier covered with bandages.

Brighton walks to him, and the young man smiles.

"Take a few of these," he says, shaking an orange bottle of pills. "I never travel without them," he jokes and removes the cap, handing Brighton several yellow ovals.

Soldiers trafficking in pills is common in the Army, but not in Brighton's unit. Getting high or encouraging a drug-infused euphoria was often a necessity to fight the fear, but Brighton didn't partake. At the bases they visited, servicemen often asked if he was "carrying," but a swift shake of the head discouraged that question being asked again. Now, with everything he has been through and all the medications that have been flushed through his body, he's curious to see if his sour mood can be improved by a simple yellow pill. He thanks the man and then finds a seat next to Baéz.

Brighton grabs the colorful paperback. "Well, brother, shall we start the story?"

"You want to read?" asks Baéz.

"Yeah, let me start. You've been doing all the work; let me pitch in!"

Brighton switches on the overhead light and begins reading, his voice echoing off the curved aluminum walls of the plane.

Abel Finley is tall; he towers over most men. His gait is strong and sure, and on this sunny morning, he follows the narrow logging trail through massive oaks and elms and shagbark hickories. The heavily trod path opens onto a vast glade, a score of grassy acres shorn of summer wheat and crushed by the footfalls and horse hooves of the temporary inhabitants who have been arriving all week. The great Harvest Crusade has drawn thousands of worshipers who are ready for three days of preaching and prayer in the wide-open wilderness of central Kentucky.

Few of the congregants have ever seen this many people. The sounds of the campground are a welcome change from the indifferent silence that echoes from these new territories. Fiddles and flutes and banjoes play as children run and scream, and young lads with full rich voices sing of temperance and glory and Christian soldiers marching onwards.

"Excuse me, Sarge, a little louder please. A few of us are eavesdropping!"

The request comes from a young man on a stretcher several rows away.

"Yeah, here too! You are tonight's 'in-flight' entertainment!" There is quiet laughter from several of the men.

Piet talks with Brighton. "I have several insomniacs who could benefit from some bedtime reading. Give me a minute to move their stretchers."

Baéz assists Piet, unclipping the litters and placing them closer together, near the center, where Brighton is seated. Several nurses also come and sit nearby.

Abel Finley is twenty-nine years of age, and, in this year of 1802, he and God converse daily. He has striking white-blond hair, worn long and tied in a tail at the back of his head. His carefully tailored clothing reveals a vanity he has been unable to vanquish. His smile projects comfort and trust. His laugh is deep and contagious.

Humming a favorite hymn, he unbuttons his trousers and makes water on a cream-colored sycamore. In his youth, he dipped his wick into every crevice, his debauchery a scandal. This was before he committed soul and spirit to his one and only Creator and before he met and married Elizabeth Beaufort. He overcame his wildness, but after seven years of wedded life, he and Elizabeth remain childless. He believes her barren womb is a judgment on his misspent youth.

Abel is a circuit rider. He teaches the Bible, speaks against strong drink, warns of the evils of slavery, and describes the deplorable conditions in prisons. He and his fellow riders are the compass and conscience of this new land.

Nearly a decade of speaking in parlors and barns and meetinghouses has taught him compassion, brought him strength, and made God's love tangible. The crowds that gather to hear him speak in this vast wilderness are far larger than those that surround the other preachers. The attraction isn't simply Abel's pleasing looks. Throngs crowd his sermons because they've been told he has the gift of healing.

A soldier smiles as he taps his buddy. "My parents warned us about these guys, the healers."
"Yup, the South was thick with 'em. Lock up your daughters, ma'am!"
Both men chuckle.

"Good morning, friends! Find a comfortable spot, settle in, and let us praise the Lord for this beautiful day. Let us be glad and rejoice."

Abel flashes his welcoming smile and waits for everyone to spread their quilts and still their children.

Brighton increases his volume when speaking in Abel's voice, imitating the gentle cadence of a country preacher.

"Yes, let us rejoice, for what a land this is! Let us rejoice in the bounty and the beauty that surrounds us. Many of you, like me, came here to begin anew. Brooklyn and Boston and Bridgeport did not satisfy; New York and New Bedford and New London were filled with transgressors and filth. And so we've come here to transform ourselves into something good, something solid. So let us praise the Lord!"

The energetic crowd calls out loud "Amens" and "Praise the lord."

Baéz watches as one young listener quietly mouths "Amen" along with Brighton. Another mumbles, "Praise him." He looks at his brother, surprised by the effect he has on these strangers.

"'Love one another,' the Master teaches us. And that love will heal you. But many false prophets are gone out into this world, and, like the serpent, they will seek to deceive you, to seduce you. Even here, surrounded by thousands of our brothers and sisters, evil will dare to tempt us. There are those who will try to sell you useless potions and sulphureous oils claiming they will alleviate your aches or grow hair on your balding head. But it is the Lord who heals, the Lord whose love will cure you and teach you the unreality of sickness."

Awed, his audience can only nod in quiet agreement. He speaks to them of the sciences beyond the physical, beyond nature; a science Aristotle named 'metaphysics.' The study of the structure of reality. Abel tells them their creator made them perfect, male and female. He gives them dominion over everything on earth. And if they align their thinking to reflect the perfection of their creator, they will never lack for anything. Not food, not health, not happiness.

"Let us stand and stretch, and sing that great hymn by Martin Luther, 'A Mighty Fortress is Our God.'"

Brighton pauses before turning the page. In that brief silence, from the center of the plane, a low voice begins singing. As it gathers strength, a few others join in.

All power is given unto our Lord,
On him we place reliance;
With truth from out his sacred word
We bid our foes defiance.
With him we shall prevail,
Whatever may assail;
He is our shield and tower,
Almighty is his power;
His kingdom is forever.

After a few quiet "Amens," Brighton continues reading.

The woman had caught Abel's eye earlier that morning. She was plain-faced with long russet hair—the color of late-autumn apples.

One soldier whistles a warning while another murmurs "Uh-Oh!" A few nurses chuckle.

Her entire brood is well behaved; they do not fidget, they do not complain. A pair of crutches lay beside one of her boys, a child of seven years, maybe eight. A perfect age, thinks Abel. An age of innocence, an innocence that is so useful in promoting healing. He points to the boy and asks, "Young man, can you join me up here?"

The boy's eyes widen in wonder as he looks towards his mother.

"And is that your brother, a twin maybe?"

Both boys nod, proud that he recognizes their kinship.

"Both of you, join me, can you? Folks, help them up. Clear a path."

One brother helps the other negotiate the uneven ground on his crutches. Abel reaches down and lifts each boy onto the platform.

"And how are you called?"

The one with the crutches answers, "Stephen, sir."

"Ah, a good name. One of our master's disciples was called by that name. He was a healer. And, brother of Stephen, what are you called?"

The boy looks down, terrified of the crowd. His mother smiles, and this calms him.

"Sanford, sir, but you can call me Sandy. Everyone does. And that's my mother, Cassandra, but she hates her name. And there are my older brothers, Joshua and Luke, and next to them are my sisters Mattie and Sarah."

He waves at his family as his shyness disappears.

The soldier nearest Piet whispers: "You know what's going to happen, don't you? He's going to heal that boy. He's going to throw those crutches into the crowd, and they are going to cheer!"

"You know this book?" Piet asks.

"These books lined my mother's shelves. It's a fine tale. Whenever I or my brother did something that disappointed her, she would upbraid us with 'I do not think Pastor Finely would approve!'"

Another soldier adds, "Yes, we were always threatened by the example of Pastor Finley."

And another: "He was a handsome devil, though. I remember growing my hair in high school so I would look like him. Him and his 'wick.' We loved that term!"

Finally, they shush one another, wanting to catch up to Brighton, who has continued reading.

"Thank you for your trust. You can rejoin your people now."

Abel shakes both boys' hands and sends them running back into the crowd. The attending flock take several seconds to register that Stephen's crutch is still lying on the stage. They stand, whooping and hollering.
"Praise Jesus, folks. Love heals."

Brighton continues reading as the story darkens and the preacher struggles with his faith while trying to diminish the loneliness that surrounded these early settlers.

A soldier lying near Brighton calls for a nurse. He points to his arm, where a bloody dressing covers a protruding bone. Brighton watches as the nurse changes the bandage and sees the bone shift into its proper position. Brighton blinks, remembering the healings he has witnessed in his grandmother's home. He looks at Baéz and realizes his brother has seen the same transformation but is not surprised.

Shortly thereafter, the lumbering C-17 touches down on US soil. The plane is silent as Piet begins unclipping the litters. He turns to the brothers.

"Thank you. I've accompanied many patients on these hospital flights. The journey can be unsettling; the men are in pain, fearful of what awaits them. But somehow you took them on a restful voyage. On their behalf, I thank you!"

Brighton keeps a tight smile in place; he understands the dread these men feel, the dread of tomorrow and of the days that follow. The effect from his yellow ovals is wearing off, but the blood in his veins is still rushing, making him dizzy. He leans on Baéz as they walk down the aluminum stairs, each unsteadied by the fear of what's to come.

17.

MOVING PICTURES

It is snowing. The large, wet flakes melt on his face and wake him. Sensing Choco nearby, Brighton stands and pulls the damp blanket close.

The dog leads the way, accustomed to his master's strange ways. The wet field is slippery, the long grass covered in ice and rime. They struggle up the hill, the elderly dog stopping to make sure his human companion is safe.

"Up we go," mutters Brighton when they reach the gravel lot where Jared parks his trucks. The seven-tonner with its two rear axles rests near the old cow shed where the crew begins and ends each day. Brighton whistles, and Choco follows as they crawl beneath the vehicle that will be their shelter for the remaining hours of darkness.

Brighton has difficulty sleeping; he roams Nonnie's many acres at all hours of the night, haunted by the visions that arrive without warning and torment him for days afterward. Choco stands guard until Rio arrives at first light, bringing Brighton a cup of coffee from the drip machine in the shed. Choco, with a pronounced limp and many gray hairs in her fourteenth year, is the only one able to offer lasting comfort. She radiates love and unquestioned affection. During the first difficult months at home, she was the only one not angered by Brighton's thoughtless behavior. He is a difficult patient. He paces Nonnie's hallways, screaming at the newsmen on the TV and cursing the President. He has the attention span of a gnat, eats like a bird, and complains about everything.

His only relief comes in the form of the little yellow ovals given to him by the injured kid on the plane. As his supply decreases, he finds an obliging provider at the VFW two towns over. He limits his intake, telling himself that the euphoria must be monitored. The intensity of the high is often excessive, and he knows to be careful.

As spring arrives, he tackles activities that tire him, allowing him to sleep. He digs new beds for the roses, removes winter's deadwood from the trees, and rebuilds crumbling stonewalls. His body aches, but the fatigue is welcomed. He can now sit through an entire meal without pacing or constantly interrupting.

At one such dinner, Baéz offers a suggestion that, like his earlier advice to play tennis left-handed, could alter the course of his brother's life.

"I'm not an actor; I wouldn't know what to do."

"Of course you do," counters Baéz. "You're a natural performer; that's why you filled tennis stadiums. The crowds love you."

"If you say so," concedes Brighton, "but to become another person, to pretend to be someone else, requires skill and training not taught at tennis camp."

"I saw you *become* Abel Finley on that plane, right in front of my eyes; I watched your fellow soldiers, rapt and spellbound by the tale you told. I also witnessed a soldier with a dislocated arm whose bones snapped into place."

Nonnie looks up with surprise. Uncomfortable, Brighton stands and leaves the room.

"Read the script," calls out Baéz. "Lonnie left a copy for you. It's good—trust me."

Over the next several days, as he and Lonnie comb the countryside seeking suitable locations for the film, Baéz keeps at Brighton, urging him to take a screen test. He claims, with a hint of jealousy, that Brighton has been starring in his own movie for so long that Center Stage is no different than Center Court. Brighton finally agrees to audition, all the while insisting he's not an actor.

A small film crew arrives from New York, and an actress who lives nearby joins them in filming several scenes. As Baéz helps Brighton slip into an old-fashioned frock coat, he advises his brother, "Just keep it simple. Abel's a charmer, and it's his confidence that makes him so attractive."

The beauty of the Bible's language assists in Brighton's transformation, the words of the preacher floating gently from his tongue. After several hours filming several scenes, Alonzo is pleased, and yells "cut" as they all return to Nonnie's house to outline a way forward.

"He and the preacher are a perfect match!" crows Baéz. "The waistcoat and those fitted breeches, along with the ribbon holding his hair in a tail, created a mesmerizing image. It's the only word for it. I believed him. I believed in his God. It was like watching him beat Sampras, he was thoroughly in control."

A start date is set, and the little town of Sterling is abuzz with the excitement of hosting a film shoot.

Tolliver Brigham knows it is Brighton's name that has secured the financing, so he negotiates a ridiculously generous profit participation for his client, fully aware that most independent films never earn a penny.

As spring turns to summer, Brighton's red beard grows fuller, hiding the distinctive scar carved by his captors that runs down the left side of his face. Lighting crews and wardrobe personnel, along with carpenters and hair stylists, begin to set up shop for their ten-week shoot.

Baéz visits the set each morning, making sure his brother has what he needs. Afterwards, he often stays on, fascinated by the process of creating a film. The attention to detail and the dedication to authenticity impresses him. He watches a team of nurserymen create a primitive vegetable garden, beautiful in its simplicity, on the sunny side of an old log barn that is being used as the Kentucky farm of the woman who has stolen Abel's heart—despite him being married.

In the first days of filming, as this large group of strangers struggles to become a family and everyone is still learning the names of their castmates and crew members, Baéz and Brighton lie on a blanket near a grove of giant hemlocks as they finish their lunch.

"She was famous in her day, right? Her books had many fans?" Brighton finishes his sandwich and throws his apple core deep into the woods.

"Yes. Her series about Eli Hammer, the Western gold miner, was a bestseller. There are eight books devoted to him. But Abel Finley sold well too. There are six in his series. Mixing religion with romance proved to be irresistible; readers couldn't get enough."

"Was he based on a real person?" asks Brighton.

"Lonnie says he's a mix of several circuit riders. They kept journals and diaries and wrote extensive letters. They were America's first historians."

Baéz collects the wrappers and bottles from their meal while Brighton opens the century-old novel to a heavily dog-eared page. He reads a portion of his rare, first-edition copy each day, seeking inspiration prior to filming his scenes. He sees a version of himself in the character, a version he prefers and admires; only occasionally does he feel he must rely on the yellow ovals to keep going. The role provides Brighton the lifeline he has needed since returning home. As he disappears behind the façade of a stranger, he finds comfort and protection. At the center of Abel's life is his faith; he is a true believer. His love for God and his devotion to two beautiful women provides an endless canvas for Brighton to explore. He embodies Abel morning, noon, and night.

A giant elm with its leafy canopy marks the way down the soft, grassy hill to her simple cabin. Here lives Joshua, Mattie, Sarah, Luke, Stephen, and Sandy. On his numerous visits to Cassandra, he stops here, releases his horse, and stares at the glorious view of this heavenly land. He feels no guilt—he is not a man cleaved in two but a servant of God doubly blessed by the love showered on him by two devoted souls.

"I have eight children, six living," Cassandra had stated when he first introduced himself. When the crowds broke up and the wagons and horses and donkeys made for home, she had waited to offer her thanks to the handsome preacher. He greeted each child, having memorized their names, and then asked where the father of such a fine flock might be.

"Wanderlust carried him and me from Pennsylvania to Kentucky, where he built us a solid home. The land was generous, our lives bountiful, but when the twins arrived, wanderlust struck again, carrying him to California."

Abel had offered to accompany them home. He rode his horse alongside their wagon, young Sarah joining him on his saddle, thrilled to receive special favor. The boys pointed out familiar landmarks, anxious to demonstrate their usefulness.

That first night, the family made the wagon their bed as he rested soundly beneath the axles. Conversations with Cassandra were easy—he simply skipped the chapter about his wife and the home they shared in Frankfurt.

Now, standing beneath the giant elm, he is content in both his homes. His delight and favor of one woman in no way diminishes his reverence and affection for the other. He tells himself his heart is sufficiently generous to meet the needs of all the dear people who love him.

Joshua takes the reins as Abel removes his saddlebags, which are packed with Bibles and Christian pamphlets as well as a much-thumbed copy of Robinson Crusoe *he plans on reading to the children. He smiles at the boy but sees he is troubled.*

"Momma needs your help, sir. She's gone all peculiar on us."

"In what way, Joshua?"

"I discovered her in the vegetable plot, past nightfall, doing strange dancing and beating her body with her fists. It was an unsettling sight, sir."

Abel sees her standing by the well, beautiful in her stillness.

"Put the horse away for me, Joshua, and then go on in the house. Let me tend to your ma."

As Joshua goes to the stables, Abel walks slowly towards Cassandra. She is trembling.

"I've brought a fine ribbon that Mrs. McClatchy asked to give you," he says. He reaches into his pocket, but she strikes him hard in the chest, her fists pummeling him.

"You promised!" she yells. "I told you I couldn't have no more. You promised not to spill. I will die with another."

He understands the dancing now. Harsh exertions encouraged miscarriages.

"A child is a blessed thing. It would be a sin to harm it. God will protect you."

"God didn't do this. We did. I cannot die and leave all my beautiful babies."

She falls to the ground, weeping. He kneels beside her, taking her calloused hands in his. She looks at him, pleading.

"Pru said if I take strenuous walks, if I run and jump, I might be able to stop this growing seed."

Prudence is the midwife. She lives on the other side of the mountain and provides the only doctoring available for miles.

"She gave me a list, things to take. Tansy, cohosh, soapwort, rue, seneca. You must get them for me."

"Cassie, you mustn't. It would be a terrible error. You won't die, I promise you!"

She shakes her head. "I'm sorry, Abel, but I don't trust your promises."

"You don't need to trust me, Cassie. But please, trust in the Lord."

Her eyes reflect her disappointment. "I thought you were different. But you're all the same, some more handsome, maybe, but in the end you're all the same. Pru will help me. Go away now, Abel. This is the cost of our pleasure."

He is startled by her words and pulls away as if slapped.

"The Lord bless you and keep you, Cassie. I will be here when our beloved child arrives!"

✳ ✳ ✳

Baéz orders a breakfast burrito from the food truck parked near the wardrobe van. Lonnie arrives with his ever-present cardboard cup of coffee.

"Do you have a minute?" he asks. Baéz nods and follows the director to an empty dressing trailer.

"Have the Army medics prescribed pain killers for Brighton?"

Baéz is confused. "None that I know of, why?"

"While screening the dailies last night, there was a scene that ended on an extreme closeup of Brighton's face. His pupils were pinpricks, and there was a slight vibration of the eyeball. Not everyone noticed, but an eye constriction is often the sign of a drug user."

Baéz's heart is racing. "I'm not aware of him taking any pain medications. Maybe the occasional Tylenol, for help in sleeping. Nothing more. But he is still suffering. I'm very aware of that. He roams my grandmother's property at night like an ill-fated creature. Still, whatever it is, I think he has it under control." He stops for a minute and then ask the question that most troubles him. "Is it getting in the way of his work?"

"No. His work has been excellent. We never have to wait for him; he's always ready, open to suggestions and direction. As I say, it is only noticeable with extreme closeups, and I can simply keep the camera back—not go in so tight."

"Do you want me to talk to him?" suggests Baéz.

"No," says Lonnie forcefully. "Leave it alone; I don't want to spook him. I don't want him to think we're watching him. Whatever it is, it's not impacting our work, so please forget I said anything."

But Baéz cannot forget. He reviews all their interactions since Germany, trying to find a clue. By the time Brighton was discharged, the doctors assured Baéz that his brother was taking only the mildest of over-the-counter painkillers; nothing that would cause eye constriction. Marijuana can cause bloodshot eyes, but not tiny pupils. Cocaine and fentanyl have that affect, but where could he have gotten those? A crew member? A fellow actor? He has no idea how to find out unless he confronts Brighton.

Her oldest son in unable to rise from bed, complaining of extreme fatigue. The boy is never sick, never misses a day in the fields, but Cassandra has heard of an outbreak of malaria in several nearby towns, towns surrounded by swamplands. Her son's head is warm, and his body is damp as she goes to the cistern to fill a pail with cool water. In the distance, she sees Abel's horse riding hard across the upper field. The challenge of caring for six children while carrying a seventh is formidable, and she is both grateful and wary of Abel's continued visits.

He carries the pail to the far corner of the pole barn where Joshua has laid his bedding roll. The boy is sweating heavily. Abel places a cool cloth on the boy's forehead while uttering words of comfort.

"He has given his angels charge over thee, lest you dash your foot against a stone.' Fear not, boy, the lord is right here with you. Listen hard and you can hear his song. Place all your trust in him, understand?"

Joshua nods as the preacher washes his face, his smile bright even in the home's darkest corner.

Brighton hears Lonnie say, "Cut!" and he relaxes, helping the young actor rise from the messy bed. As they were filming, he sensed a commotion out of his range of vision.

A tall carpenter who is on set every day is beaming and saying to everyone nearby, "I can hear you!"

A gaffer answers, "Yes, I understand."

But the carpenter responds with "No, you don't! I'm deaf in one ear, have been for more than a decade, but just now it cleared, and I can hear!"

Then the AD calls for quiet, readying for another take. Brighton and the boy playing Joshua return to their starting positions.

And yet from then on, once or twice each week, sometimes in the catering tent or the makeup trailer, and often in the deep woods, an individual finds his body slightly altered. Each person keeps silent, only sharing the event with those they trust most, not daring to "tempt fate" and have their good news reversed.

It's one of Brighton's rare days off, but he still comes to the set. Filming has consumed him, and he misses his fellow actors and crew when not working. Today, though, they are filming a difficult scene. The one where his costar, the woman playing Cassandra, dies in childbirth. He wants to be nearby, to offer support.

Brighton sits on the mossy ground and stares at the open vistas, absent any trace of modern life. He sees Lonnie climb the hill, his baseball cap worn backwards and a tired smile on his face.

"Tough scene," he says as he sits next to Brighton. "The kid was great. He's hardly fifteen; where does such understanding come from?"

"Did he sob through it all, like he did in rehearsals?" asks Brighton, his voice thick with scorn.

"Don't be such a dick. He was simple and dignified, and understands he is now responsible for the care and safety of his six siblings. The midwife hands him the motherless child as he sits in the rocker, grown into adulthood in front of our eyes. He didn't cry, but I certainly did."

Brighton has argued that his character, Abel, should have been present for Cassandra's death. He is also afraid that the young son, Joshua, is going to steal the end of the movie.

"So, did the herbs kill her or the birth?"

"I think the herbs. Some were poisonous."

"But they were thought to induce miscarriages?"

"Yes, and often they worked. Common rue is an abortifacient. The problem stems from their medical ignorance. They didn't know the proper dosage, nor which combinations were beneficial and which were lethal."

Brighton shakes his head, uncomfortable with the subject. "So tomorrow, Abel arrives home to his wife Elizabeth, Cassandra's children in tow, and he is . . . what? Contrite? A broken man? Adjusting to God's will?"

Brighton is still arguing for a more definitive ending, something heroic, something that places him back in the audience's favor.

"No, I think it is more elusive. He promised Cassandra she wouldn't die. He is blind to his own arrogance. When the Lord demanded humility, Abel found only pride. His ego dazzled him, and he ignored God's pleas that he be chaste. Now he must demonstrate contrition. He must blend these two families into one. That is his task. To save these children, to commemorate Cassandra, to value his wife."

"Is it enough for the audience?"

"If we do it right, yes, I think so. The final image should convey that a sense of grace has settled on this family."

Lonnie closes his eyes and describes what he sees. "You slowly pull into your hometown. The folks there know you, of course. They love you. There are greetings from your neighbors, and surprised looks as they see the children seated in the wooden wagon. For the kids, it's a dark adventure. They are devastated by their mother's death, but your presence in their lives has enriched them. You take the baby from Joshua as the other children slowly file out of the wagon. You stare at your home as a curtain gently sways. Someone is there. The front door opens, and your wife, Elizabeth, stands tall in the doorway. You look at each other, and then she walks to the children, holding out her hand in welcome, smiling, and saying, 'Hello, I am Elizabeth.' She accepts the situation. She forgives. Unlike Cassandra, she does not confuse her husband with God."

"But won't we hate him? I've always imagined a scene at Cassandra's grave and he's talking to her, promising to care for her kids, admitting his mistakes and begging forgiveness. Then he can go and greet Elizabeth as a new man."

"We can't do all the work for the audience. Let them discover the answers. We never explain the healings, yet I think the audience will accept them as true. He doesn't have a special gift, but he possesses a rare *understanding* gleaned from the Bible; an understanding of what he calls the divine laws of the universe. And often, when he applies them, healings do occur."

Brighton remains unconvinced. Both sit, unhappy with the other.

"Trust me, Bright. This will work. Your features are transparent. Whatever Abel understands, the audience will believe. It is written on your face. And remember, this is a love story. Nothing more."

Brighton stands, brushing the grass from his jeans. Like all actors, he must now look deep inside his character's mind and determine how to illuminate the events that are about to unfold. *How does Abel greet his wife?*

He turns to Lonnie and asks, "What is he thinking the moment he sees her?"

Lonnie doesn't hesitate. "I think he is pleased to recall how truly lovely she is. Nothing more. Keep it simple."

Brighton nods. *Keep it simple.* This is everyone's advice nowadays, yet the subject of childbirth hits too close to home for him to keep simple. The plot of their movie may be fiction, but Wynn's lies about Rebecca wishing to abort her first child have stayed with him all these years.

Why would a father lie to his children? Why would he fill their heads with such ugly tales? *Keep it simple,* he tells himself.

✶ ✶ ✶

Robert Browning is interning at *The Sacramento Bee* while studying for his master's degree at USC's Annenberg School for Communication. A devoted tennis fan, he was devastated when his favorite player joined the Army. Now, as he stares at a press release for a new film titled *The Circuit Rider,* he is mystified by a report that Brighton Bethune will play the lead in the nineteenth-century love story.

Wanting to understand this peculiar choice, Browning reads the book upon which the film is based and is the only reporter to connect the book's story about a faith healer to Nonnie's occupation as a metaphysical healer and Baéz's television appearances documenting his history of healing. The "sexiest brothers alive" are being recast as "freaks beneath a carnival tent."

He calls the film's production office and speaks with Baéz, who politely dodges his many questions. Two days later, he calls again, but the girl in the office explains that Mr. Honor has no further information for him.

"And what is your name?" he asks.

"Juliet."

"Of course it is. I should have guessed. You sound like a Juliet, emanating from a long line of remarkable women. Juliet of the spirits, Juliet and her Romeo. Well, my name is Robert Browning."

"I know." She giggles. "You've called before."

"Good, I like a girl who pays attention. You run the office? Is it fun?"

"Yes."

Her voice and vocabulary sound youthful. *Perhaps a local girl on a summer job,* he thinks.

"What are the brothers like? Are they nice to you?"

"They are. Nice. Very nice."

"You live there, do you?"

"Yes. Back from college for the summer. Everyone at school will be so jealous when I tell them. Best summer job ever!"

"'*Wake Me Up when September Ends,*' eh?"

Every girl's dream of romance is wrapped up in that summer song. Green Day and their chubby-faced lead singer. Does she understand his reference? Might she lower her guard?

"Oh yes! Don't you love it? And the music video? Jamie Bell!"

"Yes. He's terrific. '*I just want this to last forever!*' Right?"

He can hear her sigh. Maybe she'll release a few secrets.

"What are some memorable moments you've had working on the production?" he asks.

"The scar can be jarring in person. The beard covers most of it but not all. That surprised me."

"And is it red, like his hair?"

"Yes, red and blond, very full, very sexy," she says, giggling.

"He plays a preacher, right?"

"Don't act like I'm stupid. I heard Mr. Honor confirm that to you."

She is trying to act grown up.

"Yes, true, but the press release only mentions that he's a preacher from the early nineteenth century. In the book, he is also a healer. Is Mr. Bethune's character a healer?"

"The script is embargoed. People are only given the pages relevant to their job."

"Oh now, Juliet, do you expect me to believe that a clever girl like you didn't figure out a way to read the entire script?"

"Mr. Browning, you'll get me in trouble!"

"Please call me Robert. Or Robbie, if you prefer."

He chuckles to himself, having never been called Robbie in his entire life.

"Well, Robbie, tell me why *The Sacramento Bee* is so interested in our little movie?"

"Mr. Brighton Bethune is a national treasure, and whatever he decides to do with his life is of interest to our readers. Don't you think he's an interesting man?"

"That's why I took this job," she proudly answers.

People adore Brighton. In researching this story, the tone of people's voices literally changes when they speak of him.

"And Mrs. Otis swears he can heal," she says. "Happened on the set, numerous times. That's what she says."

Browning spills his coffee over the plate of bagels.

"Does Mrs. Otis live there in Sterling?" he asks, steadying his voice and trying to remain calm.

"All her life. I used to babysit her kids. Monsters. All of them. But she's sweet. Runs the bakery in the old part of town."

"And did you believe her?"

"She's not a tale teller. She says Brighton Bethune healed more than a dozen people this past Saturday when they filmed the huge crusade scene, and I believe her!"

Holy shit! he thinks, thrilled by the insane path his story is suddenly taking.

✳ ✳ ✳

Scenes in movies are shot out of order, the filming schedule determined by the logistics of weather, the accessibility of locations, and the availability of actors. For the cast and crew of *The Circuit Rider*, there is a pleasing coincidence in shooting the closing scene on the film's final day.

Brighton has a dressing space in a house nearby. He is nervous, so Baéz sits with him and listens to his brother's endless fears about the film's ending. He is driving the costume designer crazy, rejecting one outfit after another. First, he thought he should be wearing a morning coat, then simple overalls, then his minister's garb. He is struggling to figure out how Abel would meet this day, how he would handle introducing these seven children to his childless wife.

"Shave the beard," suggests Baéz, having reached his limit of patience. "You greet her as the man she met years earlier—smooth-faced and hopeful, filled with the energy of youth. Your pink scar, which the beard has hidden, will shock the contemporary audience."

Brighton's fidgeting stops. "That is perfect. Thank you! See if you can find the makeup people; it will take a while to remove this beard. Tell Lonzo to work with my stand-in; I'll get there as soon as I can. And don't tell anyone about the beard. The surprise may help the scene."

Lonnie and the cast rehearse as the sun is setting. He begs Baéz to rush his brother. "We are losing the light!" he is screaming when Brighton finally arrives.

The crew is stunned by the transformation. The blond beard with the bright red highlights is gone; the pale white skin underneath is smooth as a baby's apart from the red slash that runs from the corner of his right eye down to his chin. Brighton looks younger and supremely vulnerable, a hairless newborn. The set is silent—even the children are subdued by the scar.

After Lonnie screams, "Action!", Abel Finley steps down from the wagon and takes the newborn from Joshua, with Cassandra's many children following him up the path to his front door. A curtain rustles, and then the solid door opens. Elizabeth steps into the frame as Abel blinks away a tear. In the soft light of dusk, thousands of lightning bugs fill the humid air.

The actress playing his wife is so unprepared for Brighton's changed appearance that she freezes in the doorframe. The young actor playing Joshua senses something is amiss, so he simply steps forward, shakes her hand, and says, "I am called Joshua, ma'am, and these are my brothers and sisters."

She looks at Abel, and a small smile dares to find his face.

In subsequent takes, they shoot the ending as written, but when the film premieres in January at the Sundance Film Festival, it is the version with Joshua stepping forward that ends the movie.

✷ ✷ ✷

"**I** run a successful business—a brand recognized by many—and this allows me entrée into many different worlds. When I need something, I simply reach for the phone. When I want something to be done, it is done. When my wife became ill, I felt not only helpless but also useless. If I couldn't find the right doctor, the right treatment, the right hospital to rid her of this ailment, what good was I?"

The tall man with the thick head of curly hair stops pacing to look at Baéz and then Brighton. "And then, unexpectedly, on a summer afternoon, she is restored to health. Mercifully and mysteriously. By you!"

Mr. Parsons doesn't suffer fools gladly, nor is he intimidated by wealth or fame, but as he stands in front of Brighton, his hands are visibly shaking.

His family has owned property on the lake for generations. He is married to an attractive older woman, a sports and fitness fanatic. They have three young children. He is the fifth person in as many days to contact Brighton or Baéz to express gratitude for a sudden and dramatic recovery from a long-standing affliction.

Brighton isn't comfortable in these situations. He lacks the answers these people seek.

Meanwhile, Baéz attempts to explain the inexplicable. "Often, in an atmosphere of love, health can be regenerated. On that day of filming, your wife was not alone. Other folks also reported a positive change in their health."

A practical man, Mr. Parsons simply wants to know how his wife came to be well. His initial joy is now tempered by his inability to understand the cause of her wellness.

"But isn't your grandmother a healer? Mightn't this run in the family?"

"Nonnie doesn't call herself a healer. God, the Divine Mind, is the healer. She views her patients as perfect and then helps them understand why. God made your wife well because she has always been well. Conceivably the environment created by the film assisted your wife and others to throw off long-held beliefs about themselves."

Brighton stands. "I need some air." He shakes hands with Mr. Parson. "It was good to see you, and I am pleased to hear the news about your wife."

He leaves the room through a set of French doors that opens out onto the wide wooden porch. Baéz watches his brother, thinking how unfair it is for him to suffer from the wellness he has inspired in others. Filming ended a month ago, but already he sees Brighton struggling for something to hold on to. The only bright spot in his brother's world is the nomination of John Kerry to run against George Bush. Kerry is a patriot and, as a young soldier, testified before the US Senate about the horrors he witnessed in Vietnam, castigating the country's leaders for allowing that war to continue. His words are a beacon for Brighton, giving him permission to criticize his country for their latest war.

✳ ✳ ✳

Brock's Sports Bar is an odd place to hold a political fundraiser, especially since the candidate prefers lacrosse over football, but the room is packed with nearly two hundred Democratic high rollers. The pharmaceutical giant Afidcorp is based in Connecticut and the company's chairman organized a $5,000-per-person cocktail party, leaning on other local industry leaders to assure themselves a seat at the table should Kerry unseat Bush. Executives from ESPN, Sikorsky, and Travelers Insurance fill the room.

Connecticut is an easy win for Kerry, but the coffers of the Democratic Party need constant replenishing, so he is scheduled for a twenty-minute appearance before continuing on to New York for a larger and more important fundraiser. Most of his team had intended to skip the Stamford event, but their plans changed when they learned of an unexpected endorsement that might add some much-needed energy to their campaign.

The large-screen TVs are turned off, the overhead lights go dark, and a portable spotlight is aimed at the microphone on the dais. The crowd quiets as a young, bearded soldier in full military regalia steps onto the platform. His silver star, his purple heart, and his Ranger tag can be seen by all.

The thick red beard throws them at first, but slowly the crowd recognizes Brighton Bethune. A huge cheer follows, with whistling and clapping and stomping of feet. They won't stop, the room literally vibrating for five full minutes. Brighton raises his hands, his wide and welcoming smile breaking their hearts.

"A cold beer at the corner bar on a Sunday afternoon! Feels good, I must say. My brothers and sisters in Iraq dream of this scene. The game on TV, the Sunday comics on the kitchen table, a few hours of bliss before the work week begins."

People are smiling, their heads nodding. Kerry's people are elated.

"Soldiers dream of home. They dream of seeing their kids, their wives. They dream of playing ball. They dream of diving back into the routines that their service has helped protect. I am home, but I don't recognize it. I am safe, but I am scared by where we are heading. My wounds are healing day by day, but the wounds of America fester and chafe by the hour.

"I am a soldier, and I go where my commander in chief sends me. I trust what he says is true, and I pray that he and his team possess the intelligence to know what has to be done. And then I will do it, even if it costs my life. I trust my fellow citizens will do the same. But this is not a country at war. The American citizen and the American soldier live in separate worlds, each ignorant of the other. And that is because we are being led by men who are clueless. And I want them gone! I want a leader who can rekindle the promise that is America. And that man is John Kerry!"

A cheer rises, and Brighton takes a breath. He raises his arms, the black glove that hides his disfigured hand plainly visible. The crowd quiets.

"We assume the greatness that is America will continue. We assume the prosperity we enjoy will continue. We assume our power and leadership will always be respected. Well, that isn't true. Nations rise, but nations also fall. And I promise you, our riches will desert us if not honestly earned. We are a nation divided, a nation filled with bickering, with self-interest and an inability to listen. We don't trust our leaders and we don't respect our institutions. We don't even trust each other. This road leads to chaos. So, let's get on a new road. One that leads up."

The crowd begins cheering again.

"One that inspires. A new leader to forge a new way forward." Brighton is now screaming to be heard above the clamor of banging feet and clapping hands. "It gives me great pleasure to present to you the next president of our great nation, John Kerry."

Kerry comes out, salutes Brighton, and then takes the dais. The cheering continues as Brighton retreats to the back of the bar.

"Hey, Connecticut, how proud you should be of this fine young man. Thank you, Corporal Bethune. Thank you."

Brighton smiles, waves, and then leaves through a side door. He breathes a sigh of relief as he enters the waiting limo. It is a beautiful Sunday evening, and he is glad to be home.

As the car makes a U-turn onto the Post Road, Brighton sees Nicola Tibor talking with one of the parking attendants. Brocks had once been part of Nico's collection of sports bars.

What are the odds? he thinks. He doesn't ask the driver to stop, not even when Nico raises a hand in a friendly wave.

The noise level is unbearable, and Dušan must find an exit. He sees Nico enter from the parking lot, crushing his cigarette on the floor.

"Did you know?" he asks.

"I had no idea. He looks well, don't you think?"

After their lives were upended by Brighton's victory at The Open, they had wanted to harm him, to seek revenge. Nico was forced to sell his bars, his parking lots, his protein powders. Now his imaginative skills are aligned with the corporation that sponsored tonight's fundraiser. Afidcorp. Weight loss bars or diabetes medication, they are all the same to Nico. Something to pitch to a gullible public.

But his "Boy-O" has done all right. He came through. Nico's face and smile cannot fully express his joy. His pride.

18.

METAPHYSICS

Baéz's life is being absorbed by Brighton. No decision, large or small, is reached without measuring its impact on Brighton. Shall we have lamb tonight? Should we seed the Bleckner property? Do the roses need spraying? Baéz is embarrassed to be so exasperated by such tiny annoyances, yet they are real.

Nonnie is the one who contacted the Kerry campaign and arranged for Brighton's endorsement. That was a good day. No one traveled with him. No one wrote his speech. But endorsing politicians is not an occupation. They are trying to help Brighton find an activity that provides a level of engagement that satisfies him. Alonzo advises patience, assuring them that *The Circuit Rider* will make Brighton a star and provide many new opportunities, but Nonnie fears, like Baéz, that acting is a frivolous endeavor and will only lead to disappointment.

Baéz is seated on the dock that fronts his rustic, handcrafted home. He is finishing a bowl of cereal and a mug of coffee as Brighton arrives and sits, his face wrinkled from sleep but wearing a pleasing smile.

Baéz points to his mug. "Want some java?"

Brighton shakes his head. "Rio makes a mean brew from the Mr. Coffee machine. It is a pleasure to begin the day with him."

He sounds good. Baéz has become a careful listener.

"Some of the crew and I are putting in a grove of river birches, down where the Mulcahey estate meets the golf course," Baéz says. "Know where I mean?"

"Yup. That'll be great. Care for some company?"

"Absolutely. The guys will be thrilled. And we could use your eye."

A raft of ducks paddles across the lake as Baéz tries to act normal. Brighton interrupts the silence.

"You know, Nonnie's been sharing a number of stories about your dad when he used to sit right where we are now and wait for our mom to finish her morning swim. 'He was smitten,' Nonnie says. Good word, no? 'Smitten?'"

Baéz laughs. He likes envisioning his father as a teenager. "Is this our word for the day?"

As kids they used to flip through Nonnie's huge dictionary. The print was so tiny the book came with a magnifying glass. They would find a word they didn't know and challenge themselves to use it in conversation.

"I think so," answers Brighton.

"Okay, 'smitten' it is. Promise you won't embarrass me in front of my crew by admitting how smitten you are with me?"

"I promise. But simply hearing you say it . . . it's such a good word. Why isn't it part of our normal, everyday vocabulary?"

"Don't know. Girls can be smitten. Young men, like my father as a teen, can be smitten. But I think you and I are past the age. I think it's a youthful activity."

"We've outgrown the ability to be smitten?"

Baéz laughs, pleased by his brother's good mood. "Maybe not. Not you, at least. You have an excellent relationship with words. You apply them with conviction and gusto. The Kerry people sent Nonnie and me a video of your appearance down at Brock's. I was impressed. Perhaps you are smitten with language?"

Brighton smiles, his eyes gleaming. His gaze is inviting, but Baéz can't decipher its cause. Is his brother stoned?

"Nonnie suggested I write. She told me to set down what's going on in my head. To face it, release it, and set it free."

Baéz nods, wanting to be supportive. "Maybe write about the guys who served with you. Or your decision to enlist. I've fielded many calls asking for anything from you. A photo essay, a short story, an interview on *60 Minutes.*"

"I don't think so. Words can fail you on the spot. I need to sit quietly, hear the words in my head, and then arrange them on paper. That's what I'd like to try."

He says this with enthusiasm. Baéz thinks he should let the idea percolate. He will bring it up again at dinner.

"Good. We can figure that out."

"You know, I think I may stay behind today. Take the kayak out later. That okay with you?"

"Brighton, that's fine. The paddles are behind the lawn mowers."

"Got it. See ya later." And with that, Brighton runs up the hill to Nonnie's house.

Baéz shakes his head, frustrated. His brother is unable to focus or follow through on the many projects that claim his interest, and Baéz doesn't know how to help. He finishes his coffee and stares at the cordless phone on the table. He's been looking for an excuse to call Tolliver. He dials the number from memory.

"Ollie? Ezzie here. Got a minute?"

They had enjoyed their time together. They were polar opposites, either blending perfectly or fervently clashing, but they never tired of one another. They possessed a rare understanding of who the other was, and this knowledge set them apart from their friends. But an odd discomfort had arisen, and they never committed to understanding it or solving it.

"Of course I do," Ollie says. "Nice to hear from you. How is the world out there?"

Hearing the warm baritone again erases all hesitation and puts a smile on Baéz's face. Tolliver always teased him about the rarefied air in Sterling, saying it was not reflective of the real universe. He visited several times and loved Baéz's compact home on the lake, but he is a city boy now, needing the constant stimulation that only a thriving metropolis can provide.

"My world, as you call it, is fine and spinning around the sun same as yours."

"Any upcoming trips to the city? It would be nice to see you."

"Well, yes. We're nearly out of flax and sugar, and—"

"Oh, come on," Ollie interrupts, laughing. "I never implied you were hayseeds!"

"Fair enough. But no trips planned at present."

Baéz wonders if he should re-open that door, but then Ollie changes the subject.

"Is Kaveh Havari still in the Malibu house? Is there anything I need to follow up on?"

"No, he's fine, still at the house but not for much longer. Brighton's going out to do finishing work on the film. He's looking forward to it. And Scottie will be around, although I don't know what that means anymore."

"She's smart. She'll be a good support."

"I hope so."

They sound like family members discussing a troubled relative.

"Offers keep coming in here," Ollie says. "I assume the answer is still no?"

"Actually, that's why I called. There's an avenue that interests him. He wants to write something. A magazine piece. *Vanity Fair* maybe, or *Sports Illustrated*."

"Both have big circulation numbers, and pay well, but let me suggest *The New York Times Magazine*. Smaller numbers but greater impact."

"But not everyone lives in New York . . . which I know may be news to you," teases Baéz.

"Well, everyone who's interesting does," laughs Ollie, before continuing. "No, seriously, it will be seen and read by the folks you want. It will dominate the conversation. I can promise you. *Vanity Fair* will pay more, but he'll be sandwiched between Daniel Radcliffe and Celine Dion."

"Okay, I get that. I'll talk to him. Can you explore on your end? The level of interest, a possible timeline?"

"Got it. I'll get back. And please—promise to visit. I mean that. Come into the city. I've redone the back garden. I embraced all your suggestions. You'll like it."

Baéz closes his eyes. A garden surrounded by the city. A refuge. He had enjoyed summer nights in Tolliver's garden. He had enjoyed Tolliver.

Tolliver speaks again. "*Blessed shalt thou be in the city, and blessed shalt thou be in the field!* It's okay that we like living in different places, you know."

Baéz is pleasantly puzzled by this biblical reference. Tolliver Brigham is a complete agnostic and has never read a word of scripture, but before he can question Ollie, the lawyer explains. "Your Nonnie gave me the quote. She asked why I didn't come around anymore. I told her you and I like different things, and she gave me that line. I memorized it, waiting for you to call!"

Baéz's pleasure blooms into a huge smile.

✶ ✶ ✶

It has become Scottie's habit on Sunday mornings, if the tide is out, to walk a mile north on Flores Beach and check on the house and its inhabitant. Her "charge," as she has come to think of him, welcomes her visits. Adjusting to life in America has been challenging for Kaveh, and although the students at the university are a trusted source of information, he prefers saving his many questions for her.

As she waits for the tide to turn, she heats up two buttery croissants and, with cappuccino in hand, goes outside and sits at a salt-encrusted table where a thoughtful staff member has placed the thick bundle of Sunday papers. She gazes at the headlines and separates out the sections she wants to read first. *Times Magazine* shows two smiling teenagers on a tennis court holding a shiny silver trophy. Brighton and Baéz. Aged fifteen and sixteen. She studies the faded polaroid, probably taken by Jared, and then turns to the article. She isn't sure she wants to read it. She has worked hard to diminish Brighton's importance in her life, yet she misses him.

THE HEROES IN MY LIFE
By Brighton Esmund Bethune

On Christmas Day, when I was eleven and he was twelve, my half-brother fell through the ice behind his home in snowbound Connecticut. Through actions that I know were divinely guided, I was able to find him under the ice and restore him to safety. The local media ate it up, and I heard the word "hero" applied to me for the first time. It felt nice. For months, people on the streets of that small town smiled upon me.

More than a decade later, I beat tennis icon Pete Sampras to win the US Open. Journalists described my "heroic journey" to the top of the tennis world. This also felt nice.

On another Christmas, at the age of twenty-five, an enemy of our country broadcast to the world a video in which I was badly beaten after refusing to condemn the activities of the Army in which I was privileged to serve. From my hospital bed, I once again heard the word "hero" over the phone from the lips of this country's president as he thanked me for my service.

Classically, a hero is the son of a god, in mortal form, who possesses some extraordinary gift. More recently, we use the word to describe someone who performs a remarkable act of bravery, displaying rare courage. But in literature, a hero is simply a character around whom a plot or story is structured. Nothing more.

That is a definition with which I am comfortable. At several memorable moments in my life, I have stood in the center of a classic story filled with remarkable people. These people are the courageous ones. They are the true heroes in my life.

The article is illustrated with numerous photos of Brighton and Baéz—as teenagers at tennis camp; with Choco chasing a frisbee; with Jared sitting atop a large riding mower. There are also photos of Kaveh and Brighton smiling in front of a German museum, both caught at their peak of handsomeness. Sharply contrasting with the youthful energy of all these pictures is a devastating black-and-white photo of Brighton and Pvt. Raven Jameson—hollow-eyed and dirty—staring blankly at a medic attempting to resuscitate a fallen comrade.

My grandmother, who lost her father and brothers in World War Two, often explained to me that darkness is simply the absence of light, and this absence, this darkness, has no substance of its own. I focus on this fact when overwhelmed by ugliness. After the attacks on New York City, I found clarity and purpose by joining the Army as others in my family had done generations before. My uncles and great granddad were heroes to me, remembered in stories Nonnie lovingly told my brother and me again and again.

I am only twenty-five, but I am exhausted. These heroes of mine—Kaveh Yavari, Baéz and Jared Honor, and Pvt. Raven Jameson—provide the love that allows me to smile, and Nonnie Esmund the guidance to move assuredly forward. Look around yourself, find your heroes, let them sustain you.

Down the beach, Kaveh flips through the article, staring at the old photographs. In one, his face is still smooth and perfect, and he must turn away, gazing instead at the sparkling ocean. The waves are crashing against an enormous boulder that is home to a variety of seals, and farther out, a handful of surfers are bobbing on their boards. *Be grateful for this new life,* he constantly tells himself, but there is much he misses from his devastated homeland.

At Brighton's request, Pepperdine has hired Kaveh as an assistant coach. In the short time he has spent in Brighton's splashy home, he has adopted all things Californian. He jogs daily on the beach, he practices yoga on the sand, and he always turns the car radio up when the Black-Eyed Peas or Snoop Dogg are playing. He attends the King Fahad Mosque in Culver City and has begun to find new friendships. He still has difficulty wearing shorts, but he does feel safe, and he is grateful.

On this perfect morning, Kaveh opens the paper that Scottie insists he read each day and turns to the lengthy essay. He starts with the story about Raven.

"I'm in Yemen again. They got cooties in Djibouti. Oh brother, oh sister, O-man. Can't wait to play straight in Koo-wait."

I love the sound of his voice. He is from Kentucky and is trying to learn the names of the countries surrounding us by turning the names into songs. Tall, skinny, with paper-white skin and jet-black hair, his striking face is topped by thick eyeglasses. Private Raven Jameson left school in the ninth grade to train thoroughbred horses. He plays the banjo, guitar, fiddle, and a mean harmonica. He is easygoing and easy to like. And he can shoot a bull's eye from five hundred meters. He is our sharpshooter. A sniper who wears glasses.

We are in Northern Iraq, charting the Kurdish territory. The war has not yet begun, and our presence is top-secret

"This land is biblical, Brother Bright."

That's what he calls me. He has a nickname for everyone.

Raised by snake handlers, evangelists, and necromancers, Raven is the best thing we have for entertainment. A storyteller to match Twain and Tolstoy, though he has heard of neither.

"Never thought I'd live to see a people poorer than mine. We are back with Jehoshaphat, Brother, fighting the Syrians. Look at this place. Mud huts, outdoor cook fires . . ."

"Yeah, and Kalashnikovs aplenty. Don't underestimate them. This is their land. We are the interlopers."

"Yes, we are the flaming chariots, bringing freedom to those unfamiliar with the word. This is going to be one fucked-up incursion, and I don't like the odds playing Goliath."

We are in the hills south of Erbil, camping in rocky warrens and wondering when D-Day will arrive.

"Your job, Brother Bright, is to come out of this alive. Don't try to understand it; you'll go mad trying. Do what the man says, protect your pecker, and return home for our free college tuition. No heroics, please!"

The engineers arrive, the construction crews, the experts on electricity and water supply. Bases are built, and thousands of troops arrive to inhabit them. We stay on the road, sleep in our trucks, and sneak from village to village. We are assassins for hire.

"Do you think we're going to hell for this?" he asks one day.

"You and me?"

"Yes. You and me. We kill people. We don't know them. In our scopes we see them fall, clutching their chests."

"Well, they are the bad guys, Raven. If they had seen us first, we'd be dead."
But truth be told, regardless of my explanations, we both had trouble with the killing.

Robert Browning puts down the magazine, realizing with some discomfort that his continued research is a form of stalking, but he can't let go. He is fascinated. And a little in love.

He called Mrs. Otis as Juliet suggested. And Mrs. Otis led him to Mrs. Revson. And Mrs. Revson to Trip Murray. And Trip to Santiago. Nine people had been healed of a litany of ailments when the character that Brighton portrayed, Abel Finley, was preaching. They described the clarity of his voice, the sureness of his message, the wholeness and confidence with which he shouted down any discord or disease. And as they listened, they were cured. A bone moved, a lump dissolved, a blemish fell off, a heart pumped more efficiently. There was no bright light, and no hovering angels, simply an alteration to their body.

He doesn't know what to do with this information. He doesn't know what to think of the stories they tell him. They seem like sane people who are as mystified as he. They whisper to him, needing to share their tale, but they also fear a reversal of their condition if they speak publicly.

Is he wrong in wanting to bring their surprising stories to the world?

19.

SURFING

Nonnie and her family walk from the trendy Park City restaurant on Main Street to the quaint movie house where *The Circuit Rider* will have its world premiere at the Sundance Film Festival. In the bracing cold, flurries float gently around their heads. Attractive people, decked out in expensive scarves and hats and overlaid with colorful parkas and trendy boots, are rushing to the screening. The entrance to the Eccles Theatre is crowded, but a volunteer recognizes Brighton and leads them past the ropes.

The smell of fresh popcorn reminds everyone that this is simply a movie. Nonnie thanks an usher for his help while Baéz clings to Tolliver and Jared steers Brighton past a group of well-wishers. They all sit as the lights go down.

The audience remains in the dark for several moments before the sound of a mournful oboe emerges through the Dolby speakers, followed by serene chanting. Images of a lush green forest slowly materialize along with birdsong and the plaintive cries of soaring hawks. The luxurious forest dissolves into a pasture of violet grasses where scores of mustangs are feeding. Nearby, the surface of a quiet river is obscured by a siege of herons floating on it. Brass instruments join the choir, and the music became circular, the melody softly syncopated while the images begin changing more swiftly and the score becomes more urgent.

The audience is transported to an America they do not recognize, an America of rare and improbable abundance. Primitive landscapes fill the screen as the score segues into a familiar hymn, a chorale resembling evensong. The sound is exotic, congruous, resonating pleasingly within the ear. The visuals are breathtaking and odd, mesmerizing in an unfamiliar way.

As the opening credits slowly fade in and out, the scene shifts to a pathway leading through a bucolic wood. Here, the tall grasses are crushed flat, an ax rests on a tree stump, and the rut of a wagon wheel is filled with rainwater. A banjo plays in the distance and then human voices are heard. The camera lens settles on the bearded face of a memorable young man dressed in ministerial garb. He is addressing a large and attentive crowd.

Baéz is shaking and convinced that Tolliver can hear his beating heart. He becomes lightheaded and fears he may faint. To anchor himself, he reaches impulsively, heedlessly for Ollie's hand. He senses a smile in the dark as the hand squeezes back. He looks for Nonnie. The light from the screen illuminates her smile. He knew she would be seduced by the plain tale of a devoted preacher. He sees Brighton, lit by the image of his own self. He is slumped in his seat next to Jared, wearing a grimace Baéz cannot decipher.

The theater is quiet, the audience rapt. Baéz knows the script backwards and forwards, but he is stunned by what he sees. He finds it heartbreaking to watch his brother be so joyful, so imbued with delight and wonder, and realize he is simply acting. His scenes with the children are especially unnerving, displaying qualities that Baéz has neither detected nor observed in his brother.

While the story unfolds, he senses the audience's trepidation as the seductively arrogant preacher, blind to the troubles he has created, is unable to see the tragedy that is sure to follow. As Lonnie predicted many months before, when Joshua takes the baby from the midwife, realizing his mother has died giving birth, the theater is filled with audible weeping.

In the final scene, Abel Finley arrives home, driving the buckboard that carries Cassandra's six children and her baby. The camera reveals the thriving town from high overhead and then slowly zooms in to the wagon, focusing on the faces of the sweet children before finally finding Abel with a close-up of his striking but troubled features. His freshly shaved face, bearing the harsh scar not of Abel Finley, but the scar of Brighton Bethune, shocks the audience and an audible gasp can be heard throughout the theater.

The sobbing doesn't stop until the closing credits have ended.

The premiere party is a boozy brawl. The lobby of the wood-beamed ski lodge can barely contain the crowd. Film executives in down vests and publicists in fur boots fight for a chance to congratulate Brighton while smooth-faced young men in colorful Missoni sweaters hand him their business cards. People are pushing, and drinks are spilling, and the nervous staff begin turning guests away—there is no more room.

Phones ring with the news that Fox Searchlight has won the hotly contested bidding war, and cheering is heard, and arms are raised, and a few crazy people attempt to dance to the loud music. If films were judged by the parties that celebrate them, *The Circuit Rider* is a hit.

"I can't do this for long, brother. This is insane." Brighton speaks softly. He is having trouble breathing. A few large men run interference between the crowd and Brighton, but the circles of people around him are tightening and a few more bouncers quietly began to keep an eye out for his safety.

A scream is heard. One of the guards tries to locate the source. Then a second scream.

"I must see him! Let me in!"

The young woman forces her way through the group surrounding Brighton. She is small but determined. The music stops and the crowd stares.

"Heal me, please! I know you can. Let me touch you, and I will be well! Bless me!" She shouts these words aloud, and many folks wonder if this is a publicity stunt. "I love you! Thank you!"

She doesn't look crazy; she looks happy. Brighton sees the crowd staring at him, waiting for his reaction. He simply nods and then smiles.

"Get me out of here," he tells Baéz. "This is madness. It's only a movie."

A Sundance volunteer brings over two security guards.

"Follow me, sir," says the tall one wearing a holster and gun. "We'll have you out of here in no time."

The large men create a path, and the brothers follow until they find themselves outside, in a back alley, as snow gently falls.

Brighton doubles over, his hands on his knees, fighting for breath.

"I can't do this! I'm not some shaman. I'm just an actor!"

Baéz shushes him as a few passersby make note of his presence.

"Do you know what happened today?" Brighton asks. "While we ate a ridiculously expensive dinner and a crowd applauded a piece of fictional entertainment, thirty-one Americans were killed in Iraq! Thirty-one! Largest number since the fighting began. You should have seen the news. The country's gone crazy, demonstrations everywhere, but we elected him. Twice!"

Baéz nods to the guard, who gently takes Brighton by the arm and leads him to a waiting SUV.

He implores his brother. "Please get me home."

He hates being so weak, but the crowds have unnerved him, and he is shamed by the memory of his fallen brothers. He is collapsing, and only Baéz has the strength he needs.

✳ ✳ ✳

The odor in the hallway reminds Nonnie of burning leaves in autumn with her brothers. A sweet and pleasant smell. When questioned, Baéz explains, "Marijuana. It calms him." They need a replacement for the little yellow pills. The euphoric highs had become shorter while his dependance grew stronger. Marijuana has become his drug of choice in appeasing the dissenting voices that scream in his head. Just a few joints, laced throughout the day, allow him to function and keep the wolves at bay.

Nonnie had been unaware of the demons that torment her grandson. She is discovering many new and disturbing facts about Brighton and is upset that the boys have been less than honest with her.

Downstairs, she watches the news on the tiny TV she keeps on the kitchen counter as she prepares her morning toast and herbal tea. The black-and-white picture shows two teenagers throwing a pair of crutches into the air.

"I can walk! I can walk!" screams the girl, laughing. Her boyfriend holds her, also laughing as they exit a movie theater, ignoring the disapproving glares of the patrons waiting in line.

"This was the scene yesterday at Chicago's Logan Theater. A pair of moviegoers mocking the reports of audience members being healed while attending the recent release of *The Circuit Rider*. It may be a controversial story, and one that defies reasonable explanation, but the film's distributer, Fox Searchlight, is taking it all the way to the bank. The film continues to sell out in this, its fifth week of release. Tomorrow, the film expands from ninety-two arthouses to eight hundred commercial theaters. Fox is hoping to duplicate the success of last year's *The Passion of the Christ.*"

Nonnie turns off the television, taking her tea onto the wraparound porch and sitting in a chair that overlooks the lake. Baéz is mowing the huge field that serves as the parking lot for his Meetinghouse.

"Good grief, everyone so busy, and so early in the day!" announces Brighton as he lets the screen door slam and sits beside Nonnie with his cup of Turkish coffee.

"You would think, surrounded as I am by so many capable men, that someone would fix that door!"

He smiles. "You would think so, wouldn't you?"

An old joke. The door has slammed since they were kids.

Nonnie dislikes the heavy smell of his morning brew. "It was one of our few comforts over there, Nonnie," he explains. "We'd build a tiny fire, enough to heat the water but not reveal our location. Then we added the fine grind, let it settle in the bottom of our cups, and drank it while lying safely below our trucks at the end of day. It was a rare pleasure in a land with few."

Nonnie regrets how little she knows about his time in Iraq. Earlier that morning, before sunrise, loud thunder and heavy rain woke her and she saw Brighton and Choco scamper across the meadow, seeking shelter under Jared's work trucks.

The mower stops, and they both watch as Baéz bounds up the porch stairs.

"Good morning! Is there any more of that tar inside?"

Brighton nods, clearly amused. "Add some steamed milk; it's pretty strong."

"It's going to turn your teeth black," adds Nonnie.

"It's bad enough some folks are predicting that locusts will devour me. Now you want my teeth to rot?"

"Crazy what's going on, isn't it?" adds Baéz from inside.

"Listen," Brighton says, "you guys need to help me anticipate what they're going to ask and, more importantly, what I'm going to answer."

Baéz returns to the porch with his steaming coffee and sits on the thick balustrade, his back to the water.

"Ask what?" questions Nonnie, confused. "When?"

"We discussed this, Non. Remember? The *60 Minutes* crew is coming; that lady you like so much, Christiane Amanpour, she's interviewing Brighton."

"And then will it stop?" Nonnie asks, her exasperation plain. She sees the brothers exchange a look.

"Don't think so," Baéz answers. "Not yet. Another shoe has yet to drop. Bright and I think it might be best for him to shuffle off to California. Back to Malibu. Easier to hide at the beach."

What an odd summer, she thinks—a summer that has a large portion of the country discussing God, health, and metaphysics. "They're only talking to Brighton?"

"No. They're speaking with folks from the movie, those who were healed, and also the reporter from Sacramento and poor Clarice. I'm sure she wishes I never knocked on her door!"

"You're a part of it too?" she asks Baéz.

He nods. "Yup, the family business. They'd love to include you. As it is, they're filming a portion of my Sunday service. Hopefully we won't have any more crazies attending."

Nonnie gives him a sharp look. "Never say that, son. Never. Do not begrudge strangers coming to your door, seeking help."

"Sorry, Nonnie, but I have no patience for these folks. They're seeking an effortless answer, a magic wand that I can wave over their heads."

"Yes, and maybe one of them will be Saul on the road to Tarsus, needing to be shown the light. It is not up to you to pick and choose who you think is worthy of redemption."

"Yes, ma'am," mutters Baéz.

She sees the conspiratorial smile he and Brighton share.

"Do not say such things to Amanpour!" instructs Brighton. "It's a love story, that's what you say, not 'Saul on the road to Tarsus!' Please! I'm doing this to sell tickets! We want lots of people to see this movie. I own a portion of it!"

Nonnie finally laughs. She looks at her smiling grandsons, grateful for this time with them.

★ ★ ★

FOX INTERN SOURCE OF MANY HEALINGS FROM BLOCKBUSTER FILM

On Thursday nights, three miles from the center of the UCLA campus, a small conference room near the entrance to Fox Film Studios is filled with young college students chowing down on an endless supply of thin-crusted gourmet pizza. Fueled by heavily caffeinated drinks and a desire to wreak havoc, these horny dweebs log on to a wide variety of web sites such as Babu, Black Planet, Classmates.com, and the time-killer of them all, MySpace. Using fictional names and profiles, they begin a snarky assault on registered users. They compete to see who can create the meanest, cleverest messages. They operate quickly, typing furiously, laughing and high-fiving one another.

Angus Dramm, an intern working towards his master's degree in advertising and marketing, has created an army of scruffy students whose mission is to engage positively on the subject of The Circuit Rider. Initially they impersonated enthusiastic filmgoers, but as the film's success continues to build, Mr. Dramm has started pushing a new angle. He tells his crew to give false testimonies about ailments that were healed, mimicking some of the strange stories the unusual film has generated.

NewsCorp, the owner of Fox Searchlight and everything else named "Fox," has paid 580 million dollars for an ownership stake in MySpace, the largest social networking site in the world. And it was on MySpace that a young hipster named Guilliam Taylor told his inspiring story of limping into the Five-Acres Ten-Plex with severe asthma and walking out with his lungs clear.

The only problem is The Circuit Rider *hasn't yet opened in Terre Haute. Not to mention that, in the entire state of Indiana, there does not exist a resident with the name of Guilliam Taylor. He is fiction. Created by Angus Dramm, employee of Fox Searchlight, subsidiary of NewsCorp and proud new owner of MySpace.*

How many healings attributed to the film are actually the creative work of Mr. Dramm's Thursday-night pizza buddies? In scrambling to contain the fallout from this story, the Fox marketers put this reporter in touch with several actual, live people who testified to the validity of their recoveries from a broad array of diagnosed illnesses. But to what degree was the healing hysteria attributable to the nefarious exploitation of MySpace?

Robert Browning and *The Sacramento Bee* have struck again, and the producers of *60 Minutes* are reeling. Historic precedent suggests they pull the piece from tonight's broadcast and replace it with an old chestnut, but the entirety of the episode is focused on the movie, its box office success, and its handsome war-hero-turned-actor. CBS has been hyping the program all week, and many Sunday newspapers have full-page ads suggesting the reader tune in.

None of the pizza-chomping hackers agree to appear on camera, so CBS, lacking the luxury of time, sends several reporters scrambling after different angles. Christiane Amanpour, the lead reporter, tells her producers she wishes to revisit the "old lady with the braid."

"I know you cut her from the program, but to me, she speaks with credible authority about the enigma of mental healing. Her view of Fox's meddling will be as provocative as any, and I simply love looking at her and listening to her voice, and so will the audience. Send me up to Connecticut, and I will have something terrific by airtime."

They do, and she does. Nonnie is provocative. Beguiling. Believable.

"Mrs. Esmund, you are—"

Nonnie interrupts. "Please, I haven't been called Mrs. Esmund since my husband died. Call me Nonnie."

"Yes, of course." Amanpour smiles and then asks, "You practice metaphysical healing?"

"I do, yes."

"People come to you who are unwell, and the ailment that is troubling them evaporates. Their health is restored. Am I correct?"

"Technically, yes."

"Explain it to me, then."

"People visit me who describe themselves as suffering from a perceived lack—lack of health, lack of money, lack of harmony. I help them understand that their perception is incorrect. I assist them in altering their mental landscape and encourage them to have faith in what cannot be seen."

Christiane pauses. "There are tales of people being healed simply by listening to a preacher portrayed by your grandson."

The smile on Nonnie's face grows wide. "Yes. Amazing, isn't it?"

"But some of these reported healings were fabricated, the creation of a marketing team working for the film's distributor."

"Working in mysterious ways isn't the sole purview of our Lord. The devil can be inventive while stirring the pot."

"The young man at Fox is the devil?" asks Amanpour, hoping to generate a provocative sound bite.

"Of course not. He's probably a lovely fellow. His creativity in generating these false online personalities points to a clever and imaginative employee. Some of us, in the throes of performing our tasks, get lost in the thrill of our ambitions and turn a blind eye to the harm we may be inflicting."

"And who suffered harm in this case?"

"The faithful."

Amanpour looks puzzled. "The faithful?"

"Prayer *can* generate healing—there are many proofs of this. But the devil wants us to live in ignorance of God's power; he wants us to disregard the spiritual. Yet, for much of this past summer, wonderful tales of healing have flooded the airwaves due to the existence of this movie. If the movie can be smeared, labeled false, a lie, then the devil will have done his work."

"How do you explain them, then?"

"The healings?"

"Yes. Sitting in the multiplex while chomping on popcorn and suddenly an illness disappears? Should we not be skeptical?"

Nonnie pauses. Her smile neither wavers nor weakens. "There's a wonderful hymn that begins 'In atmosphere of love Divine, we live and move and breathe.' The character my grandson plays didn't heal those people; the film didn't heal those people. Their willingness to enter into a frame of mind where healing is normal and expected, *that* is what allowed these healings to unfold. As the stories spread and the tales grew, that healing atmosphere became more powerful. With an open heart and a sterling faith, some people were able to accept the preacher's words as truth."

"You don't find it a bit spooky?" asks Amanpour in a spirit of genuine curiosity.

"No. Not in the least. You know, the healings Jesus performed made the Pharisees and the Romans extremely nervous too. They feared his power, his ability to sway the mind of the people. That is why he often told those he healed to stay silent. 'Do not spread the word about me,' he instructed. I think many of these healings attributed to the film or to my grandson should have remained private. Gratitude is between you and God and is not meant to be announced from rooftops."

Amanpour tries to digest these words, striving to find remarks to conclude her report. "How have your grandsons responded to the charges of 'fraud' being leveled at them?"

"That is for them to answer. The brothers are private. Their struggles are not meant to become headlines for our perusal. I always advise them to 'choose carefully and know God loves them.' I think they are doing that. As are you, helping separate the chaff from the wheat!"

Nonnie again laughs as the picture fades to black.

✷ ✷ ✷

After five months in theaters and a gross of over a hundred million dollars, Brighton's film finally ends its surprising run. The new favorite at the multiplex is *The 40-Year-Old Virgin*. The audience is moving on, and Brighton is trying to do the same. His share of the profits will make him a wealthy man.

In Malibu, he swims each day as his red hair turns nearly blond and his freckles multiply. He meets with entertainment executives and sports franchises. He is a favorite on late-night talk shows. The cult that grew up around Abel Finley quiets, and the huddle of paparazzi in his driveway disappears. His sleep is less troubled, though many mornings the local surfers find him lying in the sand beside his house.

"Mr. B, wake up, sir. Tide's in; we're ready to roll!"

Brighton opens one eye, impressed by such enthusiasm. "I don't know how to surf," he admits to the rubber-suited boy with the salty hair and the peeling nose.

"We'll teach you. We all will. Come on."

Brighton stretches, yawns, and then sits up. "Let me have some coffee first. Stop by on your way home. We can discuss lessons."

"Truly?"

"Yes, honor bright. I'm called Brighton, by the way."

"Yup. Knew that. I'm called Hayden Griffiths. Are you serious about lessons?" asks Hayden.

"Yes, stop by, tell me what board to get, what I'll need. Okay?"

"You can have one of mine. After your coffee, meet me at The Ocean Inn. I live next door and have many boards. You can pick one. Okay?"

The boy's enthusiasm is contagious, and Brighton is pleased by the prospect of learning to surf. "Okay, Hayden Griffiths, you have a deal. I'll see you at The Inn."

Back at home, Brighton brews coffee in his sleek kitchen, wondering why he is doing this. Scottie claims that reinvention is one of California's specialties. But surfing? Is this what he needs? His mood swings have become more dramatic, and the lows are beginning to outnumber the highs. The specter of PTSD hovers in mind, but he tries to ignore it.

Maybe riding the frenzied waves can soothe the troubling unease that has become more and more worrisome—to Brighton and to those close to him.

20.

SUNDAY MORNINGS

Several storm systems have stalled off the coast of California, battering the residents, flooding the roads, and shutting down the Pacific Coast Highway. The only people celebrating this incursion from El Niño are the die-hard surfers.

The LA County Lifeguards are warning beachgoers to stay clear of the water, but Hayden Griffiths has been out since early morning. The heavy clouds and blistering rains do not deter him. The surf lifts him, and he rides her perfectly, a jubilant smile on his face as he maintains a delicate balance atop the roiling water.

From his vantage point, he can see Brighton's house, just north of the stone breakwater that causes so much havoc during the rainy season. Built to protect this vulnerable strip of sandy beach, the narrow jetty creates dangerous riptides that can drown even the strongest swimmer.

Suddenly, Hayden sees a person being pummeled on the granite seawall. He sees blood and bone. He heads for shore, praying the body is unknown to him.

He was fourteen when footage of Brighton, tortured and disabled, was broadcast on TV. He remembers every scary image, every scream, every drop of blood. On that horrendous day, in Hayden's eyes, Brighton transformed into one of the mutants from *The X-Men*—only better. Better than Cyclops, better than Storm, better than Iceman because he was real, and his mangled hand was way cooler than Wolverine's, even with his knives. Since that day, Hayden has been especially attentive to the needs of his neighbor, knowing Brighton's skills are not supernatural, merely human.

He maneuvers his board through the filthy debris churned up by endless days of massive tides. It *is* a body, and the raging tempests have heaved it atop the stone embankment.

Earlier that morning, before the sinister skies had lightened, Brighton was awakened by the insistent ringing of his phone.

"It's six a.m. on a Sunday morning so this better be good!" he said when he picked up.

"I am so sorry! It's nearly dinner time here in Baghdad."

Dear Ruthie! Her voice sounded troubled.

"Hey, Honeysuckle, don't listen to me. You call anytime you want!" Raven had coined the nickname, for her innate sweetness. "And a Happy New Year to you, too. Happy 2007."

There was a long silence. He wondered if their connection was lost.

"They hanged him," she said. "Hussein. Two nights ago."

Brighton was stunned by the news. "How? He's been held by the American Army for three years."

"Yup, and they simply handed him over."

With Hussein alive, some soldiers, and even some politicians, still hoped the fabled weapons of mass destruction would be discovered, but now, with him dead, they were forced to admit the truth. The invasion of Iraq had been justified by lies.

He could still see the man's dirty, unshaved face as he emerged from his hole. How proud Brighton had been, he and his men.

"That isn't the worst of the news," warned Ruthie. "The worst is that our beautiful boy, our lover of horses and cherries, has fallen. He smashed his red Ducati into a wall of stone, leaving a note begging forgiveness!"

She continued talking—he could hear her voice like static on the radio—but he simply put the phone back in its cradle. His hands shook. And then his entire body trembled. He screamed—a loud, pitiable sound.

They had been betrayed. Every single one of them. Their patriotic zeal had been harnessed by lying politicians to a foolish war and the spoils of their deceit continued to wreak havoc on innocent soldiers.

Why not get it over with? he thought. Why not join Raven? Why not simply end the nightmares, end the awful images drenched in blood? End the bursts of sniper fire he heard while sitting in the shade of an outdoor cafe on Santa Monica Boulevard. End the mystery of why he was spared.

Raven. They last spoke on Christmas Day. He said he still had a limp, but the horses didn't mind. Raven. He never told him how much he was loved, and now he would never see him again.

Brighton looked out his bedroom window as thick, impenetrable clouds of gray and black tumbled across the sky and gulls struggled against the heavy winds. He opened the tall glass doors, and rain instantly flooded his bedroom. He stared at the raging storm and decided he wanted to be part of it. He wanted to contribute his own fury to the turbulent forces agitating the ocean.

He ran onto the sand and was soaked in seconds. He headed towards the jetty, where the whetted stones are sharp and shiny. He climbed the stone pier, the crevices between the crags serving as footholds. The rough edges cut his bare feet, slowing him as he leapt from rock to rock, playing a dangerous game of hopscotch. A torrent of water crashed onto the breakwater, the spray and spume covering Brighton and swatting him down. He struggled to rise, his pajamas slipping down his bleeding body. He screamed at the invisible forces that wished to harm him and saw Raven in the distance, coming towards him, covered in blood.

When another wall of water knocked him down, his head struck granite, the pain intense as he blacked out.

The waves continue to wash over him, the salt stinging his many wounds and shocking him awake. He labors once again to stand, his knees wobbly. He hears a voice. *Be still.* He looks again at the figure in the distance, but it's not Raven; it's his neighbor, Hayden Griffiths, running down the seawall with his board beneath his arm, desperately calling out Brighton's name as the rushing tides wash the salt and blood from his inert body.

21.

WANDERING IN THE WILDERNESS

The visiting nurse hums when she bathes him, taking care not to undo his many stiches. Brighton is mortified by the erections her careful ministrations inspire; he doesn't know whether to apologize or simply pretend not to notice. His recovery has been painful and protracted, the cuts and abrasions healing more swiftly than the broken bones.

With summer finally here, he spends his days out of doors, taking long, therapeutic walks and exercising the muscles that have weakened from lengthy disuse.

Everyone is careful with him, treating him like fine china, keeping a wary eye on his activities. The worst part of being unwell, he realizes, is the fear he sees in the eyes of friends and family. He is anxious to return to Malibu and once again be on his own.

He listens as the air rustles the small lobed leaves of the white birches. He hears distant cars come to life as the parishioners exit the parking lot across the lake.

The service is over. Baéz will be here soon.

"Wandering in the wilderness." That's what Baéz has named this chapter of their lives as he instructs Brighton to celebrate the beauty that surrounds them.

Tolliver had borrowed a client's plane to rush the injured surfer home to Connecticut. Now, as he lies on the soft meadow grass, the tender mosses swaddling his body in comfort, Brighton shouts down the bitter thoughts that fight to control his mind.

"A man at rest on the Sabbath! A lovely sight on a summer's day!"

When Brighton opens his eyes, Baéz fills his frame of vision. Sunday services leave Baéz in a state of exhilaration, his entire being suffused with light. Standing within his circumference can heal a stranger, much less a brother.

"Want to sit, or shall we walk?" he asks.

Brighton knows to choose the latter—Baéz is too worked up to remain stationary. He stands, stretching, and accepts his brother's embrace. He can't recall when this habit of hugging began, but even Tolliver has become a convert.

They set off on their usual path, following the lake's edge until it meets the golf course, then turning inland through deep woods.

"Good service this morning?"

"Yes. My sermon focused on 'reclaiming your innocence.' How we accomplish that. The statement assumes that innocence can be lost, which I think is untrue. Innocence is intrinsic to who we are—simply getting older and gaining experience of the world does not nullify the purity we possess at birth."

"Maybe not nullify, but the world, and the people who inhabit this world, certainly belie the existence of innocence. Purity feels awfully distant when viewed through the eyes of man."

"Love is the animating force if we choose to recognize it. The actions of man, the history of mankind, are a constant, never-ending search for perfection."

"Interrupted by centuries of warfare and famine and disease!" argues Brighton.

"If that's what you choose to see." Baéz wears an enigmatic smile as he stares down a fearless squirrel that sits on a branch at eye level.

"I should simply decide to *un-see* evil?" Brighton says incredulously. "I am one of its purveyors!"

"Listen to yourself! These words from a man who felled a terrorist with forgiveness. The eyes and ears, the senses, are not accurate judges of what is real and true. Like tawdry journalists, they embroider and lie."

"Do you never suffer doubts?" asks Brighton with an impatient edge.

"Of course. One must be diligent in screaming them down. Rooting them out. These angry voices that scream *you are worthless*, or *wrong*, or *diseased*. We must be ever mindful of the dangers carried by these voices."

"What if they are all you hear?"

"They can seem dominant, but they're not. 'Pour in the new wine,' the Bible instructs. Fill your mind, your thinking, with love, leaving no room for this chorus of dread."

Brighton is envious of the man his brother has become. Envious and resentful. He doesn't know when this self-assurance first appeared, but he often finds it grating rather than comforting.

These walks, which fill their Sundays, always end in a clearing framed by the immense boulders left behind by retreating glaciers. Bears hibernate here. Bobcats huddle with their young. The brothers bow their heads. After several minutes of silence, they cross the lake and sit on Baéz's floating deck. These Sundays together, their arguments, their misgivings, and their individual searches for a meaningful life, have become the blueprint for Baéz's TV show on The Faith Channel. *The Honor Hour* is broadcast on Sunday mornings and offers a wide range of liberal orthodoxy to combat the fire and brimstone preached by most television pasters.

Baéz pours them each a cup of coffee as Brighton finally broaches the subject he has been dreading.

"My agent needs me back in LA. Fox wants me to play a detective in a noir-ish thriller."

Brighton can't gauge his brother's reaction. "I promise to stay away from the water," he says, teasing. "Hayden will keep an eye peeled."

Brighton knows the idea of him living on his own makes everyone nervous, even Scottie.

"I need to work," he explains. "I need to do something."

Baéz nods. "What about ESPN?"

"Still possible. Ollie is talking to them. We shall see."

"Wouldn't that be preferable to acting?"

Brighton is surprised by the comment. "I thought you liked the film?"

"I do, but I never thought you were comfortable with it. You seemed embarrassed."

Brighton sips his coffee and thinks about what his brother has said. He answers carefully.

"It is a silly occupation. And it does embarrass me; you're right. I once spent hours at the gym to become a better and stronger tennis player. Now, I do those same exercises, but the goal is to please my fans when I remove my shirt. It's degrading." He smirks. "Degrading but well paid," he jokes.

"Oh, please, don't claim you need the money!" His brother knows how many millions *The Circuit Rider* made.

Brighton laughs. "I pretend with others that money is the motivating force, but you know better."

"So why then?"

"Don't make me say it," answers Brighton, shamefaced. "The attention. I like being recognized. I like being photographed." He stares at his brother's pained face. "Not the stuff of heroes, eh?"

"No, it's not that. I think being a sportscaster might be a better fit for you. You might find greater fulfillment. Give Ollie the time he needs to convince ESPN of your value."

"I hear you. I promise not to make any rash decisions, but I'm anxious to be home and to walk on the warm sand."

22.

ROADSIDE BILLBOARDS

"Stay the night, can't you?" Baéz asks as he and Tolliver walk through Nonnie's far fields. They are holding hands.

Tolliver shakes his head. "I've got clients driving up from Philly in the morning. I need to be sharp, and isn't tonight Brighton's farewell dinner? Your heart beats quicker. You talk faster. Best I be gone."

"That's a joke, right?" inquires Baéz as he and Ollie sit on a bench made from fallen birches. *Mille Fleur*, an invasive species of rose, floods the field with its heady scent.

"Not entirely, no. Your voice goes up a notch when he's in the room. You can't be unaware of this!"

Baéz shrugs off the observation. "Old habits, I guess. I was enamored of him as a kid. Technically, I'm the big brother, older by a year, but he's the one who saved me." Baéz leans back, the sweet odor all-encompassing. "This perfume has the power to intoxicate."

"And are you susceptible to this fragrance?" asks Ollie, a large smile filling his face.

The ardent young men lean into one another like flowers drawn to light.

"No, I grew up with it. I am immune. But for you, I am simply warning you—take care. The aroma can cause foolishness. I've seen it happen." He leans in closer and notes the smell of lemon on Tolliver's lips. An afternoon beverage.

The reemergence of Tolliver Brigham in his life has been a thrilling surprise, a "gift from the gods," Baéz likes to say, which makes Ollie incredibly nervous. All mentions of God make Ollie nervous. Once, when Ollie had climaxed, he screamed "Oh God" at the top of his lungs and the two fell out of bed laughing.

In the three years that have passed since their initial attempts at being "boyfriends," each has become more versatile in their sexual appetites, and they fit together more comfortably this time around.

"Thanks for the warning. I fear I am susceptible. Some might say I incline towards foolishness and am indeed prone to a certain lunacy."

The kiss is inevitable and pleasing, and Ollie is smiling when he pulls away.

"But your ruse won't work. I still need to catch the late train."

✳ ✳ ✳

Baéz is alone and can't decide what to make for dinner or what program to watch or whether to begin the book Jared brought him. His mind is mush. He smiles. The diagnosis is love—love was making a fool of him.

He reheats leftovers from the fridge. He turns on the TV. PBS.

"Tonight, on *Frontline*—does drug advertising make you sick? An exploration into America's rising drug costs and the selling of sickness."

The impact of Brighton's movie is impossible to measure. Three years have passed, yet the questions the film raised about healing and wellness only become more urgent as America's healthcare system is constantly under attack. The documentary studies the huge sums spent on drug advertising and provides examples of the scare tactics involved in selling those medications.

As the program continues, Baéz feels a weird sensation—a tightening of his joints and muscles. He can hear his heart, the blood moving in his veins, and the air in his lungs. He is in danger.

How odd, he thinks. He is never unwell. Is the documentary triggering a response? He checks his phone, moving it close.

He feels no pain, only a familiar discomfort, the same kind he once felt when forced to take a physical exam at Wake Forest. He had found the doctor's probing a vast invasion of his privacy and had closed his eyes to silence his outrage.

"What happened to you?" the university doctor had asked those many years ago. "Your heart. Liver. They're damaged. Do you recall the cause?"

"There's not damaged now. They were *once* damaged."

"Yes, that is correct. They are fine. But whatever the traumatic event, it left markers. You should be aware. Perhaps something is hiding, perhaps something else is damaged, but without knowing the original cause, I'm not sure where to look."

"Am I sufficiently fit to play tennis or not?" snapped Baéz. "That's why I'm here."

His angry tone had embarrassed both men. He continued more carefully, knowing the doctor was simply trying to help.

"I suffered a heart attack when I was twelve," Baéz acknowledged. "I had been deprived of oxygen. A fall into freezing water. Hypothermia. I don't want to talk about it."

But the doctor's warning from years past still frightens him.

He reaches for the iPhone. He feels sweat on his forehead, and his ears are hot. He scrolls to her number and waits for his grandmother to answer. The sound of her voice always provides comfort.

"Nonnie, I need your help."

"What is it, dear?"

"Years ago, during a medical exam, a doctor warned that something dangerous might be lurking in my body, a remnant from my time under the ice. I never challenged the validity of his statement."

"He was simply declaring the truth as he understood it. I'm sure he intended no malice. Nothing inharmonious can enter into being. You've demonstrated this fact repeatedly. And that truth is just as vital, as urgent, as fundamental right now as it has ever been."

Nonnie speaks with a conviction and certainty created by years of confirming these truths and witnessing their healing effect.

"Dear boy, you take in too much of the world. We are surrounded by antagonistic thoughts and foolish lies. We must never allow them to take root. We must never consent to their existence. Paul advises, 'Come out from among them, and be ye separate.' Stand guard over what you allow into thought. You are perfect. Invulnerable. Unassailable."

He closes his eyes, the evening's damp settling on his brow. As he nods off to sleep, he hears Nonnie voice, "And in the nighttime, His song shall be with thee."

Ollie often stops at Bigelow's Apothecary near his office to pick up Nonnie's favorite soaps. He wonders what she thinks of his frequent visits. He's pretty sure she saw him and Baéz holding hands on their evening walk.

Today they are watching a water skier skim over the placid surface of the lake.

"My brothers love me, and they want me to be happy, but they wish I'd made different choices," Ollie says. "They wish I were a Raiders fan and not the Seahawks. They wish I drove a Chevy, not a Nissan. They wish I were straight and not gay."

"My brothers were twins," responds Nonnie, "and I often felt left out when they were together. Baéz and Bright are not twins, I know, but their bond is formidable. I hope they don't gang up on you."

Nonnie passes a second helping of blueberry pancakes, and Ollie drowns them in syrup. He does feel like a third wheel when the brothers are together and is embarrassed by his jealousy.

"Thank you."

"For what?" she asks.

"For understanding that fact. It is petty, and I am a fool, but my envy is real, regardless of how foolish."

"There can never be too much love, Ollie. Be grateful for their mutual affection, not begrudging."

He looks at Nonnie, impressed by the repose that is always present with her. "And why am I so fortunate as to have you as my breakfast companion on this fine Sunday morning? Why aren't you in church?"

She frowns. "Coming home the other night, I hit a deer. It limped away, the injury not fatal, but now I'm afraid of getting behind the wheel."

Ollie understands. He and Baéz have discussed whether she should still be driving. "Forget the car. No need to drive all the way to Hartford—just drop in on Baéz's service. What keeps you away?"

From the look on Nonnie's face, he knows he has struck a delicate chord and he regrets his intrusion.

"Early on, I attended his monthly sermons, to be supportive and offer advice. He and I have never discussed the causes of my absence." She hesitates. "I often feel he is preaching Christianity-Lite. His services are designed for the generation that claims they are 'spiritual, not religious.' What is that?"

Ollie raises an eyebrow, mulling an answer. "A way to understand our connection to this miraculous world, devoid of dogma?"

Nonnie smiles. "That sounds rehearsed!"

Ollie laughs, knowing she is right.

Nonnie continues, "His doctrine feels diluted, designed for easy and painless consumption. Redemption, atonement, forgiveness, these pursuits require sacrifice and dedication. They are not easily achieved. In your study and practice of the Law, do you utilize shortcuts?"

"No, but the Law is clear-cut. It is not cocooned within a world of mystery."

"Jesus gave us two commandments: Love God and Love your neighbor. How have we made it so complicated?" She dips her bacon in the amber syrup and then looks over at Ollie. "And what prevents your attendance at my grandson's services? I know you say you were raised by wolves, but what is the real reason? May I ask?"

A cloud of starlings flies noisily overhead as Tolliver thinks how to answer.

"I love Baéz. You know that. His warmth, his humor, his care and thoughtfulness. And I know these qualities have a spiritual source. But his ability to heal, his ability to make sickness disappear, is mystifying to me, even though I have been a witness many times. He is not some shaman predicting the future or some sorcerer trying to make the devil tremble. People arrive at our door, suffering with an ailment that is real, that has been diagnosed, and when they leave, they are well. And the same happens at your door."

"To those brought up in a world that relies on a material explanation of the universe, such healings can be difficult to comprehend. That is why Jesus loved children—their easy acceptance of what you call miraculous."

A voice calls to them from the Meetinghouse.

"Good morning, Nonnie!"

She waves, a bright smile on her face.

"Who is that? "Ollie asks, his body stiffening. "You know him?"

Nonnie appears thrown by the fear she hears in Ollie's voice. "Yes, since a boy. Why?"

"You can vouch for him?"

"Tolliver! What's wrong? His name is Atticus. He played Joshua in Brighton's movie, the elder son. I've known him since he was in diapers."

Tolliver uncoils, embarrassed. He won't look at Nonnie. "I am so sorry. I didn't recognize him; he's grown so. He's been hanging around, staying after services, helping clean up, chatting with Baéz. The two often share dinner, and sometimes Baéz rehearses his sermons with him."

"And this makes you jealous?"

"No! No, this isn't about jealousy. I think Baéz is in danger. The website, all these strangers seeking advice, baring their souls, wanting some piece of him—they scare me. I think there is a trap being laid to bring him down, but I cannot find it."

"Oh, Ollie, no! Fear not. I know for a fact that Baéz prays daily for protection. He is aware of the minefield he is marching through."

Now that he has expressed his fears aloud, a torrent of anxious nerves pours forth.

"Do you ever look at his website? Do you read the requests for prayer, for help, for guidance? They are chilling. Young men write to him, confessing all kinds of thoughts and desires, their wishes for sex or destruction or self-mutilation. Any concerned parent would call the police. Their fears and his prayers can be so easily misconstrued; his loving advice twisted. I fear for him. I cannot protect him."

Nonnie reaches for his hand. "It is not your job to protect him! Simply love him and leave the rest to God. I know that is hard for you, but it is true, trust me."

Nonnie rises and takes their plates inside, returning with fresh strawberries. Ollie's frenzy is spent, and he feels a weight lifted in speaking these fears aloud.

As Nonnie pours heavy cream over the berries, she looks again at the young man named Atticus, who is shepherding the late arrivals into the Meetinghouse.

"His grandmother, Laila Robertson, brought him to me as a boy. One leg was shorter than the other, causing him to limp. People stared, but he wasn't bothered. The limp never got in his way. But Laila was bothered. By the teasing. She hated that people were mean to her grandchild, this boy she loved, so she brought him to me."

"To correct the limp?"

"Yes. He was resistant at first, but I knew I had one thing he craved—Dad's seaplane. I never allowed children near it, but I told him if he worked with me for an hour every afternoon, we could end the day by touring the hangar—and he agreed! We talked about Jesus and how much he loved Atticus; how God made Atticus perfect. I pointed to the plane's canvas wings stretched over bent wood, which were also perfect and replicated the brilliant design of the inventor. Everything made to measure, nothing too short or too long, but perfect. He loved hearing about the plane and the war, and my brothers. One day I gave him one of Austin's medals. A beautiful green ribbon holding two golden bars. He ran all the way home to show Laila, not even noticing the loss of his limp."

She finishes her berries and picks a last one out of Ollie's bowl.

"People come here for healing. Whether they are seeking a handsome actor from a cult film, or a curly-headed preacher who sermonizes online, or a white-haired woman with a lengthy braid, we are here to help them in whatever way we can. Knock and the door will open. There is no right way or wrong way to approach Him. Once I was reminded of this fact, I stopped criticizing Baéz; I stopped accusing him of being a religious dilettante. And yes, you are right, I should begin attending his services!"

Baéz has cleared the branches and boughs that litter Nonnie's porch and yard. A huge storm has crippled the county, and Nonnie has lost several massive trees. Luckily Brighton has arrived for a week-long visit and can help Baéz turn these fallen sentinels into firewood.

Baéz loads Jared's Dodge Ram with all the tools they will need and then drives over the hilly fields to the far side of the property. He stares at an ancient hickory, smashed and broken, the trunk scarred, the leaves already withering. He lowers the truck's tailgate as both brothers tie oil-smudged, dirt-encrusted chainsaw chaps over their worn Levis. A hydraulic, gas-powered log-splitter is hitched to the back of the pickup. Baéz stands, adjusting the tight, leather chaps.

"I can't wear these around Ollie. Makes him crazy!" Baéz laughs.

"Lumberjacks have always been sexy!" confirms Brighton with a confident smile. He then asks, "When are you lovebirds going to officially inform Nonnie of your intentions?"

Baéz stares at his brother. "She's not blind; certainly, she is aware of our connection."

"Yes, perhaps, but folks of her generation want an announcement. Assumptions are no better than gossip; she deserves to hear it from your lips."

"Fine," answers Baéz, shaking his head.

Brighton picks up one of the hefty chainsaws fitted with a twenty-inch blade. "How do you want to attack this?"

"Let's strip the branches and boughs—Rio can grind them up later—and then you and I can cut the trunk into manageable pieces for the log splitter."

"Okay. You brought the log jacks?"

"Under the tarp. You'll be interested to know that this species of hickory generates flowers of both sexes. Highly unusual!"

"How appropriate," laughs Brighton as he pulls the cable. The loud roar of the two-cycle engine ends any further conversation. They attack the hickory, working from opposite ends and cutting the thick limbs into pieces. They are now covered in sawdust, glued to their skin with the sap of the tree mixed with their own sweat.

Baéz is a careful user of the lethal tool, employing many safety techniques to reduce the dangers, but both brothers know the inherent risk attached to all tree work. They keep a close eye on each other.

After several hours in the hot sun, with the insects buzzing around their sweaty clothes, they have a large pile of fat logs ready to be split into firewood.

Brighton opens the passenger door and retrieves water bottles and apples. He sinks to the ground, leaning against a rear tire, drinks an entire bottle of water, and then pours a second over his head.

He sits, his hair dripping as he stares at the clear sky. "This is how to live, brother, by the sweat of your brow!"

He takes a large bite of a sour green apple as they both sit in blissful comfort. On the far side of the field, a pair of goats feed on the tall grasses. Baéz fills a pail with pieces of tree bark to feed the horned animals. He unwraps a sandwich and then turns to Brighton.

"Do you think Obama can pull it off? Beat McCain?"

"California gives me a skewed viewpoint. There's not a McCain supporter within a hundred miles of my house!"

"If Obama wins, Washington will be a damned interesting place."

"Yes, and let's hope he finally brings our troops home."

Talk of the war still infuriates his brother, so Baéz changes the subject. "Did you see that *Frontline* episode last week?"

"Yes, Nonnie asked me to watch; she had read about it in TV Guide.""

"Well, they simply proved everything she's been saying for years."

"Clever approach, didn't you think?" asks Brighton. "*Does drug advertising make you sick?* Not a headline the pharmaceutical companies want you to see."

"Yes, I'm sure not. After the show, I went online to read their research. In 2003, the FDA, responding to a request from the pharmaceutical companies, approved advertising for prescription drugs on television. As an experiment. No other country allows it."

"That's five years ago! When does the experiment end?"

"Exactly! The FDA renews the Act every year without requiring any research to prove the usefulness of their experiment!"

"Really?"

"Yes. And as a result, prescription drug use has more than doubled."

"Good news for my dad and for Nico, I'm sure."

Baéz finishes his sandwich and adds his trash to the pile already covering the front seat of the truck. "Obama will have his hands full trying to overhaul healthcare."

"Yes, and while they're at it, maybe they can remove the drug ads from the nightly news!"

Both brothers laugh, having listened to the grandmother's complaints for years.

"Isn't your dad's company a drug manufacturer?"

Brighton smiles. "Yes. Afidcorps."

"Congress banned cigarette ads, why not erections and hemorrhoids?" asks Baéz.

Brighton chuckles as he refuels his saw.

"Maybe I should give Daddy a call!"

✳ ✳ ✳

An elaborate invitation with the Afidcorp logo on the envelope arrives with Brighton's mail.

Hey Boy-O, the letter begins, and Brighton smiles as he pictures Nico painstakingly printing his hand-written note. *I saw your movie a while back and I meant to write, but I didn't. I was very impressed. When you were only a teen, I knew you could do anything, and I was right. Congrats! I have also made a movie, albeit a shorter one. Ninety seconds to be exact—it's a commercial—and we are having a party to screen it at our local IMAX theater. Please come. I miss you, and even though he will never admit it, so does Dušan!*

Brighton's been looking for an excuse to take his new car, a bright yellow Porsche Boxster, for a spin on Connecticut's narrow country roads, and a trip down to Stamford fits the bill perfectly. As he scans the confusing streets of the business center, his car generates stares and turned heads, putting a smile on his face.

He finds the address. A modern glass building with the name "Afidcorp" spelled out in huge letters that stretch from the fourth floor to the sixth. From there, as the invitation explained, it is a short walk to the theater with the giant screen.

A crowd of twenty-somethings dressed in trendy clothing with bright-colored hair and painted nails are filing into the theater, but he cannot spot Nico. As he listens to the people on his left and on his right, he understands they are Nico's colleagues from Afidcorp. His breath quickens as he realizes his father might be among this crowd, but the lights dim, and the audience takes their seats, and it is too late for him to leave.

The room goes dark. Then the sixty-foot-tall screen is filled with the larger-than-life image of a rough and vigorous blue-eyed cowboy, looking like those men who sell shaving cream and cigarettes from roadside billboards. His rugged features reflect extreme concentration as he hangs precariously from a rock outcropping hundreds of feet above a desert floor. His tanned body blends into the striated gash of earth he is attempting to scale, his calloused hands and fingers coated with talc. His muscular arms slowly pull him upwards as trumpets and horns, mimicking Olympic themes, accompany his herculean efforts.

The image on the screen changes to one of blinding white snow. A tiny blue object appears, zigging and zagging down a frosty mountain. As the skier flies, leaving furrows of diamonds and ice, waves of white are chasing her—an avalanche—gaining speed and swallowing everything in its path.

As the menacing glacial mass stalks the vulnerable athlete, she abruptly pivots and zooms over an outcropping of rock. A triumphant fanfare plays as the delicate figure in blue celebrates her timely escape with an exultant thrusting of her ski poles heavenwards.

Brighton wonders what Nico is selling that warrants such an elaborate and costly commercial.

The white screen dissolves again, this time yielding to a sky dotted with cottony clouds. Suddenly a flying orb of black rubber darts across the heavens. A man encased in a flying suit, arms outstretched like some futuristic superman, soars high above the grassy landscape. A wider shot from a hovering helicopter captures the human eagle. The camera tracks this impossible flight as the sound of wind joins his screams and scores of stringed instruments join the melee of jubilant sound.

A solemn, cultivated voice speaks over the celebratory orchestra. *Conquer fear with Adrenyl. Proven effective in sublimating everything that tries to hold you back! Adrenyl. See if your doctor thinks you can take it!*

The screen goes black. A few nervous laughs punctuate the silence as the lights come back on. The audience begins wildly applauding and cheering as Nico walks onto the stage. Brighton looks for an exit. Before he can make it to the door, a strong hand grabs his arm, and he sees Dušan wearing his perpetual scowl.

"Don't leave, please. He'll want to see you."

Brighton feels trapped and isn't sure how to answer, so he asks a question instead.

"Who is this ad for? Are young daredevils at risk of heart disease?"

The *Frontline* documentary had singled out this particular drug as being marketed to an audience for which is it has never been tested.

As Dušan smirks, Brighton once again feels he is standing face to face with the devil.

"It has many uses, but Nico is preaching to the group with the highest income. Thirty-year-old males still rule the universe, and they respond to whatever they think is cool."

"So, Adrenyl is cool?"

"They're buying it by the fistful. Lightning in a bottle, babe, and it's legal."

Brighton decides to be polite. "The ad was effective, no doubt about it. Caught my attention immediately. Which agency created it?"

Dušan shrugs.

Brighton wonders if there is a "cool" approach to removing drug ads from TV. Could a campaign be designed that is hip *and* socially conscious? Could it stir people to action?

Brighton offers his hand. "So sorry, gotta go. Please send Nico my best. You've both done an incredible job. Congrats!"

He rushes to the parking lot, puts down the convertible top, and races home on the winding roads, feeling like one of the characters in the daredevil commercial as he contemplates his next steps.

23.

BRIGHTON & BAÉZ

Nonnie records both brothers' shows on TiVo, but she hates that they work on the Sabbath. There was a time, she remembers, when Sundays were sacrosanct—shops closed, liquor sales were prohibited, and theaters didn't open until sundown.

Brighton's program, *In the Zone*, airs on ESPN from ten until noon and has become a ratings juggernaut. Each week a different sports icon joins him as host and is featured in silly skits that are often re-run on the popular new site, YouTube. This season has featured Brighton and the front line of the Green Bay Packers shopping for Valentine's Day gifts in Victoria's Secret. He also invited the New England Patriots to cook a Thanksgiving meal overseen by Martha Stewart, with hilarious results.

He is a solid and knowledgeable interviewer, and sports stars are comfortable with him, letting down their guard and allowing the audience a rare glimpse into their true personalities.

Along with the weekly highlight reels is a segment that airs at the top of the second hour in which Brighton investigates the world of sports medicines. Protein drinks. Weight-loss powders. Hormone therapies. Beta-blockers. Many of these products advertise on ESPN, yet Brighton's reports often criticize these products, deeming them harmful, or at best, useless. No other sports program approaches the size of his audience, so the network is willing to take some flak from their advertisers. But savvy journalists wonder how long Brighton will be allowed to bite the hand that feeds him.

When his program ends, *The Honor Hour* begins on The Faith Channel. Although Baéz's audience is a fraction of Brighton's, the improbability of two brothers hosting television shows on the same day elicits a fair amount of free publicity.

As a goof, and to help boost his brother's ratings, Brighton pays for a series of tongue-in-cheek newspaper ads to draw attention to their programs:

**Bacon & Eggs
Sports & Religion
Heaven & Earth
Brighton & Baéz
Sunday mornings will never be the same!**

Scottie puts down the Sunday paper, pleased that the brothers still enjoy making mischief. She pours herself a lemonade and gets ready for her Sunday night lineup—*60 Minutes* followed by *The Amazing Race.* When she switches on the TV, however, she is surprised to see that the picture is in black and white. A very stylish woman is laughing. *Is that Meryl Streep?* The actress is standing on a tiny, decorative bridge that crosses over a narrow canal. A man is approaching, and she waves. Her sweet smile tells us she is pleased by his presence. He carries a gelato cone. It is Brighton, looking like a million bucks.

Older women suit him, Scottie thinks as she picks up the paper to check the listings. *What is she watching?* She doesn't remember Brighton making a film with Meryl.

"Alla fregol?" she asks. A subtitle in English spells out, "Is it strawberry?" He nods, his smile conveying the love he feels for this woman. He hands her the cone. She stares into his eyes as she licks the creamy concoction. She then touches the cone to his nose, and he wipes away the flavored gelato, laughing. A voice calls out, *"Benvenuto in Italia,"* as a shiny black gondola passes below them. Brighton waves.

His smile breaks Scottie's heart. She never sees the real one anymore.

The jazzy score is reminiscent of her favorite Dave Brubeck recordings. She still cannot figure out what she is watching, but then she sees a moving ticker tape traveling from right to left below the handsome neo-noir image. "Wouldn't you rather watch a sexy Italian love story than sit through another commercial for hemorrhoid cream? Call the number on your screen and tell Congress to get rid of pharmaceutical advertising!"

Scottie laughs as she finally understands the purpose of the short film. On screen, the seductive couple kiss as it begins to rain, and Brighton opens an enormous umbrella and the two race to safety. The picture fades to black and then the screen tells the viewer to "stay tuned for our next weekly episode!"

Patiently waiting for the perfect wave while floating on the ocean is something that fills Brighton with happiness. The water is calm as they search for the next set. Sometimes they rest in silence, sometimes Hayden talks a blue streak.

"They worry about you," says the young surfer.

"Yes, we all worry about those we love," Brighton answers.

"It doesn't bother you?"

The boy surprises him with his observations. "Yes, it does, but unfortunately, I have given them cause. And once you have done that, once you have justified their fears, there is no escape. They fear I am being careless with my life. With the gifts I have been given. That's why I love it out here. What seems so important on land dissolves in the water."

Hayden concurs with a nod. "They're awake. I see them."

Brighton looks at his house. On the upper balcony are two men. "They figured out the Jura Giga!"

Hayden laughs. "You can see that clearly?"

"I saw Tolliver raise something to his lips. Had to be coffee."

"You're not hiding a secret jar of Nescafé?"

"Never! It's like being a spy out here, though, isn't it? Look to your right, on the sand. Scottie is snooping on the boys under the guise of a morning jog."

"You are harsh!" says Hayden, laughing.

"Shall we go in?"

"Yup, 'fraid so."

"The boys," as both Scottie and Brighton refer to them, have flown out for the Fourth of July. Today is the last day of their weeklong visit, staying in Brighton's luxurious third-floor guest suite.

"Better enjoy that. Took me an hour to figure out how to operate this friggin' machine!" Ollie is wearing his vacation gear—brightly patterned board shorts, an orange muscle tee, and a baseball cap flouting the Billabong logo.

"We the first ones up?" Baéz asks, whispering.

"Hardly. Your brother's on dawn patrol!"

On their California trips, Baéz is always surprised by Ollie's transformation into a beach bum, complete with the lingo and attitude. Tolliver laughs and walks onto the large upper deck.

"Dawn patrol," he repeats, nodding towards the water. "He and Hayden went out at first light."

Baéz stares at the deep blue water as a woman jogs by on the sand's edge. She waves. It is Scottie. He returns her greeting as she heads up the outdoor stairs.

"What a day, eh? Gorgeous." She gives each man a kiss. "Are the Baywatch Boys still hoping for the perfect wave?"

"The water's been pretty glassy. They should be back soon. No action." Ollie says this with the conviction of a man who spent his youth at the beach. Scottie looks out at the water.

"Did you guys see the latest episode?" she asks.

Tolliver starts laughing. "Yes, best one yet."

"Did you know what he was working on? Or were you surprised too?" questions Scottie.

"That's the genius of what he's done," comments Ollie. "No one knew. These ads just began appearing out of nowhere, and suddenly, everyone was writing about them, talking about them, watching them. When I asked, he explained to me he was trying to create something that was 'cool,' something that would get people talking."

Scottie nods, smiling. "Well, he succeeded. From the articles I've read, the 800 number has been inundated with hundreds of thousands of calls, demanding Congress remove drug ads."

"Yup," says Baéz, "he got the audience he wanted; Capitol Hill is paying attention. That was his goal!"

"What was my goal?" calls out Brighton from the sand below. He and Hayden duck under the outdoor shower, washing the salt and sand from their boards and suits.

"Rethinking American health care!" yells Scottie over a cascade of gulls. "Shall I make you both espressos?"

"Perfect!" comes the answer.

She gets up and goes inside to the kitchen. Baéz follows.

"Which is your favorite so far?" he asks.

She answers immediately. "The first one. The only one he appeared in. As much as I like Brad Pitt, and Denzel, and even Jason Bourne, I still think Brighton is the handsomest of them all!"

"How did he get all those guys to show up for a commercial?"

"I think once Meryl agreed, everyone said 'yes.' They're only doing three more, he said, but they have so many interested stars they could easily do another dozen."

"What else did you learn?" Baéz hates asking, but Brighton tells Scottie things he tells no one else.

"Well, contrary to all the gossip, he is *not* pursuing a career as a director, or a writer." She laughs as she says this, but then her expression turns pensive. "I worry about what he does next. If this project fails, if the drug companies will still be allowed to advertise on TV, I think he will take that failure personally. I've not seen him so invested in something since tennis. That can be great, but also scary."

She fills the basket with finely ground coffee and screws it onto the fancy machine.

"I understand," Baéz says. "We need to keep a careful eye."

The sound of the boiling water being forced through the coffee stops further conversation and they return to the deck, each carrying a cup for their surfer pals.

"Thanks," says Hayden as he undoes the top of his suit. Brighton grabs the cup offered him.

"Scottie thinks I'm crazy," Brighton says. "Did she tell you?"

Scottie flashes an exasperated look. "I never said crazy. Forget I said anything. Please."

Brighton laughs. "Don't give up so easily! Hayden has heard our arguments; why should the boys be spared?"

Hayden nods, sipping his coffee. Scottie offers a wary smile and then turns to Ollie and Baéz to explain.

"I worry about how much he's spending. That's all."

Brighton fixes her with his gaze. "You don't think this will succeed?"

"Every third commercial on television is for some kind of medication," she argues. "Do you think the networks will allow anything to interfere with that gravy train?"

"Once upon a time, every third commercial advertised a brand of cigarettes, and Congress put an end to that, and the networks survived," answers Brighton.

Scottie nods. "Yes, but smoking was bad for your health. How are you going to prove that medicine is bad for your health?"

"That is our challenge," responds Brighton, "to prove they are selling illness, not wellness. And the conspiracy begins with the advertising agencies. We are looking for someone on the inside, a whistleblower. There's always one."

✳ ✳ ✳

"**I** know my division embarrasses you," says Elwynn Bethune, "but the Board has asked me to take a look at some of our older patents and see if some nugget is sitting right in front of us."

He is lunching in the corporate dining room with Sig Procopio, head researcher for Afidcorp.

"What do you suppose we are hiding?" Sig asks, his condescension clear.

"Not hiding, perhaps *mislabeling*."

They both smile at Wynn's careful articulation.

"Okay, what do you think we have 'mislabeled'?" Sig asks.

"A winter pick-me-up."

That's what Nico has requested. He has the campaign. He registered the name. Now he needs a formula of ingredients.

"And what is a winter pick-me-up?"

"Well, the concept of 'flu season' is well established. Also 'allergy season.' But sales of these remedies have plateaued. We need something new to bolster this line of recurrent health aids. We focused on the idea of winter, the short days, the gray skies. Depression sets in for many people. We want to offer them relief. Some caffeine-based remedy we already own. Something simple for over-the-counter use."

"And what is your campaign for this new drug?"

Wynn smiles. "WinterSun. Vacation in a bottle."

Sig laughs, shaking his head. "You marketing guys are impossible. But I'm sure we have some harmless tonic we invented for housewives in the 1950s."

"Exactly!" says Wynn, pleased.

"I'll put a team together, search the archives, find what you need."

"That's all I'm asking," says Elwynn, relieved.

"How's that famous son of yours?"

Wynn smiles as he knows he should. He doesn't like discussing Brighton. The topic crops up when least expected, exposing his poor choices as a parent. Instead of answering, he focuses on the pleasing view of Stamford harbor. He loves working here and living here too. Nico has remained in New York—Stamford is too small to contain his energies—but Wynn likes it.

With the help of a devoted psychologist, he has shed many of his destructive habits. More than a year of thrice-weekly sessions has rid him of all self-condemnation. He recalls advice he once heard Nonnie give to Baéz when the boy was experiencing nightmares. "We are new each day," she had said. Wynn applies this thought every morning.

He owns a two-bedroom condo overlooking an elegant marina. He has a few different ladies who enjoy the occasional dinner or a weekend in the city.

He doesn't miss Manhattan.

He doesn't miss gambling.

He doesn't miss drinking.

He misses his son.

24.

THE AFFORDABLE CARE ACT

The image of Leslie Stahl fills the TV screen as Nonnie and Baéz watch *60 Minutes* from the living room sofa.

"Senator, isn't there an uncomfortable paradox embedded in the fact that the tennis star who urged your committee to study the negative effects of drug advertising is the same man who portrayed a minister who healed without the use of medicine?"

Senator Regis Caverly smiles, his wide, friendly face welcoming all questioning no matter how foolish or misguided.

"Brighton Bethune is a sports journalist, a superb athlete, and a patriot. He played a character, as all actors do, and it is best not to confuse their persons with the characters they portray." The Senator pushes on, not allowing her to interrupt his rehearsed response. "And he is but one of many, many voices asking us to investigate the impact of television advertising on our nation's health. Congress did indeed grant a request from the pharmaceutical companies, allowing them to advertise their products on television. But what began as a limited experiment was extended without judgment. We never investigated the results of our decision."

"In the research your committee gathered, what stood out?"

Caverly looks thoughtful, then nods.

"One doctor. From Milwaukee. In his interview, he said, 'We should put Lipitor in the water. Like fluoride.' Made me crazy. Made me question the undisputed regard we hold for doctors. They're not gods. Lipitor in the water! Can you imagine? Music to Pfizer's ears, I'm sure. We are overmedicated. Over diagnosed. And that's the God's truth. And that fact will be part of these hearings."

"How does this fit in with Congress writing new healthcare legislation? Might you actually create laws that would limit advertising for drugs?"

"This is all exploratory. To write an effective and lasting piece of legislation that will impact every single person in this country requires us to study every facet of the issue, to know the repercussions."

"This will make a lot of lobbyists rich, yes?"

"I fear so. Yes. The president has kicked a hornet's nest. But if these hearings can guide us in writing a strong healthcare bill, then we will have done a good thing."

"Have you met Mr. Bethune?"

"I have not, but my wife is a big fan and will be attending the hearings in hopes of seeing him in person!"

Nonnie smiles and turns to Baéz. "Amazing what Brighton's done, isn't it?"

Baéz nods. "Yes, now let's hope all the money he spent doesn't go to waste."

✳ ✳ ✳

The Center for Palliative Care is near the Massachusetts border in Upper Falls. Located on the shore of Great Heron Lake, the old wooden buildings once served as a popular summer camp. The view is restful and suits the delicate needs of persons approaching the end of life.

Baéz has commandeered Brighton's flashy Boxster for the scenic drive up the Housatonic River to meet Nonnie's old friend Atticus Robertson. As he pulls onto the handsome grounds with their colorful flowers and fanciful wind-driven sculptures, he sees many caregivers and their charges enjoying the sunshine.

He finds Atticus sitting on a bench near the entrance. They shake hands.

"Thank you for coming. I wasn't sure what else to do."

"Nonnie's no longer comfortable driving and hoped you wouldn't mind if I came instead."

"No, I'm pleased you are here. I called today for help with my friend. We've known each other since grade school. His name is William. William Strong. He's had a wonderful life, but after a lengthy recovery from a severe skateboarding accident, his physicians prescribed Oxycodone for his pain. And like so many others, he became addicted. This is his third overdose, and the worst."

Baéz nods, listening carefully. "Tell me what happened. How is he here?"

"William and I meet for dinner every Wednesday. We work hard to stay connected. When he didn't show up this week, I got nervous. I drove to his house and found him in his cluttered living room, on the floor, barely breathing. He always has Narcan nearby, and I forced the spray up his nose and into his nasal passages, but the doctors think it might have been too late. He may have been deprived of oxygen for too long. They have him in an induced coma to see if his body can reverse the damage."

As Atticus tells the tale, his eyes water.

"What would you like from me?" asks Baéz gently.

"It may sound odd, I know, but Nonnie has always been such a help to me. I wanted her to simply sit with William, knowing it would be beneficial."

"I understand. Let's wander over to the lake. Let us first place our own selves in a balanced and congenial state of mind. Then we can sit beside William and see that he, too, is comforted."

✳ ✳ ✳

"**P**lease state your name and occupation," says the chairman.

"Mary Abigail Calhoun. Vice President, the Council on Legislation for the American Medical Association."

"Thank you for being here today, Ms. Calhoun. We are anxious to hear your advice and opinions on a range of subjects."

From their elevated dais, the Chairman and his committee members stare down at the tiny woman seated nearly thirty feet away. On either side of her are lawyers and advisors and the many, many journalists covering this first day of hearings. The television lights are blinding, but everyone can see Brighton Bethune huddled in the last row, with Scottie by his side.

The witness smiles: she is a frequent visitor to the various chambers of the House and Senate and is comfortable traveling these hallways. The AMA is the largest lobbying organization in the country.

"How many doctors does the AMA count as members?"

"Close to a quarter million, sir."

"And what percentage does that represent of all doctors in America?"

"About forty percent."

"And this membership has strongly recommended that we stop all television advertising of prescription medications, is that correct?"

"Yes, sir."

"For those of us less versed in the intricacies of the medical field, can you tell us why your members disapprove of such advertising?"

Senator Regis Caverly is a charmer, a ladies' man who nurtures his image as a humble government servant. In more than thirty years in Washington, he has amassed a mighty list of supporters and detractors, and with the Democratic Party now in power, he is using this ascendency to push forward every element of the president's challenging agenda.

"The drug manufacturers will claim that such advertising is solely for the benefit of the patient. They explain that their ads increase awareness of new diseases and the various treatments available to combat those diseases."

"Yes, I have heard those arguments. Do your members disagree? Is it not helpful for doctors to have well-informed patients?"

"We have found that such advertising has inflated demand for the newer, more expensive drugs. Also, I think you will find that these drug manufacturers are spending billions of dollars on advertising. Imagine how much less costly our medications would be if these companies reduced their expenditures by billions of dollars. We need more transparency in drug pricing; we need to know what percentage of those billions of dollars is being passed on to the consumer."

Many of those in attendance nod their heads, and Brighton is pleased that the hearings have begun in such a compelling manner.

✳ ✳ ✳

Baéz holds William's hand. The skin is cool and clammy. Baéz has a strong desire to cleanse William of the impurities that are trying to define him. Closing his eyes, he mentally washes the glistening skin.

An emanation of grace fills the room and envelops them.

When he opens his eyes, he sees Atticus hugging himself and weeping.

"Love him. Don't blame him. Don't be angry with him--he did all he could. Love him. He can carry that with him. Better than any talisman. Love."

Attie nods. Baéz releases William's hand. "I think he's gone."

"Yes," responds Attie.

"Perhaps we should notify a nurse?"

"Can we remain here just a minute more?"

Baéz aches from the pain he sees on Atticus's face. "Of course we can."

They sit silently as the sun creeps behind the tall cedars. Attie then stands and suggests they share an early dinner.

They are both quiet as they stare at their menus and order simple burgers and a pitcher of beer.

"Do you think there is a special place in hell reserved for the makers of OxyContin? They are responsible for countless deaths and destroyed lives, and all for profit," Attie asks.

"I don't believe in hell. Our consciousness simply moves forward, and the challenges we have here on earth continue until we solve them. And yes, for those who practiced evil, for those who spread suffering and death, the path will grow more difficult, joy will flee, and all comfort will depart."

A generous silence settles over the table. Atticus sips his beer and then speaks. "In the fifth grade, we moved to a new school district. I was nervous on that first day, but your grandmother told me I could never lack for love. She said, 'Invite it in, let love know that it is welcome.' I walked into that classroom and said silently to myself, 'Come on in!' William came over and introduced himself. He showed me where to hang my hat and coat. At lunchtime, he invited me to join his table. We became inseparable. I will miss him forever."

"Yes, you will. And be grateful for that. *Missing him* is simply another name for love."

A waiter comes and clears their dishes.

"Thank you for today," Atticus says. "I'm not sure I could have borne it alone."

"You can never find yourself alone. Trust that. Continue to follow Nonnie's advice. Silently whisper, 'Come on in,' and love will be there. And for those people who invented this drug, who sold this drug, no invitation will be forthcoming. No new friend will show them where to hang their hat."

✳ ✳ ✳

"**N**icola Cipra Tibor, Senior Vice President, Marketing, Afidcorp."

"Thank you for being with us today, Mr. Tibor. Is your family named for the Roman emperor or the Roman river?"

"I would be pleased with either, but I believe our name stems from a famous chain of kosher restaurants in Prague."

The crowd bursts into laughter. He is impeccably dressed, his skin radiating a healthful countenance. He always makes sure he is a walking advertisement for the wares he sells.

"So, tell us about your new drug, Adrenyl. Who was it developed for? And what does it claim to do?"

"Adrenyl is a beta blocker, designed to lower blood pressure and to assist in the recovery of heart attack victims."

"And, according to your commercial, it destroys fear, is that right?"

"Well, like many medications, Adrenyl has other uses, and minimizing fear is one of them. Lowering blood pressure often leads to a lowering of those elements in our system that create fear."

"So, this drug wasn't developed to assist daredevils diving into swimming pools from motel rooftops?"

"No, sir."

"We have seen many deaths this year from crazy stunts undertaken by folks who were prescribed your drug."

"We cannot control how our medicines are prescribed."

"No? But we read how you incentivize your salesmen and reward physicians who reach certain thresholds. Is that not correct?"

Nico's smile disappears.

Watching the hearings on C-Span as he sips a non-alcoholic beer, Elwynn shakes his head. He had warned Nico this ad campaign would get them all in trouble. He feels no regret at having leaked sensitive documents to Caverly's committee.

Baéz made the initial approach, explaining it was Brighton's wish to expose the deceptions utilized in selling healthcare and medicine. *Help him,* Baéz had pleaded.

He admired his son's campaign, his little films. They were funny, irreverent, and elegant.

Will forgiveness now follow? Does Brighton know his dad has been fired? Does it matter? For his actions to be redemptive, they must not be motivated by a specific goal. *How does salvation work?* he wonders. He stares at the definition in his treasured Oxford English Dictionary.

Deliverance from the power and penalty of sin. The act
Of preserving or the state of being preserved from harm;
12th *century. Middle English. From the Latin salvátus, saved*
As used in C.S. [Christian Science] the realization
That Life, Truth, and Love are supreme and that
They can destroy such illusions as sin, death, etc.

He stares at the TV screen and changes channels, wondering how the networks are covering the hearings and immediately regrets doing so, for there on the large screen is the image of his handsome son. He boosts the volume.

"Also in the audience today is the actor, athlete, and activist Brighton Bethune. His witty, ninety-second films are thought to be a major instigator in getting Congress to include drug advertising in their healthcare hearings. With him is the LA restaurateur Scottie Morris."

He hadn't even known her name. That's how deep their estrangement has become. *She's pretty,* he thinks.

How had he allowed his foolish addictions to come between him and his son? How had he lost him?

He knows the answer, and it shames him.

Nico's peevish testimony finally ends. Wynn continues watching as another good friend is sworn in.

"Jonathan Douglas, Senior Vice President, The Acorn Agency"

"Thank you, Mr. Douglas. Glad to have you here today. Can you tell me the revenue that your advertising agency generated in the past year?"

"Our billings amounted to $1.7 billion, sir."

"Good to hear our economy is bouncing back! And tell me, what did Americans spend overall to purchase their medications? Do you know that figure?"

Douglas looks at his attorneys and then searches his papers.

"I do not."

"Well, I do! We spent a whopping $175 billion dollars on medications. A staggering amount, don't you think, Mr. Douglas?"

"Why staggering? Compared to what, Senator?"

"Compared to what? Compared to what we spent *before* drug advertising was allowed. Ten years ago, the average American purchased six prescriptions a year. Now that number is twelve. A one hundred percent increase since your ads began flooding our airwaves!"

Elwynn's not sure where these facts will lead, but he is pleased he played a part in making them public. Now his fervent wish is for his son's forgiveness.

Attie pays the bill, and both men exit through the empty bar where a lone TV plays the news. Baéz sees Brighton's face on the screen and stops to watch.

"The hearings began today," he explains as the bartender turns up the sound. Baéz takes a seat and reaches for the bowl of pretzels. On the television, an exotic, long-haired woman sits behind the microphone and answers the Chairman's questions.

"Indigo Digger, co-founder of Message in a Bottle."

"This woman is fascinating but also polarizing," Baéz says. "Brighton pushed to include her testimony."

Senator Caverly asks: "Tell us about your company, what you do, your clients, and your unique investigations."

"Our firm evaluates the impact of corporate messaging."

She does not elaborate on her succinct answer. Tolliver had been clear with her about the dangers of providing too much information.

The Chairman smiles. "Yes. Tell us about corporate messaging. An example."

"We attempt to ascertain whether the core values of a certain client impact the likelihood of the customer base responding in a positive or a negative manner."

"Like a rating service? Like Nielsen? Did an ad cause a viewer to purchase the product? Is that correct?"

Indigo sips from her water glass. "No, Senator. More complicated than that. We are not studying the impact of a specific ad. We study the long-term effect of certain types of messaging. The effect of constant repetition and reinforcement. What impact do these messages have on the consumer that is not necessarily reflected in sales data."

The senator's impatience is clear, regardless of the polite smile. "Help me out here. I don't follow."

Indigo describes the example she uses on new clients. "The thirty-eighth president was the fittest, most athletic man to ever hold the office. Gerald Ford played football for the University of Michigan and twice led them to the National Championships. He turned down offers to play for the Detroit Lions and the Green Bay Packers. He was the physical fitness instructor for the Naval Reserve. While in the White House, he swam daily, played tennis, and enjoyed skiing. Yet he was widely believed to be a klutz. He once slipped on an airport staircase, and a popular comedian began portraying the president as an uncoordinated mass of physical shortcomings. This was inaccurate and misleading, but once the description stuck, the president *did* have a series of awkward stumbles, as if his persona was altered by the commonly held belief of his clumsiness. Whether true or false, any information that is consistently communicated through careful, repetitive messaging becomes widely accepted."

"And how does this apply to pharmaceutical advertising? Aren't these companies simply attempting to convince the viewer to purchase their cold remedy or painkiller?"

"Yes, in the short term. But the long-term message is that the human body is an extremely vulnerable vessel that is constantly under attack from illness. Their commercials portray life as a never-ending battle against an unseen enemy and medication is the only defense."

"And has your firm reached any conclusions as to the impact of this hidden, long-term 'messaging' created by the pharmaceutical industry?"

The senators and their staff members stare at this provocative woman, clearly wondering what she will say. A recent profile of her in the *Post* explained that her mother is a healer, utilizing herbs and plants to bring comfort to her diseased patients. Indigo is a believer in many types of alternative health treatments. She firmly believes the American drug manufacturers are involved in a widespread conspiracy to persuade a willing public that dependence on drugs is the best way to assure a long and lasting life. But she does not yet possess sufficient proof.

"Sir, the research is too recent. To see a true trend, to quantify the impact and its causes will take another generation. But I do think these companies have succeeded in convincing us of the necessity of medicine. Like food. Like water. Pills have become a part of America's daily intake, a block on the approved pyramid."

"But you assume that these medicines are not good for us. Are you suggesting we shouldn't take advantage of the many breakthroughs that medical research has achieved?"

"No, sir, you misunderstand me. It is not the medicine that endangers us, but the message that comes wrapped around the medicine. We are being convinced that we are frail creations."

She raises her voice as she stares at the chairman. "Big Pharma is wearing us down with their endless propaganda while you and your colleagues do nothing!"

The crowd buzzes as the cameras roll. Caverly bangs his gavel.

Sitting in the bar with his young friend, Baéz smiles, proud of Indigo's courage.

✶ ✶ ✶

The hearings continue for nearly a year. The many complex and contradictory aspects of the American healthcare system are angrily argued on TV, in barber shops, and across dinner tables. The new president is willing to employ all his political capital to achieve this single goal, but his success is far from guaranteed.

Brighton's connection to these hearings has not been lost on ESPN's many advertisers, and Disney instructs their sports network to cancel the medical segments on Brighton's show. Brighton threatens to quit and begins holding meetings with rival broadcasters, but Ollie explains the legal ramifications of violating his non-compete clause.

Ollie has driven up to Connecticut to review Brighton's options, but when he finds his client angry and upset, they sit quietly together, avoiding all mentions of the future.

"How far away our days are Pepperdine are," notes Brighton. "How thrilling that time was as we explored the endless possibilities that lay before us." He sighs and then laughs. "Don't listen to me. Go say hello to Nonnie. She'll be far cheerier company."

The day is warm and wet, and leaves are falling in glorious profusion. Nonnie sits on her wraparound porch, unfazed by the rain as she hands Ollie a fresh cup of coffee. *The Times* is damp and opened to the sports section.

"How's Brighton?" she asks.

Ollie's face reflects the pain he feels. "He's got nowhere to go. He's played out his hand."

"What will he do? Have you devised an exit strategy for him?"

Ollie ponders how much to share with Nonnie, knowing he will need her support in getting Brighton to accept his proposal.

"The UN wants to appoint him as their newest Goodwill Ambassador and send him on a lengthy tour of the Middle East. It's a perfect fit and he can legally walk away from his show. He can focus his considerable energies on those suffering from this endless war and shine a bright light where it is needed. I'm hoping he'll agree."

"Will he be safe?" she asks.

"Yes. And I think he'll find it inspiring. Nothing here enlivens him. His very public failure to regulate the advertising of drugs has saddened and depressed him."

Nonnie opens the newspaper and begins to read aloud the article that has so upset her.

"'If he were less handsome, none of this would have happened. He was a good athlete, solid but not remarkable. He earned his win at The Open, but his striking features made him larger than life, larger than his actual accomplishments. There are many tennis players of equal talent, but none as fine looking. When he went to war, his opponents were the gods of Islam, and they punished him for his actions, stealing his handsome features and making him an object of pity. But again, like a phoenix, he rose, newly minted as a prophet, idolized and worshipped, healing the sick and susceptible as he stared down from the screens of the multiplex.

And now, as Sunday sermons are preached to empty chapels, his is the voice heard across the land, and once again, a man with limited abilities has an oversized influence on a foolish populace. Thank God his wardens have finally seen fit to steal his megaphone. Now we have to hike through the hinterlands towards The Faith Channel *to catch the sanctimonious half-brother as he berates our unbelief!'"*

Nonnie puts down the paper and stares at Tolliver. "Has he seen this?"

Ollie nods. "The backlash has begun. We knew it had to happen; it was simply a question of when. The good feelings and proud sentiments he inspired will now be overtaken by the complainers, the doomsayers, and the chatterers who never create anything of value but who love to tear everything down. Stay tuned. It ain't gonna be pretty!"

Brighton returns to the welcoming sands of his beachside home as the 111th Congress of the United States votes 219 to 212 to enact the Patient Protection and Affordable Care Act. The bill is signed into law by the forty-fourth President, Barack Obama, on March 23, 2010. As part of the flurry of compromises required to pass the bill, Congress promises *not* to import cheaper drugs from Canada and *not* to use the government's purchasing power to negotiate lower prices on medicines. Congress also recommends the Food and Drug Administration extend the 2003 Act that allows for the advertising of prescription medications on television. In exchange for picking up many of the increased costs for Medicare and Medicaid, Big Pharma is assured there will be no limits on their ability to set the pricing and advertising of their products.

The selling of drugs on American television is here to stay.

Brighton's final short film begins airing on TV that same week. Baéz strongly advised him not to release it. As did Scottie, and everyone else who saw it.

"They'll just see you as an embittered loser, trying to have the last word."

"You didn't think it was funny?" Brighton asks Scottie, knowing she is the most truthful of his friends.

She smiles. "Yes, it was funny. Truly funny. You and Jane Fonda were perfect together, and the baggage you both carry was ever present without you having to say a thing."

"So?"

"No one likes the smartest kid in the class. It will take years for you to be forgiven, but that is why casting Jane was so brilliant. It's like you knew they would hate you, as they had once hated her, yet eventually came to love her again. And they will love you again too. But not today. Not today, my sweet."

✳ ✳ ✳

The bells chime at 5:46 a.m., Pacific Daylight Time, commemorating the first plane flying into the North Tower.

Brighton turns off the television and dusts his body with talcum. He pulls on his wetsuit and walks down the outdoor stairs to his rack of boards. The sun is still below the horizon, and the surface of the ocean is glassy, no waves in sight. He doesn't care. Today's not about surfing; he simply wants to float, an insignificant piece of jetsam bobbing on the gentle surface.

He recognizes one or two others drifting aimlessly on their boards. They nod to each other. He closes his eyes and listens. Gulls call out as they streak through the lightening sky. A gentle splash is heard as a fellow surfer steers his board towards shore.

Ten years. It's been ten years since he hoisted the trophy. The famous photograph of that moment, his eyes wide and watery, is a powerful embodiment of joy, yet he can't recapture the feeling.

Happiness is rarely long-lasting. Of this, he is sure. He also knows that his actions in Iraq, under orders from his homeland, are not redeemed by his successes in the world of movies and television. And, most regrettable, his efforts to assist in shaping the new healthcare bill were naïve and fruitless.

Nonnie advised him to be silent and listen. Empty his mind of all the options he sees before him and just listen. He will know what to do.

"Baéz is furious with me," he told her.

"I know," she responded, "but he will understand and support whatever you choose to do."

"You're a fool!" Baéz had screamed when Brighton told him his plans. "Don't you realize the road to inner peace is with those who love you, not with strangers?"

Brighton knows his brother's outburst was shaped by pain, not anger. As boys, they had promised to always be together, and now he is leaving. Leaving the beach, leaving his country, leaving everything and everyone he knows and loves. He will create a new life unburdened by the hypocrisy of his homeland.

Nearly three million men and women signed up for the fight in Afghanistan and Iraq. He is only one of them; as was Raven, as is Ruthie. His thoughts are with them on this chilly morning. He hopes the many who served are able to move on and lead productive lives.

As a shaft of sunlight melts the fog, he feels his heart separate from his ever-present grief. He does as Nonnie suggested—he listens. From between the waves, he gleans the simplest of instructions. *Go,* he is told, and from the stillness emerges a gentle ease he has not felt in ages.

"Here comes a nice set," he thinks as he looks at the incoming swells.

He stands, perfectly balanced, hoping the waves will carry him to a safer and more pleasant shore.

PART THREE

2011 – 2020

25.

'*I'M GOING DOWN TO THE RIVER OF JORDAN*'

The river is shallow, and the water is brown. Brighton cups the liquid in his hands, splashing it over his hair and skin, emulating a ritual baptism, but the stream feels sleek and oily, not cleansing. Naaman once lowered himself into this pool, seeking to purify his soul and rid his body of leprosy, but Brighton suspects the River Jordan has changed greatly since those biblical days.

From his spot on the riverbank, Adama watches this stranger and wonders what he has gotten himself into.

"He has come to heal a broken heart," Dierks Anderes had explained. "Take him under your wing. Stay close by his side. You can help each other."

Adama was incredulous. "He has come to the Middle East to get over a girl?" He spat three times into the sandy soil, as if to ward off the devil.

"No. Not a girl," answered Dierks. "A country. His country has destroyed his trust and crushed his faith. He has come here with hopes of recapturing them."

Dierks runs the United Nations Refugee Service, and Adama Malik, one of his trusted lieutenants, oversees several camps in Iraq, in Jordan, and in Syria. Adama is only twenty-five, but the job, with the endless needs of an ever-growing population of displaced persons, is grinding him to dust. Dierks understood that Adama needed a break, so he matched the two dissimilar men, hoping they could strengthen each other.

"He will be a huge help to us, raising money and awareness. Take him to the refugee camps. Guide him. Protect him."

Now, Adama stares at the striking man who stands naked in the muddy waters of the River Jordan. The muscled body is covered with a spatter of tiny dots in brown and red and orange. The Jordan only reaches his knees, revealing a patch of red hair that surrounds a pendulous cock. As Adama watches, the man goes to his knees and then submerges his red hair in the murky waters. Ritual bathing is a common practice in this section of the river, attracting biblical enthusiasts from around the world, but this is Adama's first visit.

He sits nearby, a towel at the ready, along with several packages of new clothing.

Brighton has tried to minimize his expectations for today, but the setting is far more modest than he had envisioned. He had seen himself submerged in deep, dark waters as he leaves behind all earthly possessions. He would be cleansed of his sins and be reborn in the perfect image of his creator. He would worship in the raiment traditionally worn in this part of the world and he would forget self. Like Naaman, God has blessed Brighton with many gifts. But, like the biblical leper, he too is unclean. This contamination took place in Iraq. He fouled himself in service to the United States and must atone for this.

He walks to shore, disappointed by the many doubts that plague him. Adama opens a large towel and rubs Brighton's skin. Like an altar boy assisting a priest with his robes, Adama opens a pair of loose black trousers for Brighton to step into. A light blue box lies at his feet. Inside are the many articles of clothing they had purchased that morning in a shop in Balqa.

Brighton's large feet drip water and sand onto the new garment as Adama gently raises it up Brighton's legs and then ties the sash around his waist. He unfurls the celadon thobe and fits the opening over Brighton's sodden hair.

As each garment settles upon him, Brighton rises taller and taller. He walks a few steps to feel the fabric on his skin as the clothes sway and move with him. *This is why women are more graceful than men,* he thinks. These garments are freeing; they do not constrict like tailored shirts and tapered pants do. From his leather backpack, he removes a small jar containing oil of vetiver and rubs some on his smooth chest. He breathes in the exotic, grassy scent.

Adama buttons the tunic up to Brighton's neck, then stands back to regard his new employer. "If the intention is to erase any sign of being an American, this is a success. Your fair skin and striking countenance still stand out, but I imagine that has always been true for you. Was disguising your identity the purpose of the traditional clothes?"

Brighton frowns. "I want to follow the dictates of appropriate dress—to wear fabric that is clean and covers me properly." Despite the sincerity, he wonders if he sounds ridiculous.

"How do you feel?"

"Naked, to tell the truth."

He begins to gather up his jeans and undergarments, his cotton shirt and the silver chain bearing the cross of Jesus. He removes the kaffiyeh and shakes the water from his hair.

"Yes, better without. You are well named, you know? Brighton. A red flag atop your head."

They walk towards the road, and Brighton asks, "What now, my young prince?"

"Don't. My father calls me that because he thinks I'm spoiled."

"Sorry, but your country is called a Kingdom. And kingdoms always have princes."

"Yes, and princesses too. But we must wait because Father, Mother, and Sister have invited us to dinner at the homestead in Amman! And all I can say is good luck to us!" He grins as he makes this announcement, slapping Brighton on the back.

✳ ✳ ✳

"We are grateful to you, Mr. Bethune. We never see my brother. This dinner is a rare occasion."

Adama's sister Leyla is beautiful. She carries herself royally, her physical presence noble and majestic. Her Levantine dialect requires careful listening, and Brighton looks to Adama to clarify certain words or expressions. Kaveh and the Army had taught him Arabic with a Mesopotamian dialect. Hers is more musical, the guttural exclamations softer and less reminiscent of the sounds he wishes to erase—the sound of soldiers screaming, of women cursing, and babies crying.

He must stay in the present, he tells himself. This ancient language means more than war, more than death. It is the language of poets, Kaveh once explained.

"What do they know of me?" Brighton had asked as Adama drove them to his parents' home high in the hills of Amman.

"The war unfolded next door, so of course they know who you are. The Angel of the Levant. They worry. They question the wisdom of your returning. They worry about my safety. They worry their daughter is easily influenced by handsome men. What can I say? They worry. It is what they do. And, as you shall see, they do it very well!"

The men stand as Basmah, Leyla's mother, brings several platters to the table. Their father, Bilal, arrives with a selection of wines.

"Sit, sit," urges the mother as she passes a platter to Brighton.

The wooden chairs scrape the tiled floor as the men pull themselves closer to the table. The aroma of za'atar and sumac fills the formal dining room. A domed ceiling sheathed in thin leaves of gold creates a warm glow, and ancient ceramic tiles surround the windows and doorways. Deep recesses in the plastered walls hold antique pottery and sculptures of ancient warriors.

No one speaks; they look to him, wanting their guest to serve himself first. He smiles nervously, the noise of his silverware clattering on fine china. Leyla is smiling to herself. Is she reacting to a private joke, or is he using the wrong implement? Or maybe the wrong word? Adama gives her a stern look. Brighton senses tension and assumes he is the cause.

Acting on a hunch, he turns to Basmah and, in lightly accented French, asks, "How have I upset your children?"

She smiles. He has guessed correctly—she speaks perfect French. "My daughter is a journalist and wants to write about you. She thinks it will bring glory to her paper, which is run by idiotic men. My son fears my daughter's interference will endanger your mission. Endanger you. But don't mind. They argue like this all the time. It is a sign of love and respect. In the end, they will do what is right."

The family listens as Basmah and their guest speak quietly in French, a language none of them share. Basmah passes the hummus, a discreet smile crossing her face. Then the lamb and the bread. Her husband pours water while staring at his wife with a wide grin.

"A clever man has entered our house," Bilal says. "We do well to listen and stop arguing."

Brighton begins eating and the conversation switches back to Arabic. He sneaks glances at the dark princess who is now talking a blue streak.

"Slower, please," he earnestly asks, trying to keep up with her rapid-fire conversation.

Adama shakes his head. "No, you do not want to know what she says. Believe me."

"My mother is a renowned beekeeper," states Leyla, ignoring her brother. "Did you know that? She is the one who taught me to speak quickly, telling me to express all my thoughts before some old man shushes me because I am a woman!"

Bilal interrupts his daughter. "Man has been collecting honey from bees for more than ten thousand years. In North Africa, in Egypt. Here in Jordan. It is an ancient art. My wife is a skilled practitioner."

In the silence that follows, Brighton turns to Leyla. Her long dark hair falls in waves on her shoulders, framing her sharp cheekbones. She speaks more slowly, wanting him to understand. "You are famous here, you know. Not as a soldier, not as an athlete, but as a naked man!"

Brighton is confused. Did he understand her correctly? He looks to Adama while Basmah and Bilal berate their daughter. She laughs at her parents' complaints.

"Ignore her, my friend," Adama says. "I have for years. She'll do anything to draw attention to herself."

Brighton looks over at her as she laughs, revealing a perfect, radiant smile that suits a woman who says what she wants and enjoys the trouble her words invite. She's earned her attention.

"A naked man? I do not understand," he says.

"Your underwear. Mr. Klein."

He is still confused, so she explains further. "The Taj Mall won't carry it. The packaging is provocative, revealing images that are disrespectful of a hero. It is banned from sale. They only carry Lady Calvin."

"A local entrepreneur stockpiled many cartons of your briefs—bought them years ago—and indeed, as my sister says, they are most revealing," Adama explains. "He sells only on the internet. They are incredibly expensive."

Adama is still smiling, but Brighton can tell the parents are embarrassed on his behalf.

"Well, since the subject seems to interest all of you, you'll be pleased to know that Al-Ahsa is now the exclusive manufacturer of my underclothes!"

The table erupts in laughter, but Bilal looks troubled as he sips more wine.

"You are a most unusual guest, Mr. Bethune," Basmah says. "This table rarely discusses undergarments!"

Brighton sneaks another look at Leyla and then addresses her mother in French. "Would it be rude for me to invite your daughter to Baghdad? For her newspaper? If it would assist her, I would be pleased to sponsor her visit."

"You would honor her with such an invite," Basmah says. "Make sure she understands it is for being a journalist, not a woman!"

Brighton nods as Bilal struggles to rise from his chair, knocking over his glass of wine. Adama quickly covers the dark stain with a linen napkin. The elderly head of the household turns and addresses Brighton. "Young man, we are rarely so frivolous. Don't get the wrong idea. We are a country in turmoil. The streets are filled with idiots trying to overthrow our king."

"Papa, enough now." Adama has suffered too many evenings ruined by too much wine. He offers his father a glass of water, but Bilal pushes it away as he begins the diatribe that is all too familiar to his children.

"Our daughter works for a paper that encourages the Brotherhood to violence, and our son quietly negotiates with government ministers. In the 70's we had the sense to throw such people out but now we sit down with them. Madness! Drive them all out, I say! Drive them out!"

Leyla rolls her eyes and then whispers to Brighton: "Do not worry. This happens all the time."

Adama begins to argue in earnest. "Papa, stop. Our neighbors are in turmoil because their rulers ignored their people, but our king has allowed these demonstrations, and his government has listened. We will not share the fate of Egypt and Libya. I am proud of this fact! I am proud of my country."

As Basmah sips from her water glass, Bilal stares at his daughter and then his son, derision coloring his features.

"I am a fool!" he shouts, slurring his words. "And my children are fools. We seek accommodation, we move forward and back, we bargain, and we adjust. Our forefathers did not bargain; they died in battle for their beliefs. They brought glory to our family, as Mr. Bethune has brought glory to his family!"

Brighton knows to remain quiet. The politics of the Middle East have never been more complicated.

"But what do we do?" asks the father, continuing his harangue. "We devote our lives to the pursuit of peace. How pathetic! We do not deserve this fine house. Our belongings are not the spoils from those we have vanquished!"

Adama tries to salvage the situation. "Papa loves the opera," he says. "The larger-than-life characters. He and Mother recently returned from the Grand Opening of the Muscat Opera House. *Turandot*. Can you imagine? Placido Domingo conducting Puccini in Oman, and my father fears *we* are too soft!"

Everyone starts talking again, Bilal stating that Domingo conducted too slowly, Leyla laughing, and Adama shaking his head. Basmah collects the plates and then returns with a platter of Kataifi—nuts and cinnamon and lemon and honey. Everyone dives in, complimenting Basmah on her bees and the flavorful flowers they have used to make their honey.

Later, Brighton is provided blankets and pillows and a pitcher of water for his bedside table. Before leaving, Adama tells him to rest, for the next day will be long and dusty.

"Your sister is beautiful," remarks Brighton.

"You will regret inviting her to join us in Baghdad."

Brighton hears jealousy in Adama's voice. "I am sorry. I should have checked with you first. Your mother emboldened me."

"Mother thinks her daughter is perfect. You think her beautiful. Her colleagues think her clever. Her last boyfriend thought she was a killer."

Brighton raises an eyebrow as he listens to these disparate descriptions.

Adama continues. "I adore my sister and hold her in high regard, but I beg you—be careful. Only she knows what lies beneath. She and I have remained close because I have no desire to uncover her secrets. Now sleep. I should never have brought you here!"

This final comment is said with a twisted smile, which Brighton sees as a sign of approval. After they say goodnight, Brighton studies his room. Beautiful, brightly colored rugs hang from the walls. Strong incense mixes with the odor of spices and exotic herbs. Bilal's words play over and over in his head: *The spoils gathered from the vanquished.* Was the Iraqi incursion nothing more than a play for oil? Had he and his soldiers risked their lives for Middle Eastern oil fields?

He takes a deep breath. He doesn't want these thoughts. Instead, he closes his eyes and sees Leyla's face. A cold princess in an Italian opera based on a Persian poet's fantasy. He had spent dinner looking everywhere but at her. He told himself he did this to honor her mother and father. In truth, he avoided her gaze because it frightened him. Her beauty is uncommon. She unsettles him; she causes a physical tightening within, a reverberation like vertigo—not unpleasant but not comfortable either.

The smell of jasmine surrounds him. Vines growing up the walls of the house are scented, Leyla is scented, and his mind is reeling from an overload of stimuli. He must sleep. Dream. Smile. He takes deep breaths of jasmine; too sweet, but oh so remarkable.

✳ ✳ ✳

The next morning, they hop in the Land Rover, and the pungent aroma of Adama's many hand-rolled cigarettes permeates their clothing. The nicotine and endless cups of coffee from the thermos his mother provided make his hands tremble as he tightens his grasp on the wheel. The windows are rolled down as they speed along Highway 10 en route to Ar Ruwayshid. From there, the Iraqi border is seventy-five kilometers to the east.

"This next town is a nightmare. One enormous gas station with a few residents scratching out a living. We will fill up and then wait for the right colleagues."

They are speaking in Arabic at Brighton's request. He needs to improve and must leave English behind.

"Colleagues for what?" he asks, thinking he has misunderstood.

"We are not driving through Iraq unaccompanied. Bandits rule. We need to create a gang, a squad of trucks and tankers and rough-looking fellows. The markings on our car will help. The red scepter is respected, but I still want us surrounded by lots of trucks. Safety in numbers. That is the expression, yes?"

Brighton nods. They are driving through Al Mafraq, Jordan's eastern province. The border is porous, and thousands of Syrians are seeking refuge. This four-lane highway connects a violent past with a dangerously unknown future. The Bedouin music blaring from the radio provides the crowning touch for Brighton's discomfort. He reminds himself that the challenges ahead are the building blocks for the enterprise of which he dreams.

Adama pulls into the large, sandy truck stop with vehicles parked in every direction. Brighton opens his door and steps outside, the air thick with the smell of diesel. He joins other drivers gathered in groups of two and three, sipping from water bottles and sharing stories.

"We will offer afternoon prayers and then we will enter no man's land. We must be off the roads by dark."

"Are we insane to be driving through Iraq?" Brighton asks.

"Every day US troops are leaving through Kuwait, taking their tanks, planes, and Porto-johns. In another month, the American presence here will be minimal, a few CIA holdovers and teams of defense contractors dismantling what took years to build. The rest will be left to rot and rust, so take a deep breath and see if you are ready for this. There is no shame in turning around. Dierks told me not to push you. We will move at your pace."

Brighton hopes his aspirations are fueled by more than willfulness.

"Thank you. I promise to be patient. And once we are settled, we shall invite your beautiful sister to come and see what we have wrought!"

Adama responds to Brighton's smile with a sharply disapproving glare. Brighton laughs as he follows Adama into the crowded shop. They buy orange sodas and sticky cakes. A few drivers ask where he is from. He says he is a doctor from Canada—he and Adama had discussed inventing this biography so as to avoid the hatred many feel for America. "Yes, your culture is everywhere, but unless you are named Bruce Springsteen or Batman, no one will know who you are. You are safe, Dr. Bethune!"

An hour later, they are back on Route 10. Three long-haul trucks are in front, and six bring up the rear. Each tails the other, forcing everyone to close their windows to keep out the sand and dust. They reach Ar Rutbah in less than ninety minutes.

Brighton sees donkeys pulling ancient wagons with smiling children who laugh and wave. He holds his breath as they speed through the barren landscape.

"You have been here before?" Adama asks.

"Yes. To invite them to join us against Saddam. Before the bombing, before the war began. We were scouts. Advance men. We spoke the language and slipped around under cover of darkness, looking for airfields, electrical plants, water storage facilities. We were moving through a foreign country with no support, existing by our wits, but not yet an enemy. Not yet."

Adama keeps a sharp lookout and stays on the tail of a water tanker. A vehicle carrying a load of Nissan trucks stays right behind them.

"What's in Ramadi? You have colleagues there?" Brighton asks.

"Yes. A village outside. Silariya, on the road to Fallujah. We will arrive before sundown. Yusef and Nabil will take care of us. They have recently arrived from Syria."

His voice betrays no fear; his posture does not signal danger. To operate in war zones demands determination and bravery, not reckless derring-do fueled by adrenalin. Brighton sees he can trust this man.

✷ ✷ ✷

In their first days in the capital city, Brighton lays out his plans to invest his considerable monies in helping the orphans of Iraq. Adama is surprised by the scale of Brighton's ambitions and pleased by the determination he sees in the eyes of his new friend.

In these early months, he and Adama lease properties across the city to house a network of childcare centers and orphanages. They meet with young, idealistic Iraqis who are determined to rebuild their country. They assemble a dedicated staff. Adama rents two apartments for him and Brighton in the upscale district of Al Karradah.

The spare apartments suit Brighton's transformed nature. The cinderblock walls painted bright white are a restful backdrop for the small paintings he buys at roadside markets. An aluminum kitchen table, a simple wooden chair, and two crates on which sit his e-reader, an iPod, and a MacBook Pro provide everything he needs.

His habit of sleeping in the Malibu sand or under Jared's diesel trucks doesn't have an equivalent in Baghdad. He cannot fall asleep under the stars in this dangerous city. Instead, when sleep eludes him, he walks for miles.

Baéz sent him a playlist, via Dropbox, of tunes from their high school years. Brighton downloads the music for tonight's walk. He and Baéz communicate via WhatsApp, and even though their texts are infrequent, each is pleased to feel included in the other's world. The news they share, however, lacks context—like reading headlines without the accompanying story.

The night is cool, and the air is filled with the loud hum of gas-powered generators. Electrical blackouts are frequent, kerosene is rationed, and lines for food are a daily occurrence. These hardships affect everyone; money does not buy freedom from shortages. Brighton welcomes this austerity. His mind is clear and his purpose plain.

He puts the buds in his ears and slips the iPod into a special pocket a local tailor has sewn into his thobe. Then he recites a brief psalm that is one of Nonnie's favorites. He repeats it each day before entering the strangely quiet streets. *And in the night, his song shall be with me,* he says as he locks the door behind him. He hits the PLAY button and walks west towards the Tigris.

Even with the music playing in his ears, he is attentive, reverting to the days when he patrolled the streets of Tikrit. He is learning the location of the many checkpoints that surround the city. Some streets are bordered by cement blast walls to protect pedestrians and sidewalk vendors from truck bombs. The twelve-foot-high structures are covered in graffiti and peeling political posters.

Mariah Carey and Boyz II Men accompany him on the route Kaveh walked years earlier to inform the Coalition Forces of Brighton's whereabouts. He walks over the Arbatash Tamuz Bridge and past the Presidential Palace as the foot traffic thins. Kaveh had described the walk many times, including his fixation on a handsome soldier from the Florida National Guard. The memory of this oft-told tale brings a smile to Brighton's face as he walks past the Danish Embassy and sees the giant Swords of Qadisiyah, the memorial to the Iran-Iraq war. Hussein viewed his troops on this very spot.

On a bench nearby, Brighton sees two young boys speaking an unfamiliar language. Kurdish, he assumes. It is late for them to be out alone. No adult is present. He walks towards them, smiling, not wishing to cause alarm.

"Are you alright?" he asks, first in Arabic, then in Hebrew.

The boys don't understand but they don't run away. Brighton sits on their bench and puts one of the buds in each of their ears. They laugh, mystified but fascinated. Brighton seeks a passerby who speaks Kurdish. A friendly student, female, translates the boys' words into Arabic for Brighton.

"They come from Sulaymaniyah, in the north. They traveled with their mother seeking relatives who live in Saddam City. Last week a truck bomb blew up the restaurant where they were begging for scraps. She was killed. Now they are trying to return home."

Brighton watches the older boy's face as he tells his story. He does not cry but holds his brother's hand. There are more than a million displaced persons within Iraq, and hundreds of thousands of orphans, yet the stories are often the same. Their home is gone, their family is gone, their city is gone.

Brighton explains to the girl that he is an American who runs several orphanages within the city and asks her help in accompanying him and the brothers so she can translate for the staff.

She agrees, smiling. "The older one is named Daniyal, and his brother is Azar. Dani speaks well, he is an educated boy, but they are hungry, and he wonders if you could buy them a sandwich."

✷ ✷ ✷

Ignoring Adama's strong opposition, Brighton invites Leyla to join them and report firsthand on the massive withdrawal of American forces from Iraq. Her initial stories are framed through the eyes of a soldier, an American corporal whose identity she scrupulously protects. Her inside view allows her dispatches to stand out from those told by her fellow journalists.

The comfortable routines and ordered habits that Brighton and Adama have established over many months are now disordered. Leyla lives one floor below and she treats the austere complex like a college dorm, running up and down the stairs to her brother's apartments to share sweets and information and ask questions of her handsome American soldier. That is how she refers to Brighton, much to his chagrin.

She has little patience for the do-gooders who are so plentiful in her brother's orbit, but Brighton continues to intrigue her. His desire to maintain a professional distance draws her closer, and his ability to make sure they are never alone feeds her appetite.

On this sunny Friday, as the mosques announce the hour of prayer, the siblings embark on an adventure with the two newest residents of the Al-Noor Children's Home, the brothers from Sulaymaniyah.

"You are going to get him killed!" Adama says with exasperated fury.

Leyla is accustomed to her brother's histrionics. He has strong emotions and cares about many things. Her smile remains unchanged as they walk through the Al-Ghazal bird market in the center of Baghdad. They cross the Tigris and stroll through the Bab al-Moatham neighborhood, allowing the clamor of thousands of birds to direct their path. Brighton lags behind, unaware of the strife between brother and sister.

"How? How will I get him killed?"

"He is lost in a dream of you. To survive here, we must be deliberate with our every action. You know this. If we don't, we end up like your Theo."

"Theo was lovely, but he was also negligent. The hashish brought his troubles. Not me. Don't blame his troubles on me."

"Yes, I know, nothing is ever your fault. But sister, listen to me—these men follow you, blinded by your sweet and deadly scent. And you love it. The last one was forced to pay a healthy ransom to save his life. There will be no ransom for Brighton Bethune. This one will be killed. He will be executed. You must release him."

"You are being ridiculous." She stares into his coal-black eyes and sees fear. Still, she shrugs off his plea. "You are like Father; you have seen too many operas!"

An unruly choir springs from the cages filled with thousands of birds—yellow and turquoise and jade, lime and apple and moss. Parrots and canaries and meadowlarks, budgies and finches and nightingales. The colorful pets are smuggled here from South America and Africa, their Syrian traffickers doing a brisk business.

Leyla looks back to where Brighton has stopped. Daniyal is on his right while Azar sits proudly on his shoulders. Sensing Leyla's eyes on him, Brighton smiles, then lets the brothers pull him towards a stall whose seller has a large Macaw standing on his shoulder and pecking at his ear. The man transfers the blue-and-gold bird to the top of Daniyal's mop of untamed curls.

Leyla turns back to her brother, who continues with his warnings.

"Sister, don't. Release him."

"You are too late, brother. He has already succumbed!"

He slaps her with his open palm.

The Macaw screeches, and Brighton drops to his knees, mistaking the slap for a gunshot while he protects Azar's body with his own.

Leyla brings her hand to her face, stunned by her brother's actions. The shock is sudden and overwhelming, and her cheek reddens. Adama grabs her and holds her close. She feels the heat of his anger as he spits out his accusations.

"I am your brother, not your confessor. This is a good man. You are dulling his senses. You are making him vulnerable. He is making unwise decisions because of you." He releases her. "We must all return to Amman. We can oversee the work from there, we can communicate via Skype, we will get his work done, and we can keep him safe. If you go, he will follow. Think of someone else for a change!"

She *is* being selfish. To feed her ambition. To prove to the men who run her newspaper that she is valuable and not afraid of working in a dangerous war zone. And she is making Brighton pay the price.

"He lives for these children," she says. "His money can buy him many things, but his moments of reading stories to them, scaring the ghosts from under their beds, and wiping their snotty noses, those are what bring him joy. Not me. Our pleasure is fleeting. Look at him. Do you ever see him delighted by anything or by anyone other than the children?"

They both turn to Brighton as he lifts Daniyal into his arms and the stall owner transfers the parrot to Azar's shoulder. Everyone is smiling now. Brighton's celadon thobe stands out amidst the garb of the Iraqi citizens, who wear mostly Western clothing. The people stare at this man who is obviously not related to these boys. Leyla knows these moments terrify Adama. The attention generated by a too-handsome face. Someone is going to recognize him. His liveliness draws attention wherever they go.

"A few days a month, he can return here," Adama says. "Visit the children. We have created an excellent organization. Fine people work with us. He no longer needs to be present. That's all I am saying. Convince him that life in Amman will allow him to continue his work free of danger. Otherwise, I am going to recommend the Embassy withdraw his visa."

The young boys and Brighton join them, loud and laughing. Daniyal and Azar each hold a small bamboo cage containing a perfect little parakeet.

"Aludra's going to kill me, isn't she?" Brighton asks while pointing at the little coops. Aludra is the overseer at the Children's Home. She adores Brighton.

"No, it will be fine," announces Leyla. "We must get a larger cage and some seed, and those little water bottle thingies the birds drink from. This is good. A project for all the children, and the lovely sound of singing in their home. Come on, brother. Help us."

And Leyla smiles, all forgotten, and everything forgiven.

Daniyal helps prepare the younger children for bed, including his brother, Azar. Then Leyla reads to them about Ali Baba. When she finishes, she moves her chair closer to Azar's bedside and tells him her own special version of Sinbad in Kurdish. Brighton watches as the boy hugs her and says goodnight.

She then joins Brighton in the large kitchen where several older boys are finishing the cleanup.

"He loves you!" states Brighton, referring to Azar.

"No, he loves my stories and that I can speak his language."

"Yes, that is most fortunate."

"Well, you know, you Americans pride yourself on speaking only one language. The rest of us have to do with several languages to make ourselves understood!"

Brighton chuckles, but then asks, "*Quante lingue parli?*"

She laughs and responds with "*Tabahaa.*" Then she leans in and kisses him on the ear, licking the lobe. He pulls back as if struck.

"Don't do that. It confuses the kids. We are *not* a couple. We are *not* loving parents." There is anger in his voice.

"It is not the children who are confused. It is you." She bites his ear again.

"Shit, that hurts." He grabs a damp cloth from the sink. He sees blood. "You know if Aludra sees you harm me, she will have you killed!"

Now they both laugh.

"Let us not fool ourselves," he says. "We are simply two needy animals who like each other. Nothing more."

She nods. "Let's go home, cowboy!"

They walk back to Al Karradah.

In the privacy of his bedroom, Brighton wears slim, button-front jeans ripped at the knee with a short, ragged T-shirt that reveals his scarred and muscular stomach.

She undresses him with an urgency that makes his heart pound. She is aggressive, fueled by fury and frustration. She is the victor enjoying the spoils of battle. She is a cruel but tender chieftain. She will bring him to the verge of climax then prevent the desired explosion. She rides him mercilessly until he begs to be allowed release. Sometimes she forces him to withdraw and spill onto her smooth belly, making him lick her skin clean.

Their erotic adventures embarrass them both, but once begun, they cannot stop. Sex has been many things for him over the years—exciting, exhausting, thrilling, needy, but never addictive. She is a drug that cures an ailment he never knew he had.

Sex, in Brighton's mind, correlates to love and tenderness. With Leyla, lovemaking is a carnal activity that releases the stress and strain of modern life. It is not a promise, it contains no hope, it is not wrapped in ribbons. And so they wrangle and spar like highly strung thoroughbreds being forced to mate while feigning indifference.

She knows he wants to keep his distance, but the more he resists, the stronger becomes her desire. She isn't even sure she likes him, but she sees the admiration her father holds for him. She knows an affair with Brighton will diminish his standing with her brother and father, and some selfish part of her wants this.

To her utter exasperation, when Bilal and Adama discover the affair, they treat Brighton even more tenderly. They call him "Leyla's boyfriend" as if they were children in school. She has expended untold amounts of energy attempting to win her family's approval, and now, because of him, she has it. She is infuriated but also secretly pleased.

✷ ✷ ✷

The miles of frayed cables conducting electricity from generators to shops and apartments creates a lacy roof above the oldest roadway in Baghdad. Rashid Street, which snakes through the city, hugging the Tigris and leading from Jumhuriya Bridge to Maidan Square, was once filled with cafes and theaters, with shops selling knick-knacks and clothing, sweets and kebabs. Now it is a scrap heap. Old cars litter the shuttered roadway, and filthy tables display auto parts and engine remnants where intellectuals once sat and drank tea and had their hair cut.

"The government announces a reclamation project every year. It is a flea market for grease monkeys," Adama says. "Mechanics wander the area, fixing cars, changing the oil, and rotating the tires. Right here on the sidewalk, leaving behind the debris of their impromptu repairs."

Brighton stares at the rusted remnants of abandoned trucks. Amidst the chaotic activity, a young man is quietly putting four new tires on a jacked-up Mercury Grand Marquis. He wears a filthy white cap with US ROUTE 66 printed on it.

"What does the government want?" Brighton asks.

"They want us to take all these roving mechanics, divide them into groups by expertise—metalwork, engine work, automotive painting—and create a series of new, registered businesses in buildings they will provide free of charge.

"And this request actually comes from the president?"

"Yes. He is impressed by what we do, by the results. It is a great honor, my friend. They are asking a private American citizen to assist with the rebuilding of Iraq."

Brighton is pleased. This is what he had hoped to accomplish.

"Only person I know with any expertise in this area is my Army buddy, Ruth Powers. She ran field maintenance, overseeing the dozens of mechanics who kept our trucks and tanks and jeeps in perfect working order. She now owns a bunch of Jiffy Lube franchises in Texas."

"Sounds perfect, brother. Bring her over. We love Texans!"

As Brighton takes one last look at the confused activity, he notices the man with the Mercury staring at him. He is heavily scarred, and sand and dirt clings to his unwashed skin. He continues staring at Brighton and then spits on the ground with a look of disgust before turning back to his car to tighten the nuts on the wheel hubs.

✳ ✳ ✳

A truck bomb blows up a food shop down the road from their apartments. If Leyla had not been fussing with her hair and procrastinating on what dress to wear, they could have been caught in the blast. It ends their nine-month sojourn in Baghdad. The city has once again become too dangerous. They will move their operation to Amman, but Brighton and Adama will return for several days each month.

Brighton invites Adama up to his rooms one last time prior to leaving the city. Leyla has already flown out; commercial air service has finally been restored. Brighton makes them each a bowl of tea from the last of his treasured leaves of Camellia. He then begins to undress, not in his bedroom, but in the living room where Adama is seated.

"You were present when I first put it on, so I thought it appropriate you be present as I lay it aside."

Adama is touched by the odd but revealing gesture as Brighton removes the thobe and his undergarments and then slowly dresses in the clothes he was wearing when they first met at the airport in Amman.

"Is this my sister's doing or your God?" Adama asks with a wicked smile.

"Leyla is more of a jeans girl, truth be told."

They laugh, but the seriousness of what Brighton is doing is not lost on either of them.

Brighton lovingly folds the soft cloth and places it back in the blue box the shop had provided on the day of his immersion in the River Jordan. Then he sits and sips his tea. The afternoon light softens the room.

"I wore it solely to erase every vestige of myself. For me, feeling invisible was unique. And freeing. It reminded me to praise God and lift my head in song. Now, I can return to the cloth that feels familiar, without losing the lessons the thobe allows."

He picks up his backpack and the blue box and they both descend the narrow stairs. The day is ending and a thick fog of diesel fumes and wood smoke colors the air.

"We will be back," Adama says. "This is not goodbye."

Their neighborhood has a new checkpoint. Once again, Brighton's height and hair and freckled skin causes people to mark his presence. And once again, Adama fears for his colleague's safety.

26.

BOONE NEVILLE

Joel Osteen saved her life, and Ruth Powers doesn't care who knows it.

When she returns from Iraq, her parents and brothers set her up in an Airstream that sits on cinderblocks in a local mobile home park, where she discovers the joys of *Ice Road Truckers* and fills her freezer with Lean Cuisines.

The guys at the VFW are good with her, and patient. They understand the difficulty of being a soldier in a country that has no idea there is a war going on. To survive this painful disconnect, they tell her to find a job, any job, something to keep her busy. They tell her about the new Jiffy Lube franchise that is soon to open. "The owner is partial to vets," they say.

Humble, Texas, is exactly what the name promises, and she had been thrilled to leave after graduating high school. Still, she follows the advice of her buddies at the VFW and rides her bike down to the Jiffy Lube that is nearing completion.

"This is my third shop. I've got one in Beaumont and one in Galveston," explains Luke Neville. "My younger brother's going to manage this one. His name's Boone. He'll need a bit of help. He forgets things. Like turning off lights or locking up or returning a call. Your skills as a mechanic make you overqualified for this job—we mostly change the oil and adjust the brakes—but I would be willing to pay extra for you to keep an eye out for him."

Luke explains his brother suffers from fetal alcohol syndrome.

"Messes with his memory. Otherwise, the sweetest man on earth. Nothing weird. I promise."

Ruthie takes the job. She is the only female mechanic and keeping an eye on the younger brother is a pleasant chore. He is a serious fellow, odd for one so young, but his smile is its own reward. He is pure Texan. He calls his elders "sir" or "ma'am" and can be seen doffing his ten-gallon hat when he spies a pretty lady. He's addicted to the Westerns Netflix ships him every week and begins emulating the laconic demeaner of his favorite shoot-em-up stars.

The best part of Ruthie's day is when Boone takes off his green-and-white coveralls with the Jiffy Lube logo and puts on his faded, low-rise skinny jeans. A large copper and brass buckle draws the eye to his fine form.

"Lookin' good, Boone," the guys tease, meaning no harm.

He's the one who gives Ruth a copy of *Every Day a Friday*. He attends Osteen's Lakewood Church and says he would be proud to escort her there on a Sunday of her choosing. A young woman working in an auto-repair shop inspires lots of jokes and whistles from coworkers and customers alike, but an offer to attend church was a new one for Ruthie.

"I hope you won't mind if I tell you how beautiful you look today," Boone whispers during that first service.

"A woman never minds being told she is beautiful."

"Get used to it, then. I'm going to remind you of how truly beautiful you are."

She smiles. "Shh. We shouldn't be talking."

He widens his eyes in mock horror and mouths, "Sorry." Osteen is instructing them to keep their visions full and their dreams big. "Commit to excellence," he exhorts, his enormous smile filling the lower half of his face. His advice and lessons are about finding success and generating an income. *God seems unusually interested in growing everyone's bank balances*, Ruthie thinks.

Boone isn't listening. He is alternating between playing with the ring he always wears and combing his thick hair behind his ears with his long fingers, all while quietly humming. He does this often, goes into his own world. When he returns, it's as if time stood still.

Sixteen thousand people applaud, and Osteen smiles as he leaves the stage. Boone takes Ruthie's hand and gives it a kiss. She laughs as she tries to remember where they parked Boone's car. Even though he is often helpful, she must not expect him to be. She can't depend on him, but she accepts this; she is accustomed to caring for herself.

As they walk to where she remembers they parked, Boone greets the many churchgoers walking beside them. He loves people, and his neighbors respond in kind. Ruth feels this affection and smiles, finally glad to be home.

Ruth Powers surprised her fellow soldiers by re-upping when her first tour of duty expired. After the miraculous Christmas rescue, she returned to her base unharmed but not unchanged. Folks went out of their way to shake her hand, but only a few noticed the subtle tremors or the always-damp brow. She was never alone. A soldier, male or female, was always assigned to keep an eye out, to chat with her, to share a meal with her, to listen to her. She welcomed the cocoon they wove around her, and finally the shaking stopped, the fevers ended, the nightmares vanished. If she had been forced to return home, she never would have recovered. Her healing came from being surrounded by other soldiers facing the same challenges. Raven didn't get that chance. He suffered from returning to a country unprepared to accept or understand him.

Boone drops by the Airstream on weekends. He invites her to square dances and Willie Nelson concerts. He takes her to Applebee's and sometimes on a walk around the messy town of Humble. She follows and lets him lead. A goodnight kiss followed by a gentle wave of the hand. He restores the years she lost by enlisting. She is a girl again. And this handsome boy is stealing her heart.

"I'm getting a dawg."

"A dawg? Is that anything like a dog?"

He smiles and doesn't miss a beat. "Yes, similar, but smarter."

"Uh-huh. And why are you getting a dog?"

"To demonstrate how responsible I am. I asked Luke what I should do to prove myself to you. You know how he worries about me. He said a woman wants to know her man can take care of her. So, I am going to start slow."

"With a dog?"

"Yes, ma' am."

Ruth smiles. They are sitting on a bench beside a miniature golf course.

"You have nothing to prove to me. You know that, right?"

He does know and is grateful to her for saying it. He is getting a dog to prove to *himself* that he can be trusted to care for her.

"Thank you, yes. I am going to call her Margaret. Maggie for short. Mags will be her nickname."

"What if it's a boy?"

"Won't be. I've already seen her. Over at Jake's. I get her on Tuesday."

"This is a big step then, huh?"

"Yes, for Mags and for us."

Mags, née Margaret, is a yellow Labrador. Boone trains her, cleans up after her, and feeds her. Occasionally he forgets to fill her bowl with water, and once he leaves her at the local dog run, simply walking home with the leash in his hand. But he realizes his mistake, turns around, and finds her playing with the other dogs, blissfully unaware her master had forgotten her. He hugs her extra hard and explains how it will never happen again.

As Mags approaches her first birthday, Boone shows up at the Airstream with his clothes in a paper bag. He explains that he doesn't have much, so most of the drawers and closet space could be hers. He has slept for a week with a Sony tape recorder to test whether he snored, and he is pleased to inform her that he does not. And he is addicted to Tic Tacs, so he knows his breath is fresh.

He is the dearest man she has ever met, and when friends or family members question the wisdom of tying herself to a fellow with diminished abilities, they receive the full brunt of her fury.

When Mags turns two, Ruth forms a partnership with Boone's brother Luke, expanding their business, which now controls seven Jiffy Lube franchises in the state of Texas and a few more in Oklahoma. When the opportunity to take over a Buick-Chevrolet dealership arises, they take it. As carmakers recover from the bailouts and Americans begin buying again, she snaps up a second and then a third dealership, all franchised from General Motors. They hire only vets, which is one of the reasons for their extraordinary success. She works hard and earns the admiration of her neighbors.

Powers Automotive becomes a trusted name, and the airwaves are filled with humorous commercials that feature Boone and Mags.

Whether it's because of his bright belt buckle, his tall, polished boots, or his shining smile, Boone's commercials get people talking and laughing and buying cars.

Please come on down, buy a car, save a buck while I take my dawg for a walk! Maggie then barks, and Boone laughs.

When Mags turns five, Ruth Powers and Boone Neville get married. As she glances down the long aisle from the back of the church, she sees Mags wearing a jeweled collar and sitting at attention by the feet of her soon-to-be husband. Her feelings of love and safety warm her heart.

Brighton offers them a fancy honeymoon in the Caribbean, but they decline, accepting instead a simple weekend at the elegant Tremont House in Galveston.

"Ruthie, you know if you ever need anything, simply call and it is yours. I mean that."

She keeps this knowledge safely tucked away. She and Brighton have an odd but comforting friendship. They had known each other for only three days—one spent at the forward operating base, one in captivity under the control of Zarqawi's soldiers, and one lying under the rubble of their jailers' base camp—but not a day goes by that she doesn't flash on some image or thought that originated in that seventy-two-hour period.

The Christmas following Raven's "crash," the euphemism they both prefer when speaking of his suicide, Brighton visited Ruthie at Camp Victory. He is carrying a brown paper bag in the hand covered by a tight driving glove.

"Hey, honeysuckle!"

That nickname is only known to one other soldier. She runs to him, holding him tight, not believing her eyes.

"What are you doing here?" she asks.

He answers with his most beguiling smile. "I was in the neighborhood."

Several Christmases have come and gone since their captivity, but for Ruth it feels like only yesterday. He holds up a bag.

"Delicious honey cakes. Fresh. From Syria.

She shakes her head, more in wonderment than confusion. To her, Brighton's life is magical.

"In the neighborhood?"

"Yeah, the Army has me visiting various operating bases, meeting with soldiers, touring the hospitals—raising morale, or something like that. I just do as they ask and hope it does someone somewhere some good.

As word of his presence spreads, soldiers begin lining up to shake his hand. He wishes each a Merry Christmas as Ruth leads him to a corner where they sit and eat the sticky cakes while drinking reheated coffee.

"I wanted to see you were okay. It has become such a strange holiday for me. When the Army called, I jumped—getting out of Dodge seemed like a good idea."

He smiles, suddenly bashful. She takes his hand, the one encased in a glove, and holds it.

"Thank you" is all she can say. She is about to cry.

"Hey, hey now, it's no big deal. I was in the neighborhood!"

Instead, she laughs. "Yeah, right!"

They sit quietly, and the other soldiers know not to bother them.

Brighton calls Ruthie every Christmas morning from that year forward. She tells her stories to Boone, explaining who Brighton is, and relates the painful details of their violent abduction. Boone looks forward to the annual call almost as much as she does. He enjoys the fact that every year, on Christmas Day, which is already such a special day, they get a call from a real, live hero. He saves up his stories and tells them to this man he has never met.

It is while watching her husband laugh during one of Brighton's calls that she realizes she had been wrong. It isn't Joel Osteen who saved her but her husband, Boone. And now, at Brighton's request, Boone agrees to the plan for Ruthie to return to Baghdad, to teach men who had once been her enemies to become entrepreneurs in the auto repair industry. The irony of the universe is lost on her, but she looks forward to spending time with Brighton.

27.

A CHANGE OF ADDRESS

Their new offices in Amman are near Rainbow Street in a stone building at the foot of the steps that lead to the many hills upon which the old city was founded. The neighborhood has trendy restaurants and lively coffee houses, and Adama's young staff blend well with the international crowd that is drawn to the area.

Brighton and Leyla rent a roomy apartment with large windows that provide postcard views of the hilly city. Once named Philadelphia after its Macedonian ruler, Amman is where Leyla and Adama were raised. Her youth was spent running up and down these fragrant hills. She was often described as a sweet girl, but, as Brighton can attest, the times have hardened her.

"Ruth is her name?" asks Leyla, her face a mask of innocence, but Brighton knows she is seething with jealousy. "Biblical, isn't it? Is she one of your fearless damsels?"

He refuses to rise to the bait. "She's an old friend who can help with an undertaking the government has asked Adama and me to oversee."

He knew she would create an issue where none existed. This is what she does. Trust is not an ingredient in her arsenal. The blame for her little jealousies and her minor disappointments falls on whoever is within earshot. Brighton tries to absorb her unhappiness and show her how useless it is, but she refuses to let go of her anger. And now, he steels himself for another fight. He cannot ignore the little gift she left in their bathroom.

"I assume I was meant to find the little test stick, the one colored blue?"

She shrugs, trying to appear indifferent.

"No big deal. I have the name of a doctor."

His heart sinks. He can't believe this is how Leyla wishes to inform him of her pregnancy.

"Please don't say that. This is a child, our child. It is not a 'thing' to be kept or tossed aside."

She shrugs again, impossible to read. "You're not going down on one knee, are you?"

She's testing him, trying to push him over the edge, but he refuses to play the part she's written for him. He knows that she is simply protecting herself, putting on her armor, but he needs her to be honest with him. How can he get her to trust him?

"A ring is the least of it. You know that. We are two adults, capable of love and care, regardless of how often we deny it. What would *you* like for us to do?"

He looks to see if there is any softening of her expression, but his stare is met with impassive eyes. A tired sigh escapes her body.

"I've worked hard to prove that womanhood is no impediment to my craft; I can handle dangerous and difficult assignments. And now, these assholes I work for, they will again see me only as a woman, bearing babies and diapers. I just hate it!" She screams the last few words, her anger clear and painful.

He understands. He does. "I know. It is tiring to continually prove your worth. But for those of us close to you, this is simply another challenge at which you will excel. And we will help you excel. God knows, running the orphanages has taught me and Adama a great deal about babies."

He hopes to get a smile from her, but she is unbending. She looks at him, her eyes questioning.

"You will be here? Regardless of rings?"

Her cheerless face breaks his heart. They are discussing a child—their expressions should be joyous. The only pleasure he has felt in these years has been created by the children in the orphanages. They are why he wakes up each day. Children are a gift, and he suddenly realizes how much he wants Leyla to keep this baby. He takes her hand and kisses it. "Of course I will be here. This is not a problem to be overcome but a blessing to be celebrated!"

Brighton wants to accept this news as a beginning, and to see Amman as the home for his new self. In the "rescue" business, he has learned there is no rest, no peace, no past, and no future. The Middle East has taught him to focus only on the present.

And in this present life, he will continue to seek penance. To practice atonement. With such meager ingredients, and with this woman and her child, perhaps he can find forgiveness.

Brighton returns to Iraq from Jordan, and along with Adama, they serve as translators for Ruth Powers while she teaches scores of Iraqi technicians, mechanics, and collision experts how to modernize, computerize, and narrow their focus so their shops can be profitable. Her templates are the vastly successful American franchises named Midas, Jiffy Lube, and Meineke.

Most evenings during her week-long stay, Adama and Brighton treat her to dinner, but on the final night several members of the Council of Ministers throw a party for all the participants as an expression of gratitude and good faith, hoping the well-attended seminars will create successful enterprises.

Adama returns early to their cinderblock apartment, but Brighton walks Ruthie back to her hotel, The Royal Tulip, in Baghdad's Green Zone. He accompanies her upstairs, and she sits on an upholstered bench and reaches to turn on a tall reading lamp. From her purse, she takes out an old-fashioned, onion-skin envelope with *"par avion"* printed in red and blue.

"It's his last letter," she explains. "I treasure them; his neat, precise writing, his odd and imaginative use of language, his ability to make you feel surrounded by his love. I will miss him for the rest of my life."

They have spent much of the evening reminiscing about Raven and answering Adama's many questions about the terror of battle. Brighton joins Ruth on the upholstered bench, staring at the artifact in her hand. "The return address always gets me," he says. "Bear Hill Hollow.*"

Ruth recites the address along with Brighton.

"Whenever I saw that postmark, I knew it was going to be a good day!" he adds.

She takes out the carefully folder letter. She smiles and then begins to read.

Dearest Honeysuckle, how splendid to get your letter! I dream of getting you out of there and bringing you home. Please. Let Uncle Sam find somebody else. You've done your bit. More than a bit, I should say—what is it now, four years? I won't rest until I hear that you have set down on fine Texan soil and are safely away from the murderous desert sand. Brighton told me he is preparing to lead a charge to come and get you. [Can't you just hear him?] Here in the holler, spring is arriving, and we shall all dance a mountain jig tonight in your honor. In the 'news you may have missed while hunkered down in an Iraqi bunker' department, our fellow abductee, Mr. Bethune, is now a movie star. He plays a preacher whose loins lead him astray. Perfect, ain't it? He is ridiculously handsome, scar and all. Was he that good-looking in our Humvee? Hollywood magic, I s'pose. I imagine that means he is also rich. Hit him up for a loan. I plan to. No shame! He has not found the air of democracy too rich a blend in the same way that I have.

Bless him. And bless you too. I pray Texas sees you soon and that it suits you better than Kentucky suits me. I feel like an extra at the dinner table—they make room for me but aren't pleased with my presence. You take care.
xxx Raven

Brighton wipes a tear from Ruthie's cheek. He wants to remove the sadness, to carve out the hurt they each feel.

Raven's image fills his mind as he slowly lowers his face to hers and kisses her lips. Her mouth welcomes him, and their eyes dare to find the other.

✳ ✳ ✳

She is still asleep in the morning as he dresses and goes down to the lobby. He finds coffee and sweet rolls and then returns to her room. He knocks. He waits. The door opens and she lets him in. She takes one of the coffees and sits in a wooden chair. He sits opposite her. Neither speak for several minutes. Finally, he ends the uncomfortable silence.

"I am so sorry, Ruthie. I don't know what we were thinking. What I was thinking."

She can't look at him. "I love my husband. I would walk through fire for him. I treasure him and I treasure his feelings for me. And now I know I don't deserve them. Or him."

The tears begin to roll down her face, but he doesn't dare hold her. He fears the suffering he has caused will rain down on Leyla, or worse, on their child.

"My brothers ate Wheaties. Breakfast was spent debating the greatness of the athletes that appeared on their boxes. Muhammad Ali. Richard Petty. Barry Bonds. I loved my brothers, so I loved Wheaties. Lance Armstrong infuriated them. 'Doesn't deserve to be on the box,' they said. 'Bike riding isn't a sport!' When I saw the picture of you, I wondered what they would think of this upstart tennis player. So handsome. More than any of the others on the box, I thought, except maybe Troy Aikman."

Brighton smiles at the mention of the great quarterback.

"When you walked in that day, muddy and unwashed but smelling good, you were a vision, but I didn't dream of you. Not in that way. Never have. And I know you've never dreamed of me."

"I have no answer for you," he says. "Sometimes we do awful things, stupid things. But forgive yourself. Forgive me. Thank God for Boone. I shall thank God for Leyla. Let us work to deserve them."

Ruth wipes her face as he continues.

"My Nonnie would say that love demands forgiveness. So let us ask a blessing from God, and a blessing for Raven too. I think he played a part in this mess, but I also think he can clear it up!"

Raven *was* the cause. He stirred up the love they feel for him—a love never consummated but carnal, nonetheless. An itch they had to scratch. Touching each other was touching him, loving him.

"There are stranger things than this. I promise you. His love was not meant to cause us suffering." Brighton states this fact with genuine conviction and then smiles at her.

A knock at the door announces Adama's arrival. He is to accompany Ruth to the airport. Brighton stands, embarrassed and wondering how to explain.

"I forgot he was coming. Let him take you as planned. I'll finish my coffee downstairs."

She nods as Brighton opens the door and signals a confused Adama to come inside.

✳ ✳ ✳

The drapes in Leyla's room are thick and the room is dark. The air is filled with incense, the smell of herbs, and the odor of medicinal syrups. Women carry trays of food in and out, wash her shiny skin, and comb her luxurious hair. Her large bed is strewn with magazines and pillows and the charger for her ever-present phone. She talks from morning until night, giving updates on her condition like a zealous reporter covering breaking news. She speaks with aunts and uncles and cousins about the child she is having with the American. All secrecy, all discretion has been abandoned.

Her doctors advised total bed rest for the final months of her pregnancy. They are worried about the weight of the baby on her cervix, so she moved back in with her parents, and mother is now taking care of daughter.

There is a knock on Leyla's door.

"It's me," whispers Brighton. He's back from Baghdad. He kisses her and then opens the heavy drapes, letting in the light.

In the kitchen, Basmah and Bilal wait in childlike anticipation for a wedding announcement. Adama knows better. He and Brighton had an awkward conversation about the future, and now each of them tiptoes around the other.

"As you know, your sister and I are having a child," Brighton said on their sandy ride home from Baghdad earlier that day. "I'm sorry, but there will be no wedding for your family to celebrate. Love has not been promised or pledged. We will raise this child with genuine care, but it is likely that we will remain two single adults. I need you to know this and tell me your thoughts. You are my brother."

Adama had remained focused on the road. He chose his words carefully.

"The situation is troublesome, especially for my parents. They do not understand the concept of having a child without marriage. And frankly, neither do I. I told them that what exists between two persons is only understood by those persons. 'We cannot know,' I said. 'Only Leyla and Brighton know.' But it is painful for us."

Brighton was saddened by this statement. "Thank you for being so truthful."

Now, in the kitchen, Adama rebukes his mother for allowing her daughter to become a spectacle. He is angry with himself for being away so long. They never should have taken on the automotive assignment. Or invited Ruth Powers.

Brighton joins them in the kitchen, smiling.

"Leyla is moving back home," he announces. "I will be by her side. There will be no more traveling."

"No more trips to Baghdad?" asks Bilal.

"No more trips. Your son and I carried out an important assignment for the Council of Ministers, but our staff can follow through from here. I am not leaving."

Adama is surprised and pleased by the news. The drive home had been unnerving, both of them irritable, and Adama had not dared ask about Brighton's presence in Ruth's hotel room.

"Whatever our little princess needs, I will try to provide. As always," states Adama with an ironic smirk.

Basmah and Bilal are not amused by their son's mocking humor—they see now that their hopes for Leyla will not be realized.

28.

A FAMOUS SANDWICH

There is no God. All your comforting words on this site are nothing more than an excuse to get clicks and hits and turn them into cash. I see thru you, and all your kind. I cannot "pray away" my problems. They are real. Your God is not. My pain is real; your solutions are not. You and everyone who depends on this site for the strength to move forward are delusional. I once believed in your God. But my wife is still sick. Sicker than before. She's dying. All of you who come here for comfort, for healing, know that Mr. Honor is a fraud, his name an affront to the purity he preaches.

Tolliver has begged Baéz to shut down the site.

"One of these madmen is going to follow through on his threats! Shut it down!"

The online harassment is becoming more frequent and often includes a promise of violence. Ollie is frustrated by his inability to protect Baéz—from these strangers but also from his own self. Baéz feels assured of his safety, but he wonders if Nonnie had ever felt threatened.

"Were you ever sued? By a patient or relatives of a patient who didn't get well or even died while in your care?"

"Like a malpractice suit?"

"Exactly. I think I'm being set up for one."

They are sitting on the porch. The sun holds them, the house, and the lake in a rosy glow. The daffodils are up, the robins have arrived, and the pussy willows are fat with fur. Jared's crews are hard at work erasing the effects of a brutal winter, and Nonnie is also restoring herself after a long hibernation. Baéz has a feeling their time together is coming to a close so he makes fewer trips to be with Tolliver in New York.

"Years ago. A local family. A daughter who died of meningitis. I visited them in their home over on Apple Lane. A string of little tenant farmer cabins. Torn down now. They were true believers. Blind believers. I often find this kind the most difficult because they believe without understanding. I sensed an ego that surrounded their prayer, a feeling that they knew better, that their god would heal their daughter while a neighbor's god might not. But she wasn't getting better, and their eyes were covered in scales. I couldn't get through. I suggested they allow a doctor to look at her, to make her comfortable and prescribe whatever steps he thought most beneficial."

"They didn't listen?"

"No. And the state sued for wrongful death and included me in the suit. In the case of children, you must be especially careful because the treatment usually involves correcting the thoughts of the parents, not the suffering child. It is their thought, their fear, which has allowed the illness to take root. With children I always insist on visiting in person, to meet the whole family, not only the sick child."

"What happened? An outbreak of meningitis must certainly have made the news."

"Yes, but the state dropped me from the suit. I felt the effects of divine protection."

"What happened to the parents?"

"They were convicted of involuntary manslaughter. Each was given a one-year sentence and allowed to serve it separately so they could care for their other children. They moved away shortly thereafter."

"What did you think? That you were simply unable to reach these parents? That their thought was not conducive to healing?"

"Well, remember what Matthew says, 'The mysteries of the kingdom of heaven are not given to everyone.' Simply believing, without understanding, can cause so much trouble."

A red-tailed hawk swoops low over the fields that adjoin the golf course. His sharp cry carries over the water and draws Baéz's eye. Tonight, Jared has promised dinner. The evening meal moves between their three kitchens, with Nonnie transported by golf cart from home to home. They don't make a big deal of it, but she is eighty-seven and certain precautions seem wise. A girl comes in daily to clean and prepare lunch. Most nights, Nonnie eats with Jared, but if Baéz and Tolliver are present, elaborate meals are prepared in the big house.

"I forgot to mention how much I loved your program last weekend," Nonnie says. "He was a genuine inspiration. I was so impressed by him, his story, his demeanor."

"Tim Tebow?"

"Yes. Such conscious faith. Such clear belief. I would think him an inspiration for many young athletes, no?"

"I hope so. He's hit a rough patch, as he mentioned, and he's thinking of leaving football. But there are no regrets. He will simply follow wherever the Lord leads."

"Was he as nice in person as he seemed on television?"

This is Nonnie's question every week. Baéz is pleased to have such a loyal viewer.

"Yes, he was lovely. Said Brighton demonstrating the ability to have many careers after leaving tennis was a real inspiration to him. He worries about finding a place for himself."

Nonnie smiles, pleased whenever Brighton's name enters the conversation. "Jared told me that your Speedo catalogue still fetches more than a hundred bucks on eBay."

Baéz laughs. "He's obsessed with tracking the price, from week to week, from year to year."

"A better investment than gold, he claims. Predictable and steady."

"For the Olympics this summer, in London, Speedo is reprinting the catalogue. As a marketing gimmick. They called Nathan for permission. He extracted a hefty fee for all of us, which is what financed the new roof on the boathouse. Don't tell Dad. It will break his heart. The price of the originals will plummet."

She laughs; the sound is easy and soft, all cares gone now. "He still finds you a miracle, you know. After you returned to the city, this was sometime after Christmas, he came up for dinner, simple leftovers. Winter is quiet here, and I think the stillness makes him nervous. On this night, he brought up a pie he had baked from the last of the apples, and he had that damn catalogue. He flipped through the pages that once made him so angry, now treating it like a treasured heirloom. He would point to a picture, the two of you lying in the bottom of a canoe, nearly naked, and say, 'Look how beautiful. What fine boys!'"

Baéz enjoys hearing that the rhythms at Hill House continue regardless of his proximity. Without the comforting continuity of Brighton's presence, Nonnie is the only connection to his history, to this land, and to what is left of his family. With Brighton's leaving, Baéz feels as if a portion of his life has been discarded and left by the side of the road.

"What is it you came up here to tell me? Something is on your mind, yes?" Nonnie asks.

"Yes. But it's good. A surprise. But a good one."

"Something about that boy over there in Nineveh?"

Nonnie refers to this period in Brighton's life as the "lost years of Nineveh," and always with a degree of bitterness that surprises Baéz. She says this to hide her hurt over the fact that he never calls.

Baéz doesn't have the heart to correct her, to point out that the ancient city of Nineveh is actually in Northern Iraq, in Mosul, not near either of Brighton's homes in Baghdad or Amman.

Baéz nods. "You are going to be a great-grandmother. Leyla is pregnant. Due this fall."

Nonnie takes this in and then quietly asks, "Have you intentionally left out the part about the wedding?"

"No, ma'am, I have not. I think that is why he has delayed calling you. He and Leyla are great partners, he says, but he doesn't think their love could withstand the rigors of marriage."

"Oh, that boy. He refuses to allow life to come gently. Listen, and then let God lead."

"I doubt any of us is able to do that anymore."

"Why do you think that is?" she asks, genuinely curious.

Baéz stops to think, knowing his statement is true but wondering why.

"The condescension I feel all around me. The disdain for people of faith. Religion has no currency in the contemporary mind. It's as quaint as finger bowls on the dining table."

"Well, the non-believers don't have it so easy either. I'm sure they also feel they are surrounded by crazy folks trying to reinstate prayer in schools and end abortion."

Baéz nods. Religion has always ignited the furies.

"The world can be a lonely place," Nonnie adds. "But focus on simply seeing what God sees, what God hears. That is what is true. That is all that matters. The rest is chaff."

She rises and goes inside. It's almost time for dinner. A chime on his laptop rings, signaling a new email. He stares at the screen, aware that Ollie's warnings have turned the messages he once welcomed into dispatches he now fears.

I told them after dinner as we watched American Idol. *They love the kids on that show. They always ask why I can't be nice and smart and talented like those kids.*

I had to tell them. So I did. Total silence. My mother left the room. Billy loves when Dad whomps on me, so he stuck around for the fireworks, but Dad didn't move. Not a sound except for the expletives he mutters under his breath. "Fucking fag!" he says as he walked to the kitchen and poured himself a beer. "Pack a bag. Take whatever you like. Get out of here. I'm going down to Biggy's. I will be back in an hour. I want you gone by then."

Mother began crying. I did as he asked.

The library is open late on Thursdays. Mondays too. So now I am here, and it is warm, and I don't know what to expect. Is anyone reading this? Can you help? The doors will be locked in an hour. Then what? Please don't tell me it gets better. I'm tired of folks telling me that. I need a place to stay. Luckily, I had dinner. But tomorrow? That creepy guy is here tonight. He looks at me. Smiles. When I look back, he touches himself. So gross. I need to find an atlas. I need to figure out the route to your house. To your Meetinghouse. I think it's only a day or two away. If I hitchhike. If I survive. Look for me. On Saturday. Friday, if I'm lucky and get lots of rides. And some pervert doesn't try to carve me up. See you then. Say a prayer for me.

My name is Reuben. Remember? Like the famous sandwich?

Entries like this terrify him. Tolliver is right—he should shut it down. The short films, the news breaks, the Bible passages, the bulletin board listing social services. Shut it all down. There is evidence that predators comb through sites like his seeking vulnerable teens to exploit. That's what the state trooper tells him when he calls asking for help in tracking down Reuben. It sickens him.

He spends the evening in prayer. For Reuben and for all lost children. "Suffer them to come unto me," Jesus had said. Children are buoyant, resilient, spirited. Qualities he prays to affirm, and trusts can protect them, and Reuben. That name stands in for all the children he's seen in unspeakable situations—refugees, orphans, slaves.

When Friday arrives, he glances over at the field that surrounds the Meetinghouse, searching for a sign of arrival, safety, a Samaritan who drove the boy all the way here. But Friday comes and goes, as does Saturday. His knees ache, but no stranger appears on their doorstep.

Tolliver Brigham has kept his client list small; only a privileged few have the ear of the estate lawyer who *New York Magazine* put on its top ten list. He rarely works on the weekends, treasuring his time with the man he now comfortably calls his "boyfriend." They still argue, sometimes over silly things, but they have honored their promise to never go to bed angry.

As Ollie pulls into the driveway after a rare Saturday in the city, he prepares himself for Baéz's fury at being so late. He had promised to be home for dinner. The headlights of his silver Volvo illuminate the cabin and the dock. Baéz has turned off all but the outdoor lights. He has gone to bed early. *In a snit, no doubt,* thinks Ollie.

He steps out of the car, his heavy shoulder bag filled with treasures from the city to assuage his boyfriend's irritation—soaps for Nonnie and the newly published Wall Street exposé, *FLASH BOYS,* for Baéz. As the dome light goes out, he sees a young man standing by the woodpile. He stares at Ollie and raises a hand in greeting.

Foundlings and orphans and strays of all sizes and ages find their way to their door, so Tolliver is not surprised by the worried face of the pretty boy standing in from of him.

"Are you Baéz?" the kid asks.

They all ask for him. They know his name from the website. He gives them hope and sound advice. They come here, seeking a miracle, looking for a father, or an older brother, and sometimes even a lover.

"Nope. Sorry. I think he's gone to bed early, so we must be quiet. Promise?"

The kid nods. "Yes, I think I saw him earlier, turning off the last of the lights. I didn't dare knock. I can wait until morning."

Ollie sticks out his hand to shake. "I'm Ollie. And I assume you are Reuben?"

The young boy nods and then smiles.

"You gave us quite a scare," states Ollie, amazed once again to see the proof of his partner's prayers.

29.

THE RED SEA

Hadeel throws the stretched dough onto the tray that holds the small, washed pebbles. In a proper clay oven dug in the ground, the dough would be thrown against the walls and baked in place, but modern homes do not allow for this. The tray of stones does create a rough texture on the bread's surface, but it's not the same. Much like everything today.

Hadeel is the weekend chef at the Restaurant Sufra—or she used to be, before a wild-haired, light-skinned man with many white teeth walked into the kitchen and asked her to teach him and his partner how to cook.

"Please," he said. "We are preparing to become parents, and we know nothing. We can pay handsomely."

She had laughed. Who is this charming man, and where did he come from? It was decided. Not by him and not by her but by the stars. She believes this.

The woman of the house is delicate, small-boned, and dressed in elegant pajamas. A scent of Shalimar graces the airy apartment, formerly an ironmongery with stone floors and thick walls of cement. A small courtyard in back could hold a taboon, which would let them bake their bread properly. She points this out to the tall man with the red hair.

"Ah, Hadeel, we do not own this apartment. We cannot simply build a clay oven out back."

She nods her understanding. This morning, as she arrived, the man from the West and the woman of Jordan greeted her warmly.

"Today we learn the wonders of Maqluba. Do I say it correctly?"

"Yes, your Arabic is good, but you speak too slowly. Everyone will wonder what you are waiting for!"

He brings fresh-squeezed juice to Leyla as she sits in a large, upholstered chair, her feet tucked beneath her. He drapes a wool coverlet over her shoulders, but she shoos him away.

"Stop fussing. I'm not an invalid! Now let's cook!"

Hadeel understands that the lessons are intended for Leyla. On her first visit, she saw how comfortable Brighton was in the kitchen: he has knife skills, an ability to use flavors and herbs, to prepare fish and break down boned meats. Still, he affects unease in the kitchen to avoid outshining Leyla. They work together on the recipes, and they share many luxurious meals. The various physicians and midwives who constantly visit are treated to superb snacks and linger in the apartment long past their scheduled appointments.

These doctors scare Leyla with their many warnings, but Brighton is always able to calm her. Hadeel is impressed by the sure hand and solid faith of her strange employer. She comes to understand that her lessons, her daily forays into teaching the art of Middle Eastern cuisine, are an inspired ruse to distract the fretful woman. Thus she dives into the campaign, assisting Brighton in creating an atmosphere of love and affection.

She brings photographs of her children, she assists Leyla in teaching Brighton to speak Kurdish, and she finds tailors and seamstresses willing to create a new wardrobe for her as the baby grows larger. The house is filled with laughter and the smell of rich foods.

Adama visits each morning, happy to sit down to an elaborate shakshuka accompanied by homemade breads, large black olives, and hummus, all washed down with pan-boiled coffee.

"I never eat so well," he states, brushing his shirt free of crumbs from the Manoushi.

"Ah, we do it to make sure you will not forget us," answers Brighton, laughing.

"No fear of that, not with my sister's skill for retaliation."

Leyla throws an old stuffed animal at her brother. "Stop this; it's not true. Like me, you do exactly as you wish."

"You see? She agrees. We teach each other terrible lessons."

In the weeks she has worked for them, Hadeel has observed a gentling in Leyla's demeanor. Her sharp edges have softened, and she smiles with greater frequency. Today, as she packs up to leave, Hadeel reviews with Leyla the finishing touches needed prior to serving the meal they have prepared for tonight's dinner with Bilal and Basmah.

"**M**ommy, it's okay. Your daughter is here; I am not moving to America. You will be able to see your little wonder every day. And Adama has promised to learn the art of changing diapers. We are not abandoning you. Your children are here."

Brighton watches as both parents look to him for confirmation; they still fear he will abscond with their daughter and grandchild to the villainous land from which he comes. He stands and raises his glass. "My activities have allowed your son to return home to Jordan. Soon your daughter will present you with a magnificent grandchild, and we will depend on you both to assist us in raising this blessed infant. My intentions are honorable."

He hopes this erases their uncertainty.

Later, after they have left and Brighton finishes washing the dishes, Leyla asks the question her parents had not dared.

"You are not going to want our child brought up as an American?"

The few candles still burning light her face like a Flemish portrait, her dark eyes reflecting the fire.

"We can't know how this will unfold," Brighton says. "I will want him to celebrate his American heritage. He will be schooled wherever we think best. He will speak English and Arabic. He will know the Bible and the Quran. I trust Adama will find an imam to assist this child. I do not pretend this will be simple, but we should be grateful for our significant resources and utilize them. My family will also want to know our child. I must promise this for them as I did this evening for your family."

She is crying. A tear catches the light, and he wipes it away. He wants to erase any impediment to their happiness and to their child's future.

He asks a blessing for Leyla and feels a stirring deep inside. For the first time he is able to envision a path that leads to betrothal. He has rarely felt so lightheaded. He smiles and kisses her perfect mouth.

✳ ✳ ✳

Jordan's only coastline, a small stretch of the Red Sea, is known for its coral reefs and deep, clear canyons filled with a wild array of brightly colored fish. Adama has suggested a weekend of scuba diving to celebrate Brighton's thirty-third birthday.

"I spoke to her doctors, all five of them," says Adama, "and they are fine with us going away. The baby is healthy and still has four more weeks before she appears!"

"She?" repeats Brighton, laughing. "We are having a girl, you think?"

"That's what Leyla tells me. Right, sis?" He turns to Leyla for confirmation.

"I think so," she answers, her voice sunny and cheerful. "Now go on. I'm tired of you both hovering and offering to make tea! Get out, enjoy yourselves!"

"You boys are worse than children. Leave us!" adds her mother, nodding. "I have always told you, daughter, boys never grow up—they simply get taller."

Hadeel joins in the laughter. The women are having a good time at the men's expense. Adama and Brighton kiss them goodbye and rush with their bags to the limousine parked around the corner. They are driving to Aqaba.

As they leave the city, their young driver asks, "Desert Road or King's Highway?"

Adama looks up from his iPad and explains the choice to Brighton. "Do you want speed or beauty? King's goes through the mountains and many quaint villages. The other is dull, full of trucks, but we will get there sooner."

"I vote for speed. Yes?"

Adama smiles and nods to the black eyes reflected in the rearview mirror.

When they arrive, Adama arranges the boat rental and the scuba gear while Brighton handles the hotel. The boat is old, used for fishing tuna, but the owner doesn't work on weekends, so his grown sons hire themselves out to tourists. Chakir and Emir know the best areas for fishing and exploring. The Board of Tourism has even sunk an old tanker as a destination for diving enthusiasts.

They load the equipment onto the boat, place the beer in an ice chest, and head south to one of the coral reefs. Azim, the chauffeur, changes into a T-shirt and jeans and comes along for the ride; he never allows anyone to understand he is part of the protection detail that follows Brighton everywhere.

The sun is bright, and in the distance other boats bob on the placid surface. With help from the brothers, Brighton and Adama don their wetsuits and tanks, jumping into the water from the back deck while holding their masks tightly in place.

The reef teems with life. Adama gives the thumbs-up, and Brighton confirms his equipment is operational. Adama goes deep, spear gun by his side, swimming through a blur of bubbles.

Brighton watches from above; he doesn't want to dive further than a single breath of air can sustain. He looks up at the surface, the sky clearly visible, a bright blue, and measures the distance in his mind. *Yes*, he confirms; he can reach the surface on one lungful of air if an emergency arose.

Being in the water always brings Baéz to mind. On their last call, after Brighton announced his impending fatherhood, Baéz had been thoughtful, cheerful, never criticizing Brighton for his infrequent contact. He suggested that a photo of Leyla would be a lovely gift for Nonnie.

Why does he have to be told these things? Why is such a simple gesture foreign to him? He disappoints people. Regardless of their close relationship and the success of their many endeavors, he knows Adama fears Brighton's relationship with Leyla is doomed.

Brighton thinks they are wrong. He hopes the world is more forgiving than his friends believe. Mistakes can be made, but the repercussions do not need to last a lifetime. A simple adjustment can have an immediate effect. *An interjection of love,* as Nonnie would say.

He gently moves through the warm waters, the lacy seaweeds caressing him as colorful fish dart and scamper about his body. The sea envelops him, mesmerizes him as he wrestles with all the negative allusions which endeavor to define him. The natural joy that was such a dominant ingredient in his childhood has abandoned him, and he must work hard to quiet the doubts that every day threaten to paralyze him. What is real, and what is a lie? These are the questions he constantly asks himself.

Flashes of soldiers and guns and hospitals and killings fill his dreams, his clammy body each morning a testament to his unrest. He doesn't feel any closer to clemency than when he first arrived at the River of Jordan. And his foolish evening with Ruth confirms his unsuitability for absolution.

Yet Nonnie would argue that these mental assassins are liars; she would tell him to fight vigorously and see the true picture of man, perfect and loving and invulnerable. He can hear her telling him that he was made in the image and likeness of a generous God and these claims that crowd his thinking are untrue; these claims of selfishness and conceit, these charges of lives he has ended and carnage he has caused are not descriptive of his real self.

The waters hold him until these somber visions dissolve into the salty sea. He accepts the love offered by Nonnie. And Raven. And Baéz and Ruthie and Leyla. Leyla most of all. He floats to the surface, buoyant and refreshed, grateful for this unexpected blessing.

Adama is cleaning a yellowfin tuna that he speared as the brothers light the gas stove. Azim pulls Brighton aboard.

When Brighton unzips his wetsuit and folds it down, the brothers see the damaged hand.

"You are safe here. We are honored to have the Angel of the Levant on board. We tell no one, not even father!"

Brighton nods his appreciation. "We are calling you '*Diya al din*,'" says Chakir as he passes a plate of buttered fish to his honored client. "It means 'brightness of the faith.' It is as close as we could translate your name."

"Diya al din," Brighton repeats. "Thank you. I like it. I like the sound."

They sit on barrels and old buoys and eat. Adama teases him, saying he is wearing the smile of a simpleton. Brighton explains that only impending fatherhood can generate such peace. "One day you will know and wonder why you waited so long!"

The circle of single men shake their heads, laughing. Brighton looks at Adama, suddenly serious.

"She said 'yes.' I asked, and she said 'yes.'" As the words leave his mouth, he can hardly believe it himself. He is either crazed or blessed. *Perhaps a bit of both*, he thinks as the men clap him on the back and clink their bottles of Petra. Adama is flabbergasted and thrilled on behalf of his parents. He gives his soon-to-be brother-in-law a heartfelt hug.

The ride to shore is quiet; only the sound of gulls can be heard. The bitter beer is strong, and Brighton drifts into a restful sleep, happily snoring.

The sound of laughter wakes him, the sun nearing the horizon as a fingernail of a moon appears in the eastern sky. Azim is helping tie up the boat as Adama throws their bags onto the dock. Brighton rises, bleary eyed.

"Thank you, brother. A perfect birthday. But don't tell Leyla how much I drank!"

"We should call. Is your phone in your bag or back in the car?"

"Don't call. Let's surprise them. Let's leave now. They don't expect us 'til morning."

"Are you up for the drive tonight, Azim?" Adama asks.

"Fine with me," the bodyguard says. "But maybe we could use our rooms to shower before we check out?"

They smell of salt and sweat and fish, and the high salinity of the sea has layered their bodies with white particles and slicked their hair in odd waves.

"No, let's be on our way. They will still be awake," answers Brighton.

"And smell our stink?"

"Nonsense. We smell like men, fishermen home from the sea!" And he beats his chest, howling like Tarzan, as the others laugh.

It is night when they pull up to the apartment, but no lights are on. Azim checks that it is safe to enter, and then they do, confused. The kitchen is filled with the smells of cooking, but no one is there. There is no note, only signs of a hurried exit. Brighton runs back to the limo and finds his phone in the carryall. There are dozens of messages, the first from much earlier that morning and continuing throughout the day. There is no time to wash or change. They speed to the Al Bashir Hospital.

"The entrance is on Al Baquer Street!" shouts Brighton nervously. He has been to the obstetrics wing of the hospital many times with Leyla, for her checkups and for the memorable ultrasound where he saw his child for the first time. Azim parks in the garage as Brighton and Adama rush into the chilly waiting room. He knows many of the nurses, and their faces signal a terrible warning.

Through a glass partition he sees Hadeel sitting with Bilal and Basmah.

"Go to them," Brighton tells Adama. "I'll find her room."

The elevator is slow. Brighton knows to calm himself; he knows to control his breathing and his heart rate.

Although he has seen death many times and soldiers have died in his arms, he is not prepared for the image that greets him in Leyla's room. The nurses have not yet cleaned, and the untidy bed is stained red. On top of the bloody sheets lies the woman to whom he proposed just two days earlier, her luxurious black hair spread over a pillow and her eyes closed and unseeing.

He holds her hand. The ring he had given her, the one she wore on her pinkie with the large topaz in the center—her favorite stone—is cold. She is cold.

He should have been here, he thinks. The grace granted him that morning in the Red Sea had been her, he realizes. Why? Is this his fault? He is weary of accepting the blame for death. He brings her hand to his mouth and kisses it. Neither had any idea of what a life together would be like, but they had said "yes." Now he would never know. *And the child? Had she wanted it?* She said she did, but he often doubted, remembering that morning with the blue stick in the waste basket.

He doesn't cry. He is immune. Life's terrors no longer threaten him.

Hadeel slips into the room and stands quietly beside him. "She saw him, before she passed. She called out to you, then she smiled and let go. Let go of all of us and of him."

"Him? It's a boy?" he asks, surprised. Leyla had been so sure it was a girl.

She nods and says, "Yes, come, meet your son."

He follows Hadeel down a long hallway that brings them to the maternity ward. Years of watching *Chicago Hope* taught Brighton the name of the clear plastic box. The hand-lettered sign on the incubator reads "2.1 kilos."

"They need a name," says Hadeel.

They had never discussed boys' names.

"Samuel, Sammy," he says without even thinking. *The boy who heard God's voice.* A solid name. Not too foreign but not specifically American either. His son will not suffer the dangers of having an Arabic name; he will not get picked out in a police raid or pulled from the passport line at JFK. Sam. Simple.

The nurse writes out "SAMI" and puts the label on the incubator. Maybe if it pleases Basmah and Bilal, he will accept the spelling the nurse suggests. Sami.

Sami is small. Tiny fingers, but they are perfect. Brighton wants so badly to pick him up but knows he can't. "Germs," a nurse explains. That's why he's in a box, to protect him. Brighton understands. He wants Sami to have a fighting chance. He needs him to live. He needs him to survive the ordeal that has stolen Leyla.

The nearby elevator opens, and Adama quietly joins him, his gaze focused on the warm incubator that holds his tiny nephew. He sees the name and says it aloud, approving. "Sami."

Brighton turns to Adama and speaks in English, his voice shaky, his body trembling.

"Raven and I once drove to the Nineveh Plains, in a Red Cross jeep. We were alone, no escort vehicle. We delivered a thick envelope of cash to a local imam. Condolence Compensation. An American drone had mistakenly fired two rockets into an ancient mosque. During prayers. More than twenty dead. Many children."

"As we sat with the imam, an angry woman burst into the room carrying a bloodied bundle of bandages. She wailed and screamed and cursed me. 'You think you can buy your way out of the hell you have created? My son shall haunt you all the days of your life!' And she unwrapped the child and thrust him in my face."

He looks at Adama. "Raven didn't understand Arabic, and I wouldn't tell him what she said, but that boy's face follows me. I see him everywhere."

Adama reaches out and holds him, sobbing, but Brighton's eyes are dry. He cannot find tears. He simply listens to the sweet cries of the many babes that surround them.

30.

'DROP BY DROP, A RIVER IS MADE'

More than a decade has passed, but the shame never leaves. The shame of being naked, the shame of dogs sniffing your privates, the shame of females posing provocatively beside you and laughing as tears stain your filthy cheeks.

He and his brothers had been rounded up at a security checkpoint and charged with "crimes against the coalition." Their only mistake was being out of doors after dark. They were transported to a military prison and kept in detention for nearly a year. He was threatened by American agents, beaten with broomsticks and made to pose wearing his underwear over his head. He was not allowed to sleep at night, often forced to stand, chained to his prison bars. He never saw his brothers again.

He is called Zaid.

Now, he walks with a limp, his head bent at an angle, his eyes dead. He rarely speaks. He washes himself obsessively, his time beneath a stream of running water his only pleasure. It is there, soapy and wet, that the concept of revenge transpires and fuses with his skull.

His initial undertakings are modest. Slashing the tires of Army vehicles, fouling food deliveries, pouring sand and honey into soldiers' gas tanks. He operates alone—an angry, ugly mutt.

When the American withdrawals begin, his sleeplessness diminishes, and the shame lessens. To keep his edge, to freshen his anger, he fouls himself to be reminded of the pain. He masturbates constantly, spilling seed in alleys and roadways and abandoned buildings. His disgust ignites the hatred, and another round of violence is born.

The thought occurs to Zaid that he is mad; all reason has left him, and he should be thrown out with the trash.

He is not yet thirty.

In the right-hand pocket of his filthy jeans, he carries a black-and-white photograph from a German magazine that shows a US soldier pissing on Kasim, his brother. If he were to die tonight, if he were to be found breathless on the side of the road, this is the message he wants to leave behind. "This is who I am. This is what has forged my life."

His father had been a mechanic—killed in the war with Iran—and all he left to his three sons was a stack of greasy car manuals and a yard filled with mismatched auto parts. When Zaid isn't masturbating or plotting revenge, he fixes cars. Any car, any make, any model. He will have a few calm months, working for one of the hundreds of car shops in Baghdad, before the darkness again descends.

In one of these bleak periods, he sees a neighbor from the old days, a friend of his elder brother, who had been a soldier, a member of Saddam's ruling Ba'ath party, disbanded by the Americans. Zaid follows Abboud for several days until the heavyset man leads him into an alley and pushes him to the ground with a gun to the back of his head.

He throws up his hands in surrender, screaming, "I am Zaid, from Abu Mushala, brother to Kasim."

Abboud puts down his gun. Many years have passed since they last saw each other. Zaid had been a gangly teenager.

"Is Kasim alive?" the man asks. "I heard the Americans got him."

"I was told he escaped prison, but he never came home. When I first saw you, I thought you might know. They killed Mem. They nearly killed me."

"Abu Ghraib?"

Zaid nods, and Abboud spits on the ground in disgust. The stories of the prison are legion.

Abboud looks at Zaid in his ridiculous baseball cap with its big red and blue ROUTE 66 logo. Abboud is now an officer with the Islamic State of Iraq and the Levant—ISIL. Many of his recruits have a history with the prison. In seeking retribution, they behead their enemies and are reviled around the world, yet they bring pride to their fellow Sunnis.

Abboud will now draw Zaid under his wing and thank Abu Ghraib, the evil fortress that inspires an endless supply of hatred. The prison is known as "the place of Ravens." Ravens. A filthy bird.

31.

ZOOM, ZOOM

Perfect timing, thinks Baéz. He is sitting in front of his iMac as he and Tolliver wait for his brother to join their Zoom call. Brighton had sent an email asking for a time when they could speak, and Baéz suggested they "Zoom." They haven't seen each other in ages, and he and Tolliver haven't had a chance to share their exciting news.

The washed-out image of his brother appears on screen. He is sitting in front of a crudely plastered white wall that reflects the glaring afternoon light and is too bright for the computer lens to handle. Baéz jots a note on the pad that lies between him and Tolliver. "He looks tired," he writes. Tolliver nods.

"Sami is with his grandparents," announces Brighton. "They take him on Saturdays."

Baéz is disappointed. He had hoped to see Sami today. He is now three years old, and they haven't seen him since last Christmas on their visit to Jordan.

"Please send more pictures. Did he get the truck we sent for his birthday?"

Brighton winces, realizing he had never thanked them.

"Yes. He's transported half the sands of the Wadi Rum in the back of that truck." Brighton laughs, takes a sip of his fruit smoothie, and then asks, "So, what's the big news? Your email was wonderfully vague."

Ollie and Baéz turn to each other, wondering who should speak first. They both burst out with the announcement.

"We're getting married! In August. And we both want you to be our best man."

"Wow!" says Brighton, looking pleased but saying nothing further. In the long pause that follows, Baéz asks, "Can you come over? You and Sami?"

Ollie draws a series of question marks on the notepad. This is not the reaction they expected. They see Brighton nod. "Yes, of course. This ties in perfectly with something I need to ask.

"What?" asks Baéz, trying to mask his impatience.

"How would you feel if Sami stayed with you?"

The question is posed so casually that Ollie must ask for clarification.

"For the rest of the summer?"

Brighton doesn't respond.

When Leyla died, Tolliver and Baéz flew to Amman to be with Brighton. They spent several weeks with him and with Leylas's grieving relatives. They interviewed nurses and nannies and helped organize a plan for the ongoing care of the tiny baby. At the time, Baéz had confided his fears about his brother to Tolliver. "It feels like he has lost more than a wife," he had said, and Ollie sadly agreed. Brighton's grief was intense; it was difficult to be near him. He fed and clothed Sami and made sure the caretakers had everything they needed, yet he rarely spoke. The silence was profound, louder than any screams he may have wished to express.

Hadeel was invaluable, her effortless support and thoughtful oversight assisted Brighton in slowly understanding the new world he had entered and must embrace. Yet, on their few phone calls and even fewer visits, Baéz has sadly watched as life slowly ebbed from his brother.

"Are you sure?" asks Baéz, realizing his brother intends to give up his child.

Brighton quietly answers, "Yes."

Tolliver probes further. "Have you discussed this with Leyla's parents and brother?"

Brighton's eyes narrow. "I haven't told them. I need your answer first."

Ollie opens his mouth to respond, but Baéz grabs his hand, discouraging him from further comment. It is Brighton who next speaks.

"You know, a few years back, I had a call from Boone Neville. He's Ruthie's husband. An incredibly brave man. He called to tell me what Ruthie couldn't. He called to say I had a son, that the night Ruthie and I had foolishly spent together in Baghdad resulted in her becoming pregnant. He explained he had forgiven her. He had no choice, he said, because he loved her. And now he was forgiving me, a man he had never met.

Baéz can't hide his surprise, wondering why his brother has never told them.

"And this is . . . when?" asks Baéz.

"Sami was six months old at the time. They would be brothers. Like you and me."

"What did you say?"

"I didn't. I was too shocked. I wondered if I should offer child support or should I apologize. But then he floored me with his next statement. He said, 'We've named him Raven, after your Army buddy. It felt right. I hope you agree.' I couldn't respond; my tears prevented speech. He then added, 'I'd like your permission to adopt him. I'll be a good father. I promise you.'"

"How did you answer?" asks Tolliver, speaking softly, but fascinated by this remarkable turn of events.

"Well, of course I agreed."

"Have you ever met the boy?"

"No. They've sent photos, of course. They are proud parents of a red-headed child who brings them great joy. There's no room for me in that picture, and that's as it should be."

Brighton pauses and then looks up, staring directly into the lens. "It would give me great peace and comfort to know that my other son is also being tended by a loving couple who, as Boone says, 'will raise him right.'"

Baéz looks at the image of his troubled brother, trying to comprehend the deep sadness that surrounds him.

"Are you sure?" he asks, for the second time

He sees Brighton close his eyes as if the answer is too painful to repeat. When he finally speaks, his voice is quiet and steady.

"On the eve of my thirty-third birthday, Leyla and I hosted dinner for her parents. I wanted to assure them that they would be part of their grandchild's upbringing. They were grateful for this promise and greatly relieved. It was late when they left. We did the dishes and then sat quietly in the living room. All I could do was stare at her. She was so beautiful and so round and so soft. I rested my head in her lap and heard the steady heartbeat of our child. I then asked her to marry me. I was as surprised as she was, but we both laughed, and then pledged our love to each other and especially to the little one who was soon to join us."

Brighton takes a sip from his drink, wiping his face with his sleeve.

"That was the last time I felt sure of anything. My proposal felt right. Her acceptance felt perfect. I knew what I was doing and knew where we were going. It felt good. Now, I no longer know anything. I am unbalanced and unprepared. How can I steer him right when I am unable to do the same for me? What if he hates everything I've ever done? How will he feel when he discovers the internet and learns his father is an assassin?"

Baéz can't listen; he can't accept this picture of his brother.

"He'll see that you're an American hero, you idiot!" he screams, impatient with his brothers' demons. Tolliver stands and leaves the room.

Brighton's eyes follow the receding figure of his lawyer. "Ollie has no patience with weakness. I remember that about him. It is his greatest fear. But war has a way of stealing the strength of even the strongest of men. If you'd known my friend Raven, if you had seen his radiant face every morning, but watched as the war, the endless killing, slowly sapped the life from his soul —"

"I did meet Raven. At Landstuhl. The Med Center. And yes, I saw what the war did to him. And I saw traces of the sweetness that had once existed in him. His story is a tragedy. Don't let yours be." A painful desperation enters Baéz's voice as he realizes what he is dealing with. "Stop this please," he yells. "You were a soldier, a proud, thoughtful soldier, and you did America's bidding. America is the sinner, not you. America is covered in blood, not you. You do not need to carry this burden; it is not yours!"

Baéz is frustrated and doesn't know what else to say. He feels helpless. He once advised Brighton to look away from evil and forgive the heinous deeds perpetrated by his father. Baéz had said, 'see only love,' and Brighton listened and then won the US Open. Today, studying the face of his brother on the computer monitor, he sees a man no longer willing to listen.

"I'm sorry brother. The only feel-good ending for this tale is for you and Ollie to raise my son. Please."

Tolliver has returned and interrupts the uneasy silence. "Let's sleep on this," he suggests.

"I've been sleeping on this for months," answers Brighton, impatient and sounding tired. "Time will not provide further clarity."

The three of them eventually agree that Sami will fly over with his dad for the wedding and then remain in the States while they explore the feasibility of such an arrangement.

They say their goodbyes, and the screen goes dark.

The joy of sharing his and Tolliver's exciting news has been stolen from Baéz, and he is upset. He knows he's being petty, but once again he is amazed by how easily Brighton's needs overshadow his own. Over dinner that night he expresses his frustration.

"You surprise me," remarks Tolliver. "You and Nonnie so often speak of forgiveness. You had a guest on your show last month who wrote an entire book on forgiveness."

Baéz recalls the episode. The writer told the horrendous tale of a mass shooting in Nickel Mine, Pennsylvania. Amish country. A neighbor marched into their schoolhouse and shot eight kids. Within a matter of hours, the parents of those students walked to the shooter's home and told his family they forgave him. When questioned, they explained it was the only way forward.

"'The only way forward,' they said. Do you think this is Brighton's only way forward? Giving up his son?" asks Tolliver.

Baéz takes a long time to respond. "You know, I was nearly adopted. By Elwynn, when Rebecca was still alive. Brighton and I spoke a lot about adoption, what it must feel like."

Ollie is quiet. "You've never told me that."

"No, but every now and then I remember, and am so grateful that Rebecca told Nonnie who my real father was."

"Brighton understands the repercussions of a neglectful dad. Perhaps he fears repeating his father's mistakes."

Both men are quiet, contemplating their decision.

"So, are we ready to become a two-child household," queries Tolliver, a smile finding his face. "Should we talk with Reuben first, allow him to feel part of this decision?"

"Oh gosh, I hadn't even thought of that. Of course we should. He's part of this family, this burgeoning household!"

"Did you ever dream . . ."

Before Tolliver can finish, Baéz swiftly answers, "No, never. I never even thought I liked children. They're so messy . . ."

". . . and noisy . . ."

". . . and costly!"

Baéz looks at his partner and laughs.

32.

VOWS

Tolliver Brigham was beginning his final year at the Pepperdine School of Law when, on a perfect autumn afternoon, he decided to jog down to the beach that connects to the campus. The sky was blue, and the water even bluer. The huge expanse of white sand was broken up by colorful blankets as a tall lifeguard wearing a bright red swimming suit stood atop his tower, making sure nothing would endanger this perfect day.

Tolliver breathed in the salty air, admiring the chiseled specimens posed atop their towels, tanned and untroubled. When he spied a familiar face crowned by memorable hair, he walked over to the recumbent form and stared at the freckles covering the man's body.

"They were knitted from wool, at first," he says. "Then cotton. Then silk. Now Lycra. The man who came up with the name won a prize of five pounds. *Speed on in your Speedo.* Not exactly memorable, but since you are their most popular model, I assume you know all this."

Brighton sat up and lowered his sunglasses. The two had only met once—Tolliver coaches the doubles team.

"And I've got a box with every size and color if you would like to visit my room and pick out your own. You clearly have more than a passing interest!" said Brighton with a raised eyebrow and a suggestive grin.

"I studied the company," explained Tolliver. "A law school assignment. Their American subsidiary was sued for selling outside their territory. I had to defend the parent company, in Brisbane, in a mock trial."

"And that led you to their current catalogue?"

"Bestselling catalogue in the history of retail merchandising!"

Brighton laughed. "Okay, okay, you've done your research."

"Do you get paid every time you wear them in public?" asked Tolliver.

Brighton stood up, brushing the sand from his arms. "Now you're embarrassing me. My name's Brighton, but you probably know that too. I am at a disadvantage. I don't recall yours."

"Tolliver Brigham. Pleased to meet."

As they shook hands, Tolliver had to look away from Brighton's body. He stared at the green towel instead and saw a Discman sitting atop a large black Bible. He pointed to it.

"A little light reading or is it a lady magnet?"

"A little of both. Certainly weeds out the dullards. Are you a fan?"

"No. You will find that we Californians believe in ourselves and little else."

Brighton smiled. "But you attend a Christian university."

"Yes, and the focus on a life of service I respect. 'Freely you have received, freely give,' reads our school motto. I can abide by that. Were you brought up in the church?"

Why was he prolonging this conversation when all he wanted to do was inspect the freckles on the man's body? There was no end to them, and they were beautiful.

"No, I was brought up in Europe. A secular crowd. But my brother and grandmother are spiritual practitioners."

This stopped Tolliver's lusty daydreams. "The same brother featured with you in the catalogue?"

"Yes. You'd like him." Brighton sat down and offered a spot for Tolliver to join.

"No thanks," Tolliver answered. "Don't let me disturb you further. It's our only day off for months. Coach loves practice, but he thinks Veteran's Day is sacrosanct. Military family, I think."

"Ah, that explains his love of crew cuts. He hates my long hair."

"Why would I like your brother?" asked Tolliver, looking for trouble.

"He has an odd name, like you. He disdains Speedos, preferring board shorts, like you. He speaks in complete sentences, which is rare nowadays, like you. He has large deep eyes, though his are blue where yours are brown. And I think he prefers the company of men."

"The counting of your freckles gave me away, didn't it? My apologies. I had not realized I was so transparent." He was dismayed by the pleasure he felt from Brighton noticing his eye color.

Tolliver looked at the large leather-bound Bible, still intrigued.

"Out of curiosity, what were you reading before I showed up?"

Brighton laughed. "Paul's letters. I spoke with my grandmother this morning. She's not pleased I traveled so far away for college. She worries about me living in this land of pleasure-seekers. She instructed me to read Paul's letters."

"His letters to who?"

Brighton seemed surprised by his lack of knowledge. "Your parents never took you to church, not even once?"

"Nope. Sorry. My three brothers are also heathens, if that's any comfort!" He laughs as he sits beside Brighton.

"My brother, Baéz, is majoring in religious studies, so maybe you two don't need to meet!" Brighton grinned, a friendly smile that undercut any implied criticism. "Paul's letters to the many churches he established. To the congregants. The people of Corinth, Ephesus, Philippi. Rome. Thessalonica. He wrote to upbraid them, to warn them, inspire them, teach them. The letters, known as *epistles,* are filled with useful advice, beautifully phrased. You could live a good and valuable life based solely on his guidance."

"We were brought up to worship the sun and the ocean and the land. Nature is what we honor. Your brother and I will do fine."

Brighton was still amused. "I agree."

On they talked, in the manner that only adults at the beginning of their lives could, the ease of making new friends being one of the particular joys of youth. They discussed their families, growing up with tennis, being a kid in Europe, freshwater lakes versus salty oceans, Agassi versus Chang, Clinton versus Bush, the precision of the law, and the beauty of the rules of tennis.

Eventually, Brighton stood, stretching his limbs and putting on a sleeveless tee.

"Got to get going. I'm on the afternoon shift today, holiday hours."

"At the Paradise? The entire team seems to work there."

"The owner's good; she lets us have flexible hours, so we sub in for each other."

Tolliver also rose, brushing himself free of sand and trying not to stare as Brighton zipped up his Bermuda shorts. "Yeah, careful with her. I hear she always has a favorite boy, one she takes under her wing. I'm told she's not the sweet young thing she appears."

Brighton folded his towel and put on a knit cap. "Another of my favorite prophets, Thomas, has a term for an activity he despised. He named it 'tale-whispering.' He said the tongue is tiny but what enormous damage it can do."

Brighton tipped his finger to his cap, a gentle salute, and then placed his earphones over his head before heading to the road.

Tolliver stood there, silent and shamed. He had rarely been so gently or effectively reprimanded.

"He quoted a disciple named Thomas as I ogled his fetching swimming togs and counted his freckles. He lectured me on the dangers of calumny. Can you imagine? St. Thomas! Me, from a family of agnostics."

The crowd laughs as the evening lengthens and the tales around the fire grow taller. The many wedding guests are sharing old stories to embarrass the best man, who has not set foot on American soil for many years.

"That's nothing," contributes Ruth Powers. "When we met, there was a war on. I'm stationed at a forward operating base, and one night, he and his unit tumble in, knackered, desperate for a shower and some shut eye. He finds an empty bunk near mine and throws his body down. When I look over, I ask, 'Haven't I seen you on a Wheaties box?'"

More laughter, louder than before, and Tolliver smiles, happy with what he started. He looks over at his old college pal, hoping he understands all this ribbing comes from a place of enormous affection. Brighton's face wears neither a smile nor a scowl.

"We met just in time," explains Baéz. He speaks softly, almost shy with this crowd of his brother's friends.

"Just in time for what?" asks the tallest of Tolliver's three brothers.

"Just in time for him to save my life. When I fell through the ice. Right out there." Baéz points to the far side of the lake.

The lake has always made Tolliver nervous. So many tragic events took place here. He wished Baéz had found a different tale with which to honor Brighton. This story always puts Baéz in a melancholy mood, which seems at odds with an evening that should be joyous.

The crowd quiets; they all know the harrowing story. Some check their watches. It is nearing midnight. The energy of the evening has diminished, and several people stand to stretch their unsure legs. A few look up at the star-filled sky.

"Going to be a beautiful day for a wedding!" announces Jared as he looks over at Tolliver.

"So it shall," confirms Ollie as he watches Reuben hand out little flashlights to assist their guests in getting to the parking area. Goodnights and tired hugs are shared, and names repeated for those who have just met.

Baéz looks over at Ollie and pokes him in the ribs.

"You were once desirous of my brother? Counting his freckles? It's like some terrible Greek tragedy! I am appalled."

Ollie laughs, pleased he told the story and loving the smile he sees on Baéz's face.

"The food was good, didn't you think?" he asks.

"Yes, and I will be the first to admit to my nervousness in having Brighton handle the main courses. I feared a groaning sideboard filled with Middle Eastern specialties none of us could digest."

"You are a terrible person! And racist," he jokes as he takes one of Sami's inflatable water toys and hits Baéz on the head with it.

Jared enjoys their gentle banter. Not since Baéz shared the boathouse with Brighton has he heard such a never-ending stream of conversation. This tall, serious lawyer has made his son happy, and he loves him for it.

Reuben returns, his face reflective of the excitement he has witnessed all day.

"Everyone's off, safe and sound," announces the youngster.

"Our guests are okay? They have what they need?" inquires Ollie.

"No complaints," answers Reuben.

Adama and Sami are staying in the big house with Brighton, as are Ruthie, Boone, and Raven. Tolliver's brothers and parents are staying at the new wellness spa that has recently opened in town while Scottie is bunking with old friends on the far side of the lake.

"Who was the dude in the red skinny jeans?" asks Reuben. "Completely dreamy!"

"Oh, don't go there. Please," answers Baéz, laughing. "That was Hayden. Surfer extraordinaire. A true rock. A solid friend. He once saved Brighton's life, in Malibu. The night his army buddy Raven Jameson drove a motorcycle into a rock wall."

"Raven? Isn't the little kid up at Nonnie's also called Raven?"

"Yes. In honor of the original," answers Jared. "He was one of the three that were kidnapped on that awful Christmas."

"Along with Ruth, yes? Raven's mother?"

Jared has tried to explain how all the weekend guests are related, but even he gets confused.

As he looks over at Reuben, Jared remembers the day Ollie found him and how grateful they were that he had arrived safely. He was an odd kid, but Jared had liked him immediately. They bonded over music when Reuben discovered Jared's collection of LPs and began sharing his favorites. Warren Zevon. Buffalo Springfield. Kim Carnes. Stephen Bishop. Hall & Oates. He once told his son he was foolhardy to think adoption was possible. Nonnie had defended him, saying, "Defining and limiting what is possible is not wisdom."

"The boy has parents, even if they have renounced him. No judge will accept this."

He was thrilled to have been wrong. He sees Reuben select an old Crosby, Stills and Nash album and puts it on Jared's ancient turntable. "Our House" plays as Reuben opens a large leaf bag and begins the massive clean-up from a day filled with games and good food and many bottles of beer.

"*. . . is a very very fine house, with two cats in the yard, life used to be so hard, now everything is easy cuz of you.*"

"I love this one. Can you imagine someone writing a song as pretty as this just for you?"

Jared holds the door for Reuben and then fills the dishwasher for the third time that day.

"It must be an honor to express your love so completely, yes?"

Jared nods as he looks at Baéz and then looks at Reuben. A new generation is emerging on the lake, and Jared can only smile at the wonder of it.

He sees Ollie looking over at him as he hums along with the song. A voice inside Jared's head whispers, *Thank you, lord.*

"**S**he is lovely. Your Nonnie. I was nervous," Adama says.

"You were good to come. Thank you. Sami is a handful and I'm grateful for your help."

"I'm honored you asked."

"You see the smile on her face? Worth all the misgivings, all the fear I felt at stepping back into America."

"Leyla would have loved your America. And your Nonnie."

Brighton is moved by Adama's simple statement. Leyla *would* have loved America. She would have thrived in the gritty, self-absorbed world he hates.

Adama sits on a long bench in one of the second-floor bedrooms. He looks over at his friend. "You should never drink," he says, "it makes your eyes sad." Brighton doesn't respond, instead looking about the room, staring at the many talismans from his childhood that are scattered about—tennis racquets with wood frames, a frayed rubber wet suit.

"This was my room as a kid, in summers," he explains. "Baéz slept down at the boathouse, and on hot evenings I would join him. We shared everything, our silly fears, our hopes, our dreams for the future. When I returned from Iraq, I needed that trust, the confidence that we could tell each other anything. I wanted to unburden myself; I wanted to tell him everything I had done in battle. But I couldn't. My actions were unforgiveable, so I remained silent, trying to imagine a world that would welcome me."

A long silence follows as Adama gathers the courage needed to ask the question he fears.

"You're leaving Sami here, aren't you?" he says. "With your brother and grandmother. As a sacrifice, a purging of your sins."

Brighton turns to face him. "No, he's not an offering, I promise, and I will make sure he visits Jordan often. He will know your country, his mother's country."

"His country," responds Adama angrily. "He was born under its flag. To a family that treasures him. This was my parents' greatest fear, and I assured them their fears were unfounded. I convinced them that you are committed to the Middle East and when you called them 'mother' and 'father' you meant it."

"And I did. I do. I am returning. Our work will continue, as will dinners on Wednesdays at their stately home on the hill. But Sami is staying here. He will be imbued with the love that my Nonnie will teach him; a love that eludes me and which I do not deserve. This will be better for him."

Adama shakes his head, furious. He hates Brighton's arrogance. The arrogance that defines America. He doesn't know how he will tell his parents.

"**T**here's a chapel at the airport filled with people who are frightened of flying. When I greeted Ruthie at customs, she took me there. She sat me down. Something was wrong; I could tell. She held me and then said, 'Forgive me.' I did as she asked. I said, 'I forgive you.' And then she wept and said, 'Thank you' and told me how much she loves me. The moment was scary, yet powerful. Nine months later, Raven was born. He was born of our ability to forgive; she had to forgive herself, and I had to see her as my loving wife, not a deceitful spouse. I knew he wasn't truly mine. It wasn't simply the shock of red hair."

"Forgiveness is powerful," Nonnie says. "And I think you are right. Forgiveness is the creator of your beautiful child."

She and Boone are sitting in two big rocking chairs that have rush seats and worn arms as the low murmur of their voices carries over the water.

"Do you like his name?"

Nonnie smiles. She loves the name, its meaning, the soldier who carried it, the bravery of this couple she is pleased to meet. "Yes, I do. Ravens are often messengers for the gods."

Boone smiles his huge, invigorating smile. "There are many stories. It is said they were the only species on the ark that copulated during the voyage and so they were punished!"

Nonnie chuckles. "I never heard that one. I did hear the bird once carried bad news to a vengeful god who became so angry, he turned the bird's feathers from pure white to midnight black."

"I read about them at the library," continues Boone. "The lady there gave me a ton of books about ravens. We had already agreed on the name, but the more I read, the more the mythology made me nervous."

"I hope both brothers have shared the many tales about the original Raven."

"They did. I loved hearing them. Neither Ruthie nor I realized that Baéz knew him, too."

"Yes, from the hospital in Germany. Two contrasting legends." She pauses. "Who are your people? Everyone tonight paid tribute to the past, unearthing old family tales. You were silent. May I ask?"

Boone sighs. "A saintly brother set me up in business and introduced me to Ruthie. The others who carry the name Neville are too tawdry to be mentioned."

She nods and then asks, "Your colossal church in Texas. Will they approve of tomorrow's nuptials?"

Boone thinks how to answer. He knows some folks disapprove of people like Ollie and Baéz.

"God loves his sons and daughters. That's what I've been taught." Boone lets loose one of his generous full-bodied laughs, and Nonnie can't help but smile.

"There is much that amuses you. My father thought laughter was a saintly ingredient in a man. I share his opinion."

Boone seems pleased. "The plane landing on the frozen, snow-covered lake. Rarely have I heard a story so oft repeated by so many people who were not present for the event."

"We are in charge of our own stories. It is good when they spread, even if they inflate the original. They still have use."

"Daddy?" asks the four-year-old looking through the screen door. He is dressed in a onesie, ready for bed.

Boone stands. "Hey, guy, did you walk down all those stairs by yourself?"

Raven giggles. "Of course! Mommy wants to know when you are coming to join us."

Boone goes inside, picks up the freckled redhead, and holds him in his arms. "Well, I think now is a good time, don't you?"

"Yes!"

"Say goodnight to your Nonnie."

He hides his head in his father's shoulder. "Night-night," he says.

"Goodnight my little man." Nonnie follows them up the stairs, leaving the porch lights on—she has lost track of how many people are under her roof this night.

✶ ✶ ✶

The next morning is sunny and clear, heralding a glorious day. The Meetinghouse is filled with the fragrance of late summer lilies. Giant sunflowers frame the entry, and swags of aromatic cedar hang from the rafters.

Nathan Winning is hovering, figuring out the best angles for his photos. The first cars are arriving, and a handful of high school boys are directing traffic. Nonnie, casually dressed, is sitting on the dock, her bare legs submerged in the dark water. Reuben is the designated babysitter for the day, and Raven and Sami are playfully splashing near the earthen dam, dressed in colorful flotation vests and water wings.

Nonnie stares at the two redheaded boys, wondering if the image is a mirage. Pairs of boys have blessed these waters for years. She wonders if these two will also discover the joys of tennis. Sons of Brighton. Or *Breetun*, as she knows Rebecca preferred.

Baéz walks onto his floating dock. He's dressed in a white seersucker jacket with a light pink stripe; he wears it unbuttoned to reveal his matching seersucker shorts. His tanned legs are framed by tall socks that disappear into white sneakers with red laces. A bright blue vinyl belt nearly upstages the shiny silver tie. Nonnie cannot hide her astonishment.

Baéz tries to scowl. "If you have nothing nice to say, best remain silent!" But a smirk breaks through as Reuben hoots his approval from the water.

Tolliver walks onto the dock and assists Nonnie in getting up. As the reality of this event and the beauty of these boys strikes her, she begins to cry.

"Don't start. We have a long afternoon ahead of us!" jokes Baéz.

She gives him a kiss. "I am sorry. This is all so new to me. Such things didn't happen in my day. You look like two perfect summer parfaits! A wedding! What a wonderful world."

Tolliver wears a light pink linen suit with a nearly invisible gray stripe. Mirrored sunglasses sit atop his healthy mop of brown hair. Deciding not to compete with Baéz's bronzed legs, he's opted for long pants and Kelly-green alligator shoes that match his bright green leather belt. A pink bowtie serves as perfect punctuation.

"Nonnie, you will have to get used to it! This is a gay wedding! We must show our colors." They laugh again, attempting to cover their increasing nervousness. Now it is Baéz's turn to cry as he looks over at his partner.

"Oh, babe, don't you start!" says Tolliver, with a smile as wide as a face can hold. "What happens now? I don't dare sit down. Why did I choose linen? Does someone come get us?"

"Yes, yes. We went through this. Brighton leads us over to the Meetinghouse. He has the rings, so don't fret. Just remember your lines!"

The children splash their way over to the resplendently attired grooms as Reuben runs interference to protect the men. "We're going to sneak in at the back once everyone's inside."

"In full bathing regalia?" asks Nonnie.

"Yes, ma'am. Me included. We want this day to be memorable." And then he starts to cry as he lifts the little boys onto the deck. "Sorry, sorry. Wasn't expecting that."

Reuben rushes the laughing children into the boathouse, wiping his wet face as he shoos them indoors.

✳ ✳ ✳

Brighton puts on his purple silk jacket with a matching straw boater. From Nonnie's upstairs windows, he can see his two sons laughing with Tolliver and Baéz. His brother and his best pal from college are getting married. That is why he is here; that is what they are celebrating, yet their togetherness causes an ache inside him. He is jealous, he realizes. Jealous of the happiness they have created; jealous of the happiness they share.

Baéz's visits to Jordan have proven painful. Their lives no longer contain a point of intersection. They express interest in each other's activities but have little in common other than a rich bank of shared memories. They talk and laugh about past events without the ability to construct new ones.

Sami, he hopes, will provide the connection. He will be the glue that binds the brothers. Picturing his son growing up on the lake, as he did, brings him great pleasure. The simplicity of this world is something he longs for.

He now teaches at two different American Universities, one outside Amman, Jordan, and one in Sulaymaniyah, in the northern provinces of Iraq. He also assists the tennis teams at each school. He visits Basmah and Bilal each week, sharing dinners and spoiling Sami. He leads a chaste life, one that is almost austere but for the trinkets required to keep a child happy.

They will never forgive him. He knows this. They lost Leyla. Now they are going to lose Sami.

He walks down the stairs and sees Jared pacing the wide wooden porch.

"You don't think this is too much?" Brighton asks, referring to his brazen colors. "I don't want to upstage the boys."

"I promise you, that's not possible. Wait until you see them!" Jared smiles then straightens Brighton's tie.

"Stop fussing," Brighton says. "You go on down and get in place, I'll go gather our happy twosome."

Music and laughter float above the water as he walks down to the boathouse. Nonnie smiles and takes his arm, a welcome support. He sees his brother and Tolliver, soon to be pronounced "husband and husband," and the hypothetical becomes real. Jared is right—they are strikingly attractive, standing side by side in soft pastels, like Necco wafers. They have their own language and signals and tenets.

"Let's get this show on the road," orders Nonnie.

She carries her shoes as the four of them slowly make their way across the freshly mown lawn to what was once a floating airplane hangar. The tall chapel and the large waterside deck are filled with friends and neighbors. As they approach, word moves through the cavernous space and people quiet and sit on the endless variety of wooden chairs and benches and pews. Roses and dahlias and asters burst from mismatched vases.

The music begins to play as both men join the minister and the best man at the front of the room.

Brighton listens to the eloquent words, the beautiful promises, and cannot stop his tears. They flow silently down his face and onto his neck. He sees the proudly gay Reuben in his exotic swimming attire carefully attending both Raven and Sami. His sons are standing atop a refractory table, one sucking his thumb and the other holding a stuffed bear.

He smiles at his two boys, their innocence so attractive and so plain. He wonders if he and Baéz had appeared similarly. Was their youth equally attractive?

No one has ever loved him so purely or so powerfully as Baéz.

Where are these thoughts coming from? he wonders, hoping he's not slipping into gloomy melancholy. The clapping of the crowd momentarily distracts him, and he sees Baéz and Tolliver kiss.

Suddenly, a wave of malevolence flows through his body, like a poisonous toxin released in his blood. A queasy sensation grabs ahold of his innards, making him feel faint. He continues to shake hands with his friends and relatives and neighbors, receiving hugs as the crowd slowly finds their way towards the enormous white tent by the clay tennis court. He pushes his way to the back of the Meetinghouse and finds Sami, bouncing on Reuben's knee, the moist remains of animal crackers covering his cheeks. The small boy smiles at Brighton and says, "Poppi," his nickname for the father who carries him everywhere, in his arms, on his shoulders, over his back. He repeats, "Poppi!" a little louder as Brighton exits through a hidden side door that leads to a private bower surrounded by tall bamboo.

A stone bench sits by a shallow pool of dark water, a gentle fountain disturbing the surface. There, Brighton sits, breathing the humid air in large gulps. He leans over himself, his hands on his knees and his head nearly to his feet. The gentle tinkle of water erases the sounds of all these people, these friends, his neighbors and old lovers, his classmates. His breathing slows; the army disciplines never leave. Sniper training. So many nights staring through telescopic sights.

Adama has begged him to see a professional regarding these lingering signs of PTSD, but as usual, he thought he knew better; he thought those days were over.

He has to flush this fear from his body. The endless images of blood. The smiling face of Raven lighting his nightly cigarette. The sense of being lost and diminished, the terror.

"Lie back. Allow me to loosen your tie. They'll miss me in a minute, but that's okay. Yes, yes, there now. Reuben was alarmed and came to me. He's a smart boy. He knew to find me, not Baéz. Stop now; just relax. Shh!"

Soft hands guide his body backwards onto the bench, his head coming to rest in the warm lap of his liberator. The hands undo his tie and open his shirt, the skin beneath damp and sticky. Brighton's eyes are shut, but his nose recognizes the lavish bouquet of Chanel. His teammate and lawyer and now brother-in-law. Ever reliable, dependable, the man you want near you in a jam. And this, Brighton thinks, is a jam.

"Nothing is going to ruin this day for Baéz. Nothing. Not the selfish needs of his globetrotting brother, needing another fix of attention; needing confirmation that he is numero uno, top of the list. Not today, dear one. Not today."

Brighton opens his eyes slowly, afraid the fresh image might hurt, but Tolliver is smiling, and there is love in his eyes, not malice. The words are spoken gently, as if addressing a spoiled child.

"We have all loved you forever. And we will continue to do so. You will be first in our prayers, first in our thoughts upon rising in the morning, first in the list of those most important to us. But today, you will leave him alone. You will ask nothing of him. You will not test him or tempt him or make him afraid. You will not share a knowing wink or use an ancient gesture or pull up an old code word. You will not blackmail him with your love and endless needs. You will find the strength to get through this day on your own, without utilizing the crutch he will gladly offer if asked."

The lack of resentment startles Brighton more than the words. Yet, the charges have been leveled, and he knows he is guilty.

"I asked Reuben to keep an eye out," Tolliver continues. "Baéz saved his life, and you are the brother of a man for whom he would do anything. Don't mess with him. Your children have taken to him with unquestioned trust. Honor that."

"You should get back," Brighton says, his voice raspy. "I'll sit here awhile. My work for the day is done. Go. Make my boy happy."

As Tolliver leaves, walking slowly back to the chapel, Nonnie coughs and then slaps an imaginary fly on her arm to warn Brighton of her presence. She'd been standing behind the bamboo.

Slowly, she enters the pleasant arbor, her footfall releasing the smell of crushed thyme. She smiles as she sits next to him.

"I'm fine. Honestly. I'm sure there is an activity or a person out there who needs you more than me," Brighton says, gesturing grandly. "Go."

Nonnie remains seated. "I'm beginning to have trouble with names. Remembering them. Today we are surrounded by history—family and old neighbors and children of neighbors, and I cannot recall the names or places to which our guests refer. I am fine here. A little rest for a little while."

"He is right, you know," Brighton says. "I am uncommonly selfish."

Nonnie puts a hand on his shoulder. "You will get nowhere with that approach, young fella. You are fishing, asking me to contradict you."

"Don't you have a special potion that I may drink and begin again? Certainly, there is a useful prayer that covers my sins."

Nonnie becomes impatient. "They're not sins. They're not even defects. They are myths that you have wrongfully accepted as true. You know better!"

"Yes, ma'am."

They smile at each other.

"I leave tomorrow night," he says. "We'll share breakfast in the morning?"

"Does Adama know?" she asks. "The family? You've told them?"

"Yes. They will see Sami in summers. Baéz will bring him to visit."

"He and Raven got on well. Do they know they are brothers?"

"Yes. Ruthie and Boone are committed to the boys knowing each other."

Nonnie is clearly thinking about what she wants to say. "You should call more. We sometimes feel abandoned, although we are too proud to complain."

"I do love you. You know that, but I can't be here. In this country," he says. "It doesn't agree with me."

Nonnie laughs. As a young boy, whenever she fed him something he didn't like, he would explain, "It doesn't agree with me." An expression one of his many nannies had taught him, in French or Spanish or Italian, he can't remember.

"I know. And I'm sorry. We are a troubled nation. We offer you no comfort. But neither can Jordan or Iraq. You will discover peace when you recognize we are ruled by one Spirit, one Mind, one God."

"Baéz made that leap. I haven't. My faith never transformed into understanding. Regardless of what you all think, I'm amazed I'm still alive. I'm functional. I laugh. I cry. And I love you and Ollie and Jared and Ruthie. Baéz and Raven and Sami are gifts. This is all I know. I can't dig any deeper into this muddled mind!"

When he points to his head, he finds his glasses resting atop the curly red mop. He smiles.

"Ah, there they are!" He laughs. "Sunglasses."

33.

NEW YORK CITY

Sami is cheering, his mouth open, his eyes bright, looking like a child chorister on a romantic Christmas card. The red hair, the pale, freckled skin, the tiny body. Brighton could stare at him for hours.

Their favorite player, Oday, has scored a goal, and Al-Faisaly is now in the lead with only minutes to play. The Stadium rocks with the loud cheering of sixteen thousand fans. Bilal is jumping up and down while Adama and Daniyal are screaming. Sami loves soccer but feels the games in Amman are much more exciting than the games Ollie takes him to in New York's Central Park. Ollie accompanied him for this year's visit, staying on for a week before returning to New York. This is Sami's second summer visiting Jordan and seeing his dad, along with Bilal, Basmah, and Adama.

Brighton has never doubted his decision to have Baéz and Ollie raise his son, but he also knows that Sami's very existence creates a high level of anxiety in many of his loving relations. Baéz fears a change of heart, worrying that a summer will come when Sami does not get on the plane back to New York. Adama fears that members of ISIL will kidnap the boy for ransom. Even Brighton has entertained images of Leyla's parents stealing the boy and settling in some far-off land.

A loud cheer rises from the stadium. Brighton takes his son's little hand and guides him through the raucous crowd to Adama's white Land Rover. A final dinner tonight, and then Daniyal and Adama will drive the boy to the airport. The flight leaves at one in the morning—two stopovers, fourteen hours in the air. Dani is accompanying him, because Brighton can't do it. He knows Baéz will be angry, but he also knows his own limits. Last year, after Sami's first summer visit, Brighton flew to New York with his son and experienced his first anxiety attack. He had to get off the plane in London while a kind steward sat with Sami for the final leg of the journey.

He stares at his son, who is getting sleepy. He dresses the boy in warm pajamas, but instead of slippers he puts shoes on his feet. Sami giggles.

"I don't wear shoes in bed. Bare feet. Or socks, sometimes, when Ollie gets me ready. Not shoes."

"I know. But you and Dani are getting on a large bird to fly you home to Ollie and Ezzie, and you will need shoes for that."

"I am going to the lake?"

"Yes. You like the lake, don't you?"

"Yes, Nonnie lives at the lake. Will she be there?"

"Yes, always. She's looking forward to seeing you."

"But you are not coming?"

"I am staying here with Lalli and Basmah. Otherwise, they would be all alone."

"But I could stay with them too," Sami says.

"And then who would take care of Nonnie and Ezzie?"

Sami stops to think for a minute. "I guess I don't know."

Brighton ties the laces of his son's new Puma trainers and then asks, "You know your Poppi loves you, yes?"

"And I love you," the boy answers.

"Yes, you are Sami, son of Brighton and Leyla, wonder of the world!"

Sami laughs until he sees tears in his father's eyes. And then he cries too.

There is a knock at the door.

"We should be going, brother," Adama says.

"The Bethune boys are coming, aren't we, Sami?"

"Yes!"

This is Sami's favorite name. He loves being one of the Bethune Boys.

Daniyal stares at the overhead signs. He doesn't know which line to get in; he's having trouble understanding the garbled announcements in English. He is exhausted. He prays for Sami to remain asleep.

At the customs booth, a stern-faced man behind a thick glass window asks questions and then noisily stamps both passports, waking Sami. Sami needs a bathroom, but Daniyal tells him to wait.

When they enter the Arrivals Hall, it is filled with people and baggage and more signs. Sami begins to cry. Daniyal would also like to cry, but suddenly a man lifts Sami—a man wearing a warm smile and holding a stuffed monkey.

"Daaaaaaa!" screams Sami, reaching out his arms.

Dani feels a wave of relief. It is Brighton's brother who holds the boy tight, as another man arrives, this one very tall, and when Sami sees him, he calls out "Ollie!"

The tall one carries the boy to the bathroom as Baéz helps Daniyal gather their luggage.

"Thank you. For bringing Sami home," Baéz says. "In a short while you can sleep, you can eat. You will be fine. I promise."

Daniyal smiles. This is the man he has heard so much about.

"Did Brighton call and explain I was coming instead of him?" Dani asks.

Baéz doesn't answer, which tells Dani all he needs to know. Adults remain an elusive species to him, even the ones he loves. He stands silently in a sea of luggage and hopes the pain that Brighton must have felt at Sami's leaving had been bearable. Ever since the night when Brighton found Danyal and his brother Azar on a park bench, starving and cold, he has seen Brighton as his father. Who else could offer such nourishing love? As he's grown older, however, Dani has realized fathers cannot solve all the problems this messy world delivers.

Ollie and Sami return, and the four of them head to a waiting limo that will take them through the traffic-clogged roads to their home in lower Manhattan. Dani stares at the iconic landmarks he recognizes from the many movies Brighton has rented for the orphanage—the Chrysler Building, The UN, and Lady Liberty way off in the distance. Ollie has the driver take a short detour so they can show Daniyal the new Freedom Tower rising from the ashes of the World Trade Center. And then, finally, home.

Their house is large, with four full floors. *They are rich*, thinks Dani. Brighton had not explained this. Everything is shiny and bright, like pictures in a magazine. The kitchen sparkles with tiles that look like jewels.

Sami often speaks of home, but Dani had not envisioned what he now sees. He wonders if there is a space where Sami is allowed to be messy and spill things.

Tolliver pulls a stool out from under the counter and points to it, then opens the refrigerator and brings out cheeses and cold chicken and milk. He puts it all on a plate and places it in front of Daniyal.

"I know how you feel. It's a brutal flight. Eat. We can talk later. I know about your appointment at the Academy tomorrow. Brighton emailed us. I'll get you there. I'll wake you. Don't think; eat, and then I'll will show you to your room. It is where Brighton used to sleep when he visited. You will be fine in the morning. I promise."

Baéz takes Sami up the green glass stairs. He waves. These are thoughtful men. He is grateful for that. He has never met homosexuals. At least, he doesn't think he has. There aren't any in Iraq. He's not so sure about Jordan.

Brighton had advised him to treat Ollie and Brighton like his tennis buddies. He smiles to himself as he realizes how ridiculous this advice had been!

"**B**righton taught me, and my little brother. We learned tennis, and then English. In that order! I am pleased to say we are good at both! I am on the tennis team, at the American University."

"In Sulaymaniyah?" asks Tolliver.

"Yes. And you pronounced it perfectly!" Tolliver laughs as their Uber driver crosses the island and then drives north on the FDR.

"We knew Brighton taught there, but I didn't realize he was also coaching a tennis team."

"Yes. We have played teams from Bahrain and Myanmar. Our match next Friday is against the Davis Cup team from Ashgabat, Turkmenistan. It will be the biggest tennis event to be held in Iraq in years!"

Daniyal doesn't know how much he should say. Brighton and Adama have had terrible fights over the upcoming match at the Al-Alwiyah Club, which was once an outpost for rich Westerners. They host Friday night bingo, they stock a bar famous for its collection of single-malt whiskeys, and they lay claim to the only clay courts in all of Baghdad. Still, the place is an offense to most Muslims.

"Do you have a death wish?" Adama had screamed in the middle of one of their arguments. "You have a price on your head. Don't thumb your nose at them by proving you live among them. We cannot protect you any longer. ISIL is out of control."

Daniyal decides not to share Adama's fears. Instead, he stares at the busy streets of New York as their taxi makes its way uptown.

"If you are accepted, when does training begin?" Tolliver asks.

"In a month."

"That's fantastic! You must stay with us. We have plenty of room. Sami will love it, and so will Reuben."

"Thank you. You are incredibly generous. First, I must be accepted."

"Yes, but I know this is in the bag!"

Daniyal squints. "And 'the bag' is a good place to be?"

Tolliver laughs. "Yes, it a good thing. Trust me."

The car pulls up to the McEnroe Tennis Academy. They are on Randall's Island. Tolliver points to the entrance.

"I'll wait for you here. It's a beautiful day. I will see you when you return."

"Thank you, Ollie."

Dani touches his right hand to his heart and salutes, expressing his gratitude.

✴ ✴ ✴

The next day is sunny and bright, so they take Sami to the Washington Square playground, where Daniyal pushes Sami on a swing as Sami screams, "Higher!" The park is beautiful and populated with a diverse collection of New Yorkers. Dani stares at the chatty mothers and the distracted nannies; he sees women in headscarves and girls revealing tanned skin. Also, men in shorts and men in business suits. Students reading thick textbooks and others nodding along to music playing on headphones. New York is a dream, and Dani is amazed to realize that he will soon be living here.

He has been accepted. They told him right away. He played, he served, he answered some questions, he filled out some forms, and they said yes. He is excited. And proud. He can't wait to tell Brighton.

Baéz arrives with several cups of ice cream and little wooden spoons. Daniyal stops Sami's swing as Baéz hands them each a cup of chocolate and a large napkin.

"Do you live with us now too?" Sami asks Daniyal between bites.

"No. I must return home tomorrow."

"Your match is on Friday?" asks Baéz.

"Yes, it is a fundraiser and will be followed by a big dinner and a 'watching' party for *Arab Idol.* Adama's girlfriend is a finalist. Shamira."

"Excuse me, I could not help but overhear, you have a friend on *Arab Idol?*"

A young dark-skinned girl holding a fair-haired baby is smiling at Daniyal.

Daniyal begins speaking in Arabic. "Yes," he answers. "Shamira. Do you know her?"

"Yes, my mother sends me tapes, but I am two weeks behind. I was cheering for her, but didn't know if she got voted through!"

"*Aosmi hu Samaa!*"

The girl looks up in surprise as Sami introduces himself in perfect Arabic.

She smiles, looking first at Daniyal, and then at Baéz. Both men laugh so she answers, "And my name is Djamila." She reaches out her hand to Sami, but he is covered in chocolate. Daniyal lifts him from the swing and onto his lap.

"Yes, this is Sami," he offers in English, "and I am Dani, and our friend here is named Baéz."

She nods. "Baéz? What a pretty name. I am not familiar with it. Are you Sami's father? His Arabic is impressive! Your wife has taught him?"

"No, his father, who is my brother and lives in Jordan. He is a tennis player." Baéz gestures to Daniyal. "And this young man is also a tennis player, taught by my brother. They both work with a man named Adama, running charities in Iraq. Adama is the boyfriend of Shamira, finalist on *Arab Idol!* Got all that?"

She raises her eyebrows, and they laugh. The baby in her arms begins to whimper and fuss.

"Excuse me, I must go feed her. Nice to talk with you!"

They nod goodbye as Baéz cleans Sami's sticky hands.

"Only in New York. People come from every country in the world. You will fit right in. When your training starts, you must stay with us. There is plenty of room."

✱ ✱ ✱

On Dani's last night, they stay home and order a large pizza with everything on it. It's what he wants. An American pizza.

"Tell us about Brighton. On our phone calls we mostly discuss Nonnie and Sami, and how much he misses them. He doesn't tell us much about his own life."

Dani thinks how to answer, knowing to tread carefully. "There isn't one. Tennis is his life. It's what he is good at."

He sees their anxious faces and wants to assure them their brother is safe. "Adama runs the orphanages, and the schools. The auto repair shops are overseen by their staff, so neither man is involved in those anymore. Brighton rarely travels to Iraq except for his commitment to the university, but that's in the north, near where I am from. Kurdistan. It is safer there."

"What is life in Baghdad like these days?" Ollie asks.

"The civil war continues; hatred between the Sunnis and Shias continues. Occasionally there are food shortages. There are no Americans anywhere, which feels odd and strangely unnerving. They were once ever-present!"

Silence settles over the room. Daniyal worries he has embarrassed his gentle hosts. They understand so little of his life. Or Brighton's.

From the baby monitor they hear Sami call out "Poppi," his name for Brighton.

"I'll go," suggests Dani. "Let me tuck him in. I'm going to miss him when I leave," and he bounds up the stairs.

Baéz finishes his wine. "I invited him to stay with us. I should have checked with you first. Sorry. But he's a great kid, and Brighton . . ."

"I did the same," Ollie admits. "I also invited him to stay with us, but I wasn't going to tell you until it was too late, which just proves you are a better person than I am!"

Baéz stands and refills both their glasses. He hears giggles from upstairs. He looks over at his husband and asks, "How'd this happen?"

"What? Parenthood?"

"Yes."

"I don't know, but it seems to find us, doesn't it?"

Baéz sits quietly for a minute, carefully choosing his words. "I never thought about children, never dreamed of having my own, or raising a brood. They were loud and messy and not possible if you were a gay man. Fatherhood was not an option, so you learned not to dream of that which is not possible."

Ollie nods. "Yes, and having a family was not the catalyst for our marriage."

"I don't think we ever discussed it, did we?" asks Baéz.

"Nope, yet here we are, a family of five."

The sound of steps on the stairs ends their conversation. Daniyal walks into the room, a sly smile on his face.

"You know, you don't really need a baby monitor. Your air conditioning ducts carry sound perfectly."

Baéz chuckles and then asks, "And what are your thoughts on parenting?"

Ollie, also smiling, adds, "You may not know this, but eavesdropping is punishable by death in many Western cultures!"

Dani laughs, amused by these two grown men. "It's a silly word, is it not?"

Baéz takes on the challenge of explaining it. "The eaves are the section of the roof that extends past the side walls, providing cover to those standing beneath. An 'eaves' dropper was one who stood there, listening to the conversations within. In the Bible it is considered a sin."

"On the night Brighton discovered me and my brother shivering on a park bench in the center of Baghdad, he tried to find out who we were. He tried 'eavesdropping' on our conversation, but unfortunately, he didn't speak Kurdish."

"Very good," comments Ollie. "And is your brother a troublemaker like you?"

Daniyal laughs, nodding his head.

Baéz then asks, "Sami is fine? He knows his Poppi is not here?"

Dani sits and takes another slice of pizza. "Yes, he's tired and a bit confused but knows where he is now."

"Thank you," says Ollie.

"Can I ask a question?"

"Of course. You've heard all our secrets!" The two men grin, pleased with their little joke. but then they see Dani's serious face and they lean in towards him.

"Was Brighton ever like this, with Leyla? Did they sit around, sipping wine, talking and teasing one another, like you two?"

"Couples have their own ways. Brighton and Leyla met at a crucible in their lives, and I assume that colored their behavior." Ollie pauses. "She was a beauty. I only met her via Skype, but she made an impression. What did you think of her?"

"I was little when I met her. In Baghdad. Soon after, she and Brighton moved to Amman, and I didn't see her again."

"I have seen Brighton be quiet and gentle, contemplative, even," adds Baéz. "He is seeking the solution to so many problems; he often gets lost. Continue being thoughtful of him," he advises. "Even if unrecognized, somewhere in his consciousness, such kindness registers and brings comfort."

On his trips to Jordan, Baéz saw the love his brother lavished on the orphans. He knows many of them think of him as their father. And yet, Brighton feels unable to raise Sami. Baéz is mystified by his brother's fear.

✳ ✳ ✳

Brighton is resting in his living room, the bright white walls magnifying the light of the late afternoon sun. Each day he tries to find time to quiet his mind and abandon the thoughts he deems detrimental to his well-being. Life, Brighton has discovered, is a process of letting go—letting go of barren beliefs, of possessions, of people, and even of memories. Lightening the load; *reducing your footprint*, as today's kids say.

Today is Sami's birthday. Always a difficult day since Sami's arrival had required Leyla's departure. He is glad his son is celebrating in New York, away from the painful memories in Jordan. On Sami's first birthday, Brighton had hosted a dinner for Bilal and Basmah, knowing how difficult the anniversary would be. People mourn differently, and different cultures commemorate death with bewildering traditions, yet no matter your beliefs, grief is a debilitating visitor. Since that first year, Brighton spends the day on his own.

There is a knock at the door. He rises from the chaise, putting the coverlet aside.

"My son wanted to come by and say thank you." Hadeel is carrying a large earthenware tagine. Her son holds a string bag containing Bedouin flat bread.

"Come in, come in!" Brighton is appreciative of the visit but also knows it has nothing to do with expressing gratitude for the tennis lessons he is giving her son.

"We won't stay, but I prepared too much last evening and thought you might enjoy an effortless meal!"

She brings it every year. The same dish that had been left on the stove when they rushed Leyla to the hospital.

"I was preparing some tea," he says. "Join me. I see friends all too rarely."

Brighton focuses on his preparations as he holds the ceramic pot high, the sound of the liquid filling the china cups both relaxing and pleasant.

"My niece, Ghena, appreciates a man who can prepare a perfect cup of tea!"

This is an old ruse, and Brighton is prepared. "Is Ghena, by any chance, unmarried?"

Even Hamsah laughs, but Hadeel is unfazed. "The joys of female company, even if marriage is not the goal, can never be underestimated. Adama says you don't ever go out, for a dance, a drink, or simply a shared meal."

"'The sensualist's affections have abandoned me,'" he says in answer. "I read that somewhere. Graham Greene, maybe? Give me a fine book, a strong green tea, and a plate of sweet Hareeseh, and I am content."

He wonders if this is true. Is he content? Living within the uncluttered silence of his thinking, he has discovered a refreshing clarity. Ambition has left. His only passion is tennis, and the only people he enjoys are those who share his passion. He loves teaching the game and he loves that young Daniyal had been accepted at the McEnroe Academy. Soon Dani will be back in Iraq for a match against Turkmenistan. The two teams are very low in the rankings, but Brighton feels it is important politically. To compete. To carry the flag. The flag of international sport.

34.

'FREELY YE HAVE RECEIVED, FREELY GIVE'

Baéz rows at a brisk pace, pushing for shore, the old wooden canoe skimming over the rough surface. The storm has come up suddenly, and they need to get off the water. They had set out under quiet skies, but now thunderclouds are forming, and loud rumbles can be felt as well as heard.

"Faster, Daah," Sami says joyfully in his bright orange life preserver.

The canoe rises up the soft, muddy incline, and Baéz jumps ashore, pulling the wooden craft clear of the water as Sami holds on, thrilled by this adventure.

"Come on, buddy. We're going to make a shelter."

Baéz lifts Sami out of the boat while dragging the craft to a giant Catalpa whose long branches gracefully bend toward the ground. Baéz places the upside-down canoe beneath the leafy covering. Brighton taught him this trick when they were boys.

The wind intensifies as heavy rains pour down on them, but Sami is unafraid. The sound of the rain lashing the surrounding woodland is exciting, not scary, and Baéz takes strength from the boy's pleasure until, suddenly, he feels a surge of electricity course through his body. He wonders if it is merely an atmospheric disturbance or if it is a warning.

✷ ✷ ✷

Nonnie walks down from her porch, staring up at the sky. The electricity hidden in the clouds flares over the lake. She feels the rumbling from repeated thunderclaps.

"Have you seen Baéz or Sami?" she asks Reuben.

"No, ma'am. The canoe's gone. I think they planned an early swim lesson at the Club."

"Well, a storm's coming up. They shouldn't be on the water."

"Baéz will know to pull in somewhere if he can't get back in time."

"Yes, and let's affirm they are safely in God's care."

"Yes, ma'am."

A powerful blast of wind blows several chairs off the dock and into the water. Reuben runs to retrieve them.

"Don't," Nonnie warns. "Leave them be. Lightning is all around us."

The heavy air releases its burden, and the rain swiftly soaks them as they seek refuge in Baéz's house. Bright bolts of electricity strike again and again, followed by loud thunder, shaking the very ground they stand on.

Nonnie looks out at the churning sky and realizes that Reuben is right—Baéz knows to pull safely ashore. He and Sami are safe. It's the other son, the one in Ninevah, who is the cause of her distress.

✲ ✲ ✲

As Brighton sits in the modernist lobby of the once-famous Al-Alwiyah Club, he notices the cabinets that once displayed bottles of single-malt scotch are empty. Regardless of this gesture, Muslims still feel unwelcomed here, although his young Iraqi players are fascinated to visit this Western institution.

Brighton is proud of his team, especially Daniyal. They played well and earned their trophy. Now the well-dressed patrons who cheered so heartily during the match are waiting for the next contest—the much-anticipated semi-final of *Arab Idol,* which is being broadcast on the Al Jazeera network.

Daniyal's teammates are freshly showered and smiling, enjoying the crowd's praise. Behind them, in a far corner by a long wooden bar, sits a man in grungy jeans and a dirty ball cap with ROUTE 66 stitched on the crown.

The lights dim as the musical theme for *Arab Idol* blares from the large-screen TVs. Adama's girlfriend, Shamira, is introduced first, but he is too nervous to watch. He leaves, nodding to Brighton with a wry smile as he lights one of his hand-rolled cigarettes. Brighton stands in back, wondering where Azim has gone. The air feels unsettled, and goose bumps cover his arms.

An electrical failure shuts the many TV's and plunges the large hall into darkness. There are no emergency lights, and the audience groans, familiar with Baghdad's unreliable utilities. A nervous laugh rises from the dark, and an ice bucket falls noisily to the floor. As the crowd waits for the singing competition to continue, a male voice calls out in heavily accented English, "DEATH TO THE INFIDELS!"

Out of habit, Brighton reaches for the gun he no longer carries. A bright muzzle flash suddenly illuminates the dining room as noisy blasts of gunfire drown out the desperate screams from the crowd. Brighton sees the man in the ball cap standing atop the bar. He wears a thick vest of explosives and a wide smile.

Brighton drops to the ground, seeking cover.

More blasts and more muzzle fire light the dance floor, and Brighton sees the panicked crowd running in all directions, tripping over those who have fallen as chaos reigns.

Brighton sees his team, terror etched on their sweet faces as they hide behind an upturned table. *I must distract the shooters,* he thinks. *It's me they want.*

"Here I am!" he screams as he stands in the middle of the dance floor, the smell of rifle propellant triggering images of his beloved marksman, while a heavy round of gunfire is aimed at him. Several of the copper projectiles hit their mark, but he is *existent elsewhere* and feels nothing.

Brighton lowers himself into a deep crouch as his shirt absorbs the blood leaking from his body. He looks at Daniyal, and their eyes lock. "Nothing can harm you," he screams, hoping Daniyal understands as he gathers every ounce of strength he still possesses. The muscles in his legs launch him straight into the air, his arms outstretched like the wings of an angel as he flies across the room.

Images from every moment he has ever lived fill his mind. He sees his brother struggling underwater, he sees Leyla laughing with her parents, and Nonnie advising him to choose carefully. He sees Raven, both the soldier and his child, smiling and breaking his heart. The bleeding doesn't stop, and he feels life slipping away, but he remains aloft long enough to land atop his players at the exact moment the bomb explodes.

✳ ✳ ✳

The violent storm ends as quickly as it began. Reuben straightens the overturned furniture on the deck. Nonnie opens her phone and squints to read the names and numbers stored there. She dials her grandson's offices in Amman, but it is Friday evening, and no one answers. She must find him; her unease is powerful and persuasive.

"Tonight is *Arab Idol*," explains Reuben. "They are in Baghdad, not Amman; there's a big party. Let me give you Adama's number."

He reads it to her, and she puts it on speaker. It rings and rings and then connects. They hear loud noises through the phone, and then sirens and the sound of people screaming. Reuben looks at Nonnie, his eyes wide with alarm. Suddenly there is a voice, distorted by fear.

"Hello? Who's there? Hello? Please!"

Nonnie is unable to respond. Neither she nor Reuben notice the green canoe as it pulls up to the dock.

Baéz puts down the oar and secures the boat to a metal cleat. He picks up Sami and holds him close, the canoe gently rocking. The two soaked passengers sit silently together, listening to the horrors a world away on a tiny cell phone.

"Adama? Is that you? It is Nonnie. What has happened?"

Baéz steels himself, his fingernails digging into his hand and drawing blood. He can hear Adama's strangled voice. "A suicide bomber. Massive destruction. We are searching for survivors."

Another voice can be heard in the background, talking with Adama. The phone crackles as the men walk on broken glass, the discordant sound interrupted by warnings in Arabic—"be careful." Then a loud cry is heard. "Oh no, please no, oh God help us." And then Adama sobs, and the connection goes dead.

Baéz looks at Nonnie, whose face is lit by a sudden streak of sunshine. Seeing that Sami is confused by all the scary noises, Baéz tries to stand and comfort him, but his body goes into shock, his legs collapse, and he falls into the water. He tries to grab the canoe, rocking it dangerously. Sami screams and falls onto the wooden ribs of the canoe's bottom. Reuben dives into the lake to assist a desperate Baéz. He holds him around the waist, trying to keep Baéz's head above the surface, but Baéz panics, his arms thrashing the roiled water and striking Reuben hard in the face. The strong blow forces Reuben to let go and Baéz begins to sink.

"Daaa! DAA!" screams Sami.

From the dock, Nonnie rushes to a terrified Sami, lifting him out of the canoe and taking him to dry land.

Their desperate cries reach Hill House as Tolliver is parking his car. He flings open the door and begins running—down the steep sledding hill and onto the wooden dock as he throws off his necktie and jacket. He dives headfirst into the lake. He goes deep, searching the agitated waters for his endangered husband. Without the sun, the muddy waters are dark as pitch, and he must rely on his hands and feet to find Baéz.

When he is forced to surface and breathe fresh air, Reuben points to his left, showing where he last saw Baéz. Tolliver dives again and this time he finds a hand. He begins to pull the body to the surface. Reuben joins him, and they drag Baéz to shore. He is shaking and trembling, coughing out lake water as he stares into Ollie's eyes.

"He's gone!" Baéz screams. "Brighton is gone!" He begins to wail and weep. Ollie pulls him near and holds him close.

✶ ✶ ✶

An enormous weight lies on top of him. He can barely breathe, and the short breaths he can manage are filled with dust. When the pounding in his head finally lessens, he can hear voices, loud voices, screaming. Frightened screams, screams coming from his own throat. He is screaming. The air is thick with smoke from the thunderous detonations. He can't see where he is. Everything hurts. He is wet. He is covered in a viscous liquid, tasting of iron. He hears sirens. And a voice he recognizes, calling out, seeking life, seeking the living.

Adama.

Daniyal tries moving, but his muscles have no strength. Wooden beams and shattered glass and cement blocks have crushed the scores of revelers that surround him. The floor of the club is littered with dead bodies. An arm is folded around him, not his own. As the dust begins to settle, he realizes the arm is connected to a body. The body is covering him, protecting him, holding him. The body has taken the brunt of the explosion, and the blood that covers Daniyal is not his own. The sticky substance leaking over his face and arms is from the body above. He keeps screaming.

"HELP!" he shouts, his throat scratchy and coated with sand.

Someone answers. He's sure of it. People are moving the debris that lies on top of him. He can't move. He is crying. He then sees a large, gold ring on the hand that holds and protects him. On the ring, the letter "P" is surrounded by bright green gems.

A school ring. He has seen it many times before.

Pepperdine.

35.

WITHOUT HIM

Ollie and Jared rush Baéz through the airport terminal so he won't see the newsstands displaying anguished headlines about his brother. Brighton's radiant face stares out from scores of front pages—not for the first time, but perhaps for a final time.

They are on their way to Amman to carry out Brighton's last wishes. On the TV that plays at their gate, a journalist explains why the world is in mourning.

"Everyone alive in the twenty-first century has a memory of Brighton Bethune, as a soldier, an athlete, a sportscaster, and an actor who touched our lives in so many positive ways and is now taken from us."

A stewardess ushers them on board the private jet. Nathan, Jared, Ollie, and Baéz flop into the large, comfortable seats as the pilot taxies to the northwest runway.

As the plane flies east and the sun sets across America, an old news item reinvigorates the armies of hatred. An interview from five years earlier, one that Brighton gave to Robert Browning in which he condemned America and pledged never to set foot on her soil again, has been re-posted, causing a furor that lacks all context.

They land at a private airstrip reserved for presidents and prime ministers. Adama, having utilized every single resource made available to him by the UN, greets them as they walk onto the tarmac in the middle of the night. He takes an ashen Baéz by the arm and never lets go.

Regardless of his promises to allow Sami to know his homeland, Baéz swears he will never visit the Middle East again. They are burying his brother. In Jordan. His every instinct tells him to strike out, so he does. He is a walking wound, a snapping dog, and the briefings by the Army and the queries from the State Department and the claims from ISIL fuel his fury. The dissonance of the streets, filled with calls for prayer and Bedouin music and the guttural sounds of the Arabic language, grate on him and feed his grief.

They bury Brighton Bethune on a hilltop overlooking Amman. Next to Leyla, facing Mecca. His body is wrapped in a shroud of cotton. The ritual bathing was carried out by Bilal and the imam from the mosque Brighton attended. Rough boards cover his body, which lies in an earthen grave. The mourners each toss three handfuls of dirt into the deep hole. No recording devices are allowed. The press is banned. Members of the Royal Jordanian Army attend the body and keep order at the burial site.

The four American men are housed in an elegant palace that is fully staffed and properly guarded. After the funeral, Adama sits with them in one of the public rooms. Nathan, unsure of how to help, simply documents their every move with his camera.

Tolliver brings Baéz tea made with sage and mint. A thoughtful woman in the kitchen has suggested the drink as a calming sedative.

"I don't want tea!" yells Baéz.

"You don't want anything," answers Tolliver. "But you must eat. You must drink. And you must rid yourself of the vicious anger that is controlling you. No one can stand to be near you. These people are Brighton's friends and family. Like us, they are seeking comfort."

Baéz shoots him a nasty look. "I cannot comfort these people. I do not *know* these people."

Tolliver puts the tea on a nearby table, taking care with his response.

"Go ahead. Finish that thought. 'I do not *like* these people.' They stole the final years of your brother's life. They were the people to whom he was devoted. You hate them. Say it. Go ahead! Your hatred is being sustained by a destructive jealousy you refuse to acknowledge. And let me tell you, as someone who loves you, it is ugly. It chokes the life from any room you are in."

Baéz's eyes betray nothing. They are a flat blue, with no depth or variation. He sips the bitter tea. "Perfect," he mutters, cursing the strong herbs that burn his mouth.

Tolliver does not give up. "You think your grief is special, unique, deeper than ours. You are rejecting the love of everyone who surrounds us. Stop shutting us out. We also loved him!"

The room is silent; no one dares speak. Finally, in a calmer tone, Baéz tries to explain, his trembling voice suddenly soft, his manner contrite.

"I wanted to be the one to save him," Baéz says. "I wanted to be the one to repair his heart. But he turned to strangers. The serenity he sought was found in a foreign land far away from everything he loved. I couldn't bear it. I still can't bear it. It is a repudiation of everything we shared. I loved him. We were supposed to die together, Butch and Sundance. A loving God would never have permitted one of us to survive the other. I'm frightened. I'm not sure how to live without him."

A tear forms in the corner of Baéz's eye and remains there, not falling.

Tolliver feels the danger of the territory they are now crossing, and he knows to remain silent. If he has learned anything from Baéz, it is to love simply, without question or limit. Do not respond to the verbal explosions falling all around you.

He sips the biting tea, allowing it to wash away all the unpleasant words he wishes to say. To express his own hurt, to say aloud how bruised and damaged he feels when his own love is rejected in favor of Brighton's. But he is not going to give credence to these aggressive suggestions. It is going to be a long night, and he will be there to hold his husband and to whisper, *I know, I know,* again and again to complaints yet to be expressed. Tomorrow, they will fly to Baghdad to meet the hundreds of people whose lives have been touched and enriched by the many charities Brighton founded.

★ ★ ★

Nonnie had once flown to England to mark the death of a daughter. That funeral offered neither comfort nor solace, so she decided against flying to the Middle East. She would not bury Brighton. Nor would she be present as others attempted to do so. She would honor his existence as she always had—by loving those around her. And tonight, that is Sami and Reuben.

Sami is perfect and understands nothing. He goes to the playground each day and challenges Reuben to send him higher and higher on the hanging swing. Cars stop at the roadside as neighbors place bouquets and hand-written cards near the rose garden at the end of the drive. Nonnie remains in the house, but Reuben takes a chair out front, introduces himself, and asks each person to tell how they knew Brighton.

He jots down these remembrances and offers hugs and tearful smiles. His presence is a blessing to Nonnie, as is that of Ruthie and Boone, who flew in from Texas to help share the burden of grief. Sami is pleased to be reunited with his brother, Raven.

Nonnie joins them for a late lunch as the doorbell rings once more.

Reuben calls out, "I'll get it," leaving his sandwich and milk on the table.

Nonnie and Ruth hear muffled voices at the front door. The ever-present soundtrack from the television mutters in the background. Boone is watching a national security analyst discussing the threat that ISIS presents to the US. "Laith Halevi" reads the caption beneath the handsome, blue-eyed Iranian. "Brighton Bethune has been a target from the moment he enlisted seventeen years ago. The enemy—"

Boone shuts off the interview mid-sentence; he turns to Reuben, who has entered the room with a new guest.

"Please, come in," says Reuben. "There are many people here who I'm sure would like to say hello."

The tall man enters, looking nervous, poised to flee.

"Ruthie, Boone," Reuben says. "I'd like you to meet Brighton's dad, Wynn Bethune."

Nonnie enters the front hall, pleased she had called Elwynn. She ushers him into the living room, offering food and drink. Boone sits with him, asking many questions. Reuben is uncharacteristically quiet, looking to Nonnie for guidance.

"Let me fetch the boys," says Ruth. "They're watching a ball game, the only safe thing on TV."

Boone explains further. "They love baseball. And today the Yanks are playing the Sox, so it's a pretty big day for them."

"Put it on in the living room so we can all watch together," suggests Nonnie.

Boone turns the flat screen back on and finds the sports channel as the young boys run into the room.

"The score is tied!" screams one.

"It's the bottom of the ninth," adds the other.

They momentarily quiet when they spot a man they don't know, but then see their game on the big screen and become noisy and animated once again.

"Raven, Sami, let me introduce a friend. Your grandfather, Poppi's dad."

The boys stare, digesting this news. Nonnie pats the cushions on the couch where Wynn is seated, suggesting the boys join him. They crawl up on the big sofa, still staring as the tall man offers his hand to shake. They snuggle up next to him as he looks at Nonnie with gratitude in his eyes. Finally, Raven breaks the silence.

"Whoever wins will be in first place!"

Wynn nods, staring at his grandsons before finally speaking to them. "It's a glorious game, isn't it? Your grandmother taught it to me. We don't play it in the country I am from."

"They don't play it in Poppi's country, either," adds Sami.

A loud cheer is heard on the TV. Wynn looks at the game.

"You see that man at the top of the screen?" he asks.

Both boys nod.

"Well, he is on second base. And his goal is to run past the next base, third base, and go where?"

"HOME!" they both answer, laughing at the easy question.

"Yes, home. The only sport whose goal is the glorious task of returning home."

He tousles their bright red hair, seeing a flash of Rebecca with her beautiful babies.

✷ ✷ ✷

The Henry Street gym is a perfect escape from the endless news coverage. Nico is lifting weights haphazardly, as if a strong body could fight off the sadness. Dušan takes care he does no harm. An old TV is tuned to the Yankees game.

Nico pushes for one rep too many, and Dušan swiftly reaches out and grabs the barbell.

"Careful, Boss. Go slow. It'll be alright."

"He was a good kid. A patriot." Nico lowers the barbell and sits, staring into the distance, a tear in his eye.

Dušan nods in agreement as a young boxer switches channels from baseball to tennis. ESPN is running the 2001 Final all day.

✷ ✷ ✷

The smell of vetiver fills the air as Hayden Griffiths welcomes each guest with a smile and a hug. The bright sunlight reflected off the ocean makes the TV difficult to see, but Kaveh knows the soundtrack by heart, the voices of Mary Carillo and Dick Enberg so familiar.

"Did she call you?" Kaveh asks Scottie.

"Nonnie?"

He nods.

"Yes. So sweet, but I can't do it. I can't get on a plane. Being here with his friends is helpful, but I think being with his family would be much too sad."

Kaveh keeps nodding. "So we're not bad people?"

Scottie reaches out to console him. "No, we're not bad," she says.

Brighton's sunny house envelopes them in soothing familiarity. The airy space is filled with actors and agents, tennis players and surfers, each a little lost but pleased to be surrounded by others who also loved him. Scottie's staff is assisting with the food and drinks at this spontaneous gathering.

"Did you guys ever hear about his great-grandfather landing a cloth-winged plane on the ice during a snowstorm?"

✳ ✳ ✳

The image of Baéz walking down the steps of the plane is broadcast on cable news all day. His handshake with the President of Iraq is condemned on Twitter by the White House.

Accolades are given, medallions are awarded, and teary tributes are offered. The American journalists are conflicted on how best to report this story. Is Brighton a hero or a traitor?

Baéz is surrounded by people desperate to say farewell. A bulletproof SUV takes them into the city, where they visit the offices of the charities Brighton founded. More speeches and tears and handshakes. Adama whispers, "We are coming to the end, I promise," as he closes the car door, and they travel to one last stop.

The sign reads "Al-Noor Children's Home" in English.

"This was our first orphanage. We were so proud of it. Brighton visited several times each week, talking with the children, tucking them in, telling them stories."

They walk into a crowded lobby filled with children and birds. Cages of all sizes and shapes hang from the ceiling and walls, and colorful plumage catches the light and arrests the eye. "Leyla and Brighton believed in surrounding the children with flowering plants and singing birds," explains Adama.

As Baéz looks at the expectant children, he hears the words Nonnie once said to a frightened Atticus on his first day of school. "Invite love in. Welcome it. You are never alone." So Baéz finally does. Welcome it. And his tired, anxious body begins to uncoil. He feels his brother's strength pouring into him, fed by the love that surrounds him. Adama brings forth each child and introduces them. He knows every name and how long they have lived here. Baéz shakes each hand, absorbing the joy that is so tangibly present. The lack of a common language is not a deterrent. The line of people wanting to say goodbye goes out the room and down the avenue.

Nathan keeps snapping pictures, and Ollie helps greet the many visitors. He walks over to Baéz with a teenaged boy.

"You must meet someone. His name is Azar. He was rescued by Brighton seven years ago. We know his brother, Daniyal."

Baéz, who has not cried since his breakdown in the canoe, feels tears forming as the fourteen-year-old hugs him. "How is your brother?" asks Baéz. "Have you heard anything? What do you know?"

As if on cue, moving slowly on cumbersome crutches, Daniyal makes his way towards Tolliver and Baéz.

The finality of Brighton's death is apparent the minute Baéz rests his eyes on the angelic tennis player who his brother had protected as his last act on earth. Baéz falls to his knees, his arms encircling the young man. Daniyal hugs him.

"I brought you something," says Dani. "I was afraid someone might steal it." He reaches into the front pocket of his jeans and takes out a gold ring studded with bright green gems. He holds it out to Baéz, who is completely overcome, tears flooding his face. He stares at the shiny ring, flashing back to a perfect memory.

"Put it on," Baéz had urged those many years ago. "We're the same size; I know it will fit. It's your college ring!" They were celebrating Brighton's triumph at the US Open, and the mid-town steak house was buzzing with excitement, filled with fans and photographers.

"The stone isn't too garish?" Brighton had asked, slightly embarrassed, having always loved shiny things. "What kind is it?"

"Tourmaline."

"What are the words that circle it? I can't see; it's so dark in here."

"Your school motto. *Freely ye have received, freely give.*"

Brighton joined him in reciting the last two words as flashbulbs popped. He smiled while putting on this perfect gift from his brother.

"I saw Rebecca," Baéz announces.

Brighton turns to him. "Where?"

"On the court. In her nurses' uniform."

"When?"

"Right after you collapsed. We could see the blood. A large cut on your knee, more on your elbow. She walked to the net, leaned down over your body, and lifted you up. She stared at the sky, and a bolt of lightning speared the dark clouds, and then the rain began."

Brighton stifled a sob. A thoughtful waiter shooed away a couple seeking an autograph. Baéz reached across the table and held his brother's hand, murmuring, "It's alright, it's alright."

"Do you think she saw me? Saw me win? Does she know?" Brighton had asked.

"Yes. Of course she knows. And so proud! Can you imagine?"

He can. Both boys had often imagined it, their mother watching over them. Guiding them. Guarding them.

As the memory of that long ago day fades, Baéz looks at all the boys and girls who fill the orphanage. He shakes each of their little hands as his grief begins to loosen its hold.

"Tell my brother the story of Brighton saving you under the ice," Daniyal says. "We all know it, but we'd love to hear you tell it. Can you?"

Baéz can't believe the pleasure he feels knowing that Brighton told them the story of the ice.

He looks over at Tolliver, who gives an affirming nod. Ollie finds a chair for Dani while shepherding the other kids to seats on the floor as he hands out several pillows. Baéz takes Ollie's hand, squeezing hard. When the other hand squeezes back, Baéz smiles, knowing he is loved. He closes his eyes, thinking back to that winter day from long ago.

"It was Christmas, and a giant snowstorm had blanketed the eastern United States. Brighton and I were sledding on the huge hill that leads from our Nonnie's house to the frozen lake . . ."

Nathan frames the image, and the shutter clicks.

About The Author

Lindsay Law has produced scores of television plays and dozens of films, in addition to a pair of productions on Broadway. Many of these works have been nominated for Emmys, Tonys, and Oscars. He was the Executive Producer for the PBS drama series American Playhouse from 1981 to 1995, and served as President of Fox Searchlight Pictures from 1995 to 2000.

His bestselling debut novel, *The Orphan from Shepherds Keep*, established him as a powerful new voice in contemporary fiction. Critics praised his "compassionate, tender, and wise" storytelling and his ability to create characters and narratives that are "impossible to put down."

With *Without Him*, Law continues to explore the sacred bonds that define us, crafting stories that are both deeply personal and universally resonant. He lives in Litchfield County, Connecticut.

Connect with Lindsay Law

Visit LindsayLaw.net to learn more about the author's journey from acclaimed producer to bestselling novelist. Discover the inspiration behind *Without Him* and *The Orphan from Shepherds Keep*, and stay connected for news about future works.

If you enjoyed this book and the time you spent with Brighton and Baéz, help spread the word online, at your local bookshop, and directly with your friends. Lindsay would love to hear about your reading experience and invites you to share your thoughts and questions about this story—and his story—at his website.

Sign up for updates to be among the first to know about upcoming releases, special events, and exclusive content from this compelling storyteller who brings the same passion for human connection to his novels that made his film and television work so memorable.

Your story matters. Share it at LindsayLaw.net.